D1234205

ꞮꞬer
King County Library System
Property of

Ransom of the Heart

AUG 0 1 2018

Ransom of the Heart, Copyright ©2018 by Susan Page Davis
Published by Tea Tin Press
Published in the United States of America

All rights reserved. No part of this publication may be
reproduced, stored in a retrieval system, or transmitted in any
form or by any means, electronic, electrical, chemical, mechanical,
optical, photocopying, recording, or otherwise, without the prior
written permission of the copyright owner. Inquiries may be sent
by email through www.susanpagedavis.com

ISBN 978-1-947079-07-6

Library of Congress Control Number: 2018904749

Ransom of the Heart

Maine Justice, Book 7

By Susan Page Davis

Chapter 1

"So, how are you feeling about this new venture, Nate?" Captain Harvey Larson looked up and nodded as the waitress filled his coffee cup. "I'll have a BLT. Thanks."

Nate Miller was nearly done with his lunch when Harvey had joined him at an outside table at the restaurant on Franklin Street. It was handy to the police station, and cops headed to "the diner" out of habit, especially in warm weather. Nate picked up a French fry and frowned. "Good. Mostly good. But I feel kind of guilty, too." He popped the fry into his mouth.

"Why would you feel guilty?"

"Well, you've put a lot into my training and everything."

"That's what got you this job offer from the state." Harvey took a sip of the too-hot coffee and set the cup down. "Look, Nate, you're a good cop, and you're a good detective. I've been proud to have you in my squad. I know this was a difficult decision for you."

"Yeah, totally." Nate eyed him warily. "I really like the Priority Unit. It's Jackie mostly. She doesn't like to think I could get shot at. It happens so often these days. Not here necessarily, but. . ."

"I know. This job has always been dangerous, but it's more so now than ever before. Believe me, I understand what that can do to marriages." Harvey picked up his coffee cup. Now wasn't the time to get sidetracked in the past. He took a quick sip. Still too hot.

"I just don't want to let you down." Nate's earnest brown eyes shone with anxiety.

Harvey shook his head. "You're not letting anyone down. You're going to be a big help to a lot of people. Kids, Nate. Parents. Educators. Even though we'll miss you, that's why I can let you go without putting up a fight to keep you here. I know this job with the Department of Education is important. And I'd never hold it against a man who chose something he thought was better for his family."

Nate pressed his lips together and nodded. "Thanks, Captain. That means a lot."

Eddie Thibodeau, Harvey's top detective, best friend, and brother-in-law, threaded his way between the tables as the waitress set Harvey's sandwich in front of him.

"Hey, Ed," Harvey said. "What have you got on the Farnham case?"

"I'm ready to pick him up, soon as I eat something." Eddie grinned and waved to the waitress. "My usual, Brooke." He sat down between Harvey and Nate.

"Well, I'd better get back to my desk." Nate pushed back his chair. "See you later."

"'Bye," Eddie said, and Harvey nodded.

"He working on ID theft?" Eddie asked.

"No, we had a new cyber stalking complaint this morning. I put him on that."

"Who's going to do those when Nate's gone?"

"I don't know. Probably me." Harvey rubbed the back of his neck and stretched a little. He picked up half of his BLT and took a bite. The diner staff made good sandwiches, but he would rather be at home, eating lunch with his wife, Jennifer.

The waitress brought Eddie's burger and set the platter, laden with fries, in front of him.

"Wow, that was quick," Eddie said.

Brooke grinned. "I saw you coming. What are you drinking today?"

"Just coffee. Thanks."

After she had filled his mug and stepped away, Eddie lifted the top half of his bun and frowned at his burger before adding a dollop of ketchup.

"Where are you going to pick this guy up?" Harvey asked.

"Fox Street. He's supposed to be at work."

"Take Jimmy with you."

"Jimmy?" Eddie paused with his burger halfway to his mouth. "Not Tony?"

"I want to get Jimmy out of the office. He's a little blue."

"What about?"

"Nate."

Eddie shrugged. "They've worked together a long time."

"Yeah. I think Jimmy figured now that they'd both made detective, they'd stick together until they retired. He wasn't figuring on Nate being such a hit with the educators."

"He does a great job when he goes out and talks at schools."

"Yeah. If he keeps one kid from getting tangled up with an online predator, then I'd say he's doing the best thing. That's a lot better than trying to catch the jerk after it happens."

A girl walked slowly up the sidewalk. She caught Harvey's attention because she eyed the diners as she approached. She wasn't roaming aimlessly or headed somewhere. She was looking for someone when she ought to be in school.

He took in her worn jeans, high-topped sneakers, and unzipped navy hoodie, but mostly he noticed her bushy, shoulder-length hair and her wary blue eyes. When her gaze met his, she stopped walking, one thumb hooked through the strap of her backpack. She looked down at her phone and then back at him.

Harvey frowned and picked up his sandwich. He had the feeling she was looking for him, but he couldn't imagine why. Teenage girls rarely sought him out.

"Okay, I'll take Jimmy," Eddie said. "What about Tony?"

"You can take him, too. You might need him." Harvey glanced at the girl. She had a determined expression, and she took a step in their direction. "Heads up."

3

"What?" Eddie stopped short of sipping his coffee.

"Company," Harvey said softly. The girl was nearly to their table. He looked up and met her gaze. "Hello," he said with a noncommittal smile. "Can I help you?"

"Are you Harvey Alan Larson?"

Harvey hesitated just long enough to process that. Harvey Larson, yes, or maybe Captain Larson, but what high school girl knew his middle name?

"Yes, I am. May I ask who you are?"

She swallowed hard. "My name is Leah Viniard."

Harvey nodded. "Nice to meet you, Leah. Did you want to see me about something in particular?"

Eddie stared at the girl, and Harvey could almost hear the gears clicking in his brain as he analyzed her appearance and her words. He felt the oddity of the situation, too.

"Yeah," she said. "I'm pretty sure you're my father."

*****

"Daddy, can you fix my car?"

Peter Hobart set down his fork and reached out for the tiny toy Mustang his six-year-old had brought him. One wheel was missing.

"What happened, Andy? Did you have a blowout?"

"Yeah." The little boy frowned up at him. "It needs a tire."

"I see that. Where'd you lose it?"

"In my room."

"Did you look for it?"

Andy nodded.

Peter looked up as his wife refilled his coffee mug. "Thanks."

"I can look for it later," she said. "If I don't find it, maybe I can empty the robot vacuum and set it loose in there."

Andy pouted his lips and stared accusingly at Peter. "You have a car store. You can fix it."

4

He smiled. "Sure, I'll ask the guys in the parts department if they've got one of these wheels in stock." If Abigail didn't turn up the missing part, maybe he could find a place online that sold Hot Wheels components. Short of that, he could surely find a replacement car on eBay. "Now, get ready for school," he told Andy. "We leave in ten minutes."

"Who's taking us?" Gary, his ten-year-old, was just finishing his cereal.

"I'll drop you off this morning, and Abigail will pick you up after school and take you to Grammy's. Remember? You're staying over there tonight."

Andy grinned. "Oh, yeah, because you and Mommy have a date."

"That's right." Peter sipped his coffee. A one-year wedding anniversary was worth a big celebration, and he intended to give Abigail an evening to remember. "Make sure you leave your p.j.s and anything else you want to take on your bed for her to pack."

"Look for me out front at 3:15," Abigail said.

"Gotcha." Gary got up and carried his dishes to the counter and then left the kitchen.

Peter wished Gary would call his stepmother Mom. Andy had called her Mommy since the day they announced their engagement, but Gary still called her Abby, like most people did. After the boys had left the room, Peter smiled at her.

"Don't work too hard on the toy wheel. I ought to be able to replace it." He tucked the crippled Mustang into his pocket. It wasn't a huge thing, but he would do whatever he could to remain Andy's hero.

Abigail leaned over and kissed him. "You're a good daddy. But you've got a lot of other things on your mind."

Peter shrugged. His biggest concern right now was Carter Ulrich, one of his salesmen at the auto dealership. "I plan to sit down with Carter today and find out what's going on with him. And I might ask Mom to take a look at the financial files."

Her forehead creased in a frown. "You think Carter's monkeying with the books?"

"Not really, but he's been asking for overtime and pushing customers on sales—I told you about that. His attitude yesterday was so odd that I reviewed his commissions."

"And?"

"He seems on track for the last couple of months, but I want to make sure everything's good before I talk to him. I can't have him getting pushy with the customers."

Abigail nodded. "I'm sure if there's anything wrong with the books, Vickie can spot it."

"Yeah." Peter's mother had been the bookkeeper since his dad started the family business nearly thirty years ago. She'd retired herself a couple of years before Peter and Abigail were married, and he had a new bookkeeper now. But his mom was still savvy, and he trusted her implicitly.

Gary poked his head in from the living room. "We going?"

Peter pushed back his chair. "Yeah." He reached for his wife and a goodbye kiss. "Happy anniversary, sweetheart. And I'll see you about quarter past five."

*****

Harvey looked deep into the girl's blue eyes. She couldn't hold his gaze, but sniffed and looked down at the table.

"What makes you think you're my daughter, Leah?" he asked, keeping his voice as neutral as he could. Across from him, Eddie was watching him closely, and his lips twitched as though he wanted to say something.

"I. . .well, your name is on my birth certificate." She finished on a more confident note and lifted her chin to lock eyes with him.

"Really?" Harvey's brain raced, though he already knew the answers to most of his questions. He sent up a quick silent prayer and managed to smile. "I can tell you with no doubt whatever, that I am not your father. As to the birth certificate, I have no explanation, but if you want to sit down and discuss it, maybe we can figure this thing out."

She hesitated, then pulled out the wrought iron chair Nate had vacated. The backpack slid off, and she plunked it on the brick sidewalk and sat down, throwing Eddie a wary glance.

"You want me to vacate, Harv?" Eddie asked.

"No, stay." Harvey took a drink of his coffee, set the mug down, and smiled at Leah. "By the way, Leah, this is my friend, Eddie Thibodeau."

Eddie nodded at her, but Leah glanced at him and then ignored him.

Harvey said, "So, tell me a little about yourself."

"Like what?" she asked.

"For starters, how old are you?"

"Fifteen. I'll be sixteen in October."

He nodded, doing some mental calculations. "And who is your mother?"

"You mean my real mother?"

He'd almost expected that and took it in stride. "Your biological mother."

"Her name was Tara Ervin when I was born."

Harvey rubbed his scratchy chin. "That name doesn't ring a bell." He caught a sheen in her eyes. She was more nervous than she wanted to let on, and probably angry with him for denying the relationship out of hand.

"She died about six months ago," Leah said. "I didn't know, but I got a packet of papers from a lawyer a few weeks ago. That's when I found out about you."

"About your biological father," Harvey said gently.

"That's you."

He pulled in a slow breath. "Leah, I'm not sure why the name on your birth certificate is the same as mine, but I'm pretty sure it's either incorrect, or it's referring to someone else with the same name."

"There's not that many." Her voice held a stubborn edge.

He nodded. "That's true, there aren't many men named Harvey Alan Larson who would be the right age to be your father."

7

"I found you online."

That wasn't surprising. As captain of the Portland Police Department's Priority Unit, Harvey had an online presence he hadn't sought. His occasional press conferences and role in solving some high-profile crimes made him easy to find. She'd probably been comparing his face with a picture a few minutes ago before approaching him.

"I don't suppose you have the birth certificate with you?" he asked.

She lowered her eyelashes. "Why do you want to know?"

"I'd just like to take a look at it."

She looked up then, defiant. "You know I could get another copy if you destroyed it."

"I wouldn't do that. I won't keep it, either. I'd just like to see it."

For a moment she sat still, gazing at him with suspicion.

"Listen to him," Eddie said. "Harvey's a good guy, and he won't do anything to your paper."

She didn't acknowledge Eddie, but she bent and unzipped her backpack. She pulled out a folded sheet of paper, hesitated, then put it on the table near Harvey's plate.

"Thanks," he said. "Have you had lunch?"

Leah shook her head.

"Would you like a sandwich?"

"No, thanks."

"They make good burgers," Eddie said. "Let me get you one."

She glanced at Harvey again, then back at Eddie. "Well, okay. I guess."

"Great," Harvey said. "What would you like to drink?"

"Coke?"

"Sure." Harvey took out his wallet and gave Eddie a ten-dollar bill. "Thanks, Ed."

Eddie moved off toward where Brooke was waiting on the uniformed officers at another table. Harvey opened the birth certificate and noted the embossed seal near the bottom. After perusing the information, he looked up. Leah was staring at him.

"So, you were born in Lewiston," he said.

She nodded. "Apparently so." She hadn't known any of it. His heart went out to her.

"Do you live up there?"

"In Lisbon."

It was fairly close to Lewiston. "When were you adopted?"

"When I was two days old."

"And when did you find out?"

She looked away, and when she spoke, her voice caught. "The day I got that in the mail."

It seemed odd to Harvey. "Your parents hadn't told you anything? Your adoptive parents, I mean. They didn't tell you that you were adopted?"

"No." Her face scrunched up, and she batted at her cheek with the sleeve of her hoodie. "I thought they were my real parents. And then I get this." She jerked her chin toward the paper. "Apparently my. . .mother. . .put it in her will for her lawyer to send me that stuff if she died."

"So, it wasn't a closed adoption."

"I don't know what it was. My mom—Mrs. Viniard—said that she—Tara—couldn't take care of me, and they adopted me. They gave her some money. What kind of person buys a baby?"

The tears filled her eyes now, and Harvey wanted to touch her and offer some comfort, but that would be a mistake. It was so easy to have good intentions misread.

"I'm sorry, Leah. And I'm sorry you found out that way. It's not uncommon for adoptive parents to give a birth mother money for her expenses, though. That doesn't mean it was an illegal transaction."

She sniffed and batted her eyelashes, as if trying to whip the tears into line. "It came in a sealed-up packet with 'To my daughter' written on the front. I don't know if the lawyer even knew what was in it."

Harvey nodded, wishing he could take away the hurt. "If it's okay with you, I'll see what I can find out about Tara Ervin."

Leah's lower lip quivered. "Her name was Tara Leland when she died, so I guess she got married sometime."

"That's good to know." Harvey took out his pocket notebook and wrote down the name and a few bits of data off the birth record. "Do you know where she lived?"

"Portland, I guess. That's where the lawyer was, anyway."

"Do you have the envelope it came in?"

"Not with me."

"Okay. How about the lawyer's name? Do you remember that?"

She looked across the street as if the answer was posted over there. "Jasper or Jacobs, something like that."

Harvey clicked mentally through the attorneys he knew. "Not Jarvis?"

Her gaze met his. "Yeah, that's it. You know that guy?"

"I've seen him in court." At her baffled look, he explained, "I'm a police officer. Sometimes I have to testify in court about people I've arrested."

"I guess I knew that." Her mouth drooped. She was probably disappointed that he didn't have a personal connection with the lawyer.

Harvey shrugged. "Mr. Jarvis and I have crossed paths a few times. I don't know him well."

Eddie came back carrying a cheeseburger plate and a tall paper cup.

"Here you go. I hope you wanted fries." He set the plate and the drink in front of Leah.

She stared at the mountain of food. "Wow. That's a lot."

Eddie shrugged. "Just eat what you want." He winked at Harvey and sat down.

Harvey waited until she'd taken a few bites. He finished his sandwich and signaled Brooke for more coffee. Finally, when Leah looked more relaxed and less famished, he leaned toward her.

"So, Leah, do your folks know you're here?"

"You mean—"

"I mean, school hasn't let out yet, has it? How did you get here?"

She froze.

"It's okay," Harvey said. "I just wondered, and I wanted to make sure you were safe and have a way home."

"I took a bus. A friend from school took me to the bus station."

"Okay." He let that percolate in his mind and drank from his coffee mug. She'd probably ditched school today and talked a friend into skipping a class or two to take her to the bus depot.

"Why are you so sure you're not my dad?" Leah asked.

Eddie arched his eyebrows, challenging him to answer that one without getting his neck in a noose.

"I was married back then, during the whole year you were born. I didn't have any relationships outside my marriage." Things had been rough with Carrie during that time, and three years later she'd left him, but he didn't think he needed to reveal that.

She sat watching him for a minute, then her shoulders drooped. She was holding a French fry, and she dredged it through a puddle of ketchup on her plate but didn't eat it.

"How do I know you're telling the truth?"

"I guess you don't." Harvey looked at his watch. He really should get back to work, but he couldn't send her back to the bus station still wondering. "Look, if it will help you, I'm willing to take a test."

"What kind of test?"

"A test that will show if we're related or not."

"You mean, like DNA?"

"Yeah. It's a pretty simple test to show paternity or not. We have a lab in the police station, right over there." He pointed toward the building. "They could do it." He wasn't allowed to use the police lab for personal favors, but he was pretty sure Chief

11

Browning would want this cleared up as soon as possible. It could affect his work if Harvey was targeted with a lawsuit.

Leah's eyes sparked. "Oh, yeah, like I want you to have your friends do it. They'd say whatever you wanted them to, wouldn't they? My dad said you're a bigshot cop."

"Really?" Score one for Mr. Viniard. He'd raised a spunky daughter, even if he'd kept the truth from her for over fifteen years. And he'd discussed the matter with Leah, at least to some degree. Harvey came to a decision and took out his phone. He clicked through a few screens and put in a search for independent laboratories in the city. "Okay, Leah. There's a private lab on Brighton Avenue. That's not too far from here. We can go over there and give samples. It will take a few weeks with them, and it will cost more, but you'll know they aren't my buddies and that whatever they tell you is the truth. What do you say? Shall we take a ride over there?"

She breathed three times and then looked him in the eye. "Okay. Yeah. You're paying for it, right?"

Harvey laughed. "Of course." He turned to Eddie. "Take the boys and go pick up your suspect. I'll leave you in charge until I get back, okay? Help Nate if he needs anything for his case, and tell Paula I'll be an hour or two." He would take Leah to the bus station personally after their foray to the lab. Still, she probably wouldn't get home until well after school let out for the day. "And, Leah, you need to call your mom and tell her where you are."

"Do I have to?"

"Yes, you do. I don't want her worrying when you don't come home from school. That's what mothers do, you know."

She had the grace to blush.

Eddie left to round up Tony and Jimmy. Harvey told Leah to finish her burger and then waited while she used the restroom. Keeping an eye on the ladies' room door, he called Jennifer on his cell phone.

"Hey, gorgeous. We don't have to go anywhere tonight, do we?"

"No," Jennifer said. "Why? Will you be late?"

"I don't think so, but something's come up that I'll need to tell you about when I get home."

She was silent for a moment and then said, "Are you all right?"

"I'm fine, sweetheart."

"Because if you're calling me from the hospital—"

"No, nothing like that. But it's a little sensitive to discuss over the phone. Don't worry. I'll tell you all about it tonight."

"Okay," she said.

Harvey smiled. Jennifer was such a relief. She could always peel through the stress he dealt with at work. "I love you," he said. "Give Connor a squeeze for me."

Leah came out of the restroom and walked over to the table. "I'm ready." She stooped and picked up her backpack.

Harvey put his phone away and stood.

"I should warn you, though," Leah said. "If this involves needles, I don't do too good with blood."

Chapter 2

Peter looked up from his computer screen as Sylvia Harding entered his office.

"Peter, your mom's here."

"Oh, good." He rose, smoothing down his necktie, and stepped to the door. His mother, trim and stylish as always, stood near Sylvia's desk at one side of the showroom. "Come right in, Mom." He closed the door behind her and indicated one of the customer chairs for her. "Thanks so much for doing this."

"No problem. I'm picking the boys up at school in an hour anyway."

"I thought Abigail was getting them."

"I said I'd do it and give her more time to get ready for your big night out. I stopped by and got the boys' things."

"Well, that was nice of you. Thanks."

"Does Sylvia know about this?" she asked.

"Yeah, she's cool with it. In fact, it was her idea." Peter sat down and folded his hands on the desktop. "I really don't think there's anything wrong with the books, but I want to make sure."

His mother frowned. "Something must have set you off."

"One of my sales reps. Carter. I just. . .Something's not right with him." Peter shook his head.

"You think he's stealing from you?"

He grimaced. "No, I don't, not really. But he's been very cagey lately about finances and going all out to make a sale."

"That's good, isn't it?"

"Sometimes he's so aggressive, the customer backs off."

She nodded thoughtfully. "I can see Carter doing that." She'd worked at Hobart Chevrolet for more than twenty years—Sylvia had her job now—building the business with her husband. She knew most of the staff. "Anything else?"

15

"Yeah. I saw him talking to a man in the lot last week. I thought it was a customer at first, but then I realized they were arguing. Carter looked positively gray. I asked him later who the guy was, and he was evasive."

"That's a red flag, for sure."

"Uh-huh. And yesterday Carter really put the pressure on a client. So bad I stepped in."

"Oh-oh."

Peter sighed and held up his thumb and index finger. "I'm this close to firing him."

His mother studied his face. "Carter's been here a long time, Peter."

"More than twelve years. And overall, he's been a good employee."

"You can't fire him on a feeling. As to the high-pressure tactics, maybe he's due for a refresher in sales techniques."

Peter leaned back in his chair. "He seems desperate. And that's why I decided to take a good look at the books. I told Sylvia I wanted a good, thorough check. She went over the accounts, and she thinks everything's fine, but she suggested I have someone else take a look to set my mind at ease." He shrugged. "You seemed like the natural choice. You know our system."

His mom smiled. "I set up that system. Of course I'll take a look. If I don't feel satisfied in an hour, I'll come back tomorrow and take the whole program apart."

"Thanks, Mom. You can use my desk. That way the other employees won't see you and wonder what you're up to. I've asked Sylvia to keep it quiet."

"Okay."

They both stood, and his mother came behind the desk.

"I've updated a few of the programs, but we're using the same basic setup we had when you left," Peter said.

"The easiest place for him to pull something funny would be in the sales and rebates, but I'll look at the shop accounts, too."

"I'll be out on the floor or in the lot," Peter said. "You can call my cell if you need me."

"Great." She sat down and pulled the chair in. "I hope you can relax and have a great evening."

"Thanks. I'm sure we will, and I'll worry less once you've looked at this."

"Abby said you're having dinner at the floating restaurant and then going to the symphony. She seemed excited about it."

His smiled broadened. Everything was good since he and Abigail had gotten married. Andy and Gary thrived under their new mom's guidance, and Peter couldn't remember being so happy. This snag with Carter was the only thing bothering him, and it had to be dealt with.

"Thanks again, Mom. I'll let you get to work."

He walked out into the showroom. Two of his sales reps, Andrea and Jeremy, were deep in conversation with customers. Carter must be outside somewhere. Andrea had the trainee, Kevin, in on her sales pitch. That was good; Kevin could learn a lot from Andrea as far as handling potential clients went. They were talking to a fortyish couple and focusing on a new model Tahoe. Better and better.

Peter nodded to Sylvia and strolled over to the coffee station beyond her desk. He hoped his mom didn't find anything in her mini audit. On the other hand, if she did, he'd have more than a nebulous feeling to go by. Either way, he was going to sit Carter down and thrash through this thing. Not today, though, he decided. He needed to simmer down and concentrate on giving Abigail a great evening. She deserved that.

*****

Abby Hobart parked near the entrance to the auto showroom and walked up to the door. Surprisingly, it opened at her pull, even though it was twenty minutes past closing time. Peter must be talking to a late customer. Usually if a client lingered after closing, it meant he was buying a new vehicle and they were finishing up the paperwork. She smiled and stepped toward her husband's office.

Her throat seized. On the floor between a bright red Malibu and a silver Corvette convertible lay a man in gray pants and a darker sports jacket. A dark pool spread from beneath his head, across the tiles, and a faint acrid scent hung in the air.

Abby looked away for a second, sucked in a deep breath, then looked again. As a nurse who had done stints in a busy hospital emergency room, she didn't flinch easily. Even so, this one made her stomach heave.

Definitely not Peter's clothing or build. She looked toward the office door. It stood wide open. The lights were on. She stifled the urge to cry out to Peter. She swept a gaze all around the showroom, but nothing moved. Cautiously, she stepped back behind the Malibu's rear bumper and pulled her phone from her purse.

It rang four times. Her brother-in-law was probably driving home from work. She almost hung up and opted for 911, but his voice came on, crisp but warm.

"Abby. What's up?"

She gulped. "I just got to Peter's store, and there's a man lying dead on the floor."

"Are you sure he's dead?" Harvey asked.

"Yes," she whispered.

"Who is it?"

"One of the salesmen, I think. It's ... well, the exit wound ..."

"Understood. Where's Peter?"

"I don't know. I was afraid to go to his office."

"Right. Get out of the store now, Abby. Get inside your car, lock all the doors, and wait for me. I'll be there in ten minutes."

"But Peter—"

"I know what you're thinking, but it's too dangerous. Get out, Abs."

"Okay."

"Did you see anyone else?"

"No, nobody."

18

"Did you try Peter's cell phone?"

"No, but I can do that now."

"No, Abby, wait. If he's hiding, that could put him in danger."

"Oh." She swallowed hard.

"You did just right. I'm hanging up to call the dispatcher," Harvey said. "I'll call you right back. Get outside."

"Okay, 'bye."

She heard his siren go on before she closed the connection. Harvey hated to use the siren in his Explorer. He said it gave him a headache.

She swallowed hard and peered around the edge of the car she'd sheltered behind. The man still lay there, exactly as she had seen him. Holding her breath, she listened. Nothing. Maybe she could sneak across the showroom from gleaming new car to car and take a peek into the office.

No. If something happened because of her carelessness, Harvey would never forgive her. But what if Peter needed urgent medical aid, and she didn't give it to him?

She sent up a quick prayer and turned to go out. As she pushed the glass door open, an engine surged. She looked right, toward the sound. A dark sedan was pulling out of the parking lot. It was too far away for her to catch the tag number. The car blended in with the rush hour traffic on the street.

Abby strode to her car. Peter had given her a new Equinox for a wedding present. She got in, hit the lock button, and looked all around the parking lot. Yards away, traffic whizzed by on the street, but the dealership's lot seemed deserted.

Her phone buzzed. Harvey.

"Hi," she said.

"I'm five minutes out. We're sending a marked unit, and they may beat me there."

"Okay. I saw a car leaving the parking lot when I came out."

"What did it look like?" Harvey asked.

"Black four-door. I don't know what kind. It was going out the far exit of the lot. I didn't get the plate number."

19

"Okay. Was it a Chevy?"

"I don't know. I'm sorry."

"It's okay," he said.

Movement caught her eye.

"The police car is here."

"Okay, why don't you go tell them what's going on. I'll be right there."

Abby got out of her car. When she stood, her knees almost buckled. She hung on to the car door and took a deep breath. Peter might be dead inside the building. She managed a wave at the two uniformed officers who got out of the black-and-white city car.

They walked over to her, looking around the lot as they came.

"Hi, I'm Abby Hobart. My husband owns this place. Thanks for coming."

The female officer said, "Are you the one who called it in?"

"Yes. There's a man lying on the floor inside. He looks like he's been shot. I'm a nurse," she added quickly.

The officer nodded. "Anything else?"

"I called Captain Larson right away. He's married to my sister. He told me not to go into my husband's office. But I did see that the office door was open."

The woman's features softened. "Mrs. Hobart, I'm Officer Dalton, and this is Officer Bonner."

Abby touched Officer Dalton's sleeve. "My husband could be in there, in need of medical help."

Dalton looked to her partner. "Should we wait for backup?"

"The shooter could still be inside," he said.

"I did see a car leaving the far end of the lot when I came out." Abby pointed. "I didn't get a good look, but it was a black, four-door sedan."

A siren announced Harvey's arrival. His Explorer pulled in with the blue strobe flashing. Harvey hopped out, his usual competent, spare self, with crisp brown hair and a rumpled suit.

"Abby." He strode to her and put his hands on her shoulders, looking deep into her eyes.

She stared back. She'd known him two years, but she still found the blue of his eyes startling.

"Are you okay?" he asked.

"I'm fine. But Peter—"

Harvey looked to the uniformed officers. "Anyone been inside?"

"Not yet, Captain," Dalton replied.

"Let's go." Harvey drew his pistol.

"Do you have body armor, sir?" Officer Bonner asked.

"Not with me," Harvey said.

"Better let us go first. Maybe you should stay with Mrs. Hobart."

Abby hoped he would stay with her. Harvey turned to her.

"We've got back-up on the way. Get in your car, Abby. I'll let you know as soon as possible what the situation is."

She nodded, her mouth dry, and walked back to her Equinox. Her hands shook as she opened the door and slid onto the seat.

Officer Bonner was already through the front door of the showroom, and Officer Dalton hurried around the side of the building. Harvey entered just behind Bonner.

Abby's lips quivered as she tried to form a prayer.

Lord, keep them safe! And please let Peter be all right.

Her phone rang and she looked at the screen. Her younger sister, Leeanne.

"Hey."

"Abby? What's going on? Eddie said he heard a call go out for officers to go to Peter's store."

"I'm there now," she said. "Harvey's here, and some patrol officers." As she spoke, another black-and-white rolled in. "Someone's been shot. Not Peter. Look, I need to go. I'll call you back, okay?"

"Sure—"

She hung up on Leeanne and jumped out of the car, striding toward the new arrivals.

"I'm Abigail Hobart, the owner's wife. Captain Larson is inside with Officers Dalton and Bonner. They said they'd make sure the—the shooter isn't still inside."

"We were told someone was shot?" The tall, dark-haired officer focused on her. His name tag read "Kelley."

"Yes. One of my husband's employees."

"And where is your husband?"

"I—we're not sure. Captain Larson is looking for him."

The door to the showroom opened, and Harvey emerged. Approaching Abby, he holstered his pistol.

"No one else is in there."

She blinked at him. "Thank God. But. . .where's Peter?"

Harvey shook his head. "I don't know, but we'll find out."

"Did you find anything in his office?"

"The lights were on, and he left some paperwork on his desk. It looked as though he may have been interrupted in the middle of something." He looked at the newly arrived officers. "Bonner and Dalton are inside. I suggest you two stand guard out here and make sure no one disturbs the scene. I've asked them to call for a medical examiner and crime scene techs, and I've called in my detective squad."

The patrolmen nodded and strode toward the door.

"Abby." Harvey drew her closer to her car. "I don't know what happened here, but we'll do everything we can to find Peter."

"Can I call him now?"

"I tried his number. He didn't answer."

She drew in a shaky breath. "You don't think he killed that man?"

"No, I don't. Now, tell me everything you know. What were your plans?"

Abby shivered. "We were going out to dinner. Sunday's our anniversary, and Peter wanted to have a special evening together."

22

"That's nice," Harvey said.

Tears rushed into Abby eyes, and she sniffed. "Harvey what could have happened here? Do you think it was a robbery?"

"I don't know. Did Peter keep a lot of cash on the premises?"

"No. Customers almost always finance. They'll make a down payment, but that's usually with a credit card or a check." She shivered again and hugged herself.

"Let's sit in my vehicle until my detectives get here. I'd like a little more background."

"Okay." Abby walked with him to his forest green Explorer and waited while he opened the passenger door for her. While he walked around to the driver's side, she took a deep breath and sent up a silent prayer.

"What do you know about the dead man?"

"Not much. I think it's Carter Ulrich, but I'm not a hundred percent sure." She shuddered at the memory of the disfigured corpse.

"I'm sorry to have to ask you questions," Harvey said.

"It's your job. I get it. I'll do anything to find out what's happened to Peter."

"Okay, then let's start with Carter Ulrich and Peter's other employees." Harvey took out a small notebook and a pen. "How many people does he employ?"

"Carter and four other sales reps and a trainee. There's a shop foreman and two mechanics and two guys in the parts shop. And the bookkeeper. She answers the phone and does filing, besides keeping track of the financials. Oh, and Peter hired the bookkeeper's daughter part time recently because the office work was getting to be too much for one person."

Harvey wrote as she talked. "It's a busy place," he said.

"Yeah. I think he's expanded quite a bit since his dad died." Abby caught a breath, but her chest felt squeezed. "Harvey, do you think they've killed him? Whoever killed that other man, I mean."

He was quiet for a moment. "At this point, I don't think anything. But we'll find out, Abby."

She nodded. Shouldn't he be doing something besides asking her routine questions?

"If that's not Carter Ulrich in there, who else do you think it could be?" Harvey asked.

"I don't know. One salesman's very blond, and one's way taller than Carter. It can't be either of them. And one of the reps is a woman, Andrea . . . Something. I can't remember her last name."

"It's okay. I'm sure we can get it from the company files."

"Right."

"What's the bookkeeper's name, in case we need her help accessing computer files?"

"Uh, Sylvia Harding. She's been here since Peter's mom retired from the job. I have her phone number."

"Great." Harvey looked up as a red Mustang pulled up beside them. "You can give me that later. Looks like Tony and Jimmy are here."

He got out of the vehicle, and Abby opened her door and hopped down. She hated having all of Harvey's men come out in the evening after they'd already put in a full day's work.

"Hey, Mrs. Hobart," Tony said with a faint smile.

"Hi, Tony. And you guys can call me Abby. Hello, Jimmy."

"Hi," Jimmy Cook said.

Harvey took them aside for a minute and gave them a quick run-down of the scene. Tony got a leather case from the trunk of the Mustang and the two detectives went inside. Harvey came back to Abby's side.

"Until we make a positive ID on the victim, I'm not really sure you can help us much," he said apologetically.

"Maybe I can." Abby frowned, trying to remember what Peter had said at breakfast. "If that *is* Carter in there, Peter was concerned about him."

"In what way?" Harvey asked.

"He was talking about it last night, and again this morning. He said Carter was kind of off the rails with a customer yesterday. Pushing him real hard to buy a truck or something like that. Peter had to speak to him about his sales pitch. And then he said he might ask his mom to come in and do an audit."

Harvey's eyes widened. "An audit? Was something going on with the bookkeeping?"

"I don't know. He seems to trust Sylvia, but something about that guy Carter was bothering him. He told me not to worry, but. . ." She looked toward the showroom.

Harvey nodded. "Seems like there was reason to worry, after all."

Tears flooded Abby's eyes, and her chest tightened. "Harvey, what am I going to tell the boys?"

Chapter 3

Peter lay cramped in the trunk of the men's car. Had he made the right decision? He hoped so. This seemed preferable to a bullet. The memory of Carter's bloody corpse made him shudder.

As soon as the two thugs had concluded that Peter could make them rich, or at least solvent, they'd led him out the back door of the showroom to a small black sedan and opened the trunk. They had duct tape inside, and one of them taped his wrists together behind him. That made his spirits plummet, but arguing seemed like a bad idea, since the other man held his gun on Peter the whole time.

"Get in," the first man said.

Peter hesitated only a moment. Anyone whose hands were free could get out of that trunk before they left the parking lot. As an auto dealer, he'd been to umpteen seminars on safety features, and he'd even done practice drills. He knew exactly where the release latch was on this model. True, with his hands bound behind him, he would have trouble pulling it. But if he couldn't get the duct tape off, he could probably kick out a tail light.

All of this ran through his mind, but he kept quiet. Talking too much might make these guys mad enough to just shoot him and be done with it.

He climbed in, his mind racing as the lid came down, shutting out the daylight. Should he have struggled? They hadn't restrained his feet, and he was grateful for that. Did the car have kick-out taillights? The manufacturer was different from those he sold, but the car was new enough that he was pretty certain it did. But if he kicked one out and couldn't wave for help, what good would it do? The men would see it when they stopped, and that would tick them off for sure.

Another dismal possibility was that he could be suffocated by exhaust fumes. Peter knew he had to stay calm and use a minimum of oxygen. As long as the car was moving, he was pretty sure there was no danger from fumes, and trunks weren't built tight enough to suffocate a quiet person. Unless there was some kind of leak and they idled the engine for a while, he thought he'd be okay. But he could imagine Abigail lecturing him on his blithe assumptions. Had he really made the right decision? He sent up a prayer, asking God to deliver him from stupidity.

The engine started, and he could tell they turned right out of the parking lot. He was sure of that. A while later, they seemed to bear right again, then hit a stop light, followed by a left turn. Peter lost track after that. He'd made the mistake of thinking about Abigail and what would happen when she arrived to join him for their date. At least these killers weren't there to confront her.

He could hear faint voices, and he thought the two men were arguing over how to proceed, over what to do with him. The car stopped at one point, and he could make out words. They didn't want to make a move toward ransoming him until they had a secure location to operate from. They agreed that neither of their residences would do. Too risky. One was called Mack. Peter thought he was the one who had held the gun on him. Mack apparently had nosy neighbors. They needed a secluded place where no one would snoop around.

That had worried Peter, but at least they weren't talking about killing him and dumping his body. Finally one of them mentioned someone he knew. This fellow could possibly help them out.

The car began moving again, and he could no longer hear their conversation. They drove for several minutes. Then it stopped, and one of the thugs got out. Only one door slammed, and Peter thought it was the driver's door. He was pretty sure the second man was still in the car. If he was going to do something, this was probably his best chance. On the other hand, if he tried to attract attention, they might decide he wasn't worth the trouble. They obviously weren't afraid to kill an inconvenient person—Carter was proof of that. Right now, he had a chance of coming out of this alive. Peter opted to remain quiet.

After twenty minutes or so, the driver returned, and they got into traffic again. Peter tried counting, but he lost track and it was hard to judge the time they drove. When they stopped, it was quiet. The traffic sounds were distant.

They opened the trunk, and Peter struggled to sit up. They couldn't have gone more than ten miles or so total, he thought. Probably less in rush hour city traffic. But they could be outside the city. Darkness was falling, but one of the men tied a rag around his face anyway, before he got a good look around. He had an impression of houses and a quiet street. He couldn't tell in his brief glimpse which way the ocean was or where the main part of the city lay. Had the lowering sun been behind him? He wasn't sure.

One of them took his arm and pushed him forward.

"Move," Mack said.

*****

Harvey crouched beside the Corvette convertible in the showroom and shined his flashlight under it, ignoring the blood spattered over the door panel and fender. The beam swept over the glossy tiles, and he halted it near the rear tire opposite. After a moment he stood and waved Jimmy Cook to his side.

"There's a shell casing next to the rear tire on the passenger side. Don't touch it, but put a marker down for the techs."

"Okay," Jimmy said and hurried away.

Harvey exhaled. They would have something to go on. It wasn't much. He walked to Peter's office. Wearing gloves, he carefully opened each desk drawer. Peter was a fairly neat person, not as fastidious as Harvey, but he didn't seem to like clutter.

Everything looked very businesslike, very efficient. The usual office supplies, a twelve-foot tape measure, a solar-powered calculator. One drawer held some files that appeared to be documents on the financing of recent sales. On the desktop were a framed photo of Gary and Andy in the formal suits they'd worn at Peter and Abby's wedding, and a closeup of Abby. She looked so much like Jennifer, but she glammed it up more. Both women were beautiful, but Harvey preferred Jennifer's natural look. He bent and peered carefully beneath the desk and chair. Nothing. No signs of a struggle, no cryptic clues.

He tried to wake up Peter's computer but couldn't get past the login password. He could probably crack that fairly quickly if he took the computer back to his office. Meanwhile, time was flying. He turned to a four-drawer file cabinet and had Carter Ulrich's address and phone number within minutes.

In the showroom, the crime scene investigators had arrived and were setting up to work. One was already taking pictures, and another was unpacking numbered markers and evidence bags. Harvey took out his phone and punched in Ulrich's number. A phone started ringing nearby.

One of the CSI's looked startled and grabbed an evidence bag he had set aside.

"That's me calling him." Harvey clicked to end the call.

"It was in the victim's pocket."

Harvey nodded. "Just send it to the lab for me." He'd made a ninety-percent certain ID, and Ulrich's recent calls would be interesting, he had no doubt.

He called Nate Miller over. He'd already sent Jimmy Cook to Sylvia Harding's house, to get a statement from the bookkeeper.

"Nate, here's Carter Ulrich's address. I'm pretty sure he's the victim. Take Tony with you and see if anyone's home. If he's got a wife, remember we don't have an official ID yet on the victim, but see what she can tell you about her husband's activities."

"Right." Nate took the slip of paper Harvey held out and wheeled to get the other detective. Harvey walked outside and breathed in the sea air off the bay. He took out his phone.

"Hi," Jennifer said almost immediately.

"Hi."

"Leeanne's here. Harvey, what's going on?"

"A man got himself killed in Peter's showroom."

"How awful."

Harvey knew she wanted more information, but she usually let him tell her what he could, when it suited him.

"It's not Peter," he said. "We've got a tentative ID, and I don't think it's anyone you knew."

"Okay. How's Peter?"

Harvey hesitated, watching Tony's Mustang leave the parking lot. "I'm not sure. Jenny, this will go public tonight—in fact, I'll probably be late because the press will be on it any minute—but I'd just as soon you didn't tell anyone beyond the family at this point, okay?"

"Of course."

"Okay. Well, the thing is, Peter's not here. We don't know what happened to him. It's starting to look like he may have been abducted."

After a moment's silence, Jennifer said, "You mean—"

"I mean he's not here. I'm pretty sure he's not responsible for the shooting, but he seems to have vanished. Abby came to meet him for dinner and discovered the body, but Peter's simply not here."

"That's not good. How's Abby?"

"She's been very helpful. I sent Eddie with her to Peter's mother's house to break the news. Gary and Andy are over there with their grandmother."

"Oh, Harvey! Those poor little boys."

"I know," Harvey said. "I would have gone myself, but I need to talk to some people connected to the business. I told Eddie to take Abby home after, and to stay with her."

"Do you think Abby's in danger?" Jennifer asked.

"I don't know. But it's possible she'll hear from Peter or from whoever's responsible, and I want to know about it immediately if that happens."

"What about the boys? Will Vickie keep them?"

Harvey sighed. "She had planned to keep them overnight anyway. I think it might be best if they stay there, at least for tonight."

"They'll be scared."

"Yeah. I told Abby if they're too upset, she can take them home with her, but I'd really like to keep them out of sight until we figure this thing out. Look, you can tell your sibs and your parents, and start everyone praying."

"I will."

"But keep away from Abby's house, okay?"

"Of course, Harvey. Is it all right to call her?"

"Best to keep her line open, just in case."

"All right."

"You could call Peter's mother, I guess. But wait a while. Abby and Eddie just left about twenty minutes ago."

"Okay, and Harvey?"

"Yeah?"

"What about that other thing, the one you wanted to talk about?"

He'd almost forgotten about Leah. He looked up at the darkening sky. A few stars were beginning to show. "I think I'd still rather talk about that in person. Sorry. I promise you it will be okay."

A white minivan he recognized drove into the car lot and parked behind a squad car.

"Jenny, the press is here. I need to go."

"I'll look for you on the late news."

*****

Abby sat on her mother-in-law's couch with one of her stepsons on each side. Seven-year-old Andy cuddled up against her side and let Abby keep her arm around him for comfort. Gary, a more dignified ten, sat with his hands folded in his lap. He fidgeted and squeezed until his fingers turned red and his knuckles white. She wished they didn't have to know what was going on. They were too old to be kept in the dark, and too young to be told the sickening details.

"Where do you think Daddy is?" Gary choked out.

Abby patted his hands. "I don't know, but Uncle Harvey and a lot of other people are looking for him. They'll tell us as soon as they know something."

"How come Uncle Eddie's not looking for him?" Gary asked.

Eddie, who had apparently made it home before he got the call and was dressed in jeans and a black T-shirt, slouched against the doorjamb. "Because I brought your mom here to be with you," he said. Abby was glad he hadn't implied that she needed police protection. The boys were taking this hard enough as it was.

Peter's mother, Vickie, came in from the kitchen carrying two coffee mugs. She handed one to Eddie and one to Abby.

"We already ate supper, but I've got some leftovers," she said.

"No, thank you." Abby took the coffee, but she wasn't hungry. She might never be hungry again if her stomach didn't unkink.

"Eddie?" Vickie asked.

"Oh, that's okay, Mrs. Hobart. I'm fine."

"Well. . ." Vickie looked uncertainly at the boys. "I was going to give the boys some cookies and milk. We didn't have dessert."

Andy swiped his eyes and stood up. Abby took that as a good sign.

"Yes," she said firmly. "I think I could eat a cookie. How about you, Gary?"

His lower lip trembled. "I don't know. I want to see Dad."

"We all do, honey," Vickie said, "but we need to eat and sleep so that we'll be feeling good when we do see him again."

"You mean he's not coming back 'til tomorrow?" Andy quavered.

Abby looked at Eddie, but he only gave her a tiny shrug.

"I can't tell you when he'll be back." Abby looked straight into Andy's eyes, then Gary's. "I wish I could. And I'm sure he wants to be here with us."

"Why can't he?" Gary's voice had an unnaturally deep timbre.

"We don't know. But we do know that Daddy loves us. He planned to be with me tonight, and he wouldn't leave any of us like this on purpose. So, he'll be back as soon as he can. Whatever is keeping him away. . ." She ran out of words. She couldn't promise them that Peter would return, but she didn't want to spark in their minds all the horrors that bombarded her own.

Eddie walked over slowly and sat down in an armchair opposite them. "We could pray. God says he listens when we pray."

Abby's breath puffed out of her in relief, and she set her mug on the coffee table. Her stomach probably would rebel if she poured the acid into it, anyway. "Thank you, Eddie. You're absolutely right. That's the best thing we can do right now." She looked up at Vickie. "Would you join us?"

"Of course." Vickie took a seat in her Boston rocker and reached for Andy's hand. He sat down beside Abby again, and she kept her arm around the little boy and took Gary's hand on the other side. Eddie took a swig of coffee and set it aside. He leaned forward and clasped hands with Gary and Vickie, completing the circle.

"Eddie, would you?" Abby could barely croak out the words, her throat ached so.

"Sure." Eddie bowed his head. They were new at this. Maybe she should have asked Vickie to lead off. But Eddie's voice came firm, though soft and pleading. "Our Father, we thank you for this family. We ask you to keep Peter safe, and to bring him back."

When he paused for several seconds, Vickie added, "Help the officers to find him, Lord. And please comfort the family of. . .anyone who's hurt or scared tonight."

Abby let out her breath. She hadn't told the boys a man had been killed at the car dealership, and she'd feared for a moment that Vickie would spill it.

"Lord, we thank you for being there, and for putting us together," she said. "Please be close to Peter and let him feel your guidance. And we thank you for Eddie and Harvey and the other officers who are working on this. Help them to find Peter." Her mind whirled with pictures of her husband lying in some obscure place bleeding and helpless. "Let him come back soon, Lord." Her voice caught.

"Amen," Eddie said.

Before she could open her burning eyes, Andy said, "Please bring my daddy home, Jesus."

Abby squeezed him.

Gary gave a little cough. "God, we just want him to be okay. Tell him to come back."

After a short pause, Vickie said, "Amen."

Abby and Eddie added their quiet amens, and they all opened their eyes. Tears streamed unchecked down Andy's face, and Gary swiped at his reddened eyes with his sleeve.

Vickie stood. "I think we should leave this in God's hands for a while. No one else is stronger or more capable. Now, how about those cookies?"

Eddie stood slowly. "Mrs. Hobart, I'd like to talk to you for a minute. Maybe Abby could help the boys with the milk and cookies?"

"Sure." Vickie sank back into her chair.

Abby hustled the boys into the kitchen. She'd filled Eddie in on the way to the house about Peter's concern over Carter and his plan to ask Vickie to look over the business's financials. As she headed for the refrigerator and directed Gary to get the cookie jar, she heard Eddie say, "I understand Peter asked you to check the company's financial records today?"

"Yes, I went to the store this afternoon," Vickie said.

Abby got out the milk jug and closed the refrigerator door. She smiled at the boys. "Do you guys have special cups here at Grammy's?"

*****

35

Jimmy Cook returned just after the medical examiner supervised the removal of the body. Harvey had shut the press conference down before the M.E. even arrived and had sent the reporters off to prepare their stories for the late news and morning papers. He'd given them minimal details on the shooting, and at the last minute he'd decided not to mention Peter's disappearance.

"Hey, Jim, what did you get from Ms. Harding?"

"Not a lot, but she seemed open and cooperative." Jimmy took out his notebook as they walked into the showroom. He paused just inside the door and leafed through his notes. "Peter asked her yesterday to go over their accounting records. She didn't find any anomalies, and she suggested he might want to have somebody else come in for a second opinion, so he got his mother. She used to be the bookkeeper here. Ms. Harding didn't seem resentful at having someone else take a look."

"Did Peter say anything to her after his mother was here?"

"Yeah, according to Ms. Harding, Peter seemed satisfied that everything was okay, but he hadn't really given her a reason why he wanted her and Mrs. Hobart to do that in the first place. Ms. Harding said that at first she was afraid he thought she'd done something wrong, but he assured her it wasn't that." Jimmy looked at his notes. "Peter said he was concerned about something else and wanted to make sure the books were okay before he got into it deeper. Ms. Harding claims she doesn't know what that other concern was."

"Did you believe her?"

"Yeah." Jimmy frowned. "I poked a little more, and she said she did overhear Peter kind of scolding Carter Ulrich the other day for coming on too strong with a customer."

"Okay, that fits with what Abby said. Anything else?"

"The trainee, Kevin Lane, is right out of school and green as grass, and I guess Peter put him with Andrea Gallis because he thought she'd be good at training him."

"Not Carter Ulrich."

"Right," Jimmy said. "And Sylvia Harding said Ulrich has been here longer than Ms. Gallis. So, I'm thinking maybe that didn't sit well? But it hardly seems like something to get shot over."

"Okay." Harvey looked at his watch. "The dead man is almost certainly Ulrich. Tony and Nate went to his apartment building, but no one was home. They reached out to a neighbor, and she said he lives alone. Divorced."

"Interesting," Jimmy said. "Maybe this financial thing has something to do with that. Divorce can be expensive."

"Yeah. The CSIs are going to be here a while longer. I'm sending you and the other guys home, and I'll meet Eddie over at the Hobarts'. He's taking Abby home, and we're setting up an overnight police presence for her. I want you and Nate and Tony to get a good night's sleep. In the morning we should have some lab reports, and we'll talk to all the other employees and see if we can get a line on what Ulrich was up to."

Jimmy nodded. "Okay, boss. Nothing from Mr. Hobart, I guess."

"Not a word. I admit, I'm worried about him."

Jimmy eyed him closely. "No chance he booked it?"

"None whatsoever. I know Peter, and he wouldn't do that. His kids and Abby are his world."

"So, what about the kids?"

"The grandmother will keep them, at least for tonight. I'm sending a patrol by her house at least once an hour." Harvey wished they could afford to keep an officer with Vickie and the boys around the clock until he found out what happened to Peter, but that wouldn't wash with the administration, unless they found evidence that Peter's family was in danger.

"So we're treating this like a kidnapping?" Jimmy asked.

Harvey nodded. "We've got patrol officers out looking for him, in case he was dumped somewhere close by."

"If they tossed him in the bay, we may never find him."

"Don't say that." The last thing Harvey wanted to think of was Peter being dead, but Jimmy was right. Never knowing would be worse for Abby and the boys. Far worse.

"Sorry," Jimmy said. "I know you were tight with him."

Harvey squared his shoulders. "Unless I see proof, I won't believe Peter left here voluntarily. I just hope he's still alive." He drew in a deep breath. He needed to call Jennifer again. She and Leeanne were probably still together. They wouldn't sleep much tonight. "Go tell the guys to go home, okay? I'll see you all at the office at seven."

He drove straight to Peter and Abby's house. The Princess Anne was probably a hundred or more years old. The details rivaled those of some of the old Victorians in Bayside, but this house was smaller. Harvey glanced at the roof brackets and mix-and-match shingle siding as he walked up to the wraparound porch. He recalled Abby saying once that Peter would have become an architect if his father hadn't died so young. This house probably satisfied some longings for Peter.

Eddie and Abby were already there.

"Hi. I checked the house over," Eddie said when he walked in the front door. "Everything's clear."

"Okay, thanks. Where's Abby?"

"Kitchen."

Harvey found her loading the dishwasher.

"I left the dishes. I guess people will be in and out of here tomorrow, though."

"You don't have to clean the house, Abby." Harvey went to stand beside her.

"Mom would." Her eyes filled with tears.

Harvey put his arms around her and held her for a moment. "We'll find him."

"I know. I just. . .I know you can't make any guarantees on *how* you'll find him. His condition, I mean." She sniffed.

Harvey pulled away and took a handkerchief from his pocket. "Here."

She took it and looked at it as if it were an oddity. "A cloth hanky."

"Yeah, I'm old-fashioned."

"Aw, come on, I know you use it to pick up evidence with." She managed a smile as she wiped her eyes.

38

He pulled a latex glove from his side pocket. "Actually, I'm not that outmoded, unless I have to be. We carry these all the time nowadays." He glanced at the wall phone over near the cellar door. "You have a landline here at home, right?"

"Yes. Peter sends faxes occasionally, and he just likes the quality of a landline better when he's talking business."

Eddie came into the kitchen. "How do you want to play this?"

"You can go home," Harvey said. "I'll stay here."

Eddie shook his head. "You've had a lot of stress today. You ought to go home to Jennifer."

Harvey wavered, and Eddie seized on his hesitation.

"Have you even told her what happened at lunch?"

Abby blinked at him. "What happened at lunch?"

"Nothing important," Harvey said, immediately feeling a stab of guilt. Even if the girl didn't belong to him, she was not unimportant. "I'll tell you about it sometime." He pulled in a breath. "Okay, Ed, I'll go home and see Jenny and get something to eat. You stay here with Abby until I get back, and then, if nothing's come up, you can—"

A tune played softly. Abby froze for an instant then clawed her phone from her pocket.

Chapter 4

Abby glanced at her phone, then she stared at Harvey.

"The number's blocked."

Harvey reached out to steady her. "Nice and easy. It might be anything, but I want you to put it on speaker."

"Okay, if I don't mess up." She squinted at the phone as it continued to ring, pushed a button, and said, "Hello?"

"Abigail Hobart?" said a scratchy male voice.

Her eyes widened.

Harvey nodded.

"Y-yes?" she said.

"Your husband is with me. If you want him back with you, then listen up."

Harvey whipped out his notebook and began writing.

"Who is this?" Abby cried.

"That doesn't matter. What matters is, you got to get us some money. You understand? Cash, I'm talking about. Your man says you can get it."

"I don't—" Abby looked to Harvey, her eyes panicky.

He turned his notebook around where she could see clearly the words he had printed. PROOF OF LIFE.

She pulled in a shaky breath. "How do I know Peter's with you? I want to know he's alive before I do anything for you."

Harvey nodded and patted her shoulder.

"Just you listen," the man said. "He's alive now, but not for long if you don't get us three hundred grand."

Abby caught her breath then steadied. "Let me speak to him."

"You just concentrate on getting the money."

"Not until I have proof that Peter's alive. I want to talk to him right now."

The man swore, then there was silence.

Abby looked down at the phone. "I think he hung up. I lost the connection, anyway." Her eyes brimmed with tears. "Oh, Harvey, what if they kill him because of what I said?"

"Easy, now. They want that money badly."

"So, this is good," Eddie said.

"What?" Abby whirled to glare at him.

"Don't get all prickly on me, BFF," Eddie said with a face of mock horror. "It's now officially a kidnapping, and we can maybe get a line on them."

Abby managed a weak smile.

"Right," Harvey said quickly, taking out his car keys. "Eddie, I had the station send surveillance equipment to me at the car lot. It's in my Explorer. Let's get set up before they call back again."

"You think they will?" Abby's voice shook.

"I *know* they will," Harvey said. "And I want a recording of the next call. You give permission for us to monitor your landline and the calls on your cell?"

"Of course." Abby handed him her phone. "Do whatever you have to."

Eddie was already out the door. Harvey called dispatch and asked for two trained officers to come to the house prepared to stay all night. Harvey didn't want to wait for the others, so he and Eddie set up the equipment. Twelve minutes after the first call, Abby's phone rang again.

Harvey looked at her. "Ready?"

"What do I say?"

"Stick to your guns. Ask to speak to Peter."

"Right." Her hand shook as she reached for the phone, so Harvey punched the speaker button for her.

"H-hello?"

"Abigail? It's me."

"Peter!" Abby's knees buckled. Harvey grabbed her arm as Eddie shoved a chair in behind her.

"Sweetheart, listen. You need to do something for me."

"Are you all right, Peter?" Her voice rose in panic.

42

"Yes, yes, I'm fine. Just do as they say. Get them money from the bank first thing in the morning."

"But—they said three hundred thousand dollars. Peter, we don't have that kind of money." Abby turned her terrified gaze on Harvey.

"You'll have to max out the line of credit for the business," Peter said.

"Will they let me do that?"

Harvey nodded and patted her shoulder. He'd instructed her to keep whoever called talking as long as possible.

"I have a quarter mil line of credit for the business. Ask them at the bank."

"But—"

"Hey, missy." The scratchy voice was back. You do what he says. Things will go badly for all of us if you don't."

"But—all right, I'll try." Tears ran down Abby's cheeks. "How—how do I get it to you?"

"We'll call at ten in the morning and tell you. When we get the cash, we'll let him go. Got it?"

"I—"

"Lost him," Eddie said.

"Did you get a location?" Abby asked.

"No."

Harvey huffed out a breath. "Okay. We'll have to go with what we've got." He knelt beside Abby's chair, took her phone from her, and handed it to Eddie. He reached for her hands. "Abby, this is a good sign."

"Yes. Peter's alive."

Harvey nodded. "You're positive that was Peter, aren't you?"

"Yes. Absolutely."

"Good. I agree. And the man said they'd call at ten in the morning."

"Why wouldn't he tell me now?"

"They probably haven't figured it out yet. They didn't plan to kidnap Peter, so they need to get their ducks in a row."

"He sounded so vile."

43

"Probably disguising his voice," Eddie said from the sofa, where he was fiddling with the recording equipment. "By the way, in case you didn't notice, that call was not from Peter's phone."

"Was it the same one as before?" Abby asked.

"Not sure yet. We may get a report on that eventually, but the number was blocked on your cell again."

The doorbell rang, and Abby flinched.

"That's probably our techs," Harvey said.

"I'll get it." Eddie headed for the front door.

Harvey patted Abby's hands and stood. "You're doing great."

"Can I tell the boys?" she asked.

He considered that for a moment. "The kidnappers are using your cell phone so far. Why don't you go use the landline, but don't stay on it too long?"

"Thanks." She hurried into the kitchen.

Eddie returned with two officers from Ron Legere's detective squad, Emily Rood and Paul Trudeau.

"Hey, you guys had this training?" Harvey asked in surprise.

Emily smiled. "Yeah, after your computer training, it seemed like a good next step."

"We both took it this spring," Paul said.

"Fantastic." Harvey admired officers who sought to improve their skills. "We've had two calls from the kidnappers, or rather one kidnapper, but he used the plural—we, us." Emily and Paul nodded soberly. "Mrs. Hobart took both calls on her cell phone. She's in the kitchen now, using the landline to tell her sons and mother-in-law the good news that her husband is alive."

"She got proof of life?" Paul asked.

"Right. They let him talk to her for about twenty seconds. We weren't able to get a location, but we recorded that second call. It's probably from a burner phone. Mr. Hobart's cell wasn't in his office, but we haven't been able to ping it. I'm guessing they disabled it."

"Okay," Emily said.

44

"The last thing the kidnapper said was that they'll call again at 10 a.m. They expect Abby—Mrs. Hobart—to raise the ransom by then, but that's tricky." Harvey gritted his teeth.

"How much?" Paul asked.

"Three hundred grand. Peter told Abby he's got a line of credit for the business, but I'm not sure the bank will cooperate on that. He probably said that in hopes of buying some time with the kidnappers and giving us a chance to find him. Only we have next to nothing to go on so far."

"What will you do if the bank won't give her the money?" Emily asked.

"I don't know yet. Peter may have quite a bit in liquid assets."

Paul whistled softly. "Must be nice."

Harvey shrugged. "Or he might not. I'm not sure why they picked that number for the ransom."

"Okay," Emily said. "We'll listen to the recording and set up to wait."

Harvey nodded. "We probably won't hear from them again until ten in the morning. I need to talk to Abby about the banking situation. We may be able to contact their banker tonight and see if he'll meet with her before business hours. If so, I'll take her to the bank first thing in the morning."

Harvey walked into the kitchen, and Eddie followed him. Abby was hanging up the wall phone.

"I talked to Vickie. The boys are in bed. She says she'll check on them, and if they're awake she'll tell them now, but she doesn't want to wake them up if they're sleeping."

"Good," Harvey said. "How did she take it?"

"She's optimistic, but still worried sick, of course. Like me."

He smiled and gave her a quick hug. "We'll get through this, Abby. Peter sounded good."

She nodded, frowning. "Yeah. I thought he was honest about his condition."

"And nothing he said triggered any red flags for you?" Harvey asked.

"Well. . .one thing."

"What?"

Abby hesitated. "I'm pretty sure the line of credit is for a million dollars. But he said a quarter million, and that I'd have to max it out."

"Are you sure it's really a million?" Harvey asked.

"Pretty certain. He had me go in last summer and sign papers for all his accounts, personal and business. I remember being shocked that he could just borrow a million dollars anytime. But why would he say the wrong thing?"

"I can think of three reasons, offhand. First, to throw the kidnappers off track. If they knew it was a million, they'd ask for a million. Second, he may have already borrowed part of the million to buy stock for the showroom."

"You're right of course."

"And third, he was protecting you. The business, too, of course, but ultimately you. Good old Peter."

"What do you mean?" Abby asked.

Harvey held her gaze and said quietly, "If things go sour and we don't get the money back, Peter doesn't want you left owing the bank a million dollars."

"He'd have to pay it back," she said.

"Or *you* would have to pay it back."

Her face tightened. "You're saying we might not get Peter back alive."

"I don't want to say it, Abby, but it's a possibility."

She inhaled slowly. "I guess I need to be prepared for that. I wish I'd been able to get more information from him."

"They didn't want the call to last long enough for us to trace," Eddie said.

"Yeah," Harvey said reluctantly. "They're not the most brilliant kidnappers ever, but they aren't out-and-out stupid, either."

"But who are they?" She turned bleak eyes on Eddie, then Harvey.

"Someone connected to Carter Ulrich," Harvey said.

46

"You're sure it was Carter?"

"Almost positive. We should get an official identification tomorrow."

"What did you tell the press?"

Harvey sighed. "That an unidentified man was killed inside the dealership showroom. That's pretty much it."

"You didn't tell them Peter's missing?"

"No. We didn't know for sure he'd been abducted then, and I didn't want to say anything that would upset the kidnappers if they were listening. And I didn't want the press hounding you for sound bites."

"Ick. I don't want reporters swarming this place." Abby's gaze darted about the room as though she expected them to pop out of corners.

"It could happen," Harvey said. "I hope we can get Peter back tomorrow, though. It's possible the press would never need to know, but if we hit a snag, we'll have to go public."

"Okay." Abby sobbed. "Sorry, I don't mean to sound like a ninny, but you guys will be with me all the way on this, right?"

"Of course."

"Abs, you know we're going to find him," Eddie said.

She placed a hand on his arm and one on Harvey's. "I'm counting on you guys. You and God."

"Do you think you can sleep?" Harvey asked.

"No."

"Okay. I'm going to leave Eddie here while I go home and see Jenny for a few minutes, and then I'll come back. Maybe you two can play checkers or something."

Abby laughed. "I don't think we even have a checkerboard. Now, if you'd said Battleship. . ."

Harvey smiled. "I also think you should let Eddie screen any incoming calls. Reporters might start calling here, trying to locate Peter for a comment on the shooting. It was at his business, after all. Are you listed in the phone book?"

"Unfortunately, yes."

47

"Then let Eddie or one of the other officers answer the phone unless you recognize the caller ID."

"Harv, you should get some sleep," Eddie said. "Those guys won't call back until ten in the morning. You'll need all your wits tomorrow."

"You should both go home if the techs are staying," Abby said.

"Turns out they're both highly skilled detectives that I respect," Harvey said. "But I'd still like to have someone from my squad here."

"I'll stay," Eddie said firmly. "I'll check the alarm system and all that."

"You could catch a few Z's in the boys' room," Abby said. She looked quickly at Harvey. "Unless you need him to stay awake every minute."

"No, I think that would be all right. Those thugs have Peter, and they've put you on notice. I don't really think they'll come nosing around here, but I want to know one of us is with you. Eddie, you should call Leeanne before I leave."

"Sure." Eddie took out his phone. "Are we telling our wives about Peter?"

"Yes, but stress to her that family only gets that intel." Harvey turned to Abby. "Now, let's talk about what Peter said. He put you on all his bank accounts, so they'll let you access that line of credit?"

"I. . .I think so." She grabbed for a tissue from a box on the granite countertop. "Peter made me a partner in the business right after we got married. I told him it was silly because we agreed I won't go to the store every day. I'll be here for the boys, and you know I've started putting in a few days at the hospital again. Only when I want to, per diem. Peter says I don't need to work, but I want to keep up my certification and maintain my contacts."

Harvey nodded. "That can be useful. But tell me more about the business partnership."

48

She shrugged and wiped her eyes. "It's just on paper. I don't do anything. I did sit in on one corporate meeting last fall, with Peter and his mom and his sister Janelle."

"Janelle's a partner?"

"Yeah. When his dad died, he left half the business to Vickie and a quarter each to Peter and Janelle. But Janelle got married, and she didn't really want to be active in the business. She sold her shares to Peter, which gave her a nice nest egg, but he's kept her on as a board member on paper. Sort of like me, I guess. And then Vickie made over half her shares to him."

"So Peter owns three quarters of the business now, and Vickie the other quarter?"

"Yes."

"Who can access the financial accounts? Specifically, the line of credit?"

"I'm not sure. We could ask Vickie."

"Do you mind if I call her?" Harvey asked.

"No, go ahead."

Abby gave him her mother-in-law's number, and Harvey placed the call. Vickie was forthright about it.

"Why, yes, I think Abby can. Any board member could."

"Really?" Harvey asked. "Even your daughter Janelle?"

"Well, I'm not positive about her. I think her name came off the financial accounts when she sold her shares to Peter. But I'm pretty sure Abby can do it, and I know I can. Captain, if you need me to go to the bank tomorrow, I will."

"Okay, I'll let you know on that. Thanks, Mrs. Hobart." Harvey put his phone away and looked at Abby. "She thinks you'll be able to get the money, and if not, she'll help."

"That's a relief."

"Come on," Harvey said. "I'll introduce you to Emily and Paul."

*****

An hour later, Harvey pulled off his necktie and sank into an armchair in his own living room. Jennifer slid onto his lap, and he

49

wrapped his arms around her. He'd told her about the calls from the kidnapper, and she'd immediately asked what she could do for Abby and Peter's sons.

"Pray," he said. "I can't believe it's after midnight. Before any of this happened—before Abby called me—"

"You'd already worked a full day," Jennifer said.

"Yeah. But here's the thing." He looked into her solemn, blue-gray eyes. "Twelve hours ago, Eddie and I were eating lunch at the diner, and a girl came up to us."

Jennifer's eyebrows drew together, but she remained silent, her full attention on him.

"She introduced herself as Leah Viniard, and then she dropped the bomb."

"Not a literal bomb, I take it."

Harvey sighed then watched her anxiously as he delivered the news. "She thinks I'm her father."

Jennifer didn't move or speak.

After about ten seconds, she twined her arms around his neck and held him close.

Harvey said, "Aren't you going to ask?"

"Ask what?"

"If it's true."

"No. You told me on the phone it would be all right."

Relief washed over him, even though he'd known deep down she wouldn't doubt him.

"If it was true, you'd have come home before midnight," she added.

He smiled at that and held her close. "That's why I love you so much. Well, part of it."

She stroked the back of his neck, then ran her fingers up through his hair. "Do you think you can sleep now?"

Harvey leaned back and cocked his head to one side. "Don't you want all the details?"

Jennifer shrugged. "When you're ready. But you must be exhausted. You ran two miles at six this morning, and you'll have a long day tomorrow."

"You're right."

Jennifer got up, and Harvey rose slowly, pulling off his suit jacket.

"I told her it's not possible. Then I took her to a lab for a DNA test to prove it. I figured we'd get that done, and I'd put her on a bus back to Lewiston."

"Heavens."

"Yeah, well, it didn't quite go that way. I called the lab first, and they wouldn't take her sample without parental consent."

"How old is she?"

"Fifteen."

Jennifer nodded. "You couldn't have it done at the police station?"

"That was my first thought, but it would be a technical no-no. Personal business. And anyway, she didn't trust my friends to tell her the truth."

"I see. So, what did you do?"

"It took a while, but I finally convinced her to call her mother—that's her adoptive mother. They live in Lisbon, and Leah caught the bus in Lewiston this morning. I made her call home before we even left the diner. The mom was appalled that Leah was in Portland. She said she would drive down and get her. We waited at the police station, and I had the unit secretary give her a tour. I didn't want any accusation of impropriety or anything like that."

"Good thinking. Paula was a good choice for that."

Harvey nodded. "When the mom got there we had a chat, and she apologized for Leah showing up like that and taking me away from my work. She was going to whisk her out of there, but I explained to her that doing a cheek swab could put Leah's mind at ease, and Mrs. Viniard finally agreed it might be the best thing. So we all went over to the lab."

They walked into the bedroom as he talked, and Harvey removed his shoulder holster and set it on the dresser. He began unbuttoning his shirt.

"They didn't have to take blood?" Jennifer asked.

51

"No. The buccal swab is what we use all the time for suspect identification from DNA. It basically gives you the same information as a blood test would."

"So, what happens now?"

"It will come back negative. But it makes me wonder if there's another Harvey Alan Larson out there."

Jennifer's eyebrows rose.

"My name is on her birth certificate, along with her biological mother's—but that woman is now deceased."

"So, no interviewing her."

"Exactly."

"Maybe someone picked your name out of the phone book fifteen years ago."

He sighed. "I wish I knew. Anyway, I know the lawyer who sent the birth certificate to Leah, Trent Jarvis. I called him after she left with her mother."

"Was he helpful?"

"Not as much as I'd like. He said Tara Ervin, the birth mom, came to him about five years ago for her divorce from a guy named Leland. Jarvis said she regretted giving up her baby, and he was afraid she wanted to start legal proceedings to try to get her back. He discouraged her from that. He implied that Tara had a hard life and still wasn't in a good position to raise a child. And anyway, the adoption was solid, or so he said."

"Was he able to talk Tara out of trying?"

"Yeah. But she insisted that he set up this thing for her with a packet of documents, to be sent to Leah on Tara's death. He says he didn't know it contained a copy of the birth certificate, but I'm sure he suspected. Leah told me she also got a copy of Tara's death certificate with it."

"That's a little morbid, don't you think?"

"Kind of, especially when Leah's so young. But Tara arranged it all a couple years ago, to be done after her death, and he was carrying out the client's orders."

"What triggered that? Was she sick?"

"Breast cancer. I guess she was scared. And she wanted her daughter to know who she was, even if she couldn't get to know her."

"Wow." Jennifer sat still for a moment, taking on Leah's sorrow. "You won't be able to let this go, even when you see the negative test results, will you?"

"Probably not. I'm sorry."

"Don't be," she said. "You feel responsible, even though you're not."

"I paid for the test."

"Okay."

Harvey continued to undress. "Leah really thinks it's true, but I know it's not. I gave her and her mother my card and told them to call if they want to."

"I would expect no less of you." Jennifer kissed him. "You'd better fall into that bed. What time are you going in?"

"I've got to be at the office at seven, and I left Eddie at Abby's with two other officers."

She heard a faint cry. "There's Connor. He was a little fussy tonight. I think it's because you didn't come home. I'll go check him."

"Bring him down," Harvey said. "He ought to see me, and maybe he'll settle down then." He wondered if Gary and Andy Hobart were sleeping, or if they were lying awake fretting over their father.

He climbed into bed with good intentions of staying awake to greet Connor, but he made the mistake of closing his eyes.

*****

Peter sat on a lumpy sleeping bag on the concrete floor in the dark and tried not to think how many people had used it before him. He flexed his arm and shoulder muscles and wriggled. If only they'd taped his hands in front of him, he knew he could break loose, but with his wrists tightly bound behind him, his efforts only caused discomfort. His hours at weightlifting had

53

built strength, but he wasn't a contortionist. Maybe Abigail was wiser to gear her workouts to flexibility and endurance.

He closed his eyes and leaned back with his head against the wall. Cold granite blocks. This house must be a hundred years old or more.

Every time he let his mind wander, the sickening sight of Carter's body came unbidden. Abigail would have seen that. She would have walked in on it.

Over and over, Peter replayed the minute after he'd heard raised voices in the showroom. From inside his office, with its door open, he'd heard Carter talking to someone. A late customer? Maybe he'd asked someone to come at closing time to sign documents.

Carter's voice rose in panic. "No, please!"

And then a loud sound that startled him, followed by a thud. He leaped up from his desk and strode to the doorway, his heart hammering. Two men stood between the new vehicles on display.

Peter took two steps into the showroom, and they jerked around toward him and he saw the gun one of them held. Before he could duck back, the gunman had trained his weapon on Peter. If only he'd had the door shut or hadn't stepped out of the room. He could have dived under his desk and called 911. But he wasn't quick enough.

What were they after?

The answer seemed obvious. Money. His stomach clenched. He'd known something was going on with Carter.

"What do you want?" He forced the words out. "If it's money you came for, I may be able to help you."

The gunman paused and flicked a glance at his partner.

At first, Peter had wished someone else had stayed late. But, no—he was glad no one else was there. They might have been killed, too. Sylvia, or Jeremy, or Andrea. Mostly, he was glad Abigail hadn't arrived before they'd hurried out the back door.

The killers' friend apparently came through with not only a secluded building with a basement, but some supplies. The one called Mack had taken Peter inside and down the stairs and sat with him. The friend they'd contacted must have driven in a separate vehicle, and Mack's buddy met him upstairs. Peter heard muffled voices and footsteps above them. Then the other kidnapper came down, and Mack took off his blindfold. That surprised Peter, but he guessed it made sense, since he had already seen their faces. Mack's buddy was holding a pistol. He aimed it at Peter's chest.

When Mack's partner handed him a chain and a couple of padlocks, Peter's hopes plummeted. Mack wrapped one end of the chain around Peter's left ankle and fixed the lock so tight he wouldn't be able to slip out of the chain. The other end of the chain went around a large vertical pipe in a corner. Great. Even worse, they left his hands duct-taped behind him.

The last thing they gave him was a sleeping bag. Mack unrolled it and laid it out, and Peter wriggled onto it, sitting on it with his back against the wall. Then they left him for a long time, turning off the bare lightbulb in the ceiling fixture. The light from the small window faded. Peter couldn't see any streetlights or stars, just a dark bit of dirty glass.

He prayed. He thought of Abigail and the boys and wondered what was going on back at Hobart Chevrolet and at his mother's house. What did Abby do when she came to pick him up at the store? He hoped she didn't see Carter's body. But she was strong. She was used to seeing blood. Even so, he hoped she didn't have to go through that.

Please, God, comfort her!

He had an idea that he might fray the duct tape on the sleeping bag zipper's teeth, since it was old enough to have a metal zipper, but he couldn't make it work. He tried for a long time, but every effort fizzled when the padded fabric crumpled on itself. With everything behind his back, he couldn't find a way to make the edge of the zipper stick up and stay solid enough to work with.

Hours later, they came back. They took the chain off long enough for him to use the small bathroom. Mack cut the tape on

55

his wrists for that, too. Afterward, they told him to sit on the sleeping bag and gave him a wrapped hamburger and a bottle of water.

"Thanks," Peter said. The young man holding the gun grunted in reply.

The wrapper was from McDonald's. Was that significant? Were they near a McDonald's? There were several in Portland. Peter catalogued them mentally.

The hamburger was still lukewarm. It wasn't bad, but it was a far cry from the dinner he'd planned with Abigail at the upscale restaurant.

After he'd eaten, his captors restrained him again and went upstairs. Peter sat in the darkness, praying silently.

He heard them talking, so they hadn't left yet. He'd offered them a bundle of cash. Were they working out how to get it? Making out their words was impossible, and he gave up trying. A few minutes later, the light switched on, and Peter blinked.

Mack came quickly down the stairs holding a cell phone.

"You're going to talk to your wife," he said. "Here's what you tell her. Do not try to say anything else. It's no skin off our nose to shoot you, and we'd rather do that than be caught. You got it?"

Peter nodded, and then they called Abigail. Peter let out a deep sigh and eased down onto the sleeping bag. The chain rattled on the floor as his foot moved.

Lord, comfort Abigail! Protect her.

He hadn't even had time to tell her that he loved her.

Chapter 5

Harvey breezed into his office at five minutes to seven. Nate Miller was already at his desk, working at his computer. He looked up and nodded at Harvey.

"Morning, Cap'n."

"Thanks for coming in early, Nate. You got anything?"

"Not much on Ulrich. I did get an address on his ex-wife. Sent it to you in an e-mail. Oh, and Jimmy called a minute ago. He's just relieved Eddie, and Eddie's coming here."

"Good. Did you check the usual suspects?"

Nate's face contorted. "The truth is, boss, we haven't had many kidnappings in the area, or in the state, for that matter. The last three were parental abductions in custody cases."

"I guess I knew that." Harvey set his briefcase on his desk. "I was hoping. But, like I told you last night, I don't think these are serial kidnappers. I think they went to Hobart's to settle their business with Ulrich last night, and Peter surprised them."

"Why didn't they just shoot him too and scram?"

"Peter's a smart guy. I suspect he talked his way out of it and offered them money."

Nate nodded slowly. "I guess that fits. He's going great guns in the business. He's expanded three or four times in the last ten years."

"I'm not saying he's loaded," Harvey said, opening the briefcase. "He puts a lot back into the dealership—inventory and so on. But he's not hurting any financially, that's for sure. He takes care of his mom and gives Abby a free hand with the credit cards. Of course, she a sensible young woman, so he doesn't have to worry much."

"Still," Nate said, "he must have put that ransom figure in their heads, based on what he thought the Mrs. could raise quickly."

"Well, this doesn't leave this room, but the truth is, his line of credit is four times what he said it is. Abby could probably have raised a lot more than they asked for."

"Huh. Maybe he figured the bank wouldn't raise their eyebrows so much if she didn't ask for it all."

"Could be. Especially when she asks for it in cash. I'll take a look at his inventory today and see if he's already used part of the line of credit for stock."

"That's a thought," Nate said. "I've got all the addresses of the other Hobart employees."

"Good. Let's ask Sergeant Legere to have some of his detectives help us out with that."

The door from the stairway opened, and Tony Winfield walked in whistling. "Hey, boss. Nate."

"Good morning," Harvey said, and Nate nodded.

"Have you seen the chief's new secretary?" Tony asked.

Startled, Harvey said, "Judith hasn't left yet, has she?"

"Not till the end of next week, but she's training her replacement. A big improvement, I'm telling you."

Harvey scowled. "What, she files better than Judith?"

Nate laughed. "I bet she won't be as good at keeping the riffraff out of the chief's inner sanctum."

"People like you, you mean?" Tony said.

"Be careful how you talk about the female employees," Harvey said. Careless remarks were being scrutinized these days.

"Right." Tony grinned and pulled his chair over near Harvey's desk. "So what's the plan, Captain?"

"We've arranged for a bank officer to meet with Mrs. Hobart at 8:30. The bank doesn't open until nine—well, just the drive-up before that—so it should be nice and quiet. I'll take her to get the ransom money, and then we'll go to her house to wait for the instructions on the drop."

"Can I go with?" Tony asked.

"Yeah, you and Eddie. Nate's got a speaking engagement in Kittery this afternoon, and I don't want him to be late."

"Sorry," Nate said.

58

Harvey shook his head. "No problem. Just keep on the research until you have to leave, okay? I'll call you if I've got any new leads for you to follow."

"What about the ex?" Nate asked.

Harvey had opened his email while they talked and eyed the address Nate had sent him. "Deering. Maybe I should send a couple guys out there while we get the money."

"Jimmy will be free while Abby's with you," Nate pointed out.

"Yeah, but I want to make sure everyone's available for the drop. We have no idea when that will be."

"There's time," Tony said. "I'll follow you to Mrs. Hobart's, and Jimmy and I can take my car to Deering while you and Eddie escort your sister-in-law to the bank."

"Maybe." Harvey leaned back in his chair and thought about it. He and Eddie would probably be plenty of manpower with Abby. He didn't want to draw too much attention to her when he took her to the bank. But he should have told Eddie to wait for him at Abby's house. "All right, that sounds workable, Tony. Thanks."

His desk phone rang, and he picked it up.

"Harv, you got a minute?" came the chief's familiar voice.

"Yeah. Are you upstairs?"

"Just got in."

"I'll be right up." Harvey stood and said to Nate and Tony, "I'm going up to the chief's office for a minute. Tell Eddie to wait for me here. Tony, you guys can go over what little Nate has on Ulrich. See if you can get a few contact names. And remember, when you see the ex, we don't have the official I.D. yet."

"What, we can't say it's him?" Tony asked.

"You can tell her it looks that way, and we'll notify her for sure later."

"I guess she can't help us with a visual of the corpse." Tony grimaced.

59

"Right, but she may know of some identifying marks. But not a word about the abduction," Harvey said, striding toward the stairs. "We need to head over to Abby's by eight—sooner if I can get away."

As he entered the chief's outer office, his phone rang. He pulled it out and glanced at the screen. "Larson."

"Captain, this is Zoe, in the lab. I have a preliminary report on the evidence collected at the shooting at Hobart Chevrolet."

"Great. Anything stand out?"

"The shell casing is from a 9-millimeter. No matches in the system. We weren't able to unlock the phone, but the fingerprints on it are Carter Ulrich's. Same with the wallet, which has his driver's license, three credit cards, a medical card, a picture of two children, and eleven dollars."

"Send me the report, please. I'll be on the move all morning, but I'll look at it on my phone."

Harvey realized that Mike's nearly retired secretary, Judith, was standing by her desk waiting for his attention. Beside her stood a twenty-something redhead that would cause more heads to turn than just Tony's. He was glad his unit secretary was a motherly woman in her late forties.

As he pocketed his phone, Judith said, "Captain Larson, I'd like you to meet Elaine Cross. She will be replacing me at the end of next week."

Harvey smiled and stepped forward. "Nice to meet you, Ms. Cross. I'm not sure anyone can replace Judith, though."

"It's a tall order," the young woman said. "Please call me Laney."

Harvey nodded. "I'm sure there's a lot to remember, but it will get easier as you go along."

"That's what I've told her," Judith said in a rare moment of warmth. "The chief is expecting you."

"Thank you." Harvey walked into Mike's office and closed the door behind him. "Hi, Mike. What's up?"

"I just got the labs on this shooting you caught last night."

"Yeah. Not a lot to go on, but it's a start."

"You're sure the victim is this. . ." He squinted at his computer screen. "Carter Ulrich?"

"Pretty sure. He's one of Peter Hobart's sales team."

"What's the word on Peter?"

"Nothing new since we talked last night." Harvey glanced at his watch. "I have to leave within ten minutes to pick up Abby and take her to the bank."

Mike leaned back in his chair, chewing his gum pensively. "I assume you'll want plainclothes backup for the drop."

"Yeah. The guy said things will go badly if Abby doesn't cooperate. I take that as a threat to Peter's life. We don't want to spook them."

"But they didn't tell her not to call the police?"

"They've got to know we're involved, because of the shooting," Harvey said.

Mike shrugged. "You're right. I'll speak to Sgt. Yeaton and Sgt. Legere as soon as they're in and ask them to have some people on standby. How many, do you think?"

Harvey had already thought about it some, but it was tricky. "I don't really know until they tell us where to make the drop. If it's out in the open—a park or something—we can use a dozen. If it's someplace more confined. . .well, we'll have to wait and see."

"Okay. I'll see that you get at least six."

"Besides my four guys?"

"Yeah."

"Thanks."

"Have you thought about replacing Miller yet?"

Harvey threw back his head and frowned at the ceiling. "Not really. Seems like I'm always looking for new detectives."

"Well, keep it in mind," Mike said. "And another thing you can think about: I know it's three months away, but Jill Weymouth called me yesterday about the Labor Day Challenge. Bangor wants a rematch in September."

"What? You're crazy," Harvey said. "We lost a good detective because of that game. No, *two* good detectives. As far as I'm concerned, you can tell the mayor—"

Mike held up both hands. "Easy now, Harvey. You know Joey would have gotten killed anyway, game or no game."

"Maybe. But the challenge gave the perfect opportunity. Accepting the invitation would be an insult to Joey's memory."

"That's a little strong." Mike popped his gum. "Well, think about it."

"No, I will not think about it. My brother-in-law has been abducted. I am going to think about that. I don't need all these distractions."

"Okay, you've got a point. Jill isn't going to be happy, though."

"Jill can take a hike. Mike, you won't even be here by Labor Day, will you? I thought your last day was August thirty-first."

"Right. It is." Mike smiled. "This isn't my headache. It's Jack Stewart's. I'll send him a memo, and he can meet with Mayor Weymouth. Sharon and I will be up at Churchill Lake, catching fish and watching the leaves turn."

"I've really got to get going, Mike."

"Of course." Mike stood and walked to the door with him. "I didn't mean to trivialize Peter's situation, Harvey. I thought maybe things were a little heavy for you right now."

"I'm okay. But thanks."

Mike patted his shoulder. "I know time's flying, but for what it's worth, I'll be praying for you."

"That's worth a lot." Harvey went briskly through the outer office calling, "Have a good day, ladies." As he dashed down the stairs, he wondered if he'd made a blunder by calling them ladies. Some people were very sensitive about things like that, especially since the harassment turmoil the department had been through the previous fall.

Eddie had just hit the third-floor landing as Harvey came down.

"Hey," Harvey called to him. "I should have had you stay at Abby's. You going with me to take her to the bank?"

"Oh, okay," Eddie said. "Or do you want me to go directly to the bank and do a little observing?"

"Yeah, that sounds good. If they're watching us, it will be less obvious how closely we're guarding her."

Eddie nodded. "And if they do watch for her to go to the bank, the fewer of us they recognize later at the drop the better."

He opened the door to the unit office, and Harvey strode in. Tony popped up from his chair. "You ready, boss?"

"Yeah. Better bring along all your gear, in case you don't get back for it before the drop."

"Already in my car."

"Good." Harvey went to retrieve his briefcase and Kevlar vest. "Nate, anything new?"

"I'm looking at the lab report."

"Okay, stay on this. Eddie, you good?"

Eddie nodded. "I'll go sit across the street from the bank."

*****

Abby greeted Harvey at the door when he arrived at her house. She was dressed in a calf-length skirt and sweater.

Harvey kissed her cheek. "How are you doing?"

"Okay. I'm ready to go whenever you are."

Emily and Paul were seated in the living room near their equipment, with coffee and muffins set out nearby. Emily put aside a book and stood when Harvey walked in.

"Good morning, Captain," she said.

"Hi. You guys must be exhausted."

Emily smiled and shook her head. "We swapped off for naps on the sofa. No calls except a couple of Mr. Hobart's employees. Abby told them the business won't open today."

Good choice, Harvey thought. "You should go home. I thought they were sending in a relief team."

"We asked to stay until the 10 a.m. call comes in," Paul said.

63

"Yeah," Emily added. "We wanted to see it through. I hope that's okay. I'm alert, really."

"Okay, but I'll have someone spell you as soon as we get that."

Harvey turned as Jimmy Cook came from the kitchen with a coffee mug in his hand.

"Oh, you ready, Cap'n?" Jimmy said. He set the mug on a coaster on the coffee table.

Abby stepped toward him. "Let me put that in a travel mug for you, Jim."

"Tony's outside," Harvey said. "Jim, I need you to go with him to talk to Ulrich's ex while we're at the bank. Eddie's meeting Abby and me there. Get going."

"Okay," Jimmy said.

"You can take your coffee with you like that," Abby told him.

Jimmy grinned. "I promise to bring the mug back."

Harvey looked at the detectives. "Emily, would you come reset the alarm, please? One of you make the rounds of every exit every fifteen minutes while we're gone."

"Right," Trudeau said, getting to his feet.

"We can take my car," Abby said. "You know, in case they're watching."

"I'd rather have my radio and equipment with me. Like I said last night, they have to know we're in this. And he didn't tell you to go to the bank alone."

She shrugged. "Okay."

They went out to his vehicle, and Harvey opened the passenger door for her. He walked around and got in the driver's seat.

"How are the boys?" he asked.

"I talked to them about a half hour ago. They asked Vickie if they could stay home from school. I wasn't going to let them, but then I thought, what are they going to do at school? They're so sad, they'll want to tell their friends what's going on, and we don't want that. And Andy would probably wind up crying. So I told them they could stay out. Vickie said she didn't mind."

"Probably for the best," Harvey said.

"And Jennifer called me. She's agonizing, too."

"We all are."

She nodded. "I told her I'd ask you if she can come over here later. I could really use somebody like her around, Harvey."

He thought about it. Abby needed her sisters. If he was missing, he would want Leeanne and Abby to be with Jennifer. Her parents, too.

"Yeah, once we're clear on their demands and the drop. We can't do anything to complicate that."

"That makes sense."

Jimmy and Tony pulled out ahead of them in Tony's red Mustang.

"Do you think the kidnappers will pull something when we leave the bank with the money?" Abby asked.

"Well, you never know. But Eddie and I will be on high alert." Harvey eased out onto the street.

"Okay." Abby frowned and adjusted her seatbelt. "I think I'll ask for the whole amount from the line of credit."

"Not the two-fifty Peter specified?"

She looked over at him. "Do you think that's a good idea? I thought about it, and I'm not sure why he said two-fifty from the line of credit when they asked for three. The only other place I can think of to get the rest is from our savings and investment accounts. But if I take it from there—" She shook her head. "I don't want the bank people to think I'm emptying Peter's savings and leaving him or something."

Harvey considered that. "I suppose it might look suspicious if you drain his personal accounts and ask for a quarter million from his line of credit. If you take it in one lump, they're more likely to assume it's for the business."

"I still wonder why he said take a quarter million from the line of credit." She frowned.

65

"I think it's so the kidnappers wouldn't know the fund was much larger."

"I suppose so. But if the bank suspects it's for a ransom, will they give it to me? I didn't tell Mr. Strickland that when I called him last night."

"I'm not sure." Harvey wished he'd checked into that. Maybe he should have talked to the banker and been up-front with him.

"This way, if we don't get the money back, Peter can start repaying them with his savings," Abby said. She stared straight ahead, and Harvey decided not to mention again the possibility that they wouldn't get back the money—or Peter.

At the bank, he spotted Eddie's pickup parked a little up the street on the opposite side. He waited until Eddie was out of his truck and had crossed the street to get out and open Abby's door.

"Everything good?" he asked Eddie.

"Yeah. Nothing unusual. No lurkers. Any cars matching Abby's description from last night, the drivers did their business and moved on."

A security guard opened the bank door for them, and the three walked in. Behind the counter, two tellers were setting up for the day and serving the early bird bankers at the drive-up window. Harvey had instructed Eddie to stand watch in the lobby while he and Abby went with the supervisor into one of the offices. A name plate on his desk read DARRELL STRICKLAND.

"Thank you for coming in early for me," Abby told him.

"Oh, I'm always here by this time," he assured her. "We don't usually open the doors until nine, but for a transaction this large, it seemed wise. I see you have some support with you."

"Yes," Abby said. "My brother-in-law, Harvey Larson."

"Have we met?" The man smiled uncertainly at Harvey.

"I don't think so."

"You look familiar. Well, anyway, that's good. I wouldn't like to think of you leaving the building unattended with so much money. Let's sit down and get to the paperwork." He pulled a file from his desk drawer and opened it. "We'll need your signature in

66

several places. Uh, I believe you said you wanted to withdraw cash."

"That's right," Abby said. "Three hundred thousand. I'd like to use Hobart Chevrolet's line of credit for the full amount if I may."

Strickland glanced at Harvey and back at Abby. "Mr. Hobart usually does this, but I don't believe he's ever made such a large cash withdrawal before. He usually exercises his credit, and we send the money to the company he is doing business with."

"He asked me to do this for him," Abby said firmly. "I do have the proper credentials?"

"Oh, yes, you are perfectly qualified to make the transaction."

Harvey sensed that the man had a feeling all wasn't right. "Mr. Strickland?"

"Yes?" The man's gaze snapped to meet his.

"If you are worried, I can assure that everything is all right. But perhaps it would allay some of your concern to know that I'm a police officer. I am also Mrs. Hobart's brother-in-law, as she said. I offered her my services today to ensure her safety. The gentleman who came in with us is a police detective with the Portland P.D."

Strickland's face cleared. "That's it. I've seen you on the news."

"That's very possible," Harvey said.

"Oh, yes, Harvey's always doing press releases," Abby said brightly.

Strickland looked from her to Harvey. "Yes. Last night, for instance. That was you, wasn't it?"

"Yes," Harvey said.

Strickland hesitated. "It's just that. . .well, Mrs. Hobart, your call came in last evening, and then I saw the news report, and I couldn't help wondering. . ."

"If there was a connection between the shooting at Hobart Chevrolet and this transaction?" Harvey asked.

"Well, yes," he admitted. "And now, Mrs. Hobart, you arrive with two policemen to accompany you when you receive the money, and. . .Oh, dear."

"It was not my husband who was killed," Abby said.

"I'm glad of that."

"We all are," Harvey said. "Now, Mr. Strickland, time is important here."

"Of-of course."

Harvey nodded. "You needn't have any worries about the money."

"Oh, Mr. Hobart is always very good about meeting his financial obligations." Strickland peered anxiously at Abby.

She managed to smile, but the strain showed in her face. "Everything is fine. In fact, Peter and I may be back in later today to redeposit this money. If not, we'll repay it on the customary schedule. It all depends on a deal he's working on, and he needs cash on hand, you see."

"Oh." Strickland slid some papers toward her. "Sign here, please."

Abby looked over at Harvey. He nodded, and she took the pen.

Chapter 6

They arrived at Abby's house at quarter past nine, later than Harvey had wanted. Abby thought he looked a little antsy. Two new techs had already arrived to take over the phone surveillance from Emily and Paul, but the detectives insisted on staying through the ten o'clock call.

"For continuity," Emily said.

"Okay, but I don't want it too congested here." Harvey paced from the door to each window, looked out, and walked to the stone fireplace, then to the kitchen door. "Any calls?"

"Just Mrs. Hobart's sister," Paul said.

"Which one?" Abby asked.

"Uh. . ." Paul consulted his notes. "Jennifer. She called on the landline about fifteen minutes ago."

"That's my wife," Harvey said.

Abby looked to him. "Can I call her back? I don't want to mess things up, but. . ."

Harvey held out his cell. "Use my phone. Keep it short."

"Okay, thanks." Abby escaped into Peter's den. She sat down in a leather armchair, surrounded by some of his favorite things. Two bookcases were filled with nature and architecture books. A Spitfire model he'd been helping Gary construct sat in its box of little plastic pieces on top of an end table. She inhaled deeply. She couldn't identify the mixture of scents, but the room smelled like Peter.

Her eyes brimming with tears, she fumbled with Harvey's phone until she found his list of contacts. Harvey probably had Jenn on speed dial, but she hadn't thought to ask him.

"Hi, babe," Jennifer said.

"It's me. Abby."

"Oh. Well, hi to you too. Why are you on Harvey's phone?"

"They want to keep mine open."

"Of course. I'm sorry."

Abby sniffed. "Jenn, I wish you were here. Or I was there. Something."

"Are you okay?" Jennifer asked.

"No. I want this to be over."

"Oh, honey."

Harvey says I can have you come here later, after the money thing is taken care of."

"Are they going to release Peter?" Jennifer asked.

"I hope so. They said they would."

"Well, if anyone can make it happen, Harvey and his squad can."

"I know. I'm just. . .This isn't real, Jenn."

"I agree. But you know, God is in control."

"Yeah."

"I keep thinking about Job," Jennifer said gently. The pastor had recently preached a series of sermons on the book of Job. "Remember what he said when everything rotten happened and his friends told him it was his fault?"

"Other than 'you all are scum'? Rough translation."

Jennifer chuckled. "They were pretty horrible friends, all right. But I was thinking more of when he said, 'I know my redeemer lives.' That was his bottom line when everything was upside down."

"I remember." Abby took a deep breath. "Thanks. I can't talk long. They should be calling soon."

"Well, I wanted to tell you that Mom and Dad want to come down."

"Isn't Dad working?" Abby ran a hand through her hair. Three of her siblings and their families already lived nearby. Would having the rest of the large family descend make things too hectic? She only wanted to think about Peter right now.

"He can take tomorrow off," Jennifer said. "They feel helpless up there in Skowhegan."

Abby gave a small laugh that came out more of a sob. "I know how they feel, believe me."

70

"Do you mind if they come down? They'd stay with us. They don't want to be in the way, but they want to be close by."

"I guess I'd like that. But make sure they understand—we don't know what's going to happen, or when Peter will be back, or what kind of shape he'll be in."

"Harvey said you talked to Peter last night."

"Only for a second. He sounded okay, but—oh, Jennifer, what if they hurt him?" The tears came hot and fast, and she couldn't hold them back. Where was Harvey with his ever-present clean handkerchiefs?

"Breathe, honey," Jennifer said softly in her ear. "They don't have anything against Peter. Just the promise of a payday."

"Yeah, okay."

"Randy might come with the folks."

"Is he moving down here for the summer?"

"Not yet. He's got a couple more weeks of school, but after that we're planning on it."

Randy was their youngest brother, and Harvey had promised to help him find a job for the summer between his junior and senior years of high school.

"I'm glad he'll be here," Abby said.

"Well, Mom wanted to know if we still want him to come down and stay. I assured her that we do. Harvey's been lining up some work for him. I don't know exactly where things stand right now, but I didn't want to bother Harvey about it."

"It will be good to see him." Randy was the youngest in the line of six siblings. Travis, who was number 5, had lived with Harvey and Jennifer for the last semester, but had gone home to the farm in Skowhegan two weeks earlier, when the university let out for the summer. He had a solid seasonal job in nearby Fairfield, but Randy was up in the air and wanted to earn some money this summer to put toward next year's college tuition.

"I miss Travis already," Jennifer said. "I almost wish Randy could stay now, but he's got finals next week."

Abby's throat hurt, talking about normal family things when Peter was in such a terrible fix. "I guess I'd better go. You'll be over later?"

"Yeah," Jennifer said. "Call me when it's okay for me to come."

"I will."

"I'll bring a casserole for supper."

"You don't have to do that," Abby said.

"I know. But you'll either have Peter and the boys back, or you'll have cops there, right?"

"Right."

"So let me bring food. I made brownies, too. Cooking and chasing Connor around has kept me from thinking too much about Peter."

"Okay, thanks. But you know you don't have to feed the cops. I'll see you later."

Abby hung up and went to the bathroom to wash her face. Horrible, she thought, looking at her blotchy skin. Jennifer would never look this awful. She quickly touched up her makeup and went out to the living room. Harvey was pacing again. He was generally very calm, and the pacing made her nervous. She held out his phone.

"Here. Thanks a lot."

"Yeah. How's Jenny?"

"Good. I told her I'll call her later. Mom and Dad are coming down, and Randy too, I guess. They'll probably all be at your house tonight."

"Okay." Harvey frowned.

"What?" Abby asked.

"I need to call Mr. Donnell. He thought he could give Randy some work at his store, but I need to finalize it. And the owner at the diner was upbeat too, but didn't promise."

"Can it wait until tomorrow?"

Harvey looked at his watch. "It will have to. We're only ten minutes out." He turned and addressed Paul and Emily. "You guys ready?"

"Yep," Paul said, and Emily gave him a thumbs-up.

"Where's your squad?" Abby asked.

"I sent Eddie to get some sleep. I want him alert for the drop. Jimmy and Tony are in the kitchen, and Nate's back at the office on the computer."

She nodded. The landline rang, and her pulse hammered. She looked to Harvey, confused. The kidnappers had been using her cell phone.

"Go pick it up," he said.

She strode into the kitchen, where Jimmy and Tony sat at the table with coffee, staring at the wall phone. Abby lunged for it before it could ring again.

"Hello?"

"Abby? It's Pastor Rowland. People are calling me and asking about something they saw on the news last night. We wondered if you and Peter are okay."

Abby threw Harvey a panicky glance. He'd followed her into the kitchen, and he couldn't hear what the pastor was saying, but Paul and Emily, in the living room, could.

"Uh, we're fine, Pastor. I can't really talk about it right now. Could you. . .could you call Jennifer and ask her about it? I think she can fill you in. I'm sorry, I have to go."

Harvey nodded, holding her gaze.

"Sure," Pastor Rowland said. "I'm sorry if I called at a bad time."

"It's okay, and. . .thanks for caring. We'd appreciate prayer." She hung up before he could ask what he was praying for. "Can Jennifer tell him?" she asked Harvey.

"Yeah. Pastor Rowland is discreet, and Jenny has good judgment on stuff like that. Are you okay?"

"Yes, but my heart's going lickety-split."

"Okay, let's get you in the other room and sit you down for a minute. Get your breath before show time." He looked at his men. "Come on, guys. I want you to hear everything. No matter which line they call on, we'll have it on speaker in the next room.

Jimmy and Tony rose. Tony scooped up Jimmy's mug and carried it with his to the sink.

"Thanks, Tony," Abby said. They were good guys, all of them. She wished Eddie was still here. She'd formed a close friendship with him before Eddie and Leeanne were married, and it had stood the tests of time and wrangling. In some ways, he was closer to her then her own brothers. But he'd stayed all night, which helped her feel secure enough to actually catch snatches of sleep. And yeah, she wanted him in top form when they went to deliver the ransom. She was thankful for her brothers-in-law, but at the same time she was glad she hadn't married a policeman.

She sat down in an armchair. "Harvey, what if they send me down near the waterfront?"

"It won't matter. I've decided that you're not going to actually make the drop."

"What?" Her lungs squeezed. "We've got the money. They'll kill Peter if we don't give it to them."

"Relax," Harvey said. "We'll give it to them—at least, we'll do what they say. But I have a female officer standing by to make the drop. She's about your build, and she'll wear a blond wig."

Abby just stared at him.

"It's going to be okay, Abby. We don't want to put you in danger, and the officer is well trained. She'll be wearing body armor, and she'll have a gun in case she needs it."

Abby pulled in two deep breaths. "So, I just stay here?"

"Yes, with a couple of officers." Harvey shrugged. "Some things might change, depending on what they tell you to do, but I really don't want you exposing yourself to these thugs. Sorry to spring it on you like that. Let's just see what they say when they call, okay?"

Her cell phone, lying on the glass-topped coffee table, rang and vibrated. Harvey picked it up and handed it to her.

"Deep breath."

She nodded and pushed the speaker button.

"Hello?"

"You got the money?"

"Yes." Her heart hammered.

"Put it in a small backpack. There's a bench near a light post on Union Street, near the used bookstore."

Abby frowned and looked at Harvey. He nodded. She ought to have known he'd be familiar with every bookstore in Portland.

"All right, I'll find it."

"You go alone, and no cops, you hear me?"

"Yes, I hear you."

Harvey was already whispering instructions in Tony Winfield's ear. Tony and Jimmy hurried into the entry, and she heard the front door open.

"Should I go right now?" Abby asked. Her voice shook, and she sucked in a deep breath.

"Not yet," the man replied. "Be there at 2:45. Sit on the bench for two minutes, then put the backpack underneath it and leave."

Startled, Abby looked to Harvey. He made the stretch-it-out signal, pulling air like taffy between his hands.

"Okay. But. . .what if someone's sitting there?"

"Wait until they go, then do it. We'll be watching."

"Can I talk to Peter again?"

Nothing.

"We lost him," Emily said.

Abby inhaled and blinked back tears. "I don't guess you know where they are?"

Paul Trudeau shook his head. "Somewhere within a five-mile radius."

"They're probably on the peninsula," Harvey said. "Maybe not too far from the bookstore."

Abby wondered if that meant Peter was that close, too. "So, what now?"

"I'll get half a dozen detectives in place early. Tony and Jimmy are already headed to Union Street. They'll scout out places where our people can wait without looking suspicious. We'll add more cops later, at intervals, in case they're watching constantly. We've got more than four hours to get everyone in

75

position. When Debbie Higgins walks to that bench with the backpack, I'll be nearby, and the others will be within sight. We won't let whoever retrieves the ransom out of our sight, Abby."

"They said no cops."

"Yes, they did." Harvey gazed at her, his ultra-blue eyes sober. "You know we can't go along with that."

She supposed not, but what if their presence put Peter in worse danger? She wouldn't insult Harvey by suggesting it, but her stomach roiled.

"What happens after the woman puts the backpack under the bench and leaves?" she asked.

"She'll take your car to get there, and afterward she'll walk back to it, get in it, and drive back here. Then we wait for another call."

She eyed him anxiously. "Will Eddie be there, at the drop?"

"Yeah. I'll call him around one. Let's let him get a couple hours of sleep."

She sighed. "I guess you've thought of everything."

Harvey's mouth skewed. "I hope so."

*****

Harvey paced Peter's study. These waiting periods were the worst. He'd insisted that Abby try to rest, but he knew she wouldn't be sleeping. He paused before a framed print and studied it. It was a floorplan of a house. An old house, he guessed, but not this one. It had a kitchen and a summer kitchen, and a parlor with two bedrooms off it. A very old house. Harvey squinted at the fine script in the lower right corner. Ah. Peter had made the drawing twenty years ago. He wondered if it was an old farmhouse that had been in the Hobart family. The drawing was meticulously neat, like Peter, and highly detailed. Two fireplaces, built-in cupboards in two rooms, a crawl space between the walls for access to wiring. An ell that probably led to a huge barn.

His phone rang. "Yeah, Tony?"

"The bookshop is too obvious, unless you want to send a plainclothes officer in ten or fifteen minutes before the drop to browse."

"Done. What else?"

"Jimmy has a spot in an upstairs office across the street. I'm going to sit in my car half a block away until around 2:30. Aaron O'Heir will drive up with a slack tire and park as close to the bench as he can get. I'll walk over and help him."

Harvey frowned. "We don't want the closest vehicle jacked up and out of commission when the drop goes down."

"Good thought, Captain. Got a suggestion?"

"Tell Aaron to put his hood up. He can tinker with his carburetor."

"Yeah. That could work."

"I want Jimmy where he's got access, too."

"As soon as he sees Debbie walking toward the bench, he'll come down to the door at street level of his building. We're just using the upstairs window for a good view and so he won't be in the way of the people who work in there."

"Okay," Harvey said uneasily. "Nothing better?"

"There's a Thai restaurant where we can put two officers at a window table, and a burger joint in the next block up. Now, there's a produce stand down half a block from the bookstore. We talked to the owner, and he'll let somebody pretend to work with him starting at two."

"Good. Who have we got for that?"

"Lloyd Gordon. And Sgt. Legere wants in, but we're not sure where to put him. There's a dress shop on the opposite side of the street from the bookstore, but we need a female for that."

"I'll ask Cheryl Yeaton if we can borrow Crocker or Benoit."

"For undercover work?" Tony said.

"Got a better idea?"

"No. Maybe Sgt. Legere could pose as her impatient husband while she tries on dresses, except she won't actually try any on."

"Yeah. Talk to Legere and work it out. And be mindful that one of the kidnappers could be using one of those same spots to observe the drop location."

"Right."

"I'll call Cheryl," Harvey said. "If they give us any more officers, put them in unmarked cars on the side streets, ready to follow whoever picks up the bag."

After a short delay, the day sergeant assured him she would have a female officer in street clothes at the clothing store by 2:15.

"Thanks, Cheryl," Harvey said. "I owe you one."

"You owe me so many, you'll never be able to repay me," Cheryl said.

A quick tap on the door made him swivel toward it. Chief Browning stood in the doorway wearing jeans and a light army jacket.

"What are you doing here?" Harvey asked.

Mike cracked a grin. "I couldn't stay away. You know me."

"Yeah, you're addicted to field work. How are you going to stand it in the woods when you retire?"

"I'll be fine, but this might be my last chance to see some action."

"You're not going near the drop," Harvey said, eyeing him from head to toe.

"I figured you'd say that." Mike pulled sunglasses from his breast pocket and put them on. "How about now? I can go book shopping."

"No way. Like nobody would recognize you just because you wore shades. Especially inside a store."

"You think?"

Harvey sighed in exasperation. "Mike, your face is better known than anyone in town's except the mayor's."

"Aw, come on, what about the news anchor or the Seadogs' shortstop?"

"They live outside town." Harvey waved a hand to indicate the entire study. "Notice anything odd about this room?"

Mike frowned and looked around. He walked over to the desk and picked up a leather case. "Nice binoculars."

"That's not it."

"Okay, I give up. What?"

"This is Peter's sanctuary, and there's nothing about cars in this room. Even the wall art is nature prints and architecture."

"And Peter makes his living with cars." Mike panned the décor. "So, what are you saying? He doesn't love cars?"

"I don't know. He was in college when his father died—studying to be an architect."

"So Dad dumped the business on him, and he's been stuck in it ever since?"

"Peter doesn't come across that way. And he's done a terrific job with the business. I'm just sayin'."

"Yeah." Mike sat down on the edge of the desk. "Peter's a good guy. So what's the plan?"

"I've got three of my men and several of Ron's getting into position gradually." Harvey glanced at his watch. "Debbie Higgins should be here soon. She's going to play Abby and deliver the ransom."

"Higgins doesn't look like Abby."

"They had a long, blonde wig in Property. And I'll get Abby to loan her one of her jackets."

Mike grunted. "Union Street."

"Yeah. Who told you?"

"Charlie Doran."

The dispatcher would have a hard time keeping something like that a secret from the chief, and Harvey hadn't asked him to. "Promise not to go there?"

"All right. I can stay here with Abby, if that will help."

"That's perfect. Thanks. I think I've covered all the bases." Harvey worked the knot on his necktie loose as he talked.

"Where will you be?" Mike asked.

"I'll pop into a dentist's office and then walk out and stroll slowly down the street to the bookstore."

"Did you eat lunch?"

79

"Huh?"

"That's what I figured," Mike said. "Eat something."

"I'm not really hungry," Harvey said.

Mike shrugged. "Don't blame me if Jennifer's mad at you. Hey, have you figured out why the car salesman was blown away last night?"

"Not exactly." Harvey walked over to the window and looked out over the Hobarts' back yard. It held a wooden play gym with a little fort on the top, like a citified treehouse. "Winfield and Cook interviewed the ex-wife this morning. She told them she left Ulrich because he was a gambler, and he'd lose his paycheck half the time before he got home with it."

"You think he was into a loan shark?"

"Good possibility," Harvey said.

"Which would make these kidnappers the loan shark's goons."

"Don't you love organized crime?"

Mike grimaced. "Do you think it's time we formed a special unit for that?"

"I dunno. We had that gang thing in the West End last summer."

"Don't remind me." Mike stood. "It's been pretty quiet this spring, though."

"Yeah. But there's always something going on around the docks."

A rustling drew Harvey's attention, and he turned toward the doorway.

"Officer Higgins is here," Abby said. She blinked at Mike. "Well, hi, Chief. I almost didn't recognize you."

"Hey, how about now?" Mike slipped on the sunglasses, and Abby smiled.

"Don't tell me you're undercover today?"

"Harvey says not, but I'll stay with you while they take care of business, if you don't mind."

"Great," Abby said. "I found Gary's old backpack. One strap is almost broken through. I was going to try to stitch it for

80

Andy. Think it will work? He's got his good backpack at Vickie's."

"That will be fine." Harvey reached for it. "Let me have it, and I'll pack the money in it. I wondered if you'd mind lending Officer Higgins something to wear that's your style. Maybe the same sweater you wore to the dealership last night?"

Abby nodded. "Sure. I had a dress on, but I wore a white crocheted sweater over it."

"I remember," Harvey said.

"She can put that on." Abby eyed him narrowly. "Did you eat lunch?"

Harvey scowled. "What is this? You're tag-teaming me?"

Mike laughed.

"Come on," Abby said. "You have time for a sandwich. Can't have you feeling woozy in the middle of the action."

"I don't get woozy."

"Yeah?" Abby took his arm and steered him toward the kitchen. "I know you, Harvey. You need some protein and some carbs before you go."

*****

Harvey walked slowly down the steps of the dental office. He glanced up the street, then down toward the bookshop. Eddie should be walking up the sidewalk on the opposite side of the street. Strolling as if he had no schedule, Harvey made his way toward the bookstore. Aaron O'Heir and Tony Winfield, dressed in jeans and chambray shirts, were huddled with their heads together under the hood of a ten-year-old Hundai.

"Yeah, that might work," Tony said when he was within earshot. "Let's give 'er a try. If that won't do it, I'll go get some jumper cables."

Tony didn't look at Harvey. O'Heir shot him a quick glance then focused on the engine again. Harvey walked on, right past the bench the kidnapper had designated. It was empty at the moment, but Deborah Higgins should be sitting on it in just a few minutes. He resisted the urge to check the time.

81

Across the street and a little farther down, a man emerged from the Thai restaurant and paused to light a cigarette. Too early, Harvey thought. It was one of Legere's detectives. He should have waited another two or three minutes.

Harvey pushed open the door to the bookstore. He liked this shop. The old building had central shelves and outlying crannies filled with new bestsellers and used books. The oldies were shelved right alongside the new stock, and you could trade in your used books for credit when you shopped. He was a regular customer.

"Good afternoon," the owner's wife called to him, and Harvey nodded. He went to a rack near the front window where they displayed Maine books. He picked up a worn copy of Thoreau's *The Maine Woods* and turned it over, as though reading the back of the chipped dust jacket. He glanced out the window. Eddie was just passing the smoker in front of the Thai restaurant. Aaron was wiping his hands on a rag and continuing the chatter with Tony.

"It's going down," Eddie said in his earpiece.

"Copy," Harvey said softly. "Spot him yet?"

"Negative."

Debbie Higgins walked past the window with a jerky stride, as if she was a little nervous. She probably was. Harvey recalled their wild excursion to Mike Browning's house last year, when Debbie was a rookie. She'd matured a lot. She didn't look exactly like Abby, but he thought it was close enough with the long golden locks, especially from a distance.

She glanced around and sat down on the bench with the backpack alongside her and looked at her watch. Harvey took a peek at his. Right on time. Could she sit still for two minutes?

A heavyset woman sat down on the other end of the bench. Debbie stiffened and pulled the backpack protectively close.

Could the woman possibly be the kidnapper? Harvey replaced the Thoreau book and picked up whatever was next to it. He took a quick glance at the cover. Van Reid. Terrific. Harvey liked his mysteries. He looked outside again. The new woman set a shopping bag beside her on the bench and nodded at Debbie, who returned a curt nod and looked away. The woman sighed heavily and shuffled her feet. Behind them, on the opposite side of the street, Ron Legere and Sarah Benoit came out of a shop with high-end women's wear in its front windows. Ron carried a shopping bag, and Sarah smiled brightly at something he said. They walked to the corner and waited for the crosswalk light to change.

Harvey stared down at the book in his hand. In his peripheral vision, he caught movement from the bench. He took a quick look. Debbie had set the backpack down and was trying to shove it under the bench with her foot without being too obvious, but the stocky woman was frowning at her.

Lord don't let a civilian blow this for us.

Harvey's heart hammered. He knew Debbie could hear him, though he'd instructed her not to talk unless absolutely necessary.

"Go, Debbie," he said.

As Debbie rose from the bench, the other woman watched her, frowning.

"Hey! You forgot something!"

Harvey could read her lips. Debbie didn't turn back.

"Find something you like?" a voice said at his elbow.

Harvey whipped around to see the owner's wife smiling up at him.

"Uh, yeah. Could you put this on hold for me? I need to go. Excuse me." He thrust the book into her hands and hurried to the door. He peered out through the glass. A dark-skinned man in black jeans and a long-sleeved navy T-shirt catapulted toward the bench. Harvey wanted to intercept him, but that could ruin everything. The woman was bending down, reaching under the bench for the backpack, and the interloper shoved her away. She flew sideways and hit the lamppost, then thudded heavily to the sidewalk.

As the man scooped up the backpack, Aaron O'Heir yelled, "Hey!" and hurried toward the sprawling woman. In that moment, the plan exploded in smithereens.

The suspect jerked the backpack to his side and sprinted down the sidewalk.

"Stay with him," Harvey said to the officers who could hear him. He shoved the door open and dashed onto the sidewalk. The man was ten yards away with Tony a few steps behind him. Eddie paralleled him on the opposite side of the street, moving fast but not in a panic.

The detective who'd been stationed at the produce stand ran up the sidewalk toward the suspect. As Harvey registered that Detective Lloyd Gordon had his gun drawn, the man with the backpack tried to turn back, but pulled up short. Tony was right behind him, blocking his retreat. The kidnapper checked and darted into the street.

"No, no, no," Harvey said helplessly as the suspect collided with a garbage truck.

Chapter 7

The truck driver braked. All around him, tires screeched and the traffic halted. Harvey reached the man first. Debbie appeared almost instantly and began directing traffic. As Harvey felt the suspect's throat for a pulse, Eddie knelt on the pavement across from him.

"Anything?"

Harvey shook his head. Eddie reached for the man's wrist. The driver barreled around the front of his truck, his mouth gaping.

"I didn't see him. He just tore into me. I didn't see him."

Harvey stood slowly. "Calm down, sir. This wasn't your fault. You've got a lot of witnesses."

Tony ran to Eddie's side, looked down at the body, and swore. Eddie jumped up, rounding on his partner with a stream of French that made Harvey wince, and he didn't speak the language. Then Eddie launched into English.

"You idiot! You crowded him. What did you expect, Winfield?"

"Easy, Eddie," Harvey said. "I'm sure Tony's going to beat himself up over this. You don't have to do it."

Eddie's eyes snapped as he surveyed Tony. "If you had to spook him, at least you could have tackled him."

"He moved too quick." Tony turned to Harvey. "I'm sorry, Cap'n. I know I blew it."

"Breathe, Winfield," Harvey said. Eddie sounded just like he had a few years ago, chewing out Eddie, and Tony's contrition mirrored times in the past when Eddie had stood before Mike.

Sgt. Legere ran to his side.

"Larson, what do you need? I called for an ambulance as soon as I saw the impact."

"I'm afraid it's too late. We'll need the medical examiner."
He looked over at Tony. "Winfield, help with the traffic until we get more patrol officers here."

Tony turned away without a word.

Eddie was already patting the dead man's pockets. He found a wallet, worked it out of the pocket, and handed it to Harvey. He flipped it open and squinted at the driver's license.

"I'm surprised he carried his I.D. on this errand," Eddie said.

"Maybe he drove here and figured he should have his license on him. We know these guys are amateurs. Name's Webster Holden." Nate would be gone already, off to his speaking engagement. Harvey handed the wallet to Eddie. "I want you on this as soon as this guy's taken away."

"Right," Eddie said.

Harvey let Ron join Eddie kneeling by the suspect. It would be futile to try to save the man. Eddie pulled a cell phone from another of Holden's pockets. He passed it to Harvey, who bagged it and called the dispatcher with curt orders.

Eddie stood. "What now?"

Two squad cars had arrived, and several officers piled out.

"I'll have the uniforms keep bystanders away and try to get traffic moving. You get this phone to the lab."

The truck driver stood wringing his hands and staring down at the body. Harvey pulled him aside. "I'm Captain Harvey Larson with the Portland Police. I want you to give a statement to one of our officers, and I'll interview you later."

The driver wiped a hand across his forehead. "Fine. Whatever you say. I just plain didn't see him."

Harvey nodded and looked around for an available detective. One of Ron's men was nearby, waiting for instructions from his boss. Harvey asked him to take the driver's statement.

Tony was waving cars onto the closest side street. "Winfield, let a uniform do that now. I need you."

Tony spoke to a patrolman and hurried to Harvey's side.

"Is that woman okay?" Harvey asked. "The one on the bench?"

86

"Jimmy was helping her."

"Find out," Harvey said. "See if she needs medical treatment."

"Okay, but boss?"

"Yeah?"

Tony's eyes darted back and forth, searching the street. "Where's the backpack?"

Harvey's heart sank.

Before he could issue an order, Tony grinned. "Is that it?" He pointed eagerly toward the truck's front bumper. Harvey saw a dark mound under the front of the truck. He walked over and stooped.

"Let me get it, Cap'n." Tony was already crawling on the pavement, reaching beneath the pulsating vehicle. He pulled out a well-worn, green backpack with an L.L. Bean logo and one broken strap. He stood, handed the pack to Harvey, and brushed off the knees of his designer jeans.

"Excellent work, Tony." Harvey loved the way the young man's mind functioned. With a few more rough edges ground down, Tony would be a great detective. He would talk to him later about tailing his suspect too closely.

He unzipped the backpack, just to be sure. The money was still neatly bundled. He glanced around. Eddie was headed for his pickup, while Ron Legere stood near the body with two of his detectives, shaking their heads. "See if you can catch Eddie and take this money to the bank. Ask for Mr. Strickland."

"What do I tell him?" Tony asked.

"I'll call him while you go and tell him we may need the cash again, but for now he'd best put it back in the vault. Bank first, lab second."

"Right." Tony reached for the backpack.

Harvey made his call while Tony rushed to flag Eddie down and tell him of their new assignment. After a quick conversation with Strickland, he touched base with Legere.

"Can you and your squad start a canvas? We need statements from everyone who saw this go down."

"We're on it, Captain," Ron said. "I'd say you had at least a dozen professionals with eyes on him."

"Yeah, I want their statements, too, but hit the civilians before they scatter. And I'll need to sit down with Gordon later."

"I'll tell him."

"Thanks. There was a woman injured at the drop. I need to check on her."

A siren wailed as an ambulance made its way slowly up Union Street. Harvey strode to the sidewalk and back to the bench. Aaron was talking to a couple on the sidewalk, taking notes as they spoke. Jimmy and a young woman were talking to the older woman who'd been shoved by the kidnap courier.

"Hey, Captain," Jimmy said as he approached. "This is Mrs. Daugherty and her daughter."

"Hello." Harvey focused on the older woman. "Are you all right, ma'am?"

"My arm hurts, and my shoulder."

"He hit her pretty hard," Jimmy said.

Harvey nodded. "Have the EMTs take a look at her."

"Thank you," the younger woman said.

Mrs. Daugherty peered up at him. "I was just sitting here waiting for Roxanne, and a girl left her bag underneath the bench. I was going to take it to her and that fellow charged into me." She craned her neck to look at the street, where the garbage truck still sat twenty yards away and the traffic snarled around it. "What happened to him? Is he going to be all right?"

Harvey glanced at Jimmy. "We'll make sure you get checked over really well, ma'am. If the EMTs say you don't need to go to the hospital, your daughter can take you home. But would you give Detective Cook here an official statement before you go?"

She leaned back and eyed Jimmy with new perspective. "You're a detective, young man?"

"Yes, ma'am." Jimmy smiled and pushed his blond hair back off his forehead. "This is my boss, Captain Larson."

"Well, I never. I thought detectives wore suits." She glanced significantly at his patched jeans and Red Sox shirt.

"Actually, I was, uh, undercover today, ma'am." Jimmy gave her a shy smile.

"Well, what do you know. I've never met a real detective before." Mrs. Daugherty reached toward him and winced.

"The ambulance is almost here," Harvey said to Jimmy. I don't think the suspect will need it, but I'll tell them to take care of Mrs. Daugherty. Meanwhile, you get the statement."

"Sure thing." Jimmy took out a small notebook.

Harvey weaved his way between stopped vehicles and met the ambulance when they were nearly to the scene of the collision. The driver rolled down the window.

"Captain! Where's the victim?"

Harvey stepped closer. "Hey, Liam. He looked past the driver and nodded grimly to his partner. "Hi, Sandy. I'm afraid he's DOA, but take a look, right smack in front of that garbage truck. We need to get him and the truck moved as soon as we can."

"Right," Liam said. "Did you call for a medical examiner?"

"Yeah. And there's a woman he slammed into who needs your attention, over there near the lamppost." He pointed. "Jimmy Cook's with her."

"Got it," Liam said. "Can you get the traffic cops to clear a spot for us to park?"

"Right." After Harvey relayed the message to the patrolmen doing their best to clear the street, he caught up with Debbie Higgins, who had removed the blond wig. "How are you holding up, Higgins?"

"Okay, sir. I heard the suspect is dead."

"I'm afraid so."

She shook her head. "What a waste. I hope we recovered the money."

"Yeah, we did. Thanks for your help today. I'd like to debrief you later this afternoon." He glanced at his watch. Unreal. It was only ten past three. "Say, about 4:30 in the Priority Unit office?"

"I'll be there," Debbie said.

"Great." Harvey had begun several mental lists. Officers to debrief, witnesses to interview personally, instructions to dole out to his squad. That was most important. They had to find out who Webster Holden was and where he lived. They had to find Peter.

He pulled out his phone and speed-dialed Mike.

"Yeah, Harv?" Mike's routine greeting was calming.

"Hey. The suspect got hit by a garbage truck. He's dead, Mike."

"I heard."

"That was fast."

"Yeah, Ron called me about ten minutes ago. Are you all right?"

"Sort of. How's Abby?"

"Confused. She wants to know what next. I told her you and your guys would find Peter."

Harvey gritted his teeth. "You know we can't make promises."

"Harv, this is Abby. You and your guys *have* to find him."

*****

Jennifer juggled her basket and tote bag so she could ring the doorbell. Mike Browning opened the door.

"Chief, good to see you."

"Hi, Jennifer. Let me take that." He reached for the basket that held her casserole. "Come on in. Abby will be glad to see you." He stood back and let her pass him.

Jennifer paused in surprise when she saw two plainclothesmen sitting on the couch. She arched her eyebrows at Mike.

"I thought they'd have left."

"Not yet. Your sister may get another call."

"Where is she?"

Mike inclined his head in the direction of the kitchen. "Baking cinnamon rolls. The boys are coming home."

Jennifer hurried to the kitchen. Abby turned from the sink, where she was rinsing a mixing bowl.

"Jenn!" Abby rushed to her with open arms.

Jennifer quickly set her bag on a chair and held her close. "How are you?"

Abby gave a little sob. "Terrible." She pulled away and sniffed. "Did you hear what happened?"

"Just that the guy who picked up the money was hit by a car."

"Not a car, a garbage truck. He's dead!"

Jennifer caught her breath. "Oh, no. What next?"

"That's what I want to know."

"Has Harvey been here since it happened?"

"No. It's been Chief Browning and me and two electronic-savvy guys all afternoon. They think there might be a second kidnapper, and he'll call to arrange another drop. But we haven't heard anything. Jenn, I'm scared."

"I don't blame you."

Abby's face crumpled. "Everyone tells me to hang in there and keep my chin up and be brave for the boys. I think I've reached my limit." She sagged into Jennifer's embrace weeping.

"Oh, honey." Jennifer stroked her hair. "Come sit down."

When she turned around, Mike was standing in the doorway holding her casserole basket and looking awkward.

"Thank you, Mike," Jennifer told him softly. "When will the boys be here?"

"Mrs. Hobart said they'll arrive in about a half hour," Mike replied.

"Okay." Jennifer settled Abby in a chair at the round kitchen table and took the basket from him. She felt the casserole dish. It was still warm. The oven light was on, and the display said 425.

"Are your rolls in the oven?" she asked.

Abby nodded, wiping her nose with a tissue. "I just put them in."

"When they come out, I'll slide this in to stay warm." Jennifer set the dish on the counter.

Abby gave a broken laugh. "I wanted to give the boys some comfort food. They love my cinnamon rolls."

91

"That's a nice thought. I can help you ice them. I brought my brownies, too." Jennifer slid into a chair next to her. Mike looked questioningly at her, and she nodded. He faded away toward the living room.

"Abby, Harvey hasn't been here at all?"

"He said he'll be tied up for several hours. I guess it was pretty awful. The guy went to pick up the money, and some woman tried to pick it up before he reached it, and he ran into her and pushed her down and grabbed it. Then he ran out in the street, and the garbage truck flattened him." She looked aghast at Jennifer. "Listen to me. The man is dead, Jennifer. I shouldn't talk about him like that."

"He's a criminal. And you're in shock."

"So he got what he deserved? I don't know. I got reading in Job again, to take my mind off things. I read the part the pastor preached from Sunday. Job said, 'if I've rejoiced at of the ruin of him who hated me, or exulted when evil overtook him'—Oh, Jennifer!"

"Shh." Jennifer hugged her again and rubbed Abby's back. "I know you're not glad he's dead."

Abby pulled away. "You're right. Because that dead man could be the only person who knew where Peter is."

"Maybe you should read something more cheerful than Job in your devotions."

"I expect you're right. But I can't manage the 'rejoice in the Lord' part right now. Not yet."

"I understand."

Abby sighed. "How does Harvey do it?"

"Do what?" Jennifer asked.

"Deal with this kind of stuff every day and not explode. How does he decompress?"

"Some days it's hard. He usually talks to me about stuff after it's over. I think that helps. And he and Eddie and Jeff getting together to run and pray in the morning does him a lot of good."

Abby's cheek twitched. "I was thinking how glad I was that I didn't marry a cop, and yet, here we are. I'm the one whose husband is in danger." Tears flowed from her eyes. "I'm so scared the other kidnappers will kill Peter now that one of them is dead. And they didn't get the money, so what good is it keeping Peter alive?"

"They can still get the ransom," Jennifer said. "They need to call again and set it up. It's not your fault that guy ran out on a busy street in front of a layo truck. Any eight-year-old knows better."

Abby nodded, a faraway look in her eyes. "I tell Andy all the time to wait and look both ways." She swallowed hard. "They'll be here any minute. What do I say?"

Mike came to the doorway and leaned in, with one hand bracing on the jamb. "Abby, your mother-in-law is here with the kids. And an officer is here to stay with you until eight this evening. I think you know Sarah Benoit?"

"I do." Abby shoved back her chair and stood.

"I'll head out after I fill in Officer Benoit," Mike said. "Would you like me to show her the basic layout of the house, since you've got family here?"

"Thanks," Abby said. I'd really appreciate it if you did that before you go. And thank you for everything, Chief."

Mike nodded. "No problem. I'm glad I could actually do something."

Jennifer smiled as Mike left the room. "As if he does nothing all day in his office. Harvey says he's the most hands-on chief they've ever had."

"They'll miss him when he retires," Abby said.

"Yeah, we all will, but I feel like Mike and Sharon deserve some down time together. That property they bought from you and Peter is their dream come true. He told Harvey they've got guests booked at the lodge from Labor Day all the way to Thanksgiving."

"He told me today," Abby said as they walked into the living room. "Sounds as if the renovations are coming along great. And he invited us to go up any time, so long as we give them a couple of days' notice. Well, hi, guys!"

93

Gary and Andy ran in through the front door, and Vickie followed more sedately.

"Mommy!" As Andy hurtled into Abby and threw his arms around her waist, Jennifer caught a glimpse of Mike and Sarah disappearing into the den.

"Hey." Abby smoothed Andy's hair. "I missed you two." She smiled at Gary over Andy's head. "Did you have a good day with Grandma?"

"We watched three videos and tried all her games," Andy said. "Then we made cupcakes. And we brought some."

"Sounds like we'll have plenty of sweets," Abby said. "How about you, Gary?"

The ten-year-old shrugged. "It was better than school. Is Dad back yet?"

"No," Abby said.

Gary's face fell.

"Where is he?" Andy asked, looking up at her with puppy dog eyes.

"Yeah, you said he'd come home this afternoon." Gary's reproachful gaze made even Jennifer feel guilty.

Abby sighed and looked to her sister. "I guess we need to have a family talk."

Mike and Sarah came from the den and headed down a short hallway toward the master bedroom.

"How come there's still cops here?" Gary asked.

"Let's go in the den." Abby took Andy's hand. "Maybe Aunt Jennifer will come with us." She gave Vickie a wan smile. "You need to know how things stand now, too, Grandma. And you should stay for supper. It's getting late. I can't tell you how much I appreciate your keeping the boys over."

"I can take them back if you need me to."

"No, no," Andy wailed.

Vickie looked helplessly at Abby. "I'm afraid I wasn't very good at entertaining them."

"I'm sure that's not true," Abby said.

Vickie held up a plastic container. "Let me put these in the kitchen, and I'll be right there."

Jennifer patted her shoulder. "We're all on edge with Peter missing. Let me take care of that for you." She took Vickie's cupcakes and delivered them to the kitchen. When she came back through the living room, Mike and Sarah were talking earnestly near the fireplace.

Mike looked up. "Jennifer, I'm just briefing Officer Benoit on the latest. Maybe you can pass the word to Abby. I didn't want to discuss it in front of the kids."

"Sure." Jennifer walked over to them.

Mike glanced toward the open doorway to the den and said softly, "Harvey reports that they've I.D.'d the dead man. His name is Webster Holden, but that's not for public knowledge. Harvey's going back to the office to see what he can find on him and interview the officers that were closest to the action. Meanwhile, the rest of his squad is taking statements at the scene, and as Harvey gets leads on Holden, they'll follow up on them."

Jennifer nodded, taking it in. Sounded like another late night for Harvey and his men.

"Do they have any intel on him yet?" Sarah asked.

"He has a record," Mike said. "You need to stay on the alert here. Harvey thinks he had a partner or two. He may decide to send another officer out for security, and I think he'll leave at least one comm person here as long as there's hope for another phone call from the kidnappers."

"Are they sure Holden had a partner?" Jennifer asked.

"Not yet, but it seems likely." Mike shook his head. "I've got to get back to the office. This thing is starting to draw a lot of media attention, and I need to huddle with our department heads and the mayor's liaison."

"Thanks for everything, Mike." Jennifer touched his hand.

"You bet." Mike winked at her. "Call in if there's the least little thing suspicious, Benoit."

"I will, Chief," Sarah said.

95

When he was out the door, Jennifer looked at Sarah and held out her arms. "I'm glad it's you here with Abby tonight." She and Sarah hugged each other and stood back. Jennifer had become quite fond of Sarah, who was Eddie's old girlfriend. Before Eddie had started dating Leeanne, Jennifer and Sarah had double-dated with Eddie and Harvey. Sarah had stumbled through some rough times since then, but they had all made peace.

"Thanks," Sarah said. "This is so stressful for Abby."

"Yeah. She's worried sick about Peter and what will happen to him now. I'd better get in there. She's torn up over how much to tell the boys."

Chapter 8

They should be back. They'd told him they would have the money by three o'clock. Peter couldn't see a clock, and they'd taken his phone and wristwatch. The only way he could gauge passing time was by the shadows from the meager strip of light that came through the small, high window.

But they'd been gone for hours. Maybe Abigail couldn't get the money. He clenched his jaw. If they did something to her when she delivered the money—if they'd hurt her—

No. Harvey wouldn't let that happen. And he was certain Harvey was in the middle of it. He was probably the first person she had called.

His stomach growled. They'd brought him an Egg McMuffin and a cup of tepid coffee this morning, but no lunch. In an effort to forget how hungry he was, he studied the shadows in the large, open room. When the killers were here, they turned on the overhead lightbulb, but it was off now. Peter had tried to notice everything he could while the bulb burned.

The building couldn't be occupied. People living in houses with basements filled the cellar with firewood, canned goods, and other junk they wanted to store—even laundry equipment. This basement was nearly empty. However, when the light was on, he had noticed a huge hulk several yards beyond the oil furnace, in the shadows deeper in the basement. He'd puzzled over it for a while and decided it was an old coal furnace, like the one his grandfather had used. Why they didn't take it out when they poured the concrete floor and installed the tiny bathroom down here, he couldn't imagine.

The chain they'd locked around his ankle gave him about ten feet of movement. It wasn't that heavy a chain, and he'd hoped it had a weak link. He'd tried to break it or to pull it free from the pipe it was wrapped around, but all he'd gotten for his efforts were painful lacerations around his ankle. When was the last time he'd had a tetanus shot? Years ago.

He hauled himself into a sitting position and for the millionth time tried to position himself with part of the chain behind him. That in itself took concentration and contortions. But rubbing the chain against the tape that held his hands securely behind him was the only option he'd come up with. He had to rip that tape off.

Apparently the chain had no rough spots or links with jagged edges. He struggled for a long time, but nothing gave way.

Peter leaned back against the cold stone wall and closed his eyes.

*****

Jimmy Cook plodded out of the stairway into the office. Harvey signed off on his eighth phone conversation and called, "What have you got, Jimmy?"

"Nothing solid, but Holden's landlord said he thought the guy did some heavy work for a financier."

Harvey frowned. "Heavy as in moving furniture, or heavy as in intimidating people who owed them money?"

"More like the latter."

Tony, who had been working quietly at his computer for the last twenty minutes, put in his two cents' worth. "Craptastic."

"Please, Winfield." Harvey rubbed the back of his neck and closed his eyes for a moment. Sometimes Tony drove him insane.

"Sorry, Captain. I was trying to get more creative with my language, like you advised."

"Try harder," Harvey said.

"Yeah, that one sounded like a junior high expletive," Jimmy said, tossing his Kevlar vest on Nate's empty chair.

Harvey threw a wordless prayer skyward and opened his eyes. "You got the name of the so-called financier, Jim?"

"Not yet. I'll get on it."

"Do that. Tony, anything?"

Tony shoved back his chair. "Maybe." He picked up a memo sheet and walked over to Harvey's desk. "I got names of three guys Holden was known to pal around with and a possible girlfriend."

"Go for the girlfriend first."

"Okay. She's a clerk at a drugstore at Market Street and Newbury."

"Go. Take Jimmy."

"You don't want me to look for the finance guy?" Jimmy asked.

"Give it to me." Harvey knew he could find something on the computer in a fraction of the time Jimmy could. Jimmy's bulky frame, however, was a great visual aid in subtly intimidating witnesses.

The two detectives were barely out the stairway door when Paula rose and walked to his desk.

"Captain, there's a Mr. Viniard coming up the elevator. He asked to see you."

Harvey paused, his mind clicking. "Viniard? Oh, yeah."

Leah's father? Had to be. He stood as the elevator opened.

A man about Harvey's age, wearing khakis and a dark polo shirt, stepped into the office. Harvey nodded to the patrolman who had escorted him, and the officer punched the elevator button to take him back downstairs.

"Captain Larson?"

"Yes."

"I'm Steve Viniard." He stepped forward. "You met my daughter Leah yesterday."

"Right." Harvey smiled. "You've raised a fine girl, Mr. Viniard. How is she?"

"She's upset, but my wife talked her into going to school today."

Harvey waved toward the interview room. "My men will be in and out of the office. Maybe we can talk in there."

Viniard followed him into the small room, and Harvey closed the door.

"Can I get you some coffee?"

"No, thanks."

Viniard sat down, and Harvey took a chair opposite him. Viniard sat for a long moment, studying him. "So, you're not going to try to get custody or anything like that?"

"Why would I do that?" Harvey asked. "She's not my child."

"How do you explain the name on the birth certificate?"

"I don't. Could be there's someone else with the same name. Could be the mother didn't want to name the real father, or couldn't, so she picked another name."

"Are you a hundred percent sure?" Viniard squinted at him. "I can almost see her in your eyes."

"I'm certain. The test we took yesterday will assure Leah of that."

"Yeah, okay." Viniard sighed heavily. "She wanted us to drive her down here last weekend, and we wouldn't. We didn't want her stirring things up." He met Harvey's gaze. "To be honest, we're a little bit afraid we'll lose her. If she finds her biological father, I mean."

Harvey pursed his lips and nodded slowly. "I can assure you, I won't do anything like that."

"Thanks. And I'm sorry she bothered you. I know you're a busy man."

"That's true, and I'm in the middle of a high-priority case right now."

"That murder yesterday?"

"Yes, that's part of it."

Viniard poised to rise. "I should let you get back to work."

"Listen, Leah's going to feel even more let down when she gets those test results. The official word on what I've been telling her, you know?" Harvey watched his face.

"You're probably right. I don't know what we can do about that except assure her that we love her. Truth is, she's a little bit mad at us right now, for not telling her about the adoption."

100

"That's understandable," Harvey said. "But wanting to find her biological father doesn't mean that she doesn't love you, and that will sink in for her as time goes by. Right now she's hurting. She lost the chance to know her birth mother and find out what she was like. She doesn't want to miss out on her father, too."

Viniard looked away, pain creasing his face. "I know you're right. But this is hard on all of us."

Harvey made a quick choice, even though it would cut in on his free time, his personal time with Jennifer and Connor. "Look, I can't be the father she hopes to find, but maybe I can help her find him."

"You would do that?"

"I'll try. I have some resources, but it would have to be on my own time. This isn't a police case."

"Right." Viniard fixed him with a questioning look. "If the bio mom picked your name, like you say, does that mean she knew you?"

"I didn't recognize her name," Harvey said. "But it could be we'd met before, or she'd heard of me. She may have read my name in the newspaper."

"I heard you're a big deal cop."

He huffed out a breath. "Not the words I'd choose, but I do show up on newscasts more often than I'd like. But that's now, Mr. Viniard. Fifteen years ago, I was a beat cop. A young patrolman in uniform. I didn't give press conferences then."

"Maybe you wrote her a speeding ticket or something."

Harvey let out a chuckle. "I suppose that's possible."

"Could she have known you earlier? In school?"

"Possible, but unlikely. I grew up in Bow, New Hampshire."

"Oh." Viniard sat back, slightly deflated. "So how'd you end up here?"

"They had openings. I applied."

Viniard nodded. "Okay. So, unless she had a New Hampshire connection. . ."

"I'll look into that when I get out from under this case. Leah probably won't hear anything for a few weeks on the DNA test. I should be able to do a little digging by then."

"Did you go to college?" Viniard sat forward eagerly, as though he may have struck gold.

"Yes. In Massachusetts. I can look into that, too, and see if she was at the university when I was there." He deliberately avoided saying "Harvard." Somehow, he doubted Leah's birth mother went there, but he could be wrong. He would make sure. He would also check the roster for the police academy during the time he was there, in case they'd come into contact during his training. But he was married then, and he didn't notice many women besides Carrie in those days.

He turned his attention back to Leah's father. "Keep in mind, this man may not know Leah exists, and even if he does, he might not want to be found."

"Yeah." Viniard sat for a moment, gazing into space.

Harvey waited until he stirred. "You know how to contact me. Give me a few days to shake this case down, and then I'll dive into it. If I find anything pertinent, I'll contact Leah." He was going to offer to contact the parents first, but Leah had had enough of being kept out of the loop. She would trust him more if he dealt directly with her.

"Okay." Mr. Viniard stood. "I appreciate your time, Captain."

"Not a problem." Harvey stood and shook his hand then walked with him to the elevator.

"I can see myself out," Viniard said.

"Oh, well, department policy," Harvey said with a smile.

"I can go down with this gentleman," Paula said, stepping toward them. "And the chief would like an update from you."

"Thanks," Harvey said. "This is Paula Dryden, our unit secretary. She'll take you down."

Mr. Viniard nodded and stepped into the elevator.

Harvey walked slowly to his desk and sank into his chair. His fingers itched to type Leah's mother's name into one of his tracer databases, but he couldn't get into that now. Peter was out there. He had a garbage truck driver to interview and several detectives to debrief.

He picked up the desk phone's receiver and dialed Mike.

"Chief Browning's office."

"Oh, hello. Laney, isn't it?" Harvey said.

"Yes, sir."

"This is Captain Larson. The chief wanted to talk to me?"

"Yes, sir. I believe he's expecting you, if you have time to come up."

"Okay, I'll be right there." He hung up with a sigh. A phone call wouldn't do for Mike. At least he could get coffee up there. He paused on the stair landing. Nate was coming up from the second floor.

"Hey, Nate. How did your speech go?"

"Great. They had parents and students there, and I took a lot of questions afterward. People are finally starting to get it. The parents really want to keep their kids safe, and I laid it on thick with the kids, that their parents weren't neurotics if they insisted on Internet filters and knowing who their contacts are."

"Preach it, brother." Harvey smiled wearily. "I'll be in the chief's office. Will you be here a while?"

"Thought I'd stay for another hour."

"I may need you tonight. Did you hear things went haywire at the ransom drop?"

Nate winced. "I spoke to Jimmy briefly. Has there been another call?"

"Not yet."

"Anything I can do?"

"Yeah, I sent you some snippets by email. Dig up whatever you can find on the dead guy, Webster Holden. I want to know every little thing about him, especially who he might be working with. Tony and Jimmy are out chasing down a girl they think he dated."

"Got it."

"Oh, and if the truck driver comes in while I'm upstairs, put him in the interview room."

"Sure." Nate went into the unit, and Harvey plodded up the stairs. For some reason, climbing that flight seemed harder than running two miles every other morning.

Laney sat at the desk in the outer office, and Judith had taken a chair near her.

"Good afternoon, Captain," Laney said with a bright smile. "You can go right in."

"Thanks." Harvey opened Mike's door with misgivings. He wished he had something more positive to report to his longtime boss and friend.

Mike turned from the window. "So. Anything on Holden yet?"

"Bits and pieces," Harvey said. "Nate Miller's back. I put him on profiling this guy. My other men are following leads."

"Okay. I'm heading home and get some supper, but if you hear from anyone connected to this, I want to know it."

"Of course."

Mike nodded. "If you have a situation, I'll be there."

"It's a situation now," Harvey said. "We just don't know where the party's going down."

Harvey's phone vibrated, and he pulled it out. "Eddie." He hit speaker. "Yeah, Ed? I'm with the chief. Go ahead."

"We found a car about a block and a half from the drop scene. We're running the plates on everything in the vicinity, and no one's gone near this one since the drop. We think it may be Holden's ride, but it's registered to a Malcolm Braley."

"Check it out," Harvey said.

"Right. Who's with Abby?" Eddie asked.

"Sarah Benoit and a comm tech. They haven't heard anything yet."

"Okay. Later."

Harvey clicked the end button and looked at Mike. "You heard him. That's how it's been going for the last two or three hours. Baby steps."

"Go home and eat dinner, Harv."

"I can't. I keep picturing Peter tied up in some cargo container or floating in the bay."

"If nothing breaks tonight, you'll need to rest. You can't be in top form if you're exhausted."

"I know. I'm hoping we find something soon."

"All right, go do it. And call me."

Harvey passed through the outer office with a wave and hurried down to his desk. Paula was taking her purse from her drawer.

"Heading out?" he asked.

"Unless there's anything else I can do for you tonight."

"Thanks, but I can't think of anything. I appreciate your hard work today."

"Goodnight, then." Paula smiled at him and Nate and left by the elevator.

"Jimmy called in," Nate said. "They're bringing the girlfriend in to talk, but she says she's not his girlfriend."

"Explain that?" Harvey said.

"Can't. Sorry."

"Did you find anything yet?"

Nate sighed, frowning at his monitor. "Holden grew up in Auburn. Had a job on the docks here for a while. I can't really find much on him, but he has been picked up before for panhandling, public lewdness, theft, and resisting arrest."

"No drugs?"

"Not that he got caught with, which is almost remarkable. But I may have a line on Ulrich's bookie. I'm going to reach out to him."

"Good." Harvey sat down and ran every name he'd ever encountered in connection with shady financial deals. Tony and Jimmy came in with a scowling young woman between them. They took her to the interview room and started the video camera. Harvey kept an eye on the conversation by way of his monitor.

105

"I told you," she said, "I only went out with Web a couple of times. I haven't seen him for a month or more."

"Just tell us whatever you know about him," Jimmy said patiently. "Where did you go with him?"

"A movie. Some science fiction thing." She shook her head. "Not my style."

"Did you go to his place?" Tony asked.

"Once. It's a crummy apartment over Libbytown way."

"Yeah? Got an address?"

She shook her head.

Harvey pulled up the information from Holden's driver's license. The address on it was for an apartment house in that neighborhood.

"How did you meet him?" Tony asked.

"He came into the drugstore one day."

Harvey turned back to the financial list, keeping his ear tuned for anything unusual.

A few minutes later, Jimmy came from the interview room. "Captain, we don't think she's going to tell us anything useful, and she's crabbing about missing work. I really don't think she was tight with this guy."

"Take her back to the store, but put her on notice."

"Right." Jimmy turned back toward Interview.

Over the next hour, Harvey talked to the truck driver, Debbie Higgins, and two of Ron Legere's detectives, but with minimal results. When the last one left, he stretched and told Nate, "I'm going to run out to Abby's again and see how she's doing. If you want to go home, go ahead."

"If you're going to keep working on this, I'll stay."

Harvey nodded. "Thanks. Take a dinner break with Jackie, then call me. If we've got something to work on, I'd be happy to have you in on it."

What would he do when Nate left for his new job? He'd be hard pressed to find someone with computer skills as good. Harvey headed down the stairs, but his phone burbled before he got to the parking garage.

106

"Whatcha got, Eddie?" he asked.

"Mr. Braley reported his car stolen yesterday. He's driving his wife's car today."

"All right. Has he got extra keys?"

"Yeah, and I just opened the trunk. Nothing but his spare and some junk.

"Okay. Give it to forensics. Get something to eat and meet me at Abby's."

Chapter 9

At the Hobarts' house, Harvey found Jennifer in the dining room with Abby, her two stepsons, and her mother-in-law. Jennifer jumped up and hurried to his side.

"Well, hi! Any news?" She kissed him.

"Afraid not." Harvey looked at Abby. "How are you holding up?"

Abby faltered, "I'm not sure how to answer that."

"We have a few leads on the—the man from the scene," he said. "We're following up on those as best we can. Sarah says you haven't had any calls?"

Abby made a sour face. "Just reporters, about the incident at the store last night. Jennifer's been telling family to call her phone, so that mine stays open."

"Good," Harvey said. "The reporters haven't connected last night to this afternoon's events?"

"I don't think so," Abby replied.

"What events?" Gary demanded. "Uncle Harvey, haven't you found my dad yet?"

"Not yet," Harvey said.

Abby stood. "We have plenty of food, Harvey. Let me get you a plate."

"Oh, that's okay."

"No, really," Abby said.

"Let me do it." Jennifer took his arm. "It will give us a chance to talk for a few minutes, and then I need to go get Connor."

"Well, all right," Abby said uncertainly.

Harvey winked at her and hoped she'd understand. Jennifer didn't just want a moment alone with him. He could tell her things he couldn't say in front of Vickie and the boys. She could clue Abby in later.

They went into the kitchen, where Jennifer loaded a plate with chicken casserole, green beans, and cornbread. It smelled great, and he gave in and took a seat at the small table. She sat down across for him and reached for his hand. Harvey closed his eyes and let everything settle for a second.

"Dear Lord, thank you for this. Thank you for Jenny and Abby, and the whole family. Please, give us something to work with, Lord. Wherever Peter is, shore him up." He didn't know what else to say.

After a moment, Jennifer gave a soft amen. Harvey looked up and gazed into her mournful eyes, gray tonight.

"Where's Connor?" he asked.

"At Beth's. Jeff is supposed to be home tonight, and they offered to keep him. Beth and Leeanne took Connor and Anna to the store and the park earlier. They're trying to wear him out and keep him from crying for us, but I feel guilty."

"I need to see him tonight. He's going to forget what I look like."

She smiled. "Can you go home now?"

"Not really. We've so many things hanging, and there's no way of knowing how much time we have to find Peter."

"To find him alive, you mean?"

Harvey picked up his fork and refused to answer that. "Did you make this?"

"Some of it, yeah. The chicken."

He took a bite and chewed, feeling revived. "It's good."

"Thanks."

"Didn't know I was this hungry."

Jennifer studied his face. "Other than half starved, how are you?"

"Going nuts."

"What if that guy was the only kidnapper?" she asked.

"Then we're in trouble. Unless Peter can get away or tell us where he is somehow, I don't have a lot of hope. But I honestly don't think it was a one-man job. That's how we'll find him.

Either the second man will make contact, or he'll make a mistake, give himself away."

"Didn't *anyone* see them go into the dealership yesterday?"

"No one we've found so far." Harvey took another bite. Maybe he should put some manpower back over there, near the store, but it was a commercial district and all the employees except Ulrich claimed to have left for the day before the gunman arrived. "I think they went to confront Ulrich deliberately at closing, or just after. They may have told him to stay after. We just don't know how it happened." He reached for the slab of cornbread, hoping his frustration didn't show. He was feeling a little ragged.

"Want coffee?" Jennifer asked.

"No, I've drunk about two gallons of it today."

"I think Abby has milk." She rose and went to the refrigerator. When she came back with a glass of milk, she said, "I guess he didn't say anything before he died?"

"No. It happened very quickly. When I got to him, he was gone. There wasn't much for the EMTs to do except get him off the street and patch up a woman he'd knocked down."

She frowned and sat down. "If that guy had a cohort, you'd think he'd have called by now. He must still want the money."

"I hope he does still want it. Because if he decides it's not worth it. . ."

"You think he'll kill Peter."

"Or just cut and run."

"Do you have roadblocks up?" she asked.

He huffed out a breath. "We wouldn't know what to have them look for. We don't even know if there's a second person involved. And we just found out they stole a car yesterday. We think Holden drove it to the drop. He'd left his car at his apartment. What vehicle do we look for now?" He took a bite of cornbread and chewed it. When he'd swallowed, he said, "Do you know how many ways there are to leave Portland?"

"A lot."

"Yeah. And not just roads. A boat could be a hundred miles down the coast by now. We alerted the airport, of course, but we don't have any I.D. on Holden's potential partners. But still, everyone on the force is watching for anyone who acts suspicious."

Jennifer was silent for a minute while he ate. When he looked up, she said, "Any boats stolen?"

"That's good thinking, gorgeous. I'll put Nate Miller on it." He pulled out his phone.

When he'd made the call, Sarah looked in at the doorway. "Eddie just drove in."

"Thanks. Send him in here, and we'll talk."

Jennifer rose. "I'd better go. I'll get Connor and take him home with me."

Harvey stood up and reached for her. He was still holding her tight when Eddie came in. He paused in the doorway. "Need a minute?"

"No, we're good." Harvey squeezed Jennifer and let her go. "I don't know if I'll get home tonight, but I'll try."

Her chin came up half an inch. "Whatever it takes, for Peter."

"Yeah."

"'Bye, Eddie." Jennifer brushed past him.

"Did you get home?" Harvey asked.

"Yeah, for about two seconds." Eddie pulled out a chair and folded into it. "No, seriously, I ate at home. Leanne's book launch is Monday."

"Oh, that's right." Harvey ran his hand through his short hair.

Eddie shrugged. "She's feeling guilty because she's excited about that, but she thinks she should be all morbid about Peter."

"I can understand that. Everybody remotely concerned feels guilty because life has to go on while Peter may be dying." Harvey shook his head. "So, talk to me. The stolen car. Are we sure Holden stole it?"

112

"Looks like it. His fingerprints are on the steering wheel."
Eddie peeled up the corner of a plastic box Jennifer had left on
the table and liberated two brownies. He got himself a glass of
milk and settled in to talk.

*****

Peter woke to the sound of pounding footsteps overhead.
Someone ran across the floor above. The door at the top of the
stairs opened, and the light came on. Peter blinked, trying to
assess the situation.

Mack hurried down the stairs.

"Something's happened to Web. I've got to get out of here."

"Let me go," Peter said.

"I can't. You'd go right to the police."

"I won't."

"Sure. Just like no police were watching when Web went to
get the money. It's all over the six o'clock news that someone the
cops were chasing got hit by a car."

So that explained why the other guy was hours late getting
back with the money.

Mack hesitated. "If I thought it would do me any good, I'd
take you with me."

"Do that," Peter said. "I can still get you the money."

"Somehow I doubt that. Good luck. Someone will find you."
He turned away.

"Wait! At least call my wife. Tell her where I am."

"No can do, buddy."

"You can't just leave me here chained up."

Mack came back two steps and threw something into his lap.
Peter looked down and saw a small brass key. It slid off his thigh,
onto the sleeping bag. He looked back, but Mack was at the
bottom of the stairs.

"Wait," Peter cried. "Don't leave me. The key won't do me
any good. At least undo my hands."

The light went off, and the door slammed shut.

113

Peter's heart pounded, and he breathed in quick, shallow gulps.

What just happened? He supposed he should be thankful Mack didn't kill him before he left.

He squinted and leaned a little to his left, concentrating on that key. It must go to the padlock at his ankle. It had to. He mustn't lose sight of it, or let it get lost in the sleeping bag. He had to get hold of it.

How on earth was he going to get out of this mess? He'd counted on the Priority Unit to follow the kidnappers back when they picked up the ransom, but that solid rock of hope had crumbled.

The Lord is my rock.

He tried not to discount that thought, but it seemed ironic. Would he die of thirst here in this basement? He looked around. The light outside the small window had faded. Dusk was coming. In an hour or so, it would be pitch black in here.

The bathroom. He could barely get to the closet-like bathroom with the chain on his ankle. He'd examined that closely when they'd let him use it earlier. Very small. Very empty. A toilet and a pedestal sink. He could reach the sink, but not the toilet while chained—he'd tried before. The small mirror over the sink was the only thing Peter saw that might possibly be useful. He'd wished earlier that he'd been able to break it while his hands were free and keep a shard to use against them. But they were too watchful, and too careful to bind his hands when they left him alone.

So now what?

*****

Abby tucked Andy in at eight o'clock. He yawned while saying a short prayer for his dad and drifted off to sleep while Abby prayed. She turned off the lamp and tiptoed out, leaving his door ajar, and made her way to Gary's room.

His light was off, but Gary sat on the window seat, peering out into the night.

"Hey," Abby said. "Time for bed."

Slowly, he climbed down and walked to his bed. He burrowed in under the quilt and looked up at her. In the light spilling in from the hall, she could see his eyes shine with moisture.

"What happened today, anyway?" Gary asked. "Something happened, but no one will tell me."

Abby took a deep, slow breath. "Honey, this is a lot to take in."

"Is Daddy dead?"

"No, no." *Lord, make me wise.*

"Well, something bad happened," he said.

"Gary, do you know what kidnapping is?"

"Yeah, sure, but. . .Dad isn't a kid."

"It doesn't have to be." She sat down on the edge of the bed. "Like I told you last night, somebody took your dad out of his office. And they want money. They said that if we took them a bag of money today, they would let him go."

"Where would we get it?" Gary asked.

"I got it from the bank this morning."

"You did?"

"Yeah. Uncle Harvey went with me to the bank to borrow it."

"Did you give it to the bad guy?"

"A police officer dropped off the money this afternoon."

"So, where's Dad?"

Abby's lips trembled, and she put a hand to her mouth. "We don't know. Something happened to the bad man before he could get back to your dad and let him go."

"What? Did he get arrested?"

Abby shook her head. "He had an accident. A truck hit him."

Gary stared at her. "Was it bad?"

She hesitated, but her years of working at hospitals had taught her to tell it straight out. "Yeah. He couldn't tell the police anything, and—and he died."

115

Gary was still for a long moment. "So. . .where's Dad? Does Uncle Harvey know?"

"No. He thinks the man has him locked up somewhere. Uncle Harvey and Uncle Eddie and all the other policemen are looking for him."

"Why don't *we* go out and look for him?" Gary threw back the quilt and started to get up.

"No, Gary. We can't. We don't have any idea where he is. We don't even know if he's in Portland. They could have taken him someplace else to hide him until they got the money."

"We could check the park," Gary said eagerly. "Dad takes me and Andy there a lot. Or the gym." He grabbed her wrist. "He really likes the gym."

"No, no, honey." Abby sighed and patted his shoulder. "It's not like that. Dad can't go wherever he wants right now. See, he has to stay with those men until they get the money. Then they'll let him go, and he'll come home."

Gary took shallow gulps of air. "You said the guy died."

"Yes, but we think he has friends. I mean, one guy couldn't keep your dad a prisoner all by himself, could he?"

Gary shook his head. "Dad's real strong."

"Yes. I didn't think I should tell Andy all of that, because it's hard to understand why anyone would do that to someone as nice as your dad. But I guess you're old enough to know." Abby swallowed hard. "Would you like to pray again? I think that's the best thing we can do right now. Because wherever your dad is, he'll be praying too. God is there with him. And if we all pray together, maybe those men will let him go."

"Or maybe he'll get away from them."

Abby considered that. Would Peter take a chance of escaping? Probably, if he thought he could do it without getting himself killed. He'd put up with a lot to stay alive, though, for the boys. And for her.

"Let's pray now," she said.

Gary lay back on his pillow, and she held his hand. "Dear Lord, we don't know what Peter needs right now, but we ask that

116

you will help him. Help the police to find him. Keep him strong and healthy, and please bring him home to us soon."

She waited, and after a few seconds, Gary said, "Don't let my father die, Jesus."

She squeezed his hand. "Amen. I love you, Gary. Now, try to sleep. We'll know more tomorrow."

She bent and kissed his cheek. Gary didn't respond. Abby rose and went out. She sent up another prayer as she went downstairs, for Gary and Andy. *And Peter, Lord. Wherever he is, let him know you're there with him, that you haven't forgotten him.*

Harvey was pacing the kitchen. He stopped when she entered.

"How are the boys?" he asked.

She hesitated. "They're taking this hard. Gary is confused. He wants to shoulder the burden, but he doesn't know how. He knew something bad had happened, and I told him about the drop, and that the kidnapper was accidentally killed. He wanted to go right out and look for Peter."

Harvey smiled sadly. "He's a boy. I'd probably have felt the same way at his age."

"Yeah. If I thought it would do any good, I'd be out there beating the bushes." Abby sat down, feeling useless and spent. "If there's another kidnapper, why hasn't he called?"

"I don't know." With most people, he'd have said something more soothing, like "These things take time." But with Abby, he had to be honest.

She looked up at him. "Where's Eddie?"

"Gone to help Nate and the other guys run down the dead man's friends and every contact on his phone."

"You got into it?"

"Yes. There was no password. The lab has printed out all the recent calls, texts, and contacts."

"And?"

"It's a burner, and there wasn't much. Most significantly, a couple of blocked numbers. If we get something solid from it, you'll be the first to know." He froze for an instant, then yanked

117

his phone from his pocket. "Speak of the devil." He put the phone to his ear. "Yeah? Really? Okay. Call me as soon as you've got an address." He closed the connection and looked at Abby. "Holden's phone rang in the lab earlier. The incoming number was one of his contacts, but the contact list just says 'MM.' Eddie's getting the name and address from the phone company."

"He can do that?"

"This company cooperates when it's a criminal investigation. Not all of them do." Harvey shrugged. "I have mixed feelings about that."

"Me, too," Abby said. "I'm all for privacy, but right now I want my husband back."

"Yeah."

Sarah came in from the dining room. "I'm going out to check the perimeter."

"Thanks, Sarah," Harvey said. After she went out the back door, he looked at Abby. "I honestly don't think anyone will come around here tonight."

"I know. But thanks. It does make me feel safer." She let out a long sigh. "Janelle called me earlier."

"Peter's sister?"

Abby nodded. "She wanted to come over, but I asked her to wait until tomorrow. I know the whole family wants to be close to the action, but. . ."

"No offense, but they tend to get in the way. They distract the officers."

"Yeah. I thought if nothing's changed in the morning, I'd have Leeanne or Jennifer come get the boys and take them to your place for a few hours. Keep them occupied and out from underfoot. My parents would like to see them, and Mom would feel like she was helping if she fed a few people."

"Oh, that's right, your folks are coming down tomorrow."

"I thought Peter would be back, and we'd have a nice celebration." She couldn't hold back a sob.

Harvey was at her side immediately. "Abby, I'm so sorry." He put his arms around her. "I know you didn't sleep much last night, but—"

She held up a hand. "I can't."

"Maybe a sleeping tablet?"

"No. No, if anything happens, I want to be alert." She leaned against his shoulder for a moment, then pulled away. "What if I tell Janelle and Vickie they can visit with the family at your house?"

"Janelle probably wants to see you in person," Harvey said.

"You're right. Tom's out of town, and she's probably feeling very left out of things and alone. It's just so hard to know what to do when everything is up in the air."

Harvey considered what he would do if Jennifer were the victim, but he couldn't imagine himself being able to function. He would, somehow. But he had resources Abby didn't have, things he could do to rule out possibilities. "Maybe tell Janelle to come here for a short visit in the morning, and she can spend more time with her mom and the boys either at Vickie's or at our house?"

Abby nodded. "I'll call Jennifer. Although, she's probably in turbo mode with Mom and Dad coming down. Leeanne has a book signing at the mall on Monday, but she may be free tomorrow."

"Big day for her," Harvey said.

"Yeah. But she told me she's so far into the next book, it's like the first one was a dream."

"Hmm. She'll wake up when people start lining up for her signature."

"Think they will?"

Harvey smiled. "Eddie's had everyone in our unit broadcasting the event on social media. I think quite a few people will show up."

"I hope so." Abby gave him a wan smile. "Go home and hug your little boy, Harvey. Sleep. Eat. Laugh. Then come back."

"Not while the boys are out there with a possible lead. But you should sleep. Try?"

Abby grasped his hand. "Pray with me first."

"Gladly."

Chapter 10

"Got it," Nate said. "Sending it to you now."

Eddie brought in the email. "Deering. The person who called Holden's phone lives in Deering. But the incoming call came from the West End. They can tell where the phone was at that time."

"Right," Nate said. "Sorry I couldn't get an exact location. But it's the same phone that sent Holden that text earlier, like around four thirty."

"Yeah. 'Where RU?' I remember. I figure whoever's on the other end is Holden's sidekick."

Eddie clicked his phone to call Tony.

"Yeah, Shakespeare?" Tony sounded full of energy, though it was nearly ten o'clock and he'd been working fifteen hours.

"Did you guys get anything at Holden's apartment?" Eddie asked.

"We found a note with a phone number on it. No name, but it's Carter Ulrich's cell number. Nothing else helpful. Doesn't look like Holden's been home much lately. Dust everywhere, and there's milk going sour in the fridge."

"Maybe he's just a slob."

"Yeah, maybe. We're not done, but there's nothing obvious. No sign of Peter Hobart."

"Okay. We've got a new address for an incoming text and call on Holden's phone—his MM contact. Leave the techs where you are and meet me there?"

"Sure."

"It's in Deering."

Tony swore. "Sounds like an all-nighter."

"Maybe." Eddie gave him the address. "I'm leaving the office as soon as I make a couple calls."

Leeanne was first on his list. "Hey, babe. Don't wait up, okay? We're following a rabbit trail."

"Okay," she said. "Be careful, huh?"

"I will be. Love you."

He called Harvey next and told him he was heading to Deering with Tony and Jimmy. "The guy's name is McCafferty. Chad McCafferty."

"I thought it was MM."

"That's what the contact list said. I don't know why."

"Are you where Nate is?" Harvey asked.

"Yeah, I'm still at the office."

"Tell Nate to work the connection between those two. How do Holden and McCafferty know each other?"

"Right."

"Do you have info on his car?"

"Not yet."

"Tell Nate to do that first. You want me to go out to Deering with you?"

"Nah," Eddie said. "Stand by and I'll call you."

He relayed Harvey's instructions to Nate and jogged down the stairway to the garage. His phone rang before he had his truck in gear. Charlie Doran in Comm—he was making a late night of it, too.

"We pinged that phone again. It's moving."

"Where now?" Eddie asked.

"Downtown."

Eddie grunted. "Call the captain, would you? He may have some ideas for following that phone."

*****

Abby woke from a sound sleep when someone tapped on her bedroom door.

"Who is it?" she called. Her clock said nearly one in the morning.

"It's Sarah Benoit. May I come in?"

"Of course." Abby snapped on her bedside lamp. After all the urging Sarah and Harvey had done to get her to rest, they wouldn't wake her if it wasn't important. Her heart raced as Sarah opened the door and walked over to the bed. "What is it? Is there news on Peter?"

"No, I'm afraid not," Sarah said. "But, do your boys have bicycles?"

"Bikes? Yes, they both do. Why?" Abby slid to the edge of the bed and groped for her slippers.

"I heard something in the garage, and when I went to check, the door was up. Not the one behind your car, the other door."

Abby's heart lurched. They'd left Peter's car at the store, but the boys' bikes had racks on that side of the garage.

"Come take a look?" Sarah asked.

"Yes." Abby grabbed her robe and flung it on as she ran through the hall, living room, and kitchen. She noted that a different comm tech, one she hadn't met, was seated on the couch wearing headphones.

She yanked open the door to the garage and looked out, beyond her Equinox. Little Andy's bike was where it belonged, which relieved part of her anxiety, but Gary's was missing.

"It's Gary." Abby glanced at the row of coat hooks on the wall. "His helmet's gone, too."

"Well, that's something." Sarah's brown eyes were full of angst. "I ran outside, but I couldn't see anyone. He must have been really quick."

"Where's Harvey?" Abby asked.

"He left to lead a manhunt."

Abby stared at her. "What happened?"

"Someone called the kidnapper's phone, and they got a fix on the other phone. They I.D.'d the person it's registered to, and they got his motor vehicle records. The captain ordered roadblocks, and they're looking for the owner. Eddie and the other guys have gone to his house in Deering."

"Deering?" It wasn't far away, but it was an outlying area of the city. "Do they think Peter is there?"

"They don't know."

Abby nodded, trying to push aside the distraction. "We've got to find Gary. Can you get some more people to help us?"

"Yes. Do you have any idea where he might be headed on his bike? His grandmother's, maybe?"

"No, not there." Abby closed her eyes for a moment. "When I tucked him in, he was talking about how we should be out there looking for Peter. He mentioned the park, and how Peter takes him and Andy there a lot."

"Which park? The one that's a block over from here?"

"Yes. And he also mentioned Peter's gym, but it wouldn't be open now."

"Would Gary know that?"

"I don't know. He might not think of that." She gave Sarah the name of the gym and its location.

"I'll request a search immediately," Sarah said. "We'll try the park first."

"I'll go get dressed." Abby headed for the bedroom, wishing she'd followed her impulse to keep her street clothes on.

"Wait," Sarah said. "The two of us can't go out looking for him. We need to stay here."

"Of course," Abby said. "Andy—"

"Yes, and there may be a second kidnapper on the loose. I'll stay with you, but we'll get a lot of people out there fast, trust me."

"Okay. Thanks." Abby trudged up the stairs feeling useless. She opened Andy's door and peeked in. The little boy slept soundly. She stood gazing down at him for a moment then turned to Gary's room. As she'd expected, his bed was empty.

"Peter, we need you," she whispered, and wiped a tear from her cheek. "God, we need Peter."

*****

124

Harvey took a call on his radio as he pulled up to the roadblock at the Franklin Street on-ramp for I-295. "Yeah, Charlie?"

"Nothing on the license plate readers."

"Okay, thanks." He scowled as he got out of the Explorer. He was a step behind the kidnapper. The man could be across the state line by now. He checked in with the officer in charge and got the same report.

"We're keeping an eye out for him, but we've got nothing so far, Captain. We've had four Acuras come through here since we arrived, but none of them matched the suspect's plate."

"Okay. Don't give up."

Eddie was calling him again, and Harvey clicked his phone on. "Yeah?"

"Hey, Harv, McCafferty's not at his house, but it looks like someone packed and ran in a hurry. Maybe two people. It's a duplex, four rooms. I'd say McCafferty has a girlfriend. There are feminine clothes and cosmetics lying around, and we found some mail with the name Emma Skerrit on it."

"Okay, I'll give that intel to Nate. Anything else?"

"Yeah. McCafferty's car is here—the Acura. Nothing suspicious on first look."

"How about the girlfriend's car?" Harvey asked.

"I was hoping you could have someone check on it for us."

"Affirmative." Harvey walked over to the officer in charge of the road block. "Hey, we're looking for the wrong vehicle. Hold on while I get some more accurate information."

It took almost ten minutes for Nate to run down Emma Skerrit's DMV records and relay the information to Harvey. She'd registered a ten-year-old Honda a few months earlier. Harvey passed on the information and noticed an incoming call from Abby. This couldn't be good at 1 a.m.

"Abby, what's up?"

"Gary's gone. He sneaked out and took his bike. I think he's gone looking for Peter."

"Okay, slow down and tell me why you think that."

125

"His bike and helmet are gone, and Sarah heard the garage door go up. Do you want to talk to Sarah?"

"Yeah, put her on," Harvey said.

"Captain, I apologize," Sarah said. "The boy got past me. I've been watching for someone trying to get in, not out."

"Understood," Harvey replied. "What are you doing about it?"

"We've got patrol officers searching the park where Mr. Hobart took the boys to play, and two have gone to his gym on the off chance Gary went there, since he mentioned it to his mother."

"Okay, anything else?" Harvey's mind clicked through places he'd seen Peter or knew his brother-in-law frequented.

"I couldn't think of any other places, and Abby didn't come up with any others. She says he wouldn't go to his Grandma Hobart's."

"I hope not. It's too far away. How about the church?"

"You think he'd go there?"

"I don't know. Call Eddie. He should be on his way in from Deering. See if he can swing by our church. And tell him to talk to the pastor, too. Wake him up if he has to."

"Yes, sir," Sarah said.

A sudden thought struck Harvey. "What about Peter's store?"

"The car dealership?"

"Yeah. Gary hasn't been there since the shooting. He might wonder if his dad would show up at the place he disappeared from."

"It hadn't occurred to me," Sarah said, "but it sounds reasonable."

Harvey made a quick decision. "I'm not too far from there, and I've got the keys Abby gave me. I'll drop by. Any chance there were more keys at home that Gary could access?"

"I'll ask."

He walked back to his car while he waited. Seconds later, Abby was on the phone.

"There's a key to the store's back entrance here, Harvey. Gary doesn't have it. I don't think there are any others around here that I don't know about."

"Okay, thanks. He's probably not there, but I'll look. And, Abby, do me a favor? Call the Rowlands and tell them Eddie will be coming by the church to look around. I think it's time to activate the prayer chain."

He drove to Hobart Chevrolet and prowled slowly through the car lot, looking for a bicycle. It would be easy to hide among the scores of vehicles. He didn't find anything, so he parked near the front doors and walked completely around the large building. When he got back to the main entrance, he stopped and listened, but heard only the sounds of distant traffic.

*****

Eddie turned into the empty parking lot at Victory Baptist. The wide expanse of pavement mocked him. He pulled his pickup into a handicapped spot near the front steps.

"Try the front doors and look around for a bike," he told Jimmy, who was riding with him. "I'll go around and check the side entrance."

"What's that building?" Jimmy pointed to an attached annex.

"That's the new fellowship hall and kitchen, and some classrooms. Check those doors, too."

Eddie walked quickly but examined every possible hiding place for a ten-year-old boy. There weren't many spots that would work. Two streetlights flooding the parking lot and spotlights illuminating the steeple made it easy to see that nothing was out of place.

"Gary," he called. "It's Uncle Eddie. Gary, you here?"

No answer. He strolled around the back of the building and tried another doorknob. He went on around the annex and met Jimmy between the Dumpster and the kitchen door.

"See anything?"

"No," Jimmy replied.

The faint sound of a door closing pulled Eddie's attention to the parsonage, a hundred yards away. Pastor Rowland had come out his side door and walked across the lawn, then the pavement, toward the two detectives.

"Eddie?"

"Yeah. I hope we didn't wake you."

The pastor came closer. "I got a call from Abby Hobart. She said you were coming to look for Gary."

"I don't suppose you've seen or heard anything odd tonight?" Eddie asked.

"No. I wish I could tell you he was safe in my house."

"It was a long shot," Eddie said. "This is Detective Cook—Jimmy. This is Pastor Rowland."

"Pleased to meet you, sir." Jimmy shook the pastor's hand.

"Abby updated me on what's happened with Peter," Mr. Rowland said. "She says Harvey told her we should start the prayer chain. That wouldn't endanger Peter worse than he already is, would it? Having more people know about it, I mean."

Eddie shrugged. "I don't see how it can get much worse. We haven't heard from the kidnappers since the drop was bungled. If that guy was working alone, Peter could be in real trouble. And if he wasn't working alone—well, I have no explanation. I don't see how it could hurt to have more people alert and on the lookout."

"That's right," Jimmy said. "This has gone beyond hushing it up so we don't upset the kidnappers."

The pastor nodded. "Abby said Harvey's considering going public with the full story in the morning if you haven't found Peter. But Gary. . .I'm so sorry she has this to worry about on top of the rest."

"Yeah," Eddie said.

Pastor Rowland looked around the parking lot. "Well, I won't keep you. Mary and I will be praying, and I'll check with Abby later this morning. If there's no word, I'll call our prayer captains."

"Thanks, Pastor."

Jimmy clapped a hand on Eddie's shoulder. "Did you hear something?"

Eddie swung around, peering in the direction Jimmy was looking. He may have heard a quiet sound during his conversation. "Where?" he whispered.

"Over there." Jimmy pointed.

Pastor Rowland stepped closer. "Sometimes we get a raccoon, if the Dumpster isn't closed tightly."

Eddie pulled his flashlight from his belt. He turned it on and walked toward the back of the annex and the Dumpster. He didn't see any movement, but he caught a soft noise. He looked at Jimmy and pointed toward the near side of the Dumpster, while he walked toward the far side.

They rounded the corners at the same time, shining their lights on the huddled form behind the container. Gary let out a little yelp and then sobbed, hiding his face from the light.

"Gary, it's me, Uncle Eddie."

Jimmy lowered the beam of his flashlight and focused on a three-speed bike that had seen better days. The front fender was crumpled, and the wheel rim bent. The tire was completely flat.

"You okay, Gar?" Eddie crouched beside the boy and reached for his arm.

Gary squawked and pulled away.

"What happened?" Eddie asked. To Jimmy, he made a "call it in" sign. Jimmy stepped away, and a moment later, Eddie heard him say quietly, "Hey, Captain? Yeah. We've got the kid."

"My arm hurts," Gary said. "I ran into the concrete steps and fell. I couldn't see where I was going."

"Why you hiding?" Eddie asked. "Whyn't you call your mom? Or go ring the pastor's doorbell?"

Gary burst into heart-rending sobs. Eddie sat down on the pavement and gently pulled the boy toward him, avoiding the painful right arm.

"It's okay, bud. It's going to be okay."

"My arm," Gary gasped, then he went back to weeping.

"Let me see." Eddie touched his bicep gingerly, and Gary let out a little gasp. "Okay, I'm going to have my friend Jimmy call us an ambulance, and we'll get someone to look at that."

"No!" Gary stared at him, his eyes glittering with tears. "I don't want Mom to know I messed up."

"Well, she already knows you snuck out," Eddie said, "and she's worried plenty. I think if you see a doctor, she might even feel a little less worried about you. Hey, maybe Uncle Jeff will come in the ambulance. You'd let him look at your arm, wouldn't you?" He seemed to remember Leeanne saying that Jeff would be off that day, and he and Beth were babysitting Connor. Still, if it would calm Gary down. . .

"No, don't call them," Gary said.

Eddie sighed. "Okay. Tell you what, you let me carry you to my truck and I'll drive you over to the hospital, and a doctor can look at you there, huh? It might even be quicker than waiting for the bus."

Gary shook his head and clutched his forearm, huddling in misery.

Jimmy walked over. "Mrs. Hobart's on the way. Sarah Benoit's bringing her."

"You hear that?" Eddie asked Gary. He looked up at Jimmy. "Tell her we're driving Gary to the hospital to get his arm checked. She can meet us in the ER."

"What about Andy?" Gary asked, a hitch in his voice.

"She won't leave him there alone," Eddie said. "They'll get someone to stay with him."

"Who?" Gary asked.

"I don't know."

"Well, I'm not going until we know my brother's okay."

Eddie held back a laugh. "Okay, buddy. Hold on."

He called Sarah. "Hey, Sarah, you with Abby Hobart?"

"I sure am. We're just getting in my car to come to the church."

"Who's staying with Andy?" Eddie asked.

"Officer Crocker. Andy's sleeping, though."

130

"Good. You and Abby come to the ER at Maine Medical. Gary's arm's banged up, and I think he needs it checked."

"Copy that," Sarah said and hung up.

Eddie looked at Gary. "It's all set. A nice lady named Allison Crocker is staying with your brother. You may have met her. She came to church here once when we were guarding Chief Browning last winter. Remember that?"

Gary shook his head.

"Oh, well, Uncle Harvey and I both know her. She's a good person. Now, let's see if I can pick you up without hurting your arm." Eddie stooped and eased his arms beneath the boy. "Upsy daisy." He stood with Gary in his arms. "Oof. You weight a ton, kid."

"Uh-uh-uh." Gary let out a little shriek.

"I'm sorry," Eddie said. He probably should have insisted on the ambulance. Too late now. "Jimmy, toss the bike in the back, will you?"

Pastor Rowland walked beside him to the truck. "Is there anything I can do, Eddie?"

"Just tell anyone who asks that Gary's safe and he's going to be okay. And if by any chance any reporters get wind of this, refer them to Captain Larson."

"Right." The pastor opened the passenger door for them.

Jimmy lifted the mangled bicycle into the truck bed and came to climb in beside Gary. "Easy, fella. I'm Jimmy. Which arm hurts?"

Eddie hurried around the driver's side, climbed in, and started the engine. "Hey, Gary, how about we put the blue light on, so traffic gets out of our way? Would you like that?"

Chapter 11

Abby ran through the emergency entrance and turned toward the triage desk. She'd worked behind it dozens of shifts, but she didn't recognize the young woman who manned it tonight.

"I'm Abigail Hobart, and my son was brought in with an injured arm."

"Excuse me." A stocky young man with blond hair approached her, holding up a PPD badge. "Abby Hobart?"

"Yes."

"I'm Detective Cook. We met at Eddie and Leeanne's wedding."

Abby recognized him immediately, since she'd actually met him several other times, at Harvey's house. "Of course. Are you here with my son?"

"Yeah, Gary's in one of the exam rooms. Eddie stayed with him."

"I'm so glad. Thank you for helping find him. I can't imagine why he would go to the church."

Jimmy shrugged. "On the way here, he told us he wanted to pray for his dad. Maybe he thinks it counts more if you pray at the church or light a candle or something."

Sarah came up beside them. "I'm parked to the right of the entrance."

"Thanks, Sarah," Abby said. "I'm going in to see Gary."

"I'll wait out here for you."

Abby made an unhappy face. "Sorry to drag you over here to spend your shift in a waiting room."

"No problem," Sarah said.

Abby could tell she meant it. She turned to the nurse behind the desk.

"Come through that door over there," the young woman said. "Your son is in exam 3."

When Abby had passed through the security door into the ER's main hallway, a nurse she knew caught sight of her.

"Abby! I met your handsome young man."

"How's he doing, Tammy?" she asked.

"Dr. Littleton just went in to check his arm. He'll probably have to set it."

"It's broken?" Abby cried. "They didn't tell me."

"Yeah. He'll probably be glad to see you."

Abby hurried into the exam room. The gray-haired doctor and another nurse consulted near the gurney, while Eddie stood back out of the way. Gary lay on the white sheet, whimpering.

"Doctor, I'm his mother," Abby said, stepping forward.

"Oh, Abby." Dr. Littleton glanced at the clipboard he held. "Or Mrs. Hobart, I should say."

"I'm still Abby. Gary is my stepson."

"Right. He has a fractured radius, and there may be something going on in the elbow. We gave him some Tylenol, and I'm sending him for x-rays. Then he'll come back here. I want to see the pictures, but I'm pretty sure I'll be casting it."

Abby pulled in a deep breath. "Okay. What do I do?"

"You can go down to the waiting room at imaging, or you can wait here." Dr. Littleton gave Gary a smile and a nod and said to Abby, "I'll talk to you in a few minutes, when we know exactly what we've got."

"Thank you." The doctor went out, and Abby moved in closer to Gary. "Hey, Gar. Does it hurt a lot?"

Gary nodded. "Are you going to spank me?"

Abby frowned. "Why would I do that?"

"'Cause I was bad, and you're the stepmother."

She laughed. "Well, first of all, I'm not sure you were bad. You wanted to help your dad. I wish you'd told me your plans, but we're here now. Second, you're a little big for a spanking, aren't you? And third, who says all stepmothers are mean?"

"Brady Huston."

"Oh, well, that's Brady for you." Gary's friend was the class cut-up.

"He's got a stepmom."

"Well, yeah."

"I told him you're a good one, but I'm not sure he believes it," Gary said.

Eddie came to her side. "Well, you can tell that punk you hit the jackpot when you got Abby."

Gary nodded. "I will."

The nurse put up the rail on the side of the gurney. "We're heading for X-ray now, Gary."

"Do you want me to come?" Abby asked. "I can't go in the camera room with you, but I can be right outside the door."

"Yeah." Tears filled Gary's eyes. "They gave me some chewy med, but it still hurts."

"Aw. I'm sorry."

"Do you want me to come, too, Gary?" Eddie asked.

"No," the boy said firmly. "I want you to find my dad."

"Okay," Eddie said softly. "I'll sure try."

Abby followed the gurney out and down the hall. Eddie tagged along.

"Thanks so much for everything," Abby said quietly. "Did I hear someone say he was hiding behind the Dumpster at the church?"

Eddie nodded. "I think he knew he'd gone about it wrong and was embarrassed that he'd messed up. His bike was useless, and he was in pain."

"So he wanted to hide."

"Yeah. I'm glad you didn't come across angry." Eddie squeezed her shoulder. "Hey, I'll grab Jimmy and get out there. They may have some more leads for us to follow."

Abby hurried to catch up with the nurse pushing the gurney. Tammy gave her a sidelong glance.

"That cop who brought him in is a looker. Do you know if he's married?"

"Yeah, to my sister."

"Oh. Sorry."

"It's okay," Abby said. "I'm used to it."

135

*****

After an update from Eddie on Gary's prognosis, Harvey sent all four of his detectives home to get some sleep. He stealthily entered his house after two a.m. and reset the burglar alarm.

Jennifer was sound asleep in their sleigh bed. He'd called her as soon as Eddie reported that Gary was found, and she must have crashed after that. Harvey was glad. Someone in the family should be getting some sleep.

He tiptoed up the stairs and looked in on Connor. The little boy lay resting peacefully, his long eyelashes fluttering with each breath. His hair was getting longer, and it was taking on a decided wave, the way Harvey's did when it got too long. He rested a gentle hand on the baby's chest for a moment and went quietly down the stairs.

As much as he longed to crawl in beside Jennifer, he sat down instead at his desk and made some notes. He had to be ready with assignments for the men first thing in the morning. He'd already canceled his Friday morning run with Eddie and told them all to meet at the office at nine, barring any earlier calls pertaining to the case.

Mike had warned him that he would probably have to hold a more detailed press conference early in the day. Ryan Toothaker, who was a good but obnoxious reporter for the *Portland Press Herald*, had wormed it out of one of Hobart Chevrolet's salesmen that the business would be closed over the weekend because the boss was somehow connected to the shooting that occurred there on Wednesday night. Harvey jotted a few phrases in his pocket notebook, things he had to make public, and things he wanted to keep out of the news reports if possible.

After that, he scanned his notes from the previous day. They needed to find out who Webster Holden was working for, and his connection to Chad McCafferty. Were they working for the same money man? And was that so-called financier a loan shark? Nate hadn't turned up anything as far as stolen boats went, and the car Holden had driven to the drop hadn't told them much.

Emma Skerrit, McCafferty's girlfriend, seemed like a safer bet. She was out there somewhere with McCafferty. Harvey had asked a tech at the police station to ping her phone and McCafferty's repeatedly. If things went his way, that pair would be hauled in before daylight, and they would get some solid information. McCafferty was in this up to his neck, or Harvey was badly mistaken. Again he reviewed everything they'd learned so far about Carter Ulrich and his finances. Nothing concrete there, just rumors and speculation. Harvey had a short list of bookies and money launderers that could be connected to this, but so far he had no clues pointing to any of them.

He paused when he came to the notebook page where he'd copied the names off Baby Girl Ervin's birth certificate. Her adoptive parents had named her Leah Viniard. He almost wished he had a right to look out for her. Thinking back over his brief meetings with Steve and Denise Viniard, he knew they loved Leah, no question there. He had no reason to think they wouldn't do right by her, so why did he feel so protective? He ripped out the page and set it aside. He would think about Leah's family after Peter was found.

He got up and walked out to the living room, where he kicked back in a recliner. He didn't want to wake Jennifer, and he didn't want to waste time having to dress if he got a call during the next few hours. Responding slowly might result in Peter's death.

*****

Harvey woke to the smell of coffee and sat up to stretch. Jennifer poked her head in from the kitchen. She looked like a kid in her Piglet T-shirt and denim cut-offs, with her hair in two long braids and bare feet.

"Hey." She walked toward him smiling. "I wouldn't have cared if you woke me up."

"Aw, I just wanted to be ready to spring into action if I got a call."

137

The sun streamed in through the front window, and he looked at his watch. It was almost eight.

"I guess I got a few hours in."

"Yeah. Connor's in the highchair. Want to eat breakfast with him?"

"Terrific." He rose, wondering how she'd managed to get the baby up without waking him.

Connor burst into a huge grin when he saw his father and bounced up and down in the highchair, babbling.

"Hey, buddy." Harvey stooped to kiss the top of his head. He'd have unbuckled the harness and lifted him out, but Connor was halfway through a very messy breakfast of sliced banana and oatmeal.

"I'll have what he's having." Harvey sat down in his usual chair and scooped up a spoonful of cereal for Connor. Jennifer set a mug of black coffee beside him.

"Thanks, gorgeous."

She put her arm around his shoulders and bent to kiss him soundly.

"How's everything?" he asked.

"Fine. I talked to Abby a few minutes ago. Gary's at home with a cast on his arm. She's keeping him and Andy home today, but they might come over here later to see the folks if Gary feels up to it. I expect Mom, Dad, and Randy this afternoon."

"Not Travis?"

"No, he's started his job up there, and he's working today and tomorrow, but he's torn up about Peter. Randy's really eager to get down here."

"I'd better give Mr. Donnell a call."

"Do you have time?"

"Dish me up some oatmeal and I'll do it now. Then I'm hitting the shower."

The call to set up a twenty-hour-a-week job for Randy took three minutes, and Harvey sat at the table with his son for another ten. If not for Connor, he'd have been out the door, but watching his son mug at him and say "dadada" kept him glued to

138

the chair while he ate not only oatmeal and a banana, but a scrambled egg.

"Are you all set for the Wainthrop invasion?" he asked Jennifer as she wiped the oatmeal and banana slime off Connor's hands, chin, and cheeks.

"I think so. Beth is going to do some cooking. I guess we'll put Randy right into Trav's room, huh? He'll be moving in there next week, after he finishes his finals."

"Yeah. It'll be good to have Randy for a while. I can get to know him better." Travis, the 19-year-old, had stayed with them for the spring semester, from January to mid-May, while pursuing his degree in business. After being disappointed that he wasn't offered a sports scholarship, he'd bounced around a little, trying to decide what courses to take. Before he'd left them for the summer three weeks previously, he'd decided to change his major to computer science. Harvey didn't know if that was a good fit or not.

Unlike Travis, Randy knew exactly what he wanted to do. For some time, he'd wanted to be a police officer and was taking steps to make sure he succeeded. Harvey wasn't certain if his own profession had influenced Jennifer's youngest brother or not, but it made him happy to see a kid so enthusiastic about law enforcement. He tried not to go overboard in showing his pleasure, but he thought Randy would do well. He was a serious, studious young man who thought deeply about topics like justice and serving the public. Already he was reading books about ethics and criminal psychology. Harvey knew his idealism would fade somewhat when he got a dose of the job, but he thought Randy could handle it.

Jennifer lifted Connor from the highchair and handed him to Harvey. "Give him a hug and then go get your shower. And don't toss him around. Remember, he just ate."

Harvey grinned. "I wouldn't do that, would I?" He nuzzled Connor and kissed his clean cheek with a loud smack. "What's your day going to be like, Connor? Are you going to help

Mommy get ready for company? Your grandpa and grammy will fuss over you and tell you how big you're getting."

Jennifer laughed. "He's growing like the proverbial weed."

Harvey stroked Connor's back, thinking about Gary's misguided foray. "I've been thinking a lot about Leah."

"So have I," Jennifer said.

"Gary isn't that much different from her—they both want to find their dads, but they're not sure how to go about it."

"Those kids are hurting so badly." Jennifer's eyes misted. "I know you'll want to keep helping Leah when this is over."

"I'm worried that if she does find her father, she may not like what she finds." Harvey leaned over to kiss her and flicked a glance at the clock. "I hate to put Connor down, but I'd better." He handed her the baby and made a quick call to the dispatcher. "Anything new on the Hobart case?" No one had found Chad McCafferty or Emma Skerritt, and no one had called Abby about the ransom money.

Fifteen minutes later, Harvey kissed Jennifer with ardor at the door. "I'll call you."

"Okay. I'll be here."

She held Connor while she watched him go to the garage. They waved when he drove out, and Harvey got that leaving-home feeling. He hadn't hit the street yet, and already he longed to return.

He walked into the office at ten to nine. Tony and Jimmy were already in, and Tony was saying, "I ran into her in the parking garage this morning, so we walked up together. I think she's super."

"Who's that?" Harvey asked as he passed Tony's desk.

Jimmy answered for him. "Laney Cross, the chief's new secretary."

"I've met her," Harvey said. "She seems like a nice girl. Woman."

"Watch it, boss," Tony said.

"Right."

140

Friday. A week from today would be Judith's last day on the job, and Laney would be on her own in Mike's outer office.

Harvey looked up as Paula approached him with a cluster of phone messages in her hand.

"Oh, I'm sorry, Paula," Harvey said. "I should have let you know we'd all be coming in a little late."

"It's okay," she said. "I knew you'd been putting in extra hours, and somebody needed to answer the phones here. They've barely stopped ringing."

To prove her point, the phone on Harvey's desk rang. He picked it up, and Paula's phone started in. She dropped the messages on his desktop and hurried back to her own station.

"Larson," Harvey said.

"Hey, Captain, it's Ryan Toothaker."

Harvey grimaced. "Not now, Ryan. I just got to my desk, and I've got nothing for you."

"Press conference later? The day sergeant said to ask you."

"Yeah, I suppose so."

"The earlier the better," Ryan said.

Harvey sighed and drummed his fingers on the desktop. He really wanted to get some things in motion before he talked to reporters. "Two o'clock, I think. In the station lobby."

"I was hoping for earlier."

"Should I send you a formal apology?"

Ryan chuckled. "Nah, I'll cope."

"Good, because the more time I have to work before we meet, the more information I'll have for you."

"Can't you give me a little something now to get started with? You must have an I.D. on that man who was run over on Union Street yesterday."

"I do."

"Well?" When Harvey didn't respond immediately, Ryan said, "Come on, Captain. The place was swarming with cops when it happened. I was there five minutes after the collision, and you and Sergeant Legere were both on the scene already. I

141

counted at least five detectives and half a dozen uniforms. Either that was a superfluous response, or something was going down."

"His name was Webster Holden," Harvey said. "Now I'll expect you to give me anything you find out about him before the press conference."

"Deal. He's a local?"

"Yeah. Have fun with it." Harvey hung up.

The messages were a mixed bag, and between incoming calls he returned them. One from Mayor Jill Weymouth was on the top of the stack. Paula usually ranked his messages in what she perceived as order of importance. Jill's secretary put him right through.

"Captain, good morning."

"Morning, Mayor," Harvey said. "How can I help you?"

"I spoke to the chief a few minutes ago, and he apprised me of the kidnapping situation. Does your squad have anything new on that?"

"No, ma'am." Harvey scribbled himself a note. If Jill knew about Peter's kidnapping, the world may as well know. Not that she was indiscreet, but too many people were in on it now, and it would leak out and be common knowledge soon. If he didn't lead with it at his press conference he'd be accused of a coverup. "It's our top priority right now."

"I won't keep you long. Chief Browning implied that the traffic accident victim yesterday afternoon was mixed up in it."

"Yes, ma'am. I've scheduled a press conference for 2 p.m."

"All right, I'll expect to hear more then," Jill said.

"Okay. We have several leads to follow today."

"I'll let you get to it. Keep up the good work, Captain."

"Thank you." Harvey hung up with a sigh. He tossed the top message in his wastebasket and eyed the second one. A TV reporter. He set that one aside. His phone rang.

"Paul Trudeau here, Captain. I'm at the Hobarts' again, monitoring calls until noon. We haven't had any incoming, and Mrs. Hobart says there's nothing new from your end. Is that right?"

"That's correct. How's Abby holding up?"

"She seems pretty Stoic. Plans to take the boys to her sister's after lunch."

"How's Gary?"

"I don't think he's up yet. Abby said he didn't sleep well because of the pain. Too bad about his arm."

"Yeah. Maybe someone in the family should pick up the boys so that Abby can stay near the phones there." He didn't want Abby halfway across town when the kidnappers rang her cell phone.

"I'll suggest that," Paul said.

"Well, she won't want to get Gary up if he's sleeping now. I'll trust her judgment."

Nate walked in, and Jimmy walked over to talk to him. Tony got up and hovered by Harvey's desk until he closed the conversation with Trudeau.

"You got something, Tony?" Harvey asked, riffling through the messages.

"Maybe. Eddie just called in. He's got a lead on Holden's boss."

"Great. Where is he?"

"Eddie? He's on his way in."

Harvey handed him three memo sheets that held messages from reporters. "Could you please give these to Paula? Ask her to call them all back and tell them I'll hold a press conference in the lobby at two o'clock. Then we'll sit down together, and I'll give assignments."

"Sure."

Tony took the messages, and Harvey decided only one more message really needed a speedy response. By the time he'd made the call, Eddie was in and the four detectives had drifted into the interview room where they could sit comfortably around the table.

"Eddie, talk," Harvey said as he sank into a chair.

"Yeah, I went to see my C.I., Silver. He didn't have much, but it may be a fleck of gold."

143

"Silver's always steered you straight. What did he give you?"

"Web Holden provided muscle for that guy they call the Falcon."

Harvey scowled. "Lionel Prewitt? I thought he was in jail for money laundering."

"He is," Eddie said. "The word is, he's running his concerns from inside."

"Who's his lieutenant?"

"Silver says it's a guy named Talbot."

Harvey took out his phone and tapped into the computer network. "Davey Talbot?"

"Could be," Eddie said.

"He could be running Prewitt's insurance rackets and high-interest loans," Harvey said.

Eddie nodded. "That's how I see it. Peter's salesman, Ulrich, probably owed him."

Harvey rubbed his sore neck, regretting spending several hours in the recliner. "Okay, let's get a 20 on him."

Nate rose. "On it." He hurried out to his desktop.

Harvey looked across the table at Tony. "You had a couple of names last night—buddies of Holden's."

"Right," Tony said. "We didn't get anything helpful, but there's a couple more guys we could lean on."

"See what you can find out, but take Jimmy with you."

"Will do."

"All of you stay on the alert, in case we get something on Chad McCafferty and Emma Skerritt."

Jimmy and Tony nodded solemnly.

Nate came to the door of the interview room. "Prewitt's got an estate in Cape Elizabeth. Talbot's living in it. Runs his operations from there."

Harvey didn't like it. The man's base was outside the city, and therefore outside his jurisdiction. But the fact that he was living in the Falcon's house pretty much clinched the hunch that Talbot was conducting business for him.

"We could ask him to pay us a courtesy call," Eddie said.

"Me and Shakespeare can go to Cape Elizabeth," Tony said.

Harvey turned his frown on him. "I thought you were the grammar whiz, Winfield."

"Sorry." Tony smiled sheepishly. "Shakespeare and I can go. It just doesn't have the same ring to it."

"No, it doesn't," Harvey said. "But I don't think we're ready for that. We don't have anything solid that connects this Talbot to the kidnappers, even if he is hand in glove with the Falcon."

"What if they're keeping Peter down there?" Eddie asked.

Harvey let out a breath, not liking the suggestion. "If we spook Talbot now, it could spoil things later. Unless we find a connection and can get a warrant, I don't see getting permission to search that place. Now, what else have we got?" He skimmed the print-outs of reports that had come in that morning from the lab and the night patrol sergeant. "Why can't they find Emma Skerritt or her car?"

"Dunno, boss," Jimmy said. "She might have gotten past our roadblocks last night, before we realized she was mixed up in this."

"In which case, she could be in Canada," Tony said.

"And the phones?" Harvey asked.

"Ms. Skerritt and McCafferty must have wised up and turned them off," Nate said.

"Maybe." Harvey had yet to be convinced that the people who'd kidnapped Peter had high IQs.

"If they're using burners, maybe they ditched those and started using new ones," Eddie said.

Harvey grunted. "That's more likely. McCafferty probably tossed his. But apparently Emma Skerritt's was a smart phone through AT&T. Women don't like to give up their phones."

"Or anything else," Tony said.

"Shelley had fits when we got new ones," Jimmy said. "All her apps and contacts. . .She had to make sure every single thing got transferred to the new phone."

145

Harvey straightened the papers. "Nate, tell the techs to keep trying her phone. She may turn it on this morning, thinking she can give her messages a quick look."

"Got it," Nate said.

"And try to find out if Chad McCafferty also worked for Falcon Prewitt or his flunky, Talbot."

"Silver didn't know anything about McCafferty," Eddie said. "He did say he heard Holden mentioned in connection with someone called Mack, though."

"Could be our guy. 'Mack' McCafferty. The MM caller." Harvey looked questioningly at Eddie. "Are you ready to ride down to Cape with me?"

"Sure." Eddie stood. "Think we can get a warrant?"

"I don't know, but I think it's time to talk to Davey Talbot anyway."

"Boss, what about the other phone?" Tony asked.

Harvey looked at him blankly for a moment, then his mind connected Tony's words to a loose end. "Carter Ulrich's." He looked at the lab report again. "There's nothing here on it."

"Maybe it was low priority," Eddie said.

"Nate, find out about that. I want every contact Ulrich made." As he rose, Harvey said, "Jimmy, you help Nate compile every single report that's come in overnight on this thing. Check every night shift cop's report."

"Instead of going out with Tony?" Jimmy asked.

"Yes. Tony, you're on McCafferty. I think that's more promising right now. Any little tidbit you find, you call me."

"Copy that," Tony said.

They moved into the outer office, and Harvey paused for a moment by Eddie's desk. "I'm going to touch base with Abby. You go through what Silver told you, and cross reference with Tony about Holden's friends. You may have an overlap, and something might pop out. We already know Holden and McCafferty were communicating. I need anything that will connect either of them solidly to Talbot."

He sat in his swivel chair and called Abby's landline.

"How you doing, kiddo?" he asked when she answered.

"We're okay," Abby said. "Gary's having some pain and a little trouble adjusting to wearing a cast and having his activity restricted. I'm keeping both boys home from school again, though I don't know how long I can do that."

"Pray that something breaks over the weekend."

"I am. I'm praying all the time." Her voice cracked.

"Jennifer says she looks for the folks after lunch," Harvey said.

"Yeah, she said they'd come get the boys later if I need to stay here," Abby told him. "They need some distraction. I got on the school's website a few minutes ago and got Gary's homework assignments."

"Good," Harvey said.

"Well, he just got up, and he doesn't really feel like doing schoolwork, but maybe by tomorrow."

"It would probably do them good to see your parents and Randy and Jeff and Beth and the babies."

"Yeah." Abby's voice took on new decision. "I want to see everyone, too, but I feel like I need to stay here."

"The officers will notify us both immediately if anyone calls."

"I know." Abby sighed. "Janelle's coming here soon. Maybe I should go to Jenn's with the boys later."

"I suppose so, if the kidnappers haven't called you by then."

"If Gary feels up to it, we'll go over after we eat lunch."

Abby's voice was firmer, and Harvey decided that getting away from her house and the constant presence of law officers might be good for her.

"Sounds like a plan," he said. "We've got some leads we're following up on. I'll keep you posted if we learn anything."

"Thanks, Harvey."

He could hear imminent tears in her voice again.

"Chin up, Abby."

"Yeah. I'm doing my best, for the boys."

"You've got a lot of people who love you and will do anything you ask to help you."

"I know. Thanks."

When Harvey hung up, Eddie and Tony were leafing backward through their pocket notebooks.

"You got something?" Harvey asked.

"Don't think so," Eddie said.

"Well, I really want a warrant for Talbot's place. Get me something."

"Don't worry, Cap'n," Tony said with his crooked grin. "We'll look under every rock."

Harvey clicked open a database on his desktop. "Don't forget to look up once in a while."

"Hey, Captain," Nate said from across the room.

"Yeah?"

"I may have what you need. Jennifer's program is showing me that Webster Holden was arrested for assault three months ago, and the victim said it was connected to a debt he owed. And Holden was bailed out by Davey Talbot."

Harvey looked at Eddie. "Get my gear and stand by. I'll put the warrant app in, then we go."

*****

Peter's left ankle throbbed. If he moved it the slightest bit, pain stabbed him. What he'd give for a handful of aspirin!

The window was bright now. This must be Friday, but he wasn't certain. It was hard to keep track of the days. He must have slept a long time. He was hungry, very hungry.

He had to work harder to sit up this time. He ought to use the bathroom, but he wouldn't be able to undo his belt. He hadn't drunk anything for twenty-four hours, and it didn't seem urgent. He supposed he was dehydrated. Abigail would have fits if she knew.

He leaned back against the cold wall.

Where was Harvey Larson? Peter had convinced himself that Harvey was the greatest detective since Hercule Poirot, but he

148

hadn't been near the vacant house. Was Harvey losing his touch? Was this house even in Portland? Maybe they took him farther than he'd estimated. He could have passed out for a while during the ride and not realized it. But, no, he didn't think he'd lost consciousness during that harrowing trip in the trunk of Mack and his buddy's car. It seemed like a fading dream.

The only sensible conclusion was that he was on his own. He couldn't count on Harvey and the Portland P.D. to find him before he died of thirst, any more than he could count on Mack to come back and release him. He had to free himself.

He dreaded even trying, because he knew how much it would hurt. And he was getting weaker. Did it make any sense to fight the chain again?

He'd heard of animals caught in a trap chewing off a foot to get free. Well, he couldn't do that. At one point he'd managed to get hold of the chain and pull against it with all his weight, but nothing gave. So much for his years of weight training. He'd chafed his wrists so much on anything he could reach—the chain, the sleeping bag's zipper, the edge of the sink—that he was sure his arms were bloody. But the flimsy strips of tape still held him. That didn't seem right.

Eddie had shown them as a party trick how to get loose when your wrists were wrapped with duct tape. It was simple. Even Beth Wainthrop had done it. But Eddie had noted that it didn't work if your hands were taped behind you. Peter had tried anyway, but he couldn't get the leverage he needed.

Carefully, he rolled onto his knees. By leaning his forehead against the wall, he was able to push himself up slowly. He stood panting on the concrete floor. It shouldn't be this hard. He stooped to be sure the key was still on the sleeping bag. So far so good. He squared his shoulders. The chain would let him get a couple of steps into the bathroom. If nothing else, he might be able to bump the faucet on and get some water.

Chapter 12

Abby's landline rang, and she picked it up in Peter's den.

"Hi, Mrs. Hobart. This is Anita Spelling, Gary's teacher."

"Oh, hello." Abby's mind raced. How much should she tell Ms. Spelling?

"I was hoping Gary would be in school today," the teacher said.

"I'm sorry. Gary's had an accident."

"Oh, dear. Not serious, I hope."

"Well, he broke his arm. He won't be back until Monday at the earliest."

"I see. Well, we're going to announce the winners of our school-wide story contest on Monday, and we especially hoped Gary would be there."

Abby swallowed hard. Would Peter be home by Monday? Or would they all be in mourning? Anything but this uncertainty. "I'll try to make sure he's there."

"That would be great. I'm so sorry he was hurt. Is he doing okay?"

"Yes. He's got a cast. It was a bicycle accident. But we'll see how it goes. What time is this happening?"

"At two-fifteen. We're having an assembly in the multi-purpose room."

Abby tried not to think about the chaos that could erupt after Harvey revealed to the world this afternoon that Peter had been kidnapped. Reporters would probably flock to the house. Maybe she should keep the boys somewhere else until this was over. And if there was a second kidnapper, as Harvey seemed to think, was he ever going to call? Surely he'd have done it by now. She didn't want to follow that thought to its logical conclusion. She would cling to hope.

The boys couldn't isolate themselves forever, even if the worst happened. She came to a decision. Surely Peter would be home before then, and he would want to help celebrate. If not, this sounded like something Gary would want to tell his father about when he was able. Miss Spelling wouldn't call if there wasn't good news in store for Gary, would she? Abby didn't want this to be something their son regretted missing years later.

"All right, I'll make every effort to have him there. If he's not up to a full day of school by then, is it okay if he doesn't come in until time for the assembly?"

"Of course. I understand. And if he's in too much pain—"

"He is on pain medication. But—actually, I guess it's all right to tell you, since it will be on the evening news. We're having a bit of a family crisis."

"Oh?"

"Yes. Gary's father has been kidnapped."

"No! I'm so sorry."

"Thank you. Gary took his bike out last night and went looking for his father, and that's when he fell and broke his arm."

"My goodness." Ms. Spelling sounded truly flummoxed. Abby would bet she'd never heard this good an excuse for a child missing school before.

"I know it sounds weird, but it's true. Our whole family has been hit pretty hard with this."

"I'm so sorry. Is there anything we can do to help?"

"I don't think so," Abby said. "The police are working on finding him."

"We can wait to present the award if this is too much for Gary right now."

"No, don't do that," Abby said. "You've got everything planned, and I think it would be good for him to have something else to think about."

"Under the circumstances, I think I should tell you, Gary will be receiving the highest award for his grade."

"That's wonderful. I won't tell him, but I'll bring him in Monday. Please don't tell the other children about his father until the police make it public. I think that will happen this afternoon, but I wouldn't want the class to be upset and distracted."

"Of course," Ms. Spelling said.

"Thank you." Abby hung up. Had she done the right thing? She immediately punched the button for Jennifer's home phone.

"Good morning." Jennifer's voice was normal and comforting in her ear.

"Hi," Abby said. "What time are Mom and Dad getting there?"

"I'm not sure exactly. After noon. Why, what's up?"

"Nothing with Peter. It's Gary."

"Is he okay?"

"Yeah, but the school called. His teacher, actually. Ms. Spelling."

"Did she want to know why Gary's been out for two days?" Jennifer asked.

"Kind of. They're awarding prizes for a story contest Monday, and Gary's one of the winners. She said they especially hoped he'd be there."

"He should be up to it by then," Jennifer said.

"I hope so. He's got a lot of pain today, but I'm trying to keep ahead of it with the medicine. The assembly is at 2:15 that day. I'm going to try to get him there, unless—well, unless the very worst happens." She sniffed.

"I understand," Jennifer said, "but you've got to keep on hoping, Abby."

"Would you keep Andy that day?"

"Sure, but can't he go back to school Monday? If you don't want him to, I could keep track of Andy. In fact, I bet Mom and Dad would like to be there if they can stay that long."

"Wow, I didn't even think of that," Abby said.

"Dad may have to go back, but I'll ask Mom to stay if she wants to," Jennifer went on. "I can drive her home the next day."

"Let me call the school back and see if it's okay if extended family comes."

153

"Okay. Call me back. I was just going to turn on the vacuum, but I'll wait until I hear back from you."

Abby hung up and called the school. Yes, grandparents and aunts and other various relatives were welcome. And yes, Gary would receive a very special award, but the school would appreciate it if she kept that a surprise.

"Wow, that's great," Abby said. "We'll be there."

But when she'd replaced the receiver, she walked slowly to the living room door. Detective Trudeau sat in Peter's usual chair with earphones on, sipping coffee. He looked at her, smiled, and lowered the earphones so that they circled his neck.

"How's it going?"

"Okay," Abby said. What if they did get bad news on Peter, or no news at all? She walked up the stairs and looked into Gary's room. He was sitting up in bed, with his cast on top of the covers. Andy crouched on the rug, running some toy trucks back and forth. He looked up.

"Mommy, did Daddy fix my toy car?"

Abby's throat burned, and she pulled in a quick breath. "I don't think so. Not yet."

Andy went back to his play, but Gary met her gaze. His eyes held the sheen of tears.

"Are you going to feel like getting up later to go see Grandpa and Grammy?" she asked.

"I guess."

She turned away. Jennifer would be waiting for her call. Abby felt like she might dissolve into tears at any moment, and she hated that feeling, especially when the boys would see her weakness. She went down to the master bedroom and closed the door before calling her sister.

*****

Harvey's extension rang, and he picked up his desk phone, his eyes still on the monitor and the warrant application he'd filled out for Davey Talbot's house.

"Larson."

"This is Sergeant Yeaton. Two of my officers responded to a call at a gas station on Congress Street. The complaint involves a woman on your BOLO. Emma Skerritt."

That got his attention. "Have them hold her until we get there. What's the exact location?"

She gave it to him, and Harvey scribbled it in his notebook. "Thanks, Cheryl."

He rose, reaching for his jacket. "A couple of uniforms have got Emma Skerritt. Eddie, you're with me."

"Can I come, boss?" Tony asked.

"Not this time, but stand by in case I need you to do something else. And keep on with those connections."

Tony didn't try to hide his disappointment.

"We'll be here if you need anything," Jimmy said.

Harvey checked in on the 911 call while Eddie drove his truck toward the service station with his lights flashing and siren wailing. The station's manager had called in saying he'd foiled a kidnapping at the gas pumps outside. The woman was shaken but wanted to leave.

"We're lucky she stayed until the patrol car got there," Eddie said.

Harvey shook his head. "No luck at all. God's on our side, and we're going to break this thing."

They pulled in at the gas station, and Eddie parked in the empty spot in front of the air pump. Harvey scanned the license plates of the vehicles in the lot.

"That's Emma's car." Harvey nodded toward a Honda sitting in front of the entrance to the convenience store. He shoved the door open, and they went inside.

A harried-looking woman stood behind the checkout counter. Three customers waited in line. Harvey looked around and spotted two uniforms in a cluster of people near the refrigerator cases. Officer Bill Theriault looked his way and broke away from the others.

"Hey, Captain. Glad you're here. The woman wants to leave, but I told her she needed to speak to you first."

"Is she all right?"

"Yeah, apparently the suspect tried to snatch her and drag her into his car, but the manager saw it out the window and got out his shotgun. The woman was fighting the man, but he was about to shove her into his vehicle. The manager told him to leave her alone, and he jumped in his car and took off."

"Did he get a license plate?"

"The first three digits."

"Okay," Harvey said. "Let me talk to her, and Eddie will take the manager."

Eddie leaned in close. "How picky do you want me to be about the shotgun?"

"Not very. We owe this guy."

Eddie nodded and took the manager aside.

As Harvey approached the woman, he nodded to Officer Alicia Peterson and focused on the victim.

"Emma Skerritt?"

"Yes." She was small-boned, about five-four, maybe thirty years old, short brown hair, and she eyed him warily.

"I'm Captain Larson." He showed his badge. "Could you step outside with me, please? I'd like you to show me where you were when you were assaulted."

"I told the officers," Emma said. "Some man drove up while I was gassing up and grabbed me."

"Right. I'm sorry you had to go through that." Harvey guided her out of the store and stopped beside her car. "Which pump were you at?"

"That one." She pointed to the nearest gas pump. "I had pulled in facing the store."

"Did you know the man who grabbed you?"

"No. I'd never seen him before."

"Could you describe him for me?" Harvey asked.

"I told the other officers. He was pretty big. At least as tall as you, maybe taller. And heavier. White."

"How old?"

"I don't know. Maybe forty or so?"

156

"Okay." Harvey figured it was another one of Talbot's errand boys. "Our people are working on the partial plate number the store manager reported. Were you aware that we've been looking for you since last night?"

"Me?" she squeaked. "No."

"You and your boyfriend, Chad McCafferty."

She swallowed hard but said nothing.

"We need to know where he is, Emma."

"Is he in trouble? I figured something was up." She twisted the strap of her woven purse.

"What made you think that?" Harvey asked.

"He came home last night and told me we had to leave pronto. And he'd been away a lot the last couple of days, but he wouldn't tell me what he was up to."

"Where is he now?"

She let out a sob. "You won't hurt him, will you? He's really scared. I know he owes money, but I didn't think that was against the law."

"We're not talking about that," Harvey said. "This is something else."

"Are you sure? Because I thought the guy that attacked me was probably who he owes the money to."

"Well, that could be," Harvey said, "but I don't think that's the reason Chad insisted on leaving home yesterday. Now, when you left the house with him, you took your car. He left his car there. Where did you go?"

"We went to a friend of mine's house and slept there, but Chad said we couldn't stay there very long. I think those guys are looking for him."

"What guys?"

"I don't know. Loan sharks or something." Emma pulled in a shaky breath. "He told me to go gas up the car and we'd try to get out of the city." She squinted up at him, and Harvey waited. After a few seconds, she shrugged in defeat. "He said something about getting different license plates for my car."

"I see. Well, that is against the law, you know."

157

Tears escaped Emma's eyes, and she batted at her cheek with the back of her hand. "Please, he's going to think they got me."

"Who?" Harvey asked.

"That guy he owes money to. Talbot. Chad's scared of him."

"I thought you didn't know who he'd borrowed the money from."

"I didn't. I don't."

"Is there a chance Chad is working for this Talbot, rather than being in debt to him?"

"Working. . .? I don't know. But last night he said something about a job he was supposed to do, but he couldn't, and Talbot would be mad. That's all I know."

Harvey supposed both possibilities could be true. McCafferty could be working for Talbot to pay off a debt. "Okay, I'll ask you again. Where is Chad now?"

Emma's shoulders quaked.

"Listen to me, Emma." Harvey stooped and looked into her watery eyes. "I am the best chance Chad has of living through this day. Tell me right now where he is, and my men and I will go and get him."

"Are you going to arrest him?"

"We'll put him in custody, and he'll be safe from Talbot." Eddie came out of the store as Harvey spoke. "Trust me, Emma, this is the best thing you can do to help him. You can save his life right now. Give me the address."

*****

Tony stepped out into the police station's lobby and paused. Laney Cross was headed toward the stairway, and he couldn't keep a big grin from sprouting on his face.

"Hey, Laney."

She smiled back. "Hi, Tony."

He shot a glance at the wall clock. Way too early to ask her to lunch. Or was it? "Uh, will you be going out for lunch today?"

She hesitated. "Probably. That diner down the street is handy."

"Yeah, I'll probably be down there, too. Around noon, if I don't get called out before that."

She gave a little shrug, and her smile lingered. "Maybe I'll see you there."

"Yeah, maybe."

She took a step toward the door, and Tony made a split-second decision. "Hey, listen."

As he'd hoped, she turned back toward him, her delicate eyebrows arched expectantly.

"Uh, I know this is kind of off the wall, or off the cuff, or whatever." Confusion started to replace the anticipation in her eyes, and he rushed on, "My cousin's getting married in a couple of weeks, and I need a plus-one. I wondered if by any chance you'd be interested in going with me."

She hesitated, and his hopes plummeted.

"I know it's not much of a date."

"So, what day is it exactly?"

Her simple question bolstered his confidence. "Two weeks from Saturday. Oh, and it's in Augusta."

She blinked. "Augusta?"

"Yeah, an hour each way. If you don't want to—" His phone rang, and he pulled it out and glanced at it. "Oops. It's my boss. Sorry."

"No, that's okay. Can I think about it?"

"Sure."

"We can talk at lunch." She hurried into the stairwell, and Tony pushed the talk button.

"Yeah, Cap'n?"

"Eddie and I have a lead on McCafferty. Meet us at this address, and bring Jimmy."

"Copy." Tony signed off and hit speed dial for Jimmy Cook.

"Yeah?" Jimmy sounded a little groggy. Probably staring at reports had mesmerized him.

"Get downstairs, Jimbo. The boss wants us to meet him. We're bringing in McCafferty."

159

Eddie concentrated on his driving while Harvey called Nate with instructions on getting more warrant applications expedited. They'd left the patrolmen to take Emma to the station and have her held until they returned.

Eddie parked his truck a block below Emma's friend's house. She'd told them the woman who rented Unit A of the duplex had gone to work.

"Think McCafferty's in there?" Eddie asked as they waited for backup.

"I don't know. He may be off looking to pinch a license plate to put on Emma's car." Harvey checked the side-view mirror. "There's Jimmy's truck."

Eddie was glad they hadn't come in Tony's red Mustang. It drew too much attention. Jimmy's silver Ford pickup was almost fifteen years old and looked it. Nobody would pay any attention to it in this neighborhood.

When Tony and Jimmy joined them on the sidewalk, Harvey pointed out the house. "It's the one with green shutters, Unit A on this side. You two take the back."

Two minutes later, Harvey hammered on the door while Eddie stood to one side. "Police. Open up."

No one answered. Harvey huffed out an exasperated breath and grabbed the doorknob. To Eddie's surprise, the door swung open. Most people didn't leave their front doors unlocked in the city. He held up a hand to Harvey and stepped forward, leading with his pistol.

Eddie checked the kitchen and stepped toward the living room while Harvey turned to check a bathroom off the kitchen and open the back door for Jimmy and Tony.

Eddie saw a dark, wet patch on the tan living room rug. Definitely blood. The landlord wouldn't like having to replace the carpeting.

"In here, Harvey." When Harvey came in, Eddie went to check the two bedrooms. Messy, but vacant, and no blood that he could see.

160

Tony was coming out of the hall bath. "Clear."

When Eddie walked back into the living room, Harvey was bending over the stain.

"All clear, unless there's a cellar," Eddie told him.

"There is," Jimmy said, coming from the kitchen. "The door's locked on this side, but we checked it. Nobody down there."

Harvey frowned. "This is fresh, and it's a lot of blood."

"What do you think happened?" Jimmy asked.

"I'm not sure."

"Was somebody besides us after McCafferty?" Tony asked.

"Maybe there were three kidnappers," Eddie suggested.

Harvey shook his head. "More likely Talbot knew he and Holden botched up Ulrich's execution. He probably sent out some runners to shut Mack up before we could get to him. Call for some crime scene techs, Jim. I want to know if this is Mack's blood."

While Jimmy made the call, Eddie joined Tony in a more thorough search of the kitchen and the bedrooms. Their diligence was rewarded when they found some plastic bags of drugs behind a row of canned goods and a wad of cash in a trinket box. Eddie took the items and met Harvey in the living room.

"Got some swag, Harv." He held up the two bags of powder and one of pills. "Looks like heroin and a bunch of assorted prescription pills."

Harvey looked around at the three detectives. "All right, when the techs get here, make sure they know the drugs could belong to whoever's name is on the lease for this place. I doubt Chad and Emma brought it with them, and if they had that bankroll, they wouldn't be so desperate."

"I found it in the renter's bedroom," Eddie said.

Tony raised his eyebrows. "We'd better look up the friend who lives here."

Harvey nodded. "Emma gave us her name and said she went to work this morning."

"I got it." Eddie took out his notebook and flipped through to the information he'd written down before Harvey handed Emma Skerritt over to the patrol officers. "Her name is Stiles. Rose Stiles."

"Tony, you and Jimmy sit down and count that money together right now."

Eddie was glad Harvey had given the order. It would protect them all from another who-shorted-the-cash scandal, like the one they'd had last fall. Through the window, he caught sight of a black-and-white pulling into the driveway. "Back-up's here."

"Okay," Harvey said. "I'll brief them, and then we've got places to go. You call Nate about the renter."

Harvey went outside, and Eddie relayed to Nate the information they wanted about the woman who rented this half of the duplex. When he wrapped up his conversation with Nate, he told Jimmy and Tony where to find the woman. They went out to where Harvey stood near his vehicle, talking on the phone. By the time he was done, Tony came to the truck to hand Harvey the bag of money.

"Three thousand, seven hundred, on the nose. Jimbo's talking to the neighbor in the other apartment. She says she was home all morning but didn't hear anything until we got here."

"How could she not hear anything?" Eddie asked.

Tony raised his shoulders. "I have my doubts. But, anyway, we found out where the renter on our side works."

"You and Jimmy go find her. Tell her what happened and what to expect when she comes home."

"You want us to bring her in?" Tony asked.

Harvey gritted his teeth. "I'd have said no if she was just doing her friend a favor by letting the two of them spend the night, but those drugs. . ."

"We'll bring her in," Tony said.

"Yeah. Probably better. And let Nate know where you're going. I'll see you at the station." Harvey climbed wearily into the passenger seat.

Eddie went around and got in behind the wheel. "Think we'll find Chad?"

"I hope so," Harvey said. "We'll have to start calling around to hospitals and clinics. Whoever bled all over that apartment needs medical attention."

"If he's not dead."

While Eddie maneuvered his way back to the police station, Harvey called Jennifer. "I doubt I'll get home before suppertime, gorgeous," he said. "Maybe not then. Looks like Eddie and I will be going out of town this afternoon. . . . Oh, just following up on a lead. And then I've got to talk to the press."

When they got to the station, Harvey went to the top floor to give the chief a quick update. Eddie had Nate send him some documents and printed out copies of the warrants that had been approved.

Harvey came back looking alert and ready to move. "Warrants?" he asked.

"Yeah," Eddie said. "We're all set to go to Davey Talbot's place in Cape Elizabeth. They'll have several officers meet us there. And Cheryl sent an officer to the duplex owner with a hard copy of the warrant for that place, in case he wants to know what we're up to."

Harvey's face wrinkled. "Like he could keep us out with criminals hiding out in one of his apartments. I hope he doesn't think we left the blood there." He picked up his flak vest. "Let's go."

Tony came in from the stairs.

"Where's the renter?" Harvey asked.

"Jim's got her down in booking," Tony said. "She cops to the drugs."

"Okay. Work through it and get her out of here as soon as you can. We're heading for Talbot's place."

"Oh, Captain, I've got a ton of messages for you." Paula hurried toward him with a handful of note slips.

"Great." Harvey took them with a scowl. "Look, if I want to get to Cape Elizabeth and back before the press conference,

163

we've got to leave now." He shuffled quickly through them. "Nate!"

"Yeah?" Nate called from his desk.

Harvey peeled off two of the messages. "You can handle these calls for me. Tony, run upstairs and give the chief an update."

"Yes, sir." Tony looked inordinately happy with his assignment, and Harvey remembered the redhead.

"Be quick about it. And as soon as you're done, you two get Emma Skerritt up here and get a written statement from her. She says she doesn't know anything about the kidnapping, but she may not realize what she knows."

"Okay," Tony said. He was out the door before Harvey could put the rest of the messages back in Paula's hand. "These will have to wait. If you need me urgently, call my cell."

"Will do," Paula said cheerfully, and Eddie strode to the stairway door. If he was lucky, he could persuade Harvey to eat a burger on the fly.

Chapter 13

Peter sagged against the stained white sink in the bathroom. He'd managed to bump the nearest faucet with his head until it moved enough to deliver a trickle of water. Now he had a blinding headache from hitting it so many times, and he was sure he had deep contusions on his forehead.

He was tempted to sink to the linoleum and lie there until he regained some strength, but if he did that, he might never get up. He stretched upward, pulling against the chain on his ankle. He still couldn't quite reach the framed mirror.

At least it wasn't a solid medicine cabinet. It was just a flat mirror in a white nine-by-thirteen frame. If he only had one more inch of tether, he was sure he could knock the frame off its support, but with his most vigorous attempts he'd only brushed the nearest corner.

He lifted his head and squinted in the darkness. Only a little light found its way in from the outer room's small window, and he could barely make out his outline. Probably best that he couldn't see himself clearly. He certainly wouldn't want Abigail to see him in this state.

At once he knew that wasn't true. He would give anything to see her—or any other person—at that moment.

Peter coiled his muscles and drove his head toward the mirror. It lifted and teetered. He prayed that it would not fall to the floor on the far side of the sink, where he couldn't reach it. He drew back. It swayed a little on whatever device it hung from, but it didn't leave the wall.

One more time. He would soon be exhausted. This effort had to count. Peter stood on his right foot and stretched his chained left leg as far as he could. He bent his knees and launched himself again, slamming his forehead into the wall at the bottom of the wooden frame as the chain tore into his battered ankle, halting his momentum. The mirror tipped and fell on his head, then skittered down his shoulders and back. On the floor behind him, it shattered.

Thank you, God!

Sweat or blood trickled down into his left eye, and he blinked rapidly. Now he only had to find a suitable shard that he could pick up with his hands bound behind him, hold it in a position so it contacted the tape, and work it back and forth enough to cut through the filaments without slicing his wrists wide open.

He sank to the floor and slumped against the wall, breathing deeply and thinking out how to do it.

*****

Tony tried to hurry Jimmy down the sidewalk. They'd booked Emma Skerritt's friend, Rose Stiles, for drug possession, and talked Emma through her statement. He hadn't gotten a chance to talk to Laney on his trip up to Chief Browning's office, and now it was quarter to one. He was in a hurry to get to the diner.

"That Rose didn't even try to blame it on McCafferty and Emma," Jimmy noted.

"No, she missed a good chance there." Tony looked ahead and spotted Laney seated at a table with one of lab techs. By the time he and Jimmy got there, she had risen and was gathering up her trash.

"Hey, Laney," Tony said. "We got hung up."

"Oh, there you are." She smiled uncertainly at him and Jimmy. "I figured you weren't going to make it."

"Almost missed you," Tony said. "This is Jimmy Cook. We work together."

"Hi," Jimmy said, eyeing her with open speculation.

"Well, listen, I've got to get back to the office," Laney said.

Tony tried not to let his disappointment show. "Okay. Did you think about it?"

"Yeah. I guess it will be all right. We can talk again sometime about the details."

"Sure."

"Okay, then. 'Bye." She included Jimmy in her parting smile. Tony exhaled.

"So, you got a date with her, or what?" Jimmy asked.

"Yeah."

"The chief's new secretary."

"Yeah." Tony scowled at him. "What's wrong with that?"

Jimmy held up both hands. "Nothing."

They found a table and put in their orders. After the waitress brought their sodas, Jimmy ripped the end off his straw's paper covering and blew the wrapper at Tony. It hit him between the eyes and bounced off onto the table.

"Watch it," Tony snarled.

Jimmy laughed. "So, where are you taking her?"

"My cousin's wedding."

"A safe first date, or what?"

Tony shrugged. "I have to go, and I figured I had a better chance inviting her to that than for a drink or something."

"Really? And would this cousin happen to be on Uncle Bill's side of the family?"

"Yeah. His daughter, Amy."

Jimmy nodded sagely.

"What?" Tony asked.

"Where's the wedding?"

"At the Blaine House."

"And of course, Laney knows this."

"Well, I . . ." Tony lifted his paper cup and took a swig of Moxie.

Jimmy's jaw dropped. "Does she even know about the family connection?"

"We didn't get around to it yet."

"Oh, I see." Jimmy picked up the straw wrapper and crumpled it. "So, when were you planning to tell her that this wedding will take place inside the governor's mansion?"

Tony cleared his throat. "We were supposed to talk about it at lunch, but you saw. We were late, and she had to get back to the office."

"Right."

"Maybe someone told her," Tony protested. "You know the office gossip."

"Yeah."

Mercifully, the waitress arrived with their lunch plates.

"I will tell her," Tony said when she'd left them.

"You'd better." Jimmy picked up his burger and took a big chomp. After he'd chewed and swallowed, he looked over at Tony. "And why did you think this would be a good first date?"

"Oh, come on." Tony wasn't hungry anymore. "I needed a plus-one, okay?"

"Yes, and you've been salivating over that girl all week. I can just see the two of you alone in that Mustang for an hour, tooling up the interstate, and you let drop that the father of the bride is Governor Johnson."

"I'll tell her before that."

"Make it soon," Jimmy said darkly. "Women need time to prepare for stuff like that."

"Yeah, point taken."

Jimmy nodded and poised for another bite of his burger. "Oh, and don't be surprised if she changes her mind about going."

"She wouldn't."

"I would if a girl did that to me."

Tony felt like flinging his fries at him. Jimmy was a married old fuddy-duddy past thirty, that was all. It must have been at least ten years since he'd had his last date.

*****

Eddie was a little nervous as he and Harvey were ushered into Davey Talbot's house. The man who showed them in didn't exactly look like a butler. More like a bouncer from a bar down on the waterfront. But Harvey didn't hesitate to follow him into the big stone mansion, so Eddie tagged along. The back of his neck prickled, and he turned around to look. Nobody was behind him, but he did spot a camera above the decorative transom window over the door frame.

Talbot was seated in a lavishly furnished living room on a fancy, old-fashioned wing chair. He looked about sixty, with brown hair going silver and baggy brown eyes. Nice suit, though. In one hand he held a rocks glass half full of amber liquid, and in the other he held the business card Harvey had sent in ahead of them.

"Come in, gentlemen." He didn't get up, but waved toward the sofa opposite him. Antique, Eddie thought. Harvey could probably name the style and maker. The painting over the fireplace would probably impress people who liked that sort of thing. It reminded Eddie of a landscape they'd recovered in an art theft case, except this one looked kind of blurry. His homework for that case surfaced, and his brain popped out "Impressionism." That was the style.

"May I offer you a drink?" Talbot raised his glass slightly. If he started drinking hard liquor this early in the day, how did he keep his head clear enough to run the Falcon's empire?

"No, thanks," Harvey said easily. "We're here on business."

"Of course." Talbot took a sip and set the glass on the end table. "How may I help you, Captain. . ." He flicked a glance at the card. "Larson."

Instead of sitting down, Harvey took a couple of photos from his pocket and walked over to him.

"I wondered if you know this man."

Talbot made a show of focusing for a moment on the picture Harvey had gotten from the DMV.

"Hmm."

"Maybe you'd recognize him in this one." Harvey held out a picture of Holden taken by a crime scene investigator right before they moved Holden's body off the street.

"I say."

"Yes, it's a bit graphic," Harvey said. "Did you know him?"

169

"Holden."

"That's right. Was he working for you?"

Talbot drew in a deep breath and exhaled with a weary air. "I think he may have run a few errands for me from time to time."

"Huh." Harvey took the pictures back. "What errand was he running on Wednesday?"

"Wednesday, Wednesday." Talbot picked up his glass, as if another sip would help his memory. He sipped his drink and shook his head.

Harvey held out another picture. "How about this man?"

Talbot frowned. "He looks somewhat familiar. Can't place him, though."

"And this one?" The last picture was of Carter Ulrich. They'd gotten it from his apartment.

Talbot's eyes narrowed. He rubbed his chin.

"Was he Holden's errand on Wednesday?" Harvey asked.

"I believe I saw that man's picture in the *Press Herald*."

"Yeah," Harvey said. "In the obits. But unlike your errand boy, he wasn't hit by a truck. He was shot in the showroom at Hobart Chevrolet on Wednesday evening."

"Shot? By whom?"

"I'm asking the questions," Harvey said. "Did you know him?"

"I was aware of him, yes. His name's Ulrich."

"That's right," Harvey said. "Bonus question: *How* did you know him?"

"Please, Captain, it would be much more congenial if you sat down."

"Funny, I was thinking it would be much more efficient if you came to the station with us."

Talbot arched his eyebrows. "But your precinct is in Portland, is it not?"

"I'm sure they'd loan us an interview room here in Cape Elizabeth. We're here under their auspices. I've got warrants for your arrest and a search of this place. Captain Hillman and his men are on the way to assist us."

170

Talbot sat still for a moment then drained his glass and set it aside. "All right, stand up if you want. Ulrich did some business with us."

"Us?" Harvey asked.

"Please. I have a rather large array of business dealings."

"You and Falcon Prewitt."

"I couldn't speak for him."

"I'm sure you do, and often. He owns this house."

Talbot waved a dismissive hand. "Ulrich was a gambler. He came to one of my employees for money. Several times."

"I see," Harvey said. "How much did he owe you as of Wednesday?"

"I'd have to check my records, but I'm thinking somewhere in the neighborhood of three hundred thousand."

"Interesting."

"Is it?" Talbot asked, taking a phone from his pocket.

"Excuse me, but I'll have to take that. It's included in our warrant." Harvey reached for the phone, and Talbot's eyes flickered, but he didn't resist. Eddie knew the warrant included specific authorization to seize Talbot's computers, phones, and any records they could find on paper. No doubt Harvey anticipated their suspect using his cell to instruct his flunkies to get rid of any evidence on the premises.

"Thanks." Harvey tucked the phone in his jacket pocket. "So, you sent Holden and his pal to collect from Ulrich."

"What? No. Why would you say that? I haven't heard a word from Holden since well before Wednesday. That was the day you mentioned, wasn't it?"

"It was. So, why did you think you hadn't heard from him?"

"I didn't have any errands for him," Talbot said.

"Right. And you expect me to believe you just let it ride for two days, when he didn't bring you the money?"

"I told you, I didn't sic him on Ulrich."

Harvey paced to a large window and looked outside. He swung around and met Talbot's gaze. "When a man owes you that big a debt and he can't pay, what happens next?"

"We would make other arrangements."

"What, you set up a payment plan for him?"

"That would be one option."

"How many times does the guy have to skip a payment before your goons kill him?"

Talbot's face hardened. "I assure you, whoever shot that man did not do it on my orders."

"Hmm." Harvey frowned and paced a little. "Why do you suppose Holden didn't report in to you after he failed to collect from Ulrich?"

"Why should he, when I didn't send him there? I didn't expect him to contact me."

"I think you did send him there. And now he's dead."

Talbot held up both hands. "I didn't kill Holden."

"No." Harvey frowned. Eddie recognized his frustration. Holden's death was accidental.

Eddie's phone whirred softly and vibrated in his pocket. He turned away, took it out, and looked at the screen. Nate was texting him. He opened the message.

"Tell Cap CU called DT's # Tue."

Eddie puzzled that out and texted back, "U got the ID?"

A few seconds later another text came in with "SP cooperated" and a seven-digit number. The area code would be 207, Maine's one and only.

Eddie considered interrupting the conversation, but Talbot had suggested that Ulrich's debt was due to his love of the racetrack, and Harvey was trying to extract some information on Talbot's connection to the betting world.

Eddie hesitated and decided it was worth a risk. He punched in the 207 and then the number Nate had sent him. A couple of seconds later, a jazz tune began playing in Talbot's vicinity. He frowned, stood up, and pulled a second phone from his other pocket. He scowled at it for a moment.

"It's okay," Eddie said from across the room. "It's just me calling you."

172

Talbot pushed a button. The music stopped, leaving a tense silence.

"What's up, Eddie?" Harvey asked softly, taking the phone from Talbot's limp hand.

"Carter Ulrich called an unlisted number on Tuesday. The lab report is finally in on his phone. Nate couldn't get a name, but the State Police apparently had it on record from another case, and they cooperated. It was Mr. Talbot's phone. That one."

Harvey's chin rose a centimeter, his blue eyes icy. "Why did Carter Ulrich call you?"

"I didn't know he did," Talbot said.

Eddie quickly texted Nate, "How long did CU call to DT last?"

"Yes, you did know," Harvey said, "and we'll prove it, because we've got Ulrich's phone, and yours. Did he call to tell you he needed more time to pay up?"

Talbot eyed him keenly for a few seconds. "You know what? I think it's time to call my attorney."

"Then it's time to take you into custody." Harvey turned to Eddie. "Go find the fellow who let us in. Make sure he's not destroying any evidence."

"Sure," Eddie said, walking toward the door. "Nate says Ulrich's call here lasted thirty-five seconds."

"Long enough to state his business," Harvey said as Eddie left the room.

Two Cape Elizabeth cops waited in the entrance hall.

"Where's Jeeves?" Eddie asked.

"Who?" one of the officers asked.

"The guy who tends the door."

"He went that way." The officer pointed across the room toward an archway.

"One of you come with me," Eddie said. He and a patrolman whose nametag read "Runyan" strode through the spacious rooms, looking for Talbot's man. They found him in a comfortably furnished office with another man, cleaning out an armoire. The smaller man was packing weapons into a large

173

duffel bag, and the butler-type was in the act of guiding some papers into a shredder.

"Hold it," Eddie said, drawing his gun. "Hands up and take a step backward, both of you."

Jeeves shoved the papers into the slot on the shredder. Eddie swore and stepped forward to turn it off before the documents were more than a third through the teeth. He held his pistol on the bulky man, who stood with his hands high and his jaw set.

"We've got a warrant," Eddie said. "Hands behind your back." While he handcuffed the man, he looked over at Runyan. "Soon's I secure these two, call your captain. We need more men. And when they get here, check out back." He nodded toward a door that led outside. "They're packing up an arsenal here, and who knows what else they've got in a vehicle outside already. Make sure nobody leaves the property."

Runyan handed him his own handcuffs, which Eddie used on the second of Talbot's men. By the time he'd finished and recited the Miranda, the patrolman had made his call.

"We've got people on the gate, so nobody leaves here," Runyan said, "and six more officers to help out with the search. Captain Hillman is just arriving."

"Great," Eddie said. "Keep these two handy until we're ready to transport them, but don't let them get in the way."

*****

Jennifer threw the door to her house wide. Her parents and her youngest brother, Randy, stood in the breezeway.

"Hey! Come on in."

Her mother had Connor out of her arms before even saying hello.

"Oh, you're such a precious little fellow!"

"Hey, pumpkin," Jennifer's father said, giving her a quick hug. "Anything new on Peter?"

"Not yet." Jennifer held out her arms to Randy. "Are you set to move down here next week? Because Harvey's got work lined up for you."

"Terrific." Randy returned her hug and stood back. "I've got finals next week, but my last day of school is Thursday."

"Take a day or two to unwind and pack," Jennifer said.

"I thought I'd probably move down on Saturday, if the job was a sure thing."

"It is. Your room is ready whenever you are. You'll sleep in there tonight."

Her father and Randy went out to get their luggage, while her mom carried Connor to the sunroom and sat down on the wicker settee.

"Can we see Abby?" Marilyn asked. "I feel so bad for her."

Jennifer nodded. "She's going to bring the boys over soon, if there's no word on Peter. If there is, then we'll go over and pick up Gary and Andy." Abby had changed her mind several times on the arrangements, but apparently Harvey had persuaded her to get out of the house, and Jennifer was glad. She hadn't told her folks yet about Gary's adventure the night before, and she realized she'd better clue them in before the Hobarts arrived.

"Uh, did anyone mention to you about Gary's arm?"

"His arm? No." Her mother's attention jerked away from Connor and settled on Jennifer.

"He broke it last night."

"What happened?"

Jennifer swallowed hard. "Uh, bike accident. When Dad comes back in, I'll tell you all about it."

A knock at the patio door drew her attention. Beth stood outside, smiling brightly and holding six-month-old Anna.

Jennifer walked over and opened the door for her. "Hi! Come on in."

Her parents and Randy greeted Beth, and Jennifer's mother passed Connor off to George and took Anna in her arms.

"Is Jeff off tonight?" Randy asked.

175

"He doesn't get off until late, but he'll be home tomorrow, so you can spend some time with him then." Beth pulled a rocking chair over next to her mother-in-law and settled into it.

"Jennifer was just saying that Gary broke his arm," Marilyn said.

"What?" Jennifer's father, George, scowled. "When did this happen?"

"Last night." Jennifer launched into the tale and concluded with, "So he's going to be okay, but he's still very upset about his dad. They've got to find Peter soon."

"Those poor little boys," Beth said.

"Should we not mention Peter when they get here?" Randy asked.

"Well, they know about it. Abby gave Gary more details last night, so he wouldn't be thinking wild thoughts about it, although what can get wilder than a kidnapping like this, I don't know." Jennifer shook her head. "She hasn't told them about the salesman who was shot at Peter's showroom, though, so please don't mention that."

Randy nodded soberly.

"Terrible thing," George said. He looked down at Connor, who was plundering his pockets. "I guess this guy's too little to understand any of it."

"True, but he knows his daddy hasn't been home much for the last three days." Jennifer tried to smile, but it was hard.

"How's Leeanne doing?" Marilyn asked.

"Okay. Eddie's been mostly absentee, too. I'd hoped they'd get here for lunch today, but Harvey called me around noon and said they had to go out of town for a while. I had to trust Eddie to get some lunch into him. Now I'm hoping for supper together. Leeanne promised to come over at five, whether the guys are coming home or not."

"Good," her mom said. "Well, we'll help with the food and babies."

"Would you like to sleep over at our house, Marilyn?" Beth asked.

176

Jennifer's mom shook her head. "If Jeffrey's changing shifts tonight, he'll want to sleep late in the morning. We'll be fine here."

Her husband set Connor down carefully. "I'll take the bags upstairs."

"You and Mom are in the guest room," Jennifer said, following him and Randy into the living room. "I put out clean towels for everybody in the bathroom up there."

Beth watched the two little ones while Jennifer helped her mother unpack a cooler of food and a pie carrier. A few minutes later, Randy wandered into the kitchen.

"Is it okay if I play a computer game?"

"Sure," Jennifer said. "Did you bring something with you?"

"No."

"Okay, but don't use my computer. I was right in the middle of some new software I'm working on for John Macomber. I think you can use Harvey's desktop, though." She set down the apple pie she was holding and hurried into the study. She sat down at Harvey's desk and clicked a few keys. "Yeah, looks okay to access the games."

Harvey almost never played video games, but he had a nice selection for Jennifer's younger brothers and Abby's boys. She stood, and Randy slid into the rolling chair.

"What's this?"

"What?" Jennifer asked.

Randy frowned, pointing at a slip of memo paper. "Who's Leah Viniard and Tara Ervin? I know who Harvey is, but not Dr. Joseph Menard."

Jennifer's heart lurched. Harvey must have done some online searching when he came home late last night.

"He, uh, was probably looking up some stuff." She hesitated. Should she tell him those were the names on a birth certificate?

"Sorry," Randy said. "I didn't mean to snoop."

"It's not your fault he left it there. It's just..." She glanced toward the doorway that opened on the entry next to the kitchen, where Beth and her mother were chattering away. "It's kind of

177

sensitive. Would you mind not bringing this up with Mom and Dad?"

"Sure. I wasn't trying to pry into his business."

"I know. And it's not police business." She sighed. "Can you handle something a bit mind-blowing?"

"I don't know. Can I? Maybe you shouldn't tell me."

"Yeah. Okay, I'll leave that up to Harvey." She opened a desk drawer and dropped the paper inside. "Thanks for your discretion, Randy."

"No probs."

Chapter 14

Harvey consulted his phone and leaned sideways so he could look into the entry. "I'm going to go talk to Captain Hillman. The Cape Elizabeth Police will have to complete the search."

Talbot held his gaze. "I don't get the personal touch?"

"Oh, yeah. You're coming with us." Harvey smiled. "But don't worry. They've got half a dozen officers to handle things here."

Talbot huffed his disdain. "I'm surprised they have that many men in uniform."

Harvey shrugged. Cape Elizabeth's police department would be stretching its resources thin to accommodate his request, it was true. That was probably one reason the Falcon—and now Talbot—had chosen to locate here. That and the unbeatable views of the ocean.

At that moment, Captain Hillman and two patrol officers entered the room.

"Thanks for coming, John." Harvey shook hands with the captain.

"No sweat," Hillman replied. They'd met several times before, and Harvey had confidence in his professional skills.

"Keep an eye on Mr. Talbot," Harvey said to the patrolmen. He stepped into the entry to tell the captain exactly what he wanted to accomplish.

"I've got a press conference scheduled for two o'clock at our station, so my detective and I will have to leave here soon."

"Sure. Go ahead, and we'll get the job done. I'll deliver any evidence recovered personally."

"Thanks." Harvey detailed exactly what he was looking for. "Of course, if you find anything else of interest, that's covered, too. This guy is known to run financial and protection rackets, and his boss who's now in the slammer was also into drugs, so. . .Whatever looks good."

John nodded. "Yeah, I'm familiar with Mr. Prewitt, and I got the warrants that your office forwarded to me. Nice work, Harvey. We've been trying to get something solid on this guy for months."

"Let's make it stick." Harvey strode back into the parlor. "Let's go, Talbot."

"What, you're really taking me in?"

"Yeah, let's go."

Talbot spread his hands. "Look, I'll tell you what you want to know. Those guys have worked for me some, but I would never tell them to kill anyone."

"What guys are we talking about, specifically?" Harvey asked.

"Webster Holden and Mack McCafferty."

Harvey's brain ratcheted a notch. "That would be Chad McCafferty?"

"I suppose so. I know him as Mack."

"All right, so where is he now?"

"I have no idea. I expected to hear from him or Holden Wednesday night, but they never checked in."

Harvey inhaled carefully. It wasn't quite a confession, but it was one step away. And if Talbot had underlings out hunting down McCafferty, he wasn't letting on. "They should have checked in after their visit to Ulrich at Hobart Chevrolet, you mean."

"I didn't say that."

Harvey let it pass. "We know what happened to Holden yesterday. You didn't hear from either him or McCafferty since five o'clock Wednesday? Think carefully, now."

Talbot shook his head. "I made a few calls myself, trying to locate 'em. Then I heard about Holden on the news last night. Got himself run over."

"And you said a few minutes ago that you'd heard Ulrich was dead."

180

"Yeah."

"So you weren't expecting him to pay off his account."

"I'm not saying anything about delinquent accounts without my lawyer."

"Okay, but answer me this." Harvey stared into Talbot's eyes. "Did you ever have your employees abduct anyone in an effort to settle a delinquent account?"

"What?" Talbot's eyebrows shot up. "What are we talking about? Someone snatch a kid or something? I didn't know Ulrich had any kids."

"And you'd have known if he did."

"Of course. I make it a point to know who I'm doing business with."

Harvey paused, staring out the window toward the rocky shore a hundred yards away.

"So, you think my guys kidnapped someone?" Talbot asked.

"Right now, I think Holden and McCafferty may have seen a crime of opportunity."

"Those bums. They thought they could squeeze Ulrich and cut me out?"

Harvey turned toward him but said nothing.

Talbot rolled his eyes ceilingward. "Let me call my attorney."

"Sure. But I'm taking you to Portland with me. You can call from the station."

"What? No. I'm cooperating."

"We still need you in Portland." Harvey took out his handcuffs. "You got any weapons on you?"

"No. I'm not that sort."

"Of course not."

Eddie entered the room with Captain Hillman.

"We've got two laptops, a desktop, half a dozen flash drives, and four cell phones," Eddie said. "That's not counting about thirty handguns we'll have to check to see if they've been reported stolen. And the big guy, Cartwell, he did some shredding. He may have wiped some stuff off the computers, too, before I got to him."

Harvey blamed himself for not keeping an officer with that man from the minute they arrived.

"We may be here a while," John Hillman added. "It's a big house, and Mr. Talbot likes electronics."

"We'll take what you've got so far with us to Portland," Harvey said. "If we find evidence of crimes committed in Cape, we'll loop you in right away."

"Okay," John said. "Want us to keep the guns? My boys can run them."

"Sure. Let us know if it's too much, or if any connect with past crimes. No sign of Hobart?"

"My men did a quick search and didn't find anything, but we'll check everything more thoroughly."

"Okay." Harvey clicked the handcuffs around Talbot's wrists. "Search him, Eddie. You may find another gadget or two."

*****

Peter gritted his teeth and tried to adjust the shard of glass he held behind him. He'd sat down on the sleeping bag to ensure he didn't drop his new tool while standing and destroy it. His fingers where slippery with blood, and he had trouble telling where the best edge was. Was it possible he could bleed to death through his fingers before he ever got the tape off? Abigail would be so distressed.

He paused to rest and tried to picture his hands behind him. The piece of glass was about three inches long, the biggest one he could reach after breaking the mirror. It felt about half an inch or so across at the widest part, and it tapered to a lethal point. With sharp edges on every plane, it endangered him no matter how he held it.

God, you've got to help me. If I don't get this soon, I'm done.

Cautiously, he adjusted his grip on the glass. It seemed to be contacting the tape; he felt some resistance, but no sharp pricks. It was so easy to slice himself before he realized it, and his reactions seemed to be getting slower.

182

"Today, Lord," he said aloud. He held his breath and worked the shard back and forth.

Something gave. He was so shocked, he dropped the glass. "No!"

He sat still for a moment, breathing deeply. Then he started patting the thick fabric beneath him. Where was it?

Another filament in the tape parted, loosening the bond. Peter sat still. Was it really weakening? He struggled to his knees and lifted his bound hands as high as he could behind him—a matter of inches. He thrust downward, forcing his wrists apart as he did.

He tumbled forward and landed on his face, knees still on the sleeping bag. Pain radiated from his nose, almost blocking out the realization that his hands had come apart. He lay for half a minute with his face on the rough concrete, just breathing, trying to quiet his gasps.

With excruciating slowness, he brought his arms forward. Blood covered his hands, wrists, and lower shirtsleeves. He put his hands on the floor to push himself up, but the fingers of his left hand hurt so badly that he used his elbow instead. Finally he was sitting up, staring down at his bleeding hands.

Stop the bleeding first, he told himself. Pressure. With what? There was only the sleeping bag, and he pressed all his fingertips against the outside of it. His blood soaked into the green cloth, and pain nauseated him. Were there bits of glass in his fingers? In this dim light, he wouldn't be able to see them. He sagged forward and clenched his teeth. He had to stop the bleeding.

*****

Tony glanced around the office. Nate had gone to the locker room, and Jimmy had gone down to the lab. Paula had also left on a break. He wouldn't have a better chance to talk to Laney. He didn't have her cell number, so he picked up his desk phone's receiver and punched in the number for the chief's office.

"Chief Browning."

Startled, Tony nearly dropped the phone. "Oh, uh, Chief. Hey. This is Winfield. I, uh, didn't expect it to go through to you direct."

"Oh, Judith took Laney down to the records room to introduce her to the staff down there. What's up, Winfield?"

"Uh, well, I, uh ... wasn't sure if you'd heard from the captain that they're bringing Talbot up here."

"Yes, Captain Larson called me a few minutes ago."

"Great," Tony said. "Just wanted to make sure you were in the loop, sir."

"Thank you."

The chief hung up on him, and Tony stared at the phone for a second then replaced the receiver. He took a deep, slow breath in an unsuccessful effort to calm his raging pulse.

He could run downstairs and wait outside the records room for Laney to come out, but she would have Judith with her. And waiting in the stairwell wouldn't work. Since she was with the older woman, Laney would use the elevator.

Nate came out of the break room. "So, do you think the Captain will make it back in time for the press briefing?"

Tony eyed the clock. "Have you ever known him to be late?"

*****

Harvey had a headache by the time they got back to the police station. Talbot had complained all the way there. If only he'd been allowed a backup team from Portland to transport him.

He hated press conferences to begin with, and he hated headaches. Taken together, they made him irritable, which was not good if your words might be splashed all over tonight's local newscasts.

They were a mile from the station when his phone rang. He looked at it and grimaced.

"Yeah, Mike?"

"You're cutting it close on the press conference, Harv. The lobby's full of reporters."

"I know, and I'm sorry. What have I got, ten minutes?"

184

"Yeah. I hope you know what you're going to say."

"Pretty much. Can you have Cheryl send a couple of officers to meet us in the garage to escort Talbot? Eddie will supervise the booking."

"You're booking me?" Talbot howled from the back seat.

Eddie swore in French, and Harvey shot him a disapproving glare. "We're almost there, Chief. I'll go right to the lobby."

He hung up and swiveled to scowl at Talbot. "Put a sock in it, would you?"

"No! I want my lawyer as soon as we get there."

Harvey rubbed the bridge of his nose. It was impossible to focus on what he would say to the press. Eddie parked in the garage and got Talbot out. Harvey paused only long enough to speed-dial Abby.

"Hey, I'm about to do a press conference. Anything you want to say?"

"Just bring Peter back alive."

"Yeah. That's what we all want. I'll appeal to public. We're releasing Peter's picture, Abs. You might not want the boys to see the six o'clock news."

"Can I offer a reward?" she asked.

"Of course you can."

"I'd give the ransom money—"

"Whoa! Abby, remember, that's not your money."

"Of course, you're right. How about ten thousand? I could take that from our savings. What do you think?"

"Sure."

Cheryl Yeaton, the day sergeant, looked up as Harvey entered the hallway door from the parking garage. She spoke to one of the journalists and turned toward the lectern, which a patrolwoman was setting up for Harvey. He was glad to see Nate Miller in the front row with a laptop set up on a rolling stand, which meant he was ready to show Harvey's visuals on the blank wall behind him. Harvey went over to speak to him for a moment then approached the lectern.

"You all set?" Cheryl asked.

185

He nodded. He was confident things were well organized on this end, if not in his mind. "One new wrinkle. Mrs. Hobart wants to offer a reward. Can you set up a hotline and get the phone number to Miller, so he can project it on the wall? And we'll need two or three people to field calls."

"Right away?"

"If you can manage."

Cheryl pulled a sour face. "Of course I can manage the impossible." She walked straight to the front of the audience. "Thank you all for coming. Captain Larson is in the building."

A low murmur of laughter swept the gathering of about twenty reporters and videographers. Harvey thought he detected a note of relief. He smiled and stepped up to the lectern.

"Am I late?"

"You're right on time," Cheryl assured him. She leaned in and whispered, "But I was getting a little worried."

"I'm sure you could have handled things, Sergeant Yeaton," Harvey said smoothly, and Cheryl threw him a grim smile and hurried to the door that would put her in the area that held her office, the duty room, and the communications room. He'd given her an assignment that would push her limits over the next quarter hour.

Harvey focused on the press. "So. We're in the middle of a breaking case, and I'll give you the latest developments. You all know about the shooting that took place Wednesday evening at Hobart Chevrolet. This is a photo of the man who was killed, Carter Ulrich. He was an employee at the car dealership. Detective Miller will post it on our liaison website for you."

Right on cue, Nate had the photo of Ulrich displayed on the wall.

"We now believe that the owner, Peter Hobart, was kidnapped that same evening," Harvey said. "This is a photo of Mr. Hobart." Nate swapped out the pictures. "He has not been seen since before the shooting. His wife was to meet him at the showroom at close of business Wednesday, but when she arrived, she found Ulrich's body. Her husband was missing."

The reporters were furiously scribbling in their notebooks.

"We knew for certain he'd been kidnapped a few hours later," Harvey said. "A call came in to Mrs. Hobart for ransom about 9:40 p.m. She was able to speak to her husband for a few seconds at that time. It's the last time we're certain that Peter Hobart was still alive."

He paused for a moment. Stating the bald truth cut deeply. He looked out at the reporters. He knew most of them, had worked closely with some.

"We need your help. We'll give you photos of Mr. Hobart, and we ask you to publicize them. Tell your audience, if anyone has seen this man in the last two days to please contact the Portland police. We'll set up a hotline in our comm room and staff it starting at the close of this press conference. We'll have that number for you in a minute—"

Nate lifted a hand, pointing behind him. Harvey swiveled and looked at the 800 number on the wall.

"Well, there you go. Our day sergeant, Cheryl Yeaton, is her usual efficient self today. If you get calls in your newsrooms about this kidnapping, please refer them to us."

"Captain—" Half a dozen reporters waved their hands.

"I'm not finished." Harvey looked out over them. "The family is offering a ten-thousand-dollar reward for information that leads to Mr. Hobart's safe return. Anyone who contacts us through the hotline with details that take us to the victim will be eligible."

He paused considering how much more to tell. He figured they were running out of time. The kidnappers had cut off communication twenty-four hours ago, and that usually wasn't good. The more he revealed, the better Peter's chances of some good Samaritan coming up with a clue.

"My detectives and I helped Mrs. Hobart prepare to meet the kidnappers' demands on Thursday, but unfortunately, things did not go as planned. The man who tried to retrieve the ransom was struck by a vehicle and killed. We believe he wasn't working alone, and that there's at least one more kidnapper still out there.

He hasn't contacted us, and we figure he's afraid." He nodded to Nate, and Chad McCafferty's photo came up.

"This man is a person of interest in the case. His name is Chad McCafferty, nickname Mack. We'd like to be notified immediately if anyone knows his whereabouts."

Harvey paused and looked over the group. Some were veteran reporters, and others looked like rookies fresh out of journalism school. For better or for worse, he was giving them a chance to help solve several crimes. He only hoped he wasn't putting Peter in deeper danger.

"I'd like to say right now that if anyone involved contacts our hotline and gives us information leading to the return of Peter Hobart, we will take their cooperation into consideration. Someone has abducted Mr. Hobart and is holding him against his will. But if we don't find Mr. Hobart alive, this will become a homicide case. So whoever knows anything needs to step forward now."

He opened the forum for questions, calling on a woman from Channel 2 first.

"Is this McCafferty the other kidnapper you're looking for?"

"Right now, he's just a potential witness. I can't give you details, but we do believe he has some connection to the case."

The questions rained thick and hard. Harvey revealed that they had several leads they were following, and that they were questioning some contacts. But he didn't mention Emma Skerritt or Davey Talbot by name or get specific about their leads. He did admit that the roadblocks on the I-95 ramps Thursday night were connected to the case.

Nate had sent him a fact sheet he'd prepared with minimal biographical information on Peter Hobart, Carter Ulrich, and Webster Holden. Harvey released that to the journalists. He saw Mike leaning against the wall near the stairway and nodded to him. Like old times.

"Thank you, folks," Harvey said. "Help us out by filing your stories with as much information as you can and referring any inquiries to us."

He turned away. Mike had slipped inside the stairwell, and Harvey wished he'd escaped with him. Ryan Toothaker chased him to the door that would take him to the comm room to talk over details of the hotline with the head dispatcher.

"Captain, hold on a sec."

Harvey sighed. "Well, Ryan, did you find out anything interesting about Holden?"

"I guess not. Nothing you didn't already know. But do you know who the second kidnapper is?"

"I told you, we have someone in mind."

"That McCafferty guy."

"I didn't say that."

"You don't want us to broadcast that he's the kidnapper and have people be on the lookout for him?"

"I've given you his name and his picture. We would like to talk to him. I did not ever say we think he's one of the kidnappers." Harvey shook his head. "Ryan, we don't to want to spook him. But we have some leads we're following, and we hope to track him down soon. We don't want civilians getting in the way of that."

"You said you're talking to some other people. Can you tell me who?"

"No."

"Relatives of the dead kidnapper?"

"I can't reveal that."

"If you could just—"

"No, Ryan. Go write up your story."

"But I don't have anything the others don't have."

"That's right." Harvey reached for the keypad beside the doorjamb.

"Just one little tidbit, Captain. You know that if—"

"If you say that I'd give my sister-in-law an exclusive if she still worked for the paper, I'll have you banned from this building."

Ryan gulped. "You could do that?"

"Yes. And I will, if you bring Leeanne's name into this."

"Okay." Ryan held up a hand and took a step backward.

Harvey felt sorry for him, but not that sorry. He punched in the key code and hurried toward the comm room. His cell phone's vibrations halted him. He checked the screen and was surprised to see Captain Hillman's name.

"Larson. That you, John?"

"Yes. I have something for you to look into. One of Talbot's men checked in—that is, he thought he checked in. He called Talbot's henchman. You know, the big guy, Cartwell."

"Right, the heavy. What'd he say?"

"Seems this guy was out on a so-called errand and didn't know about our raid on Talbot's place."

"He didn't catch on when you answered Cartwell's phone?" Harvey asked.

"No. He was a little shook up. Said he'd located McCafferty, but he got away."

"I just came from McCafferty's hideaway half an hour ago," Harvey said. "We found some blood there."

"Well, this guy said he was pretty sure he'd hit Mack, but he lost him."

"What did you tell him?"

Hillman chuckled. "I told him the boss wanted him to come back to headquarters. We'll pick him up when he gets here to Talbot's house."

"Great. Hold him and anyone with him," Harvey said. He went on into the busy comm room to speak to Charlie about the hotline workers.

*****

Peter stirred. He must have drifted off again. He looked toward the window. It was still bright outside, but he couldn't tell what time.

His hands hurt like crazy. He flexed them. The left hurt more than the right. He held them up and studied them. They were so caked in blood that he couldn't tell where the cuts were, but his fingertips had suffered for sure. He also had a few lacerations on his left wrist. But the bleeding seemed to have stopped, so that was something. What now?

He lay still, thinking. There was something he had to remember.

The key!

Even a small movement like turning his head hurt, but he had to find it. It was somewhere here on the sleeping bag. He eased back and looked carefully over the rumpled fabric, stained with his blood. The light from the high window wasn't strong enough to help much from across the room. Slowly, methodically, he patted the folds of fabric. It had to be here.

Ten minutes later, he nearly despaired.

I know it's here, God! Mack threw it down.

Maybe if he stood and shook out the sleeping bag. The little key would fall out on the floor. He'd have to be careful, though, so it didn't bounce away to where he couldn't reach it.

He crawled to the wall and leaned against it. After two failed attempts, he managed to get to his feet and pull the corner of the sleeping bag up with him. He pulled it in slowly, clutching a wad of the quilted cloth and listening for the key to plink on the floor. If it didn't hit the concrete, it must be down inside the folds of the bedding.

He caught a faint sound and froze. Swaying slightly, he moved his head from one side to the other, searching for it. Carefully he crouched with the sleeping bag in his arms a peered at the floor. At last he saw it and leaned forward.

Chapter 15

Three off-duty officers had volunteered to come in and take the first shift on the hotline. Relieved, Harvey thanked Charlie Doran and was half way out the door of the comm room when Charlie called him back.

He nodded toward one of the regular dispatchers. "We just took a call from a woman on Hatch Street, near the place you were looking for McCafferty."

"Yeah?" Harvey said.

"Her car was stolen within the last twenty minutes."

"That's got to be Mack," Harvey said.

"I put out a BOLO," Charlie said. "He can't have gotten far."

"Good. So, when will the hotline be operational?"

"I've got one guy on it now. We'll have a couple more within the hour," Charlie replied. They hashed out a few details, and Harvey went upstairs. He'd barely reached his desk when Paula transferred a call from Charlie.

"Sasha's got a call from an officer placing that stolen car about a mile from your scene on Hatch Street."

"Is McCafferty in it?" Harvey asked. It was almost too good to be true.

"He's rolling. If it's him, he's headed toward Deering. We've got a car tailing him."

"Current location?" Harvey got it and took out his phone and called Eddie. "You done with Talbot?"

"I can be," Eddie said.

"Leave him to Cheryl's men. I'm going to start my vehicle. Go straight to the garage exit, and I'll pick you up."

Eddie didn't ask where they were headed until he'd piled into the front seat of Harvey's Explorer.

"McCafferty, on Danforth. A squad car's trying to pull him over."

"That could be tricky in traffic this time of day."

"Yeah." Harvey flipped on his siren. "Put the flasher up."

Eddie lowered his window and fastened the blue light to the Explorer's roof. "So, how'd they get on to him?" he yelled over the siren's wail.

"He stole another car, and the owner called it in right away. A sharp-eyed cop spotted him. They're tailing him now."

"Who's on him?"

"Marston and Needham."

Eddie nodded. Both the patrolmen had been with the department several years. Voices sounded on the radio, and they listened.

Harvey scowled at what he heard. "The car belongs to a neighbor near the duplex. They must have left the keys in it."

A minute later, Eddie said, "Sounds like they stopped him."

Charlie called Harvey's code.

"Take that," Harvey said, and Eddie reached for the radio. "What have you got for us, Charlie?"

"Unit 14 stopped your suspect and is requesting backup." Charlie gave the location.

"We'll be there in two minutes," Eddie said.

"Good. Shots fired. I'll send a bus."

"You got your vest?" Harvey asked.

Eddie shook his head.

"Mine's on the back seat. Grab it."

Eddie stretched to reach the vest while Harvey concentrated on traffic. On the radio, Charlie's call went out for an ambulance.

"You want me to put this on?" Eddie asked. "It would save time."

Harvey shook his head. Only one of them could wear it, and he didn't want Eddie jumping into the fray while he watched.

Up ahead, he saw the strobe lights of the patrol car and a slight snarl in traffic as cars slowed to go around the stopped vehicles.

Harvey pulled to the curb several yards back and grabbed his Kevlar vest.

"Stop the traffic," he told Eddie. As soon as he had the vest on over his jacket, he dashed toward the patrol car with his gun drawn. To his relief, the officers had already apprehended McCafferty. Ted Marston had him prone on the ground and was handcuffing him.

"You guys okay?" Harvey asked the other patrolman, Brock Needham.

"Yeah. But he drew a gun. We had to shoot."

"The bus is on the way. I take it he's not dead?"

Needham shook his head. "Winged him, but he has a wound in his thigh, too, Captain. Ted only fired once."

"You sure?"

"Yeah."

"He was wounded earlier. Where's the prisoner's weapon?" Harvey asked.

"Under the car. We didn't touch it."

"Good. Now, you go help Detective Thibodeau with traffic until another uniform gets here." Harvey went to retrieve the handgun and bag it. "You all right, Ted?" he asked as Marston stood and wiped his brow with his cuff.

"Yeah. It was dicey for a few seconds. Is the ambulance coming?"

"They'll be right here," Harvey said. "How bad is it?"

"He jumped, and I hit him in the arm instead of the chest, but his leg's bleeding, too."

"Okay. You guys have a first aid kit?" He noticed that Ted was shaking.

"Yeah. In the trunk."

"Give me your keys. I'll get it. You sit down." The prisoner wasn't going anywhere, and Harvey walked with Ted to his squad car, where the patrolman sat down on the passenger side with the door open.

"I swear I only fired one bullet, Captain."

"I know. He was already hurting when he got in that car. You're even on that score." Harvey grabbed the first aid kit and hurried back to the prisoner.

He leaned over McCafferty. The man had a rag tied around his leg, and though his pantleg was soaked with blood, that wound seemed under control. He was bleeding on the pavement, however, from the fresh hit. The wound seemed low in the shoulder, possibly near the top of Mack's lung, rather than his arm. His eyes were closed, and he moaned softly.

"Hey, Mack." Harvey grasped his other shoulder. "Do you hear me, Mack?"

McCafferty howled.

Harvey gritted his teeth. "Where is Peter Hobart?"

Mack didn't respond.

The ambulance's swooping siren flared louder as it rounded a corner. Eddie joined Harvey just as he fished a roll of gauze out of the first aid kit.

"Hey, Harv, don't wreck your suit," Eddie said.

"Well, I'm not going to stand here and let him bleed."

"I'll do that." Eddie snatched the gauze from his hand. "You've got to talk to the press. You got this guy's gun?"

"Yeah." Harvey turned as the two EMTs approached. Jeff Wainthrop and Mark Johnson walked toward him with their gear.

"This the only patient?" Mark asked.

"Yeah. One of our officers shot him. He's a little shaky. Hi, Jeff."

"Yo, Harvey. Beth called and said the folks got in all right."

"Good. I expect you'll take the prisoner to MaineGeneral?"

"No doubt," Jeff said as he and Mark crouched to tend to the wounded man.

"I'll talk to him there," Harvey said. "That leg wound is older. We found blood in his apartment. The shoulder shot is fresh, from one of our officers."

"Thanks," Jeff said. Mark was quickly checking vital signs.

"I expect I'll see you this weekend," Jeff said. "I'm off at midnight."

"Okay. And just give Officer Marston a quick look before you go."

"Got it," Jeff said.

Harvey walked away and called Cheryl Yeaton. "Our prisoner is under the EMTs' care. He'll be heading for the ER soon. I'm going to have Needham drive Marston in. He's the one who shot the suspect, and he's a little shaky. I didn't see it, but it sounds like McCafferty fired first, or at any rate pulled his weapon. I've got the prisoner's gun. I'll bring it in, and I'll touch base with you before I go to the hospital."

As he signed off, Eddie caught up to him.

"You drive," Harvey said and tossed him the keys.

*****

Peter fumbled with the padlock key several times before he managed to insert it correctly and turn it, unlatching the mechanism. His fingers on his left hand were oozing blood again. As much as possible, he avoided using them as he unwound the chain.

At last, he was free from the restraints. He looked toward the stairway and knew he would need to rest for a while before attempting to climb it. He sat for a long time, rubbing his ankle and praying in silence. The light from the window beckoned to him. If only he had something to stand on. The window ledge appeared to be very narrow—only an inch or two. He doubted he could climb up there and break the window. Even if could, he doubted he could fit through the small opening. But he might be able to attract attention if he was up there.

Hopelessly, he gazed at the window while massaging his raw ankle and thinking. The bottom of the window was six or seven feet off the floor, and it consisted of only four small panes, aligned horizontally. There was no way.

The chain. He followed it back in the shadows to where it was looped around a pipe. He'd tried to break it before, or to pull the pipe loose, without success. But if the lock on that end was keyed the same as the one on his ankle. . .

197

He crawled to it and seized the lock, ignoring the stabbing pain in his hands. After a moment, he slumped with his back against the wall. It would have been too easy.

The stairs were his only hope, and he made himself rise, holding onto the wall, and then stagger toward them. The steps had no risers behind them. A rail ran up the wall on the right, but the left side of the flight was open. He would have to go slowly and be careful.

He took the short walk into the bathroom first and ran cool water over his hands. His cuts stung, but after the initial shock, the bath felt good. After a couple of minutes, he dried his hands and looked at them. They would take time to heal.

But he didn't have much time. His tightening stomach reminded him that he hadn't eaten for thirty hours or more. At least the water worked. He bent to slurp from the faucet.

It took him several minutes to undo his zipper so he could relieve himself. His fingers throbbed, and he bathed his left hand again at the sink and wrapped toilet paper around it. It was time to face the stairs.

He clung to the railing and put his foot on the first step. Pulling his weight up taxed all his strength. Each step seemed to grow larger than the previous one, until the next seemed insurmountable. He crawled up the last two. When he finally reached the top, he lay panting, longing to open the door yet dreading the attempt. He refused to think that it might not open at his touch.

Finally he hauled in a deep breath and used the railing to pull to his knees. He reached for the doorknob. Cringing at the pain, he turned it.

Of course it was locked. He'd known it would be, hadn't he? But he'd needed to try.

The knob had the standard button latch. With great care, he turned the button and once more tried the knob. Still, the door didn't budge.

His gaze traveled upward. Several inches above the knob was a round brass fitting. A deadbolt. From this side, it could only be unlocked with a key. No doubt there was a turn lever on the other side. It made sense. He had one on the cellar door in his own house.

Christine had insisted on it. He'd taken her on a couple of business trips, but after Gary was born, she'd stayed home. But she didn't want to be alone overnight unless that cellar door was secure. Of course, their house had an outdoor cellar entry, and this one didn't seem to have that. Peter looked down the stairs at the shadowy basement. Had he missed something?

A sudden thought made him look up, hoping to spot a light switch on the wall beside the door. But, no. The switch was outside the door, probably on the kitchen wall.

He hadn't thoroughly explored the basement. He remembered the old furnace. Was the house old enough to have a coal chute? Maybe there was something he could climb on—a box or something in a corner.

The thought of having to climb the stairs again disheartened him. But if there was an outdoor cellar entry or something else that would help him, he would be foolish not to use that.

Still sitting, Peter lowered himself one step at a time. At the bottom of the stairs, he grasped the railing and pulled himself up. His hands were on fire, and his ankle throbbed. He pulled in several deep breaths. He would have to go slowly, around the edge of the room, so that he would always have the wall for support.

He took the first step.

*****

Harvey sat at his desk, scowling as he listened to the doctor's report over the phone. McCafferty's wound was worse than he'd thought at the scene and required surgery. Going to the hospital now would do him no good. The kidnapper was still in the operating room and might not be conscious and able to answer questions for a couple more hours.

Harvey ran his hand through his hair. "Okay, doc. Thanks. I'll come by this evening."

He called Captain Hillman to see what the Cape Elizabeth police had found out.

"We'll have plenty of evidence against Talbot for the weapons and the rackets," John Hillman told him, "but we haven't found anything to link him to your kidnapping."

"I was afraid of that."

"Can you hold him over the weekend and set the arraignment for Monday?" Hillman said. "That would give you a couple more days to work your end of it."

"Yeah, there's no way he'll be in court before then." Talbot's attorney was probably already screaming for a speedy arraignment and bail hearing, but the convenient timing of the weekend was on Harvey's side.

When he hung up, Nate came over to his desk.

"We got a call while you were on the phone."

Harvey looked up at him. "And?"

"It was the lab. They've got results on the gun our guys took off McCafferty."

"Thanks, Nate." Harvey jogged down the stairs and into the lab. "Zoe! What have got for me?"

She turned toward him, smiling. "Nice to see you. I was about to head home."

"I won't keep you. You got something on the nine-millimeter?

"Yes." Zoe turned to her computer screen and hit a few keys. "Its fired casings match the one you picked up at the homicide."

Harvey's pulse picked up. "The Ulrich shooting from Wednesday night?"

"That's the one. This gun was used to kill your victim."

He scrutinized the screen and nodded. "Fantastic."

Zoe grinned. "Glad I made your day. Now I'm getting out of here. Have a nice weekend."

"I plan to."

Five minutes later, Harvey was seated across the desk from Mike in the chief's office.

200

"You might as well go home and eat with your family," Mike said. "You can't talk to Talbot any more until his lawyer's on the scene."

"I thought he'd have been here and left by now."

Mike shrugged. "He was in court this afternoon and sent a junior partner over, but they stipulated no questioning without the lawyer present."

"I let Emma Skerritt go, now that we've got her boyfriend."

"You wouldn't get anything else out of her, anyhow."

Harvey sighed. "You're right. I told her Chad was in the hospital, but I wish I hadn't. She's probably over there now, and I really don't want her to be the first one to talk to him." He shook his head. "Why'd I do that?"

"Because you're a kind person."

"Ha." Harvey squinted at him. "Who'd ever have thought?"

"Well, I wouldn't have, five years ago. I'd have said you were a good detective and a decent man then, but now you're a genuinely good person."

"I'm getting soft."

Mike shook his head. "You're showing the work God's done on you, that's all. Emma Skerritt was caught up in this, and it wasn't her fault, other than falling for an idiot. Did you tell her you picked up her friend, too, for drugs?"

"Yeah, and I told her to stay away from the duplex."

"Well, your fatigue is showing, I won't deny that. You could call whoever's on duty outside his hospital room and tell them not to let her in."

Harvey thought about it. "Nah, I think it's okay. Anyway, I called a minute ago, and he was still in surgery."

Mike opened a drawer, took out a manila folder, and slapped it on the desk. "Take a hard look at these, Harvey."

"What is it?"

"Your interviews for Nate Miller's position. Next Tuesday at nine, ten, and eleven a.m."

201

Harvey stared at him for a moment then opened the folder. His jaw tightened as the looked through the three sets of paperwork. "Two of these are women."

"Don't start, Harvey."

"No, sure. It's okay. I know everyone's harping on diversity right now."

"That's right." Mike shrugged. "You've been busy, and I didn't think you had a lot of time to put in on this, but we need to move on it. Thought I'd help you out."

"You didn't take my short list into consideration?"

Mike opened his top drawer and took out a pack of gum. As he unwrapped a stick, he leaned back in his chair. "Ron Legere got the best of the candidates for his squad after the shakeup last fall. I'm not letting any more kids like Winfield skip a grade. It causes discontent down the ranks."

"Yeah, I know. Sorry about that. I don't think we have any more geniuses working for us now, anyhow. And Crocker didn't pass the exam. I might have taken her."

Mike's eyes narrowed. "There's only two more officers in this department who've passed it."

"Sarah Benoit and Max Farington," Harvey said.

"You told me you weren't comfortable putting Sarah in your unit, given her history with Eddie."

"Well. . ." Harvey took a big breath, trying to look at things impartially. "They've gotten past all that, I think, and Jenny's gotten close to Sarah."

"Is that a problem?"

"I guess not. I mean, Eddie's my best friend, and we work together all the time."

"But you got to be friends because you were partners," Mike pointed out. "If it weren't for that, you and Eddie probably wouldn't have much to do with each other."

"That would be my loss."

"His, too. But anyway, what do you think now about Eddie and Sarah working together?"

"I don't know, to be honest. You put her file in here. I guess that means you want me to consider her."

"She deserves a chance. But we can wait until Ron has another opening. Of course, we might lose her to another department if we hold her back too long."

"Yeah. She's smart," Harvey conceded.

"Not as brilliant as Winfield or as street-smart as Eddie." Mike chewed thoughtfully for a moment. "I know it's tough bringing a woman into an all-male unit. But we all need to grow up a little and figure it out. I was probably wrong not to take a woman into Priority when I was the captain."

"You had the squad you wanted, and we did good work." Harvey eyed the photo of Sarah clipped to her test results.

"Do you think she'll understand if you don't pick her?" Mike asked.

"Does that matter?"

Harvey didn't like the thought of sitting down to explain that to Sarah, though, and she would deserve an explanation. "Let me look at these two profiles you've got from outside. It could be one of them is more qualified." He flipped through the file again. "I notice you didn't put Farington in here."

"To be honest, I weeded him out with about ten other outside applications. He barely passed the test, and I didn't think he was the best choice. There were several from other departments with very high scores, and one of those candidates has detective experience but wants a change of venue."

"Hmm. Okay."

"I can give you a couple more of the top profiles if you want, or is three enough?"

"Give me your next highest two."

Mike opened the drawer and selected the files.

"Take those home." Mike slid the additions across the desk. "It's after five o'clock. Send your boys home, too. You rounded up a good batch of suspects today, and Cape Elizabeth will work with you on Talbot and his crew."

"But we haven't found Peter."

203

Mike threw his hands in the air. "I can't help you. I wish I could."

"Me too."

"Do you think he's still in the city?" Mike asked.

"We haven't found anything that makes us think he was in Cape Elizabeth, or that Talbot knew anything about the kidnapping. I think he's being square with us on that."

"Still," Mike said, "if they got out of Portland, Peter could be anywhere."

"Yeah." Harvey tried not to think of Peter starving to death in some old barn or his friend's body being dumped in a rural location. "Well, I'll be over at the hospital by seven. I sure hope McCafferty is awake and able to talk by then."

*****

Peter rested on the sleeping bag for a while before attempting the stairs again. He hadn't found any more exits to the basement. He'd tried twice to work his way up to the window, but it needed more strength than he had left. He considered wrapping his shirt around his hand and trying to break the glass, but he could barely reach the window. Would he be able to attract attention if he shattered it?

After much thought, he decided to try the stairway door again. He wasn't sure he was thinking clearly, but it seemed his best chance. He wouldn't be able to pick the locks without a locksmith's tool kit. But he had to try.

What did he have that he could use? If he had the right implements, he might be able to do it, or at least he imagined he might. He couldn't lose all hope now.

He put the padlock key Mack had left him in his pocket without much faith that it would help, but he had to try every possibility.

Slowly, he stood and took one step at a time, staying close to the wall. When he reached the stairs, he took hold of the railing and painfully inched up the steps. When he reached the top, he went to his knees on the uppermost tread.

He took the padlock key from his pocket, but it wouldn't fit into the slot, no matter how he tried. His pockets were empty now, except for the Matchbox car Andy had given him on Wednesday morning. It seemed years ago. Peter drew out the little toy, careful not to drop it. The only thing that might possibly help him was the axle. Even his swollen fingers told him it was the wrong shape and too thick, but after some work he had the axle free of the chassis, with the second wheel still attached. He shoved the car back in his pocket, but the tiny wheel fell, bouncing off a step and onto the concrete floor below.

Peter pulled himself higher, feeling the deadbolt lock in the dimness. He tried to put the end of the axle into the key slit on the lock. No way.

Now what? He stuck the tiny axle in his pocket and studied the door. It was a plain, flush panel made of plywood. Of course it would open inward. The hinges showed on this side, but he would need tools and steady hands to take them apart. They were on the side of the stairway that had no railing, and the brass seemed to taunt him. He couldn't take them apart, and he knew he couldn't break the door in from this side.

Peter closed his eyes and rested his head against the door, summoning courage to try a hopeless task. Mack had disappeared and apparently had no plans to reveal his whereabouts to anyone. The other kidnapper was dead. No one could help him.

The light was fading. He looked down the stairs and toward the window. Which was more likely to give him his freedom—the door or the window? He was more likely able to break the window than the door. But then what? If he could somehow crack the door, he could get out. He knew he could.

And he had climbed to the door. He reminded himself of his futile attempts to hoist himself up to the window. He was up here, and he needed to try.

Peter's stomach rumbled, and he knew he had to act soon. Each minute that passed drained more of his energy. Holding on to the railing, he pulled himself up. On TV, they kicked the door, but he was on the wrong side for that and standing a step below the threshold. Still, the door wasn't all that sturdy. Maybe he could crack the plywood on this side.

He clung to the railing and braced for a kick. His attempt was almost laughable. The angle was wrong, and he was exhausted. Even so, the effort would have thrown him down the stairs backward if he hadn't held to the railing so desperately. His forearms and hands felt almost useless now. He wasn't sure he could hang on through another kick.

Shoulder? He wasn't sure a healthy man could force the door from this side, and he was weak and in pain. But his boys and Abigail were out there. He couldn't die here without knowing he'd tried everything.

He drew back, pulled in a deep breath, and shoved against the door with his left shoulder. The door rattled.

Well, that did a lot of good.

He let go of the railing and grabbed the knob with his right hand. All or nothing. He pulled back and launched himself. He hit the panel and fell back. Unable to keep his hold on the doorknob, he sprawled backward, clutching for anything and grasping only air. His hip hit the edge of the stairway halfway down, and he did an awkward back somersault over the side.

He lay on the concrete, gasping. He couldn't have hit his head too badly, or he'd be unconscious. Wouldn't he? The side of his head hurt, but the pain seemed worse in his limbs. What hurt most, his leg or his elbow? The slightest twitch of either his left arm or leg caused excruciating pain. It wasn't just his raw ankle. He must have broken some bones.

Dear Lord, I'm going to die here. Comfort my boys and Abigail.

Chapter 16

Going home was a good decision. Harvey greeted his in-laws and took off his jacket, tie, and shoulder holster. It felt good to sit around the table with Jennifer's extended family, even though a few were missing.

Abby's eyes looked hollow, and dark half-circles had formed under them. She hadn't bothered with makeup today, and if he hadn't known better, he'd have thought she was the oldest of the three sisters.

"You caught the guy, right?" Her voice cracked. "Eddie said you have him in custody."

"We've got McCafferty, yes, and we're ninety-percent sure he's the second kidnapper. But he's recovering from his surgery, and I haven't been able to question him yet. His girlfriend insists she knows nothing about a kidnapping."

Eddie sat down the table a couple of places, where he was eating with one hand while the other arm stayed around Leeanne's shoulders. "She knew he was on the run, but she didn't know why. She thought he was on the outs with Davey Talbot."

"Which he is," Harvey noted. "If we hadn't gotten to him, Talbot probably would have had him taken out." He looked around the table, self-conscious suddenly of his harsh words in front of several children. "Sorry. I should have left business at the office."

"It's okay," Jennifer's father said. "You're carrying a big load."

"I'll go over to the hospital with you after we eat," Eddie said.

"You don't have to. You've already put in a lot of hours this week. I'll call in one of the other guys. Tony, maybe. He's the only one without a family."

"I can go," Eddie said.

"No, you stay with Leeanne. You two are still newlyweds."

Leeanne nodded to him. "Thank you, Harvey."

He smiled. "So, how's the new book coming?"

"Okay."

"Are you ready for the book signing on Monday?" Marilyn asked.

"Well, I'm nervous, but I guess I'll live through it." Leeanne made a face at her mother.

"Do you have to take the books?" Beth asked.

"No, the bookstore ordered them."

Marilyn said, "Well, your father will have to work Monday, and Randy has school, but I thought I might stay over."

Leeanne smiled. "I'd like that."

"Yeah, Mom, that would be terrific." Jennifer stood. "I'm going to take out the next round of biscuits. Anyone need anything while I'm up?"

George held up his water glass, and Jennifer walked over and took it from his hand with a smile.

Harvey looked toward the boys. Gary had begged to sit beside Randy, and his younger brother claimed their uncle's other side. Gary looked a little droopy now. Randy was buttering a biscuit for him.

"Gary, how's the arm?" Harvey asked.

"It hurts all the time."

"He just had his pain meds about fifteen minutes ago," Abby said. "It should kick in soon. But I don't want to stay late. He needs to get to bed early tonight."

Beth turned her head toward the living room. "Oh, there's Anna. I'd better go get her."

The baby's wails increased while Beth hurried from the room, then they stopped abruptly.

"Mommy solves the problem," Leeanne said.

When Jennifer offered dessert and coffee all around, Harvey pushed back his chair.

"I'd better get going."

"So soon?" Jennifer asked.

He looked longingly at the family. "I hate to." He'd only held Connor for a few minutes before the meal began, and he hadn't even seen Anna. Beth and Jeff's baby was napping when he arrived. "I just feel guilty wasting even a minute when I could be looking for Peter."

"It's not wasted time," Jennifer said softly.

"I'm sorry."

Her wistful expression tugged at him, and he stooped to kiss her. Jennifer hugged him for a moment, then let him go.

"I know how you feel," she said, "and we all want you to find him. But we'll miss you."

"I know. Thanks." He stepped back and met her father's gaze. "George, Marilyn, thanks for coming down. I'll see you later—or tomorrow, depending on what happens."

Eddie set down his fork. "Don't you want me to go, Harv?"

"No, but you can call Tony for me and tell him to meet me there."

On the way to the garage, He keyed in Charlie Doran. "Hey, Charlie. How's the hotline going?"

"Busy," Charlie said. "We've had a hundred and fifty calls."

"Really?" That surprised Harvey in a way, and then again, it didn't. "Anything helpful?"

"Anything that seems pertinent, Sergeant O'Heir is sending a unit out to check on it. The chief had him call in two extra teams tonight."

"Great."

"Yeah. So far, we've turned up a break-in, an assault, and two cases of vandalism. That's in addition to everything else the front desk has been dealing with. But nothing yet that seems related to the Hobart case."

"Okay, call me if you get something."

Harvey got in the Explorer and started the engine. Was this only the third day? It seemed like Peter had been gone a year.

*****

209

Eddie sat and chatted with Leeanne and the folks for a few minutes after Harvey left, but he was restless. Randy took his dish of pie and ice cream into the study, and after a couple minutes, Eddie excused himself and followed him.

"So, Randall, my man, you're going to spend the summer down here?"

"Looks like it." Randy was sitting at Harvey's desk holding his bowl and spoon, but he wasn't looking at the computer screen. He was frowning at a small sheet of paper on the desk.

"What have you got there?" Eddie leaned in to look over his shoulder.

"Jennifer said it was something Harvey was working on. Do you know what it is?"

Eddie hesitated. A couple of the names jumped out at him. Leah Viniard and Harvey Alan Larson.

"Jennifer started to tell me about it earlier," Randy said, "but then she put it in the drawer. I was just looking for a pencil, and I saw it again."

"Uh, those are names off a birth certificate someone brought Harvey the other day." Eddie wondered if he should have hedged.

Randy looked up at him, his eyebrows lowered. "Birth certificate? Which one's the baby?"

"I believe it's Leah Viniard. That's her name now. She was adopted, though."

Randy puzzled over it for a few more seconds.

"She's a kid about your age," Eddie said. "I met her."

"So Tara Ervin is her mother?"

"Yeah."

"Is Dr. Joseph Menard the father?"

"No."

Silence hung between them as Randy stared at the names. At last he met Eddie's gaze. "So, why is Harvey's name on this list?"

Eddie pulled over Jennifer's chair and sat down. "That's a funny story. I probably shouldn't be telling you, but you probably shouldn't be asking, either."

Randy gritted his teeth and cringed, definitely an admission of guilt.

"Well, we've gotten this far," Eddie said.

*****

At the hospital, Harvey went up to the surgical ward, where he stopped at the nurses' desk and showed his badge.

"I'm Captain Larson. I'm here to see Chad McCafferty."

"Oh, yes, they're expecting you. Room 312."

So he was out of the recovery room, at least. Harvey walked briskly down the hall and found Allison Crocker, in uniform, seated outside the door. She rose as he approached.

"The doctor said you can talk to him, Captain, but he's still kind of groggy."

"Thanks."

"His girlfriend's in there," she added. "She came about an hour ago."

Harvey nodded. "Okay. You stay alert. We arrested his boss and several of his flunkies, but you never know who's still out there with a grudge."

Allison nodded gravely. "I'll be on my toes." Her eyes flickered at something beyond him, and she smiled. "Oh, there's Detective Winfield."

Harvey turned and nodded to Tony.

"Hey, Captain. Hi, Allison." Tony gave her a friendly nod.

"Let's do this," Harvey said, and he and Tony went into the room.

The bed nearest the door was empty, and McCafferty lay on the one near the window with his eyes closed. His left arm and shoulder were heavily bandaged.

Emma Skerritt's eyes widened when she saw them, and she jumped up. "They said I could sit with him."

"Yeah, that's fine," Harvey said, "but we need to ask him a few questions. Has he been talking?"

"Not much. Just, 'What happened? Where am I?' That sort of thing."

"He knew who you were?"

"Yeah. I didn't say much about the stuff you asked me. He's still dopey, you know? The doctor said it's just a flesh wound in his leg, but the other business is serious stuff."

Harvey took that to mean Marston's shot had affected Mack's lung. "Well, if you don't mind, we need a few minutes. You can wait right outside the door."

She hesitated. "You're not going to hurt him again, are you?"

Harvey sighed. "No, Emma, we won't hurt him. He wouldn't have been hurt in the first place if he hadn't tried to shoot our police officers."

She looked down. "I guess."

"It's the truth. In fact, he already had the leg wound when we caught up to him."

Her eyes flared. "What do you mean?"

"I mean someone else shot him first. He bled all over the rug in that duplex you were staying at."

"Who did it?" she asked.

"We don't know yet, but it wasn't us. Did you know he had a gun with him?"

Her lips twitched. "I'll be right outside."

Harvey watched her go. Tony stepped over and shut the door behind her.

"Wake up, Mack," Harvey said, bumping the side of the bed intentionally.

McCafferty flinched and his eyes flew open. "Who. . ."

"I'm Captain Larson, and this is Detective Winfield. Where is Peter Hobart?"

"Who?"

"The guy you and Holden kidnapped."

McCafferty blinked. "Uh. . ."

Harvey gave him five seconds. "You'd better start talking Mack. You're already looking at murder one on Carter Ulrich. You don't want to add Peter Hobart to the list."

"What? No!"

"Yes," Harvey said.

"Hobart's not dead."

Harvey smiled. "Now you're talking my lingo. Where is he?"

"I—wait! Is Web Holden dead? Because I heard it on the news, that he was dead. Is it true?"

"Was he your friend?" Harvey asked.

"No. Not really. But—"

Harvey waited.

McCafferty's eyes darted about the room. "It was all him."

"What do you mean by that?" Harvey asked. "Be specific."

"Holden was the one who shot the guy, not me."

"What guy?"

"At the car showroom. The guy owed big bucks, and he'd been given umpteen chances to pay."

"To whom did he owe the money?" Harvey asked. He saw Tony's flicker of a smile when he said *whom*.

"Talbot. Davey Talbot."

"And Talbot sent you and Holden to collect?"

"Not that time. He said the guy wasn't going to pay, ever. He'd run out of chances."

"So what exactly was your assignment?"

McCafferty's lip quivered. "We were supposed to take care of him."

"Kill him, you mean," Harvey said.

Mack didn't say anything, but he looked away, his breath coming in choppy gasps.

"So you shot him," Harvey said.

"No, it was Web Holden, not me. It was all him."

"Then why did you have Web's gun today?"

"Huh?"

"The gun you had in the car you stole today is the same gun that killed Carter Ulrich at the car dealership."

Mack swallowed hard. "Web left it behind when he went to pick up the ransom. If things went bad, he didn't want to be caught with a gun on him."

"You expect me to believe that?" Harvey asked.

"It's the truth.

213

"Okay. And whose idea was it to grab the business owner and demand a ransom for him?"

"It was his idea, actually." McCafferty clutched the edge of the blanket and looked up at Harvey, his expression pleading for mercy. "We didn't know he was in there, but—but after—Well, he came out of some other room, and he says, 'What do you want? Do you want money?' Well, of course we wanted money."

"And what did you say?"

"Not me," McCafferty said quickly. "Holden said, 'Sure. How much you got?'"

"So where is Peter Hobart now?"

"He's—he's in a house."

"Where?" Harvey was becoming impatient, and his tone hardened.

"It's ... it's in the West Side."

"I need the street address."

"It's a one-story brick house on Baldwin Place. I can't remember the number."

Harvey looked at Tony and nodded. Tony hurried into the hallway.

"Whose house is it?" Harvey asked.

"I don't know. Holden knew a guy."

"What do you mean, he knew a guy? The guy who owned the house?"

"No, he didn't own it. He was a real estate agent, and he knew this house was empty."

Harvey's brain clicked and whirled. "Is there a For Sale sign in front of this house?"

"Yeah, I think so." Harvey's scowled, and McCafferty said, "Yeah, there is. I'm sure."

"What agency?"

"I dunno. Red and white sign."

"You'd better be telling it straight." Harvey turned on his heel and strode into the hall.

Tony had his phone to his ear. "Dispatch is sending four units, boss."

214

"Tell them there may be a red-and-white for sale sign out front, and the house is empty. See what they can get us." Harvey threw Allison Crocker a glance. "You stay alert. Nobody goes in but medical personnel and cops."

"Yes, sir," Allison said. "And the girlfriend?"

Emma was hovering a little way down the hall. Harvey wished he had a reason to hold her, but he believed that she hadn't known about Peter. She'd have cracked when they questioned her, before she knew where Mack was.

"Only after we get another officer here with you. I don't like the two of them in there and you alone out here. I want one officer in there all the time."

He made a quick call to Aaron O'Heir, who had come on duty as night patrol sergeant. While he arranged for another officer to help Allison hold things down at the hospital, Tony told Emma she couldn't go back inside the room until another patrolman came. One of the officers would stay with her while she was inside the room.

Harvey shoved his phone in his pocket and dove into the nearest stairwell with Tony on his heels.

"You ride with me," he told Tony. "As soon as we're in the car, call the rest of our squad."

Some of the patrol units would beat them to the neighborhood. They would be looking for a vacant brick house. Harvey wished he could be first on the scene, but that was impossible with the moments he'd used to give orders and the distance from the hospital. He put on his lights and siren and clenched his teeth.

Tony yelled over the noise, "Hey, Cap'n, Eddie wants to know, should he tell Abby?"

"Is he still at my house?" Harvey asked.

"He's wherever Abby is."

Harvey hesitated. "Okay. He can tell her, but have him stress that it may come to nothing. But I want him to meet us there pronto."

"Right." Tony relayed the message as they roared out of the parking lot.

*****

"Take me with you, Eddie."

The strain in Abby's face ripped him to pieces. "I can't, Abs."

"Please. You can't leave me out of this." She looked around wildly and grabbed Leeanne's arm. "Tell him. He *has* to take me."

Leeanne looked at him, speechless. She never interfered with his police work, and Eddie was glad she kept quiet this time. Still, Abby had been through so much this week. If he was the one who'd been kidnapped, he would want Leeanne to come to him. And giving in would be quicker than arguing.

"Okay," he said. "But you have to stay in my truck when we get there, until we know it's safe for you to get out."

"I'll do whatever you say."

She didn't even take her purse, just ran for the door.

Eddie gave Leeanne a quick kiss.

"Thanks for dinner, Jenn."

"We'll be praying. Go." Jennifer patted his shoulder as he strode past her.

Abby was already buckled in. "Where is it?"

"In the West End. I don't have an exact address, but it's a vacant house with a For Sale sign. We've got patrol units there now, looking for it."

"That could take a while."

"I hope not. Call Harvey and see if they've got an address yet."

"He won't get mad?"

"Has Harvey ever gotten mad at you?"

"No." Abby took out her phone and punched in a call to Harvey.

"Now, me he might yell at," Eddie said, "but you, no."

The ghost of a smile touched her lips.

"Harvey, it's Abby. I'm with Eddie. Do you have an address?"

"Just the street name—Baldwin Place. When you get close, you'll see police cars." She told Eddie. "Do you know where that is?"

"I know the area. I've got a cousin that lives over that way." He reached over and fumbled the glove compartment open. "There's ear plugs in there. You might want 'em." Leeanne had insisted he carry several packages of the cheap foam inserts, so that he wouldn't be deaf by the time he hit thirty.

Abby got a package open and handed him the plugs then put a pair in her ears, and he let loose the siren. He drove across town, and the traffic pulled over out of their way. They were soon in a residential neighborhood. In the distance he caught a telltale flash of blue.

"There's one of ours."

Abby said nothing but stared ahead and clung to the handle on the door frame. A minute later, he pulled up behind a squad car and got out.

"Stay put." He shut his door and hurried to the cruiser. A patrolman was just getting off the radio.

"Hey, Jerry," Eddie said. "You got anything? Where's Captain Larson?"

"They think they've found the house. Two streets over." He gave a precise address, and Eddie bounded back to the truck.

"They think they found it." He put the truck in gear.

"How far is it?" Abby asked.

"Not far." He took a cross street two blocks and saw the lights from several police vehicles down the street to his right. "That's got to be it." He rolled as close as he could get and stopped his truck in the street next to Harvey's Explorer. He left it running with the flashers on. The house was lit up, and several patrolmen were posted in the driveway and at the door.

Eddie climbed out. "Where's the captain?"

"Inside," one of the officers yelled back.

Eddie bent and looked in at Abby. "You stay here. I mean it. I'll come tell you the second I know something."

"Eddie!"

Something about her voice stopped him. He stooped lower and looked at her. The blue and red lights made weird shadows on her face.

"What?"

She made a choking noise in her throat and pointed. "That sign."

Eddie squinted. "The For Sale sign?"

"Yeah." She turned toward him. "It's Redmond Realty."

"So? They sell a lot of houses around here."

"But, Eddie."

She was crying. Eddie stared at her for a moment. This was serious. He got in and shut the door.

"What is it, Abby?" He put his arm around her. "What's going on?"

"Tom," she said. "Tom Merrick."

"Who—" Eddie caught his breath. "You don't mean. . ."

Abby nodded. "Peter's brother-in-law. Janelle's husband works for Redmond."

Chapter 17

"Eddie?" Abby's face was streaked with tears, and her hand shook as she reached toward him.

"*Sacre bleu.*" Eddie exhaled.

"What do we do?"

He swallowed hard and gave her a little squeeze. "Okay, you listen to me. Do not move. I'll lock you in, and you stay here. I'll make sure Harvey knows."

"Eddie, I'm a nurse."

"I know. Just let me find out what's what."

She sobbed in earnest then, big shaking sobs. Eddie wanted to comfort her, but he knew the best thing he could do was get to Harvey.

"Here." He snatched a tissue from the box in the console and shoved it into her hand. "I'll be right back. I promise."

He got out and ran for the house, holding his badge up in case any of patrolmen didn't recognize him, though there was a fat chance of that after all the publicity he'd gotten last winter as the Heartbreaker Hero. He would probably never live that down.

An ambulance pulled up, siren wailing. His hopes rose. If Peter was dead, Harvey would have called the medical examiner, not the EMTs.

He asked the cop at the door, "Any hostiles inside?"

"No, but they found a guy in the basement. Might be the kidnap victim."

Eddie hurried inside. He found the cellar stairway quickly. Two uniforms stood near the door, in the bare kitchen.

"Down there?" Eddie asked.

One of them pointed. Eddie strode to the open doorway. Lights flooded the basement below, and he heard voices. He went down the stairs. Harvey, Tony, and two more cops were crowded around a man on the concrete floor. Eddie stepped

219

closer and looked down at Peter's haggard face. His eyes were closed, and he wasn't moving. Eddie laid a hand on Harvey's shoulder.

Harvey looked up at him.

"EMT's are here."

"Good."

"He's breathing, then?"

Harvey stood. "Yeah, but he's in rough shape."

"Harv, Abby's in my truck outside, and she told me something that may be important."

Harvey moved a few steps away, toward the oil furnace, and Eddie went with him. Harvey cocked his head to one side and quirked his eyebrows.

"That Realtor's sign outside—Redmond."

"Yeah?" Harvey asked.

"Peter's brother-in-law works for them."

Harvey stared at him for a moment. "Tom? Janelle's husband?"

"Yeah. Tom Merrick."

Harvey let out his breath in a puff. "We'll have to pick him up. McCafferty told me at the hospital that Holden knew a guy in real estate. He told them about this place, maybe even let them in." He rubbed his chin. "Guess I'd better go talk to Abby. She would know his address."

"It might not be him," Eddie said.

"It's too coincidental."

"Yeah, but coincidences do happen. That's why circumstantial evidence isn't usually enough."

Harvey grimaced. "Yeah. Where's your rig?"

"Right by yours."

A shuffle at the top of the stairs drew their attention, and Jeff Wainthrop and Mark Johnson hurried down, carrying their equipment. Jeff zeroed in on Harvey and Eddie.

"Is it Peter?"

"Yeah," Harvey said. "Abby's outside, and I'm going to go talk to her. "I'll be back. You can tell Eddie and Tony anything pertinent." He nodded to Mark and jogged up the stairs.

*****

Abby had the pickup window down and was staring toward the house.

"Harvey," she called as soon as he hit the front steps.

He beelined toward her and stopped beside her door. "Abby. We've found him."

"Is he okay? I want to see him." She unlatched the door, but Harvey stood in front of it so that she couldn't open it.

"Not yet," he said gently. "Jeff and Mark just went in. Let them take his vitals and get an IV in."

"An IV?"

"I think he's dehydrated. And, Abby, he may have some broken bones."

"They beat him up?" Her voice rose in outrage.

"I don't know. It looks more like he may have taken a bad fall. He may have been trying to escape. He wasn't bound, but we saw evidence that he had been."

"What do you mean? Ligature marks?"

Harvey reached through the window and touched her shoulder. "Let us gather the evidence. I'll tell you all the details when we've sorted them out. I promise."

She pulled in a shuddering breath. "Can I call and tell the boys?" Her chin jerked up sharply. "He's going to make it, right? Harvey, tell me. Is Peter going to be okay?"

"I'm not a doctor. He was unconscious when we found him. He may have hit his head pretty hard. You know that's serious. He has other injuries, too."

"What kind of injuries?" Abby's eyes hardened.

"His hands are bleeding, and there are cuts on his wrists, his palms, and his fingers. One ankle is lacerated. We think they had him chained by one foot. Knowing Peter, he probably fought it and tried to break the chain."

221

She took two breaths and met his gaze. "Okay. What else?"

"I don't know. If he fell from the stairway, which looks like a good bet, he could have internal injuries. Broken ribs, anything."

She pushed on the door. "Let me go in."

"Why don't you call the boys first? I can go in and get a report from Jeffrey."

She hesitated. "Should I ask my mother to bring Gary and Andy to the hospital? I think they need to see him, too."

"I don't know. Will they let the boys in if Peter goes to the ICU?"

"I'll make them allow it."

Harvey nodded. "All right, but remember it's possible Peter will need surgery. I'm sure they'll do X-rays and run tests, anyway."

She sighed. "Okay, I'll tell them not to come until I call again. Maybe morning would be better, but I know the boys won't sleep tonight."

"Listen, Eddie said you mentioned Tom Merrick."

Her eyes focused on his, and her lips thinned. "Yeah. That's his real estate company."

"Can I ask you not to tell Janelle yet that we've found Peter?"

She eyed him keenly. "You're going to go find Tom?"

"That's the plan, as soon as Peter's in the ambulance."

She nodded slowly. "Janelle said he was out of town this week."

"Where?"

"Boston. Some real estate seminar."

"It's Friday night," Harvey said. "Think he's home yet?"

"I don't know."

"When did he leave?"

"Wednesday? Thursday?" Abby frowned. "Do you think he was gone when this happened?"

"Maybe." Or maybe he wasn't gone at all, Harvey thought, but he wasn't about to say that.

"Well, that would be good, wouldn't it?" Her hopeful tone made his stomach churn. He didn't want to disillusion her.

"Let's just see what we see. If Tom was in Boston all this time and had nothing to do with it, that would be great. But let's hold off on telling that side of the family for a few hours, okay? Say, 8 a.m.? If Peter's mom calls you before then, don't lie to her, but I want time to figure this out."

Abby nodded.

"What's Janelle and Tom's address?"

She gave it to him, and Harvey was glad it was within ten miles of where they were.

"It's not late," he observed. "When we're done here, I'll probably ride over there and have a little chat with Tom if he's home."

"Okay. I'll call the boys now."

"Good. And I'll see what I can get out of Jeff. If he gives the go-ahead, I'll come get you and take you in the house. Deal?"

"Deal."

*****

Abby called the Larsons' house, and Jennifer answered on the first ring.

"Abby? What's going on?"

Abby smiled. "I have some news, but I want to tell the boys first, if you don't mind."

"Of course," Jennifer said. "I can put Andy on here in the kitchen and take Gary to the extension in our bedroom. Will that work?"

"It's perfect. Thanks."

"Hold on."

Abby waited, watching as more officers arrived and residents gathered to chat in small groups on the sidewalk across the street.

"Mommy?" Andy said on the phone.

"Hi, honey. It's me. Is Gary there yet?"

"Aunt Jennifer is getting him another phone."

"Okay. Are you guys doing okay?"

223

"Yeah. We had ice cream."

"Great!"

She heard a click, and Gary said tentatively, "Hello?"

"Hi, Gary," Abby said. "You can both hear me, right?"

"Yeah," both boys replied.

"Good. I wanted you to hear it at the same time. The police have found your daddy."

Andy gave a little whoop, and Gary said gruffly, "About time."

Abby smiled. "Uncle Harvey and Uncle Jeff and Uncle Eddie are all with him right now. They're going to let me see him soon."

"Can we come and see him?" Gary asked.

"Not yet, but soon, honey. They're going to take him over to the hospital and let some doctors check him out."

"Is he hurt bad?" Gary asked.

"Well, I haven't seen him yet, but Uncle Harvey told me that he probably needs to see a doctor. They think he fell down and bumped his head, and he has a few cuts."

"What from?" Andy yelled in her ear.

"I don't know yet, sweetheart, but they'll fix him up. I'll call again when it's okay for you to see him. Probably that will be at the hospital. Okay?"

"Yeah," Gary said.

"Okay," Andy echoed.

"All right, now whichever one of you is with Aunt Jennifer, please put her on the phone now."

"She's with me," Gary said.

"And who's with you, Andy?" Abby asked.

"Aunt Leeanne."

"Okay, give them the phones, please. I'll see you later."

A moment later, Jennifer said, "Abby? They found him?"

"Yes."

"Thank God!"

"Amen to that," Leeanne said.

224

"Well, what I didn't tell the boys is that he's in pretty rough shape. I haven't seen him yet myself, but Harvey says he's unconscious, and he has some pretty severe injuries."

"Oh, dear," Jennifer said.

"I'll know more later. I'll call you again after I see him. I don't want you to take the boys to the hospital until I give you the word, all right?"

"Sure," Jennifer said.

"We'll be praying," Leeanne added.

"Thank you." Abby sobbed. "Jeff and Mark are here, tending to him."

"That's good," Leeanne said. "I'll tell Beth."

"Thanks. There's a lot more to tell you later, but I'm going to get off now. Just pray hard, okay?"

"We will," Jennifer assured her.

Abby closed the connection and held the phone to her chest. She sucked in a big breath and blinked against burning tears. Eddie came out of the house and down the driveway. She opened the truck door and hopped out.

"Can I go in now? Please?"

"Yeah. I'll take you. They're getting him ready for transport. Jeff says you can ride in the ambulance."

"Good." She grabbed his hand. "How bad is it really, Eddie?"

"Well, prepare yourself."

"Is he awake?"

"No. Mark and Jeff think he may have a skull fracture."

She couldn't hold back a sob. Eddie stopped walking and put his arm around her.

"You okay?"

She sniffed and nodded.

"If you're going to crumple on me, I'd better take you back to the truck."

"No. No, I'll be fine. I need to be with Peter."

"Okay." He eyed her uncertainly. "You sure you can do stairs?"

225

"I'm sure. Let's go." They walked slowly up the driveway to the front stoop.

"They also think one leg is broken, and they're not sure about his arm," Eddie said.

She stopped in the doorway. "What else aren't you telling me?"

"That's most of it. There's blood."

"Harvey said his hands have cuts."

Eddie nodded. "We think that's from trying to get loose. There's a broken mirror, and we found a piece of it near where he was chained."

Abby's heart clenched. "Let me see him."

"This way." Eddie guided her into the empty kitchen.

He preceded her down the cellar stairs. Abby held the railing with one hand and clung to Eddie's hand with the other. She could see the EMTs below them, huddled over a form on the floor, but between them and several police officers, she couldn't actually see Peter, other than one foot and his bandaged right arm.

Harvey met them at the bottom of the stairs and drew her toward him.

"You okay, Abby?"

She nodded, her eyes on the EMTs. Jeff stood and turned toward them.

"Hey, sis." His smile wavered. "Looks like you'll get him back."

Abby brushed past him and went to her knees on the concrete floor. Peter's face was ashen. He had an IV line in his left forearm, and Tony Winfield was holding the bag of saline fluid. Mark Johnson was wrapping Peter's splinted right leg.

She swallowed hard and looked up at Jeff. "Is there a skull fracture?"

"If there is, it's hairline. Concussion, minimum. But we'll treat him extra careful. We want to make sure he's stable before we lift him up the stairs."

226

She nodded. Both Peter's hands and wrists were wrapped in gauze, and there was no place for her to hold on to him. Tears streamed down her cheeks.

"Can you hold this, Jeff?" Mark asked, and Jeff crouched to help him. Abby eased over a little to give them room.

"The ER's expecting him," Mark said as he worked. "They'll probably take him straight to X-ray, if his vitals are okay when we get there."

Abby cleared her throat, but a painful lump remained. "How's his blood pressure?"

"Not great," Mark said.

Jeff handed her a clipboard, and she looked down at the notes he had made.

"His oxygen's low," she said.

"Yeah, we'll get him on oxy in the bus." Jeff winked at her. "He's going to make it, Abby."

"Are you sure? That head wound. . ."

"That's the worst thing," Jeff agreed.

"Okay, I'm done." Mark sat back on his heels and put his scissors and tape back in his kit. "Let's get the stretcher down here."

"Eddie, give me a hand?" Jeff said. He and Eddie bounded up the stairs.

Jimmy Cook came down the stairs and went straight to Harvey. "Hey, boss. You need Nate and me down here?"

"Let's wait until they get Peter out," Harvey said. "You two start looking around up there. It's hard to protect the crime scene with this many people responding, but we need to know if the kidnappers left anything behind up there. As soon as the EMTs clear out, we'll take this basement apart."

Jimmy nodded and went back up the steps.

Abby reached out toward Harvey, and he bent toward her. "What do you think you'll find?"

"Well, there's a sleeping bag over there, and the duct tape they probably had on his hands. We might get some prints off that. And in the bathroom, there's a broken mirror. I expect Peter

227

used the glass to get himself free, but we'll look it over real well, anyway."

"He had a bathroom?" Abby looked around and homed in on the doorway a few yards away. On the floor near it was the crumpled sleeping bag and a slack chain. "They chained him up."

Harvey's hand came down on her shoulder. "It's over now, Abby. Just think about Peter, and what he needs from you right now."

She looked back at the man she loved so much. Peter pulled in a shuddering breath and exhaled, his eyes still closed. She reached out and gently smoothed his hair. He was filthy. Peter hated that. She looked up at Harvey.

"Probably the first thing he'll say is, 'I need a shower.'"

Harvey chuckled.

Abby looked toward the stairs. Eddie and Jeff maneuvered their way down, carrying the collapsed stretcher from the ambulance. "Remember when you guys went running together and you thought I'd be grossed out because Peter was all sweaty?"

Harvey nodded, smiling. "Eddie was sure you wouldn't marry him after that, but he was wrong. I'm glad you hung in there."

"Me, too." Abby stood.

"Okay, let's clear out and give the EMTs some space," Harvey said.

The uniformed officers trooped up the stairs. Jeff laid the stretcher beside Peter, and he and Mark lifted the patient onto it.

"You need help getting him up?" Eddie asked.

"We've got it," Mark said.

Jeff looked over at Abby. "You want to ride with us?"

"Yes, please."

She waited until they were nearly to the top of the stairs and squeezed Eddie's arm. "Thank you. You, too, Harvey. I'll see you later."

Her phone hummed in her pocket as she followed Jeff and Mark out of the house. Patrolmen lined the driveway as Peter was rolled to the back of the ambulance. Abby pulled her phone out and looked at it.

She caught her breath and looked over her shoulder. Harvey was only a couple of steps behind her.

"Janelle is calling me."

"Don't answer it," Harvey said.

She nodded. "I won't talk to anyone but my family. That includes you guys."

"Good." The stretcher was in the ambulance. Harvey gave her a boost up. "I'll probably see you later at the hospital."

"Sit here, Abs," Jeff said, indicating the jump seat near Peter's head. Abby sat down and touched his forehead.

"He's cool."

"Yeah, no fever," Jeff replied as he hung the IV bag. "There'll be a neurosurgeon standing by when we get there."

Mark shut the door, and Abby pulled in a deep breath. "I'm glad it was you who came."

Jeff gave her a crooked smile and sat down beside her. "Me, too." He reached for Peter's wrist and gently positioned his fingertips to take a pulse. "Holding steady."

Chapter 18

Harvey and Nate approached the front door of Tom Merrick's house. Nate and Jimmy went around to the back. Harvey missed having Eddie beside him, but he'd sent him to the hospital to watch out for Peter and Abby.

The porch light came on, and a moment later Janelle Merrick opened the door.

"Captain Larson? Is there news on Peter?"

"May we come in, Janelle?"

"Of course."

She led them into the living room. Upscale, modern furnishings, Harvey noted. Contemporary art, but no big-name artists except the one Sofia Areal print. He didn't like it, but that was just him. Harvey liked realism.

Janelle turned to face him. "It must be bad."

"Why do you say that?" Harvey asked.

"Otherwise you wouldn't be here. I tried to call Abby a while ago, and she didn't pick up. Is Peter. . ." Tears filled her eyes.

"I'm actually here to see your husband," Harvey said.

She raised her chin and blinked. "Tom?"

"Yes. Is he home?"

"No, he's in Boston."

"A real estate seminar, I believe?"

Janelle eyed him keenly. "That's right. But I don't understand."

"When do you expect him home?"

"Tomorrow night. They're wrapping the seminar at four tomorrow."

"What day did Tom leave to go to Boston?"

"Thursday morning. What is this about?"

231

"Janelle, I need to ask a few more questions. Would you mind if my men did a walk-through of the house? They won't disturb anything."

She stood there for a moment, staring at him. "You think Tom's done something."

"It's more a matter of ruling him out."

She sank into an armchair. "Does this have anything to do with Peter? Because Tom wouldn't—he just wouldn't."

Harvey sat down on the sofa, kitty-corner to her.

"I know this is stressful, Janelle. Believe me, I wouldn't be here if I didn't think it was necessary. Can my men come in and look around?"

"Is there a warrant?"

"No," Harvey said. "We could get one, but it would be better if we had your permission."

She hesitated. "Are you looking for something in particular? Just tell me what you want, and if we've got it, I'll get it for you."

"Does Tom have a computer here at home?"

"A laptop. He took it with him."

"Could you give me his boss's home phone?"

"Mr. Redmond?" Janelle asked.

"Yes."

"I don't understand. This has something to do with Tom's job? Harvey, what are we talking about?"

If Janelle was trying to stall him, she was doing a pretty good job of it. Harvey tried not to let his frustration show.

"We're talking about Tom's boss's phone number."

"He probably has it on his phone, but. . ."

"Okay. Forget that." Nate could find it in two minutes or less. "Can my guys take a quick walk-through? If everything's okay, we'll leave then."

"I. . .I guess so. You'll tell me if you're taking anything?"

"Of course. Thank you." Harvey nodded to Nate, who went out the front door.

Harvey looked up at the Areal print. "Nice picture."

"Thanks," Janelle said. "It was expensive, even though it's only a print. I mean, expensive for us. I'm still trying to decide if I like it there or not."

Nate, Tony, and Jimmy came in. Harvey nodded to them, and they separated, Nate taking the kitchen and the other two heading for the stairs. Janelle sat on the sofa, swiveling her head to follow as much of their movements as she could.

"Have you spoken to Tom since he went to Boston?" Harvey asked. A three-day seminar seemed a little intense to him for real estate agents.

"Yes. He calls me every evening."

"Did he call you tonight?"

She frowned. "Yes, about six o'clock. Why?"

"Do you have the name of the hotel where he's staying?"

"The Marriott on the Long Wharf."

"Okay, thanks." He didn't want to upset Janelle further by taking out his notebook, but he was pretty sure he could remember that.

Nate emerged from the dining room. He stood near the doorway without coming any farther, so Harvey stood and walked over to him.

"Downstairs is clear," Nate said quietly. "And I found that phone number you want—Redmond."

"Send it to my phone. Thanks."

Jimmy and Tony came down the stairs, Tony jogging light-footed, and Jimmy following with heavier, slower steps.

"All clear," Tony said cheerfully.

Harvey turned to Janelle. "And we're out of here. Thanks so much for your cooperation, Janelle."

The detectives were nearly to the door. Janelle jumped up and grabbed Harvey's sleeve.

"Wait! What about Peter?"

Harvey didn't like to deceive her, but if Tom was involved, telling his wife that Peter had been found could damage their investigation. And he had no doubt Janelle would tell him.

"We have some promising leads," he said. "I may have some news for you in the morning."

She let them go, and he heard her lock the deadbolt behind them.

As they walked back to their cars, Harvey put in the call to Tom Merrick's boss.

"Hello?" came a cautious voice.

"Mr. Redmond?" Harvey said.

"Yes."

Harvey explained who he was and asked if he could go to the man's house to talk to him.

"Is it my son?" Redmond asked. "What's happened to Brent?"

"No, it's not about your family, sir," Harvey said. "This is more of a business concern. I just have a few questions about a house your agency has listed for sale."

"Oh," Redmond said. "Would you rather meet me at my office? All my records are there. It might be easier to access what you want."

"Sure." Harvey got the address and signed off. "Eddie, you come with me. Bring your own vehicle, though. And I'm going to call Boston P.D. first. You guys wait."

After he made the second call, he put his phone in his pocket and faced his men. "All right, Boston P.D. will try to pick up Merrick at his hotel. Until we know they've got him, Nate and Jimmy, I want you two to sit here, just in case he comes back early. Don't let him get in the house, okay?"

"Okay," Jimmy said.

"Do you need to make any arrangements with family?" Harvey asked.

Nate shook his head.

"I'm good," Jimmy replied.

"Okay, and if Boston doesn't have him by midnight, Tony and Eddie will spell you." Harvey arched his eyebrows at Eddie, then Tony, and both nodded. "Good. Nate, do you have your tablet?"

"Yeah," Nate said. "It's in my car."

"While you're sitting, see if you can find any links between Tom Merrick and McCafferty or Holden or Talbot."

"Got it."

"Now, Tony, go to the office and tell the head dispatcher what we're doing. Tell him Nate and Jim will check in every twenty minutes and that I'll be at the hospital, where he can reach me on my cell. Then put in a warrant application for this place and file a preliminary report on the house where we found Peter. Then you can take a nap if you want. Just be ready to go back on duty at midnight."

"Sure," Tony said.

"All right. Call me if anything comes up." Harvey got into his SUV and headed for Redmond Realty.

*****

Tony hurried through the Priority Unit office to the locker room and stored his gear. He came back out and went to his desk. A pink message slip lay smack in the middle of his keyboard. Odd. He picked it up.

To: Detective Winfield. From: Laney Cross. His pulse accelerated. In the box for the message, Paula had written, *Laney asks that you call her personal phone whenever you get this.* It was followed by a number with a prefix reserved for cell phones.

Okay, this was a step forward. Wasn't it? She'd left her private number for him. On the other hand, what was so urgent that she'd left a message for him at the office?

Tony sat down. His stomach felt a little queasy, not as bad as when he'd attended an autopsy with the captain, but worse than when he smelled vinegar, which he loathed.

He took out his cell phone and started to enter Laney's number. No, maybe he should hold off on that. If she was mad at him and wanted to break the date, he wouldn't want her in his contacts. He picked up the desk phone and carefully punched in the number.

"Hello?" she said.

"Hi. It's Tony."

"Oh, hi, Tony. Thanks for calling."

"No probs."

"How's your case going?"

"We found the guy."

"Really?" she almost squealed.

"Yeah, but I don't think that's public knowledge yet. We're still following some leads on the parties responsible. It may be a long night." He hoped he and Eddie didn't have to relieve Nate and Jimmy at midnight. They couldn't keep Janelle from alerting Tom to their visit, but they could stand by in case he came home from Boston early.

"Wow, I'm so glad you found him. Is he okay?"

"I wouldn't say okay, but he'll make it."

"That's great."

"Yeah. So, why did you want me to call?" he asked.

"Oh, that." She hesitated. "I, uh, told Judith that I was going to your cousin's wedding with you."

"Yeah?"

"Uh-huh."

"Did she tell you that was a mistake?"

"No, but she did ask me which side of the family the cousin was on, and I said I didn't know."

"Okay." Tony had a bad feeling.

"Then she asked if the governor would be there."

He swallowed hard. "Yeah, I expect he will be. Is that all right?"

After a moment's silence, Laney said, "I guess so. I mean, I just wish I'd known. Judith told me, and I felt so stupid. It's like everyone but me knew he was part of your family tree."

"I'm sorry. I didn't think about it the first time we talked, and then at the diner we only had a second. I'm really sorry. If you're not comfortable with going to the Blaine House—"

"We'd be going to the Blaine House?"

"Sure. The wedding is there."

"Oh."

"It's just going to be a small wedding," Tony said.

She was silent.

"I mean, they can't fit that many people into the parlors."

"Okay."

"Really, I'm surprised they're letting me bring someone," he went on. "It's mostly family and close friends. Not a lot of political connections. That's the way Amy and her fiancé want it."

"Amy?"

"She's the bride. Uncle Bill's daughter."

"Wow."

Tony waited a few seconds. When she didn't speak, he asked hopefully, "So, are we good?"

"What do I wear?" She sounded scared. Tony hated that he'd done that to her.

"Just anything. Uh, do you go to church?"

"Yes, why?"

"Just whatever you'd wear to church, then." Which was an odd thing for a man who rarely attended church to say. "Or a concert or something. Not formal."

"A dress, though."

"I'm sure there'll be women there in dresses and in pants. It's an afternoon wedding."

"Whatever that means." He could barely hear her.

"Look, do you want to think about it?" he asked, dreading her answer.

"Yes. No. I don't know." She cleared her throat. "I just. . .Oh, man."

"If you don't want to go, it's okay," Tony said. "We could do something else next weekend. A movie or something. Oh, hey, what about Monday? Eddie's wife is having a book signing, and we're all going to try to get to the bookstore on our lunch hours. You want to ride over there with me? It's on Congress Street."

"Yeah," Laney said. "That sounds really fun. What's the book about?"

"Uh, it's a. . .true crime story. About a case we had last year."

"Are you in it?"

237

"Maybe a tiny mention. Harvey and Eddie are the heroes, I'm sure."

"Sounds interesting."

"Great. We'll aim for noon on Monday, at the door to the garage. If my schedule is messed up, I'll call you."

"Okay. Thanks."

"And you can think about the wedding. If you want to change your mind. . .well, let's see how it goes Monday."

"Yeah." She sounded more cheerful now. Tony fiercely hoped she wouldn't break the date for Amy's wedding.

His cell phone rang. He hit a button and winced. Harvey. "Hey, listen, I need to go. We're working late tonight, and I've about used up my break time."

"Okay. Thanks for calling, Tony. I'll see you Monday."

He smiled. "No probs." He hung up and picked up his cell.

*****

When Harvey and Eddie arrived at the hospital, they found Abby and Leeanne in the family waiting room on the med-surg ward.

"Peter's still in X-ray?" Harvey asked.

"No, he's out," Abby said. "The doctor is setting his leg, and then they'll move him up here. It should be soon."

"What did the tests show?" Harvey sat down beside Abby, and Eddie wrapped his arms around Leeanne and kissed her as if they were all alone in the break room. That was where Eddie usually took Leeanne for a few minutes if she visited him at the office.

Abby looked pointedly at them, but they ignored her, so she just smiled and turned half away from them, toward Harvey.

"There's no skull fracture."

"Praise God for that."

"Yeah," Abby said. "I was worried after what Jeff and Mark told me. He's concussed for sure, and very dehydrated. But the worst part is his leg. It's a pretty bad break, in his femur. And his hands and wrists are a mess, but they'll heal." Tears spilled down her face, and she brushed them away. "Sorry."

238

"Hey, no need to be." Harvey took out his handkerchief and handed it to her.

Abby laughed and took it. She jerked her head toward Leeanne and Eddie. "You'd think those two were in love or something."

"Yeah." He grinned, glad Abby was able to make jokes. "Was Peter conscious?"

Her smile widened. "Yeah, I got to talk to him for a couple minutes after they got done in Imaging. He was a little strung out, but he's lucid. I didn't get many details on what happened, though. He just kept saying, 'I thought I would die there.' I didn't push him, because I knew you'd want to hear it all firsthand."

"Thanks. I'll talk to him tonight if they don't drug him up so much he can't stay awake."

"I haven't told him about Gary's arm yet." Abby looked up at him, her eyes shining with tears. "I didn't want to give him more to worry about."

"Are they putting a cast on his leg?"

"Not until tomorrow. They need to wait until the swelling goes down."

"Okay," Harvey said. "So, he'll be here a while?"

"A few days, anyway." Abby let out a deep sigh. "So, what did you find out about Tom?"

"The Boston police are going to pick him up, if he really is at the Marriott."

"You have doubts?"

Harvey gritted his teeth and shrugged. "Hard to say. I talked to his boss, Miles Redmond. Otherwise I'd have been here sooner." He took Abby's hand. "I'm glad Leeanne's here with you."

"She insisted, and I knew that if I said no, either Mom or Jennifer would come instead, and they've got our boys and Connor and Randy. Not that Randy needs a sitter. And Dad's there, too." She stopped and shook her head. "Sorry. Chattering."

"Hey, kiddo, you've been through a lot. Chatter all you want."

Abby squeezed his hand. "So, what about Tom? Do you really think he was involved in the kidnapping?"

"Involved, yes. To what extent, I don't know yet. Mr. Redmond gave me the scoop on that house. It's been on the market three weeks. He thinks the asking price is a little high. They showed it several times the first week, but not much since."

"So, Tom thought he could get away with using it to stash a kidnap victim?"

"It's too early to tell what Tom thought," Harvey said. "It looks like the two kidnappers, McCafferty and Holden, may have talked him into finding a place for them to use."

Eddie released Leeanne and flopped down in a chair, then pulled his wife onto his lap. "Those guys really went at this caper backward," he said to Abby.

"How do you mean?"

"Mr. Redmond didn't even know someone had used the keys from that house."

"The set the owner gave the agency was at the office," Harvey confirmed. "I figure Tom or one of the other two made a duplicate key the night they took Peter."

"They didn't have them in a lock box at the house?"

"I guess not." Harvey frowned. "I got the impression that this house was on the low end of the scale for properties they handle. And Redmond said something to the effect of the owner not being in a rush to unload it."

"What if Tom made duplicate keys before all of this happened?" Abby asked.

Harvey frowned. "I'm not following." He was pretty sure that the kidnapping wasn't planned, and that the men hadn't intended to take Ulrich with them the night they shot him.

"Peter and I don't see much of Tom. He's kind of an odd bird, as Grandpa Wainthrop would say."

"He does sell houses, doesn't he?" Harvey asked.

"Apparently. He must sell enough to keep the job. But Janelle told me once they'd had trouble with finding a mess in a vacant house they'd listed."

Harvey eyed her carefully. "So maybe someone rented the space on the side or what?"

"Maybe. It's one possibility. She said they couldn't find signs of a break-in."

"Hmm."

Eddie apparently didn't have all his attention on Leeanne. He sat up a little straighter and said, "I can see that. Someone who works for the agency might let it out for a party."

"Wouldn't they get caught?" Harvey wasn't quite buying it. "If the neighbors knew the house was empty and suddenly one night there's a wild party going on, they'd be suspicious."

"And call the cops," Eddie added.

"Maybe that isn't what happened." She scrunched up her face. "I just thought maybe. . .I guess it would depend on the house and the neighborhood."

Harvey nodded. "And the reason the renter wanted it. If it was something that wouldn't attract a lot of attention—no loud music blasting or dozens of cars parking on the street."

"Yeah," Eddie said. "He could let them stash something there overnight, for instance. Stolen goods or an incoming shipment of contraband. Something they were going to move fairly quickly, but they needed an innocent-looking place to store it."

"So you think Tom's been taking money to let people use vacant houses for their nefarious purposes?" Leeanne asked.

"I don't know," Harvey said. "I still think it would be simpler to rent a storage unit. Less chance of getting caught."

"But for a kidnapping victim, they needed a place with a bathroom," Abby pointed out.

"Yes, and a place where other people wouldn't be passing by within a few feet of the door."

"What if Tom owed those guys a favor?" Eddie asked.

Leeanne shifted on his lap. "Or money," she said.

Harvey nodded slowly. "They might offer to cancel a debt or a favor if he got them a place to use at short notice." His phone whirred, and he looked at it. "I need to take this. Excuse me."

241

As he stepped out into the hallway, a man in blue scrubs approached. Peter's doctor? When Harvey went back to the waiting room a couple of minutes later, the doctor was talking to Abby. Leeanne and Eddie stood near her, listening.

Harvey sidled up to Eddie. "Boston P.D.'s got Merrick. They'll hold him overnight, but we need to pick him up in the morning."

"Tony and I can go," Eddie said.

"Okay. You'll have to take Merrick to the hotel to check out, and one of you will have to drive his car back here."

Eddie nodded.

"Call Tony now," Harvey said. "Tell him you don't have to surveil the Merrick house tonight, but you'll leave early in the morning."

Eddie eyes focused on the far wall for a moment, and he nodded. "If we leave around seven, we should have him back here by mid-afternoon."

"Good. Call me when you get back, and I'll come to the station. If I'm not already there." The doctor was leaving the room, and Harvey walked over to Abby. "Sorry. That was business. What's up with Peter?"

"He's all set in his room, and I can go in. You can come in for a few minutes if you want, but they don't want a lot of people at a time. Peter needs to rest."

"You go in with her, Harvey," Leeanne said. "Eddie and I can wait."

"Actually, I'd better go home and sleep," Eddie told her. "I seem to have a full day laid out for me tomorrow."

"Oh, okay. I got to see him for a minute in the ER. I don't have to see him again tonight." She pulled Abby into a hug. "It's going to be all right."

Abby gave a little sob. "I know. Thank you. And thanks for sitting with me and praying with me."

"Any time at all." Leeanne smiled and stepped away.

"Goodnight, Abs," Eddie said. "I'm ecstatic that we found him."

"Me, too." Abby kissed his cheek. "You guys did a super job."

"Well, it's not over yet. Harvey can fill you in."

"Don't forget to call Tony now," Harvey said. "It's almost eleven, and he needs to know."

"Right. Come on, Leeanne. You got your car here?" Eddie and Leeanne walked out together, hand in hand.

"What's the room number?" Harvey asked Abby. "I need to make a few more calls, and I'll join you there."

"It's 410."

"Great. I'll be right there."

She pressed his arm and hurried out of the waiting room. Harvey pushed the speed-dial for Nate.

"Hey, Captain," Nate said.

"You still sitting on the house?"

"Right where you left us," Nate said. "Nobody in, nobody out, and all the lights are out except the back bedroom."

"You can go home," Harvey said. "Boston P.D. picked up Merrick. Eddie and Tony will drive down and transport him in the morning."

"Perfect," Nate said. "What do Jim and I do tomorrow?"

"Sleep in. They'll be putting a cast on Peter's leg tomorrow. There's no skull fracture. I'm hoping to talk to him now, but if not, I'll see him in the morning. You guys go ahead with your weekend plans unless I call you."

"That sounds good," Nate said. "Goodnight, boss."

Harvey gave Jennifer a quick ring.

"I'm so glad you called," she said breathlessly. "How is Peter?"

"I haven't seen him yet, but I'm going in now. Abby's in there." He gave her a quick rundown on the medical situation as he knew it. "If he's too groggy to talk now, I'll come home. Even if he can talk, I shouldn't be here much longer. How are the boys?"

"Beth took them over to her house around nine. She called me a few minutes ago and said they're finally asleep."

243

"Good. I expect Abby will give the word for them to come in first thing in the morning."

He had only taken a few steps toward Peter's room when his phone rang. With dismay, he realized the caller was one of the techs he had left on duty at Abby's house that day.

"Michele, so sorry," he said.

"Will there be someone relieving us?" Michele asked.

"No, I think we've got this one about wrapped up. You can pack up the phone surveillance equipment and take it back to the station, then enjoy your weekend."

"You're done?" she asked in surprise. "We heard you caught one of the kidnappers, but I thought there was some question of there being more people involved."

"We had one guy picked up in Boston," Harvey said. "I'll be surprised if we get more than that."

"Nice work, Captain."

"Thanks," Harvey said. "And thanks for your patience."

He found Peter's room easily. Abby was sitting in a chair close to the bed with one hand resting gently on Peter's head. She glanced up at Harvey and smiled.

"It's hard to find a place to touch him that doesn't hurt."

Peter's eyes looked droopy, but when he looked up at Harvey his smiled flickered. "Hey, bro. I'd offer to shake hands, but. . ." He lifted his arms slightly, displaying not only his bandaged hands and wrists, but an IV port and a line to the cardio-respiratory monitor.

Harvey grinned. "Even though you're wrapped up like a mummy, it's terrific to see you again."

"I'm pretty sure I'd be dead by morning if you and your boys hadn't found me."

"Well, I don't know about that," Harvey said, "but I'm sure glad it didn't take us any longer."

"He's probably right, with his injuries," Abby said.

"There's no way I could have gotten out of there," Peter added. "I tried to get up to the window, but I was too weak, and I

244

didn't think I could fit through it anyhow. If I'd had something to stand on. . ."

Harvey patted the leg that wasn't broken. "Quit fretting about it. You're safe now."

"That's right," Abby said. "You should be resting, not going over and over the last few days in your mind."

"It's hard to let it go." Peter's apologetic smile faded as he gazed up at Abby. "I am so thankful, Abigail. I need to see the boys, too."

"I'll have them here first thing in the morning. I want you to be a little perkier when they see you. And Gary needs rest, too."

"Yeah." Peter glanced at Harvey. "Abigail was telling me about Gary going out and breaking his arm."

"He was very intent on finding his dad," Harvey said.

Peter winced. "That's another thing. I keep thinking about that deciding moment at the store. Was I stupid to offer them money?"

"No," Harvey said firmly. "They'd have shot you without remorse. You saw what they did to Carter Ulrich?"

"Yeah. That's what made me do it. I figured it was my only way to stay alive. But I hadn't really thought it out—I didn't realize they would chain me up for days and then leave me to starve to death."

Abby sobbed, and Peter's expression darkened.

"I'm sorry. I shouldn't talk about it."

"Yes, you should," Abby said. "Talking is good. It's just hard to think about you in that situation."

"I know you need rest," Harvey said, "but I'd like to ask you a few questions, if you don't mind."

"Sure," Peter said.

"Let's start at the store. How many of them were there?"

"Two. Mack and his buddy."

"That would be Mack McCafferty and Web Holden," Harvey said. "Who did the shooting?"

"Mack."

"Really?" Harvey frowned. "Because Mack says Holden was the gunman. And yet, he had the gun that killed Ulrich when we arrested him today."

Peter's eyebrows drew together. "Well, I didn't actually see the shot fired. I heard it, and I ran out to the showroom, and those two were standing there over Carter's body. It was obvious they'd killed him. Mack had the gun in his hand. I suppose the other guy could have had a gun, too, but I didn't see it."

"Did you know them?" Harvey asked.

Peter shook his head. "I only know the one guy's name, Mack, from when they were talking later. Oh, wait—he said . . . Is today Friday?"

"Friday night," Harvey said.

"It seems like longer ago than that, but I guess it was yesterday. The other guy was supposed to go get the money, and hours later Mack came to the cellar and he said it was on the TV news that Web was hit by a car. That would be on Thursday, right?"

Abby nodded. "Yesterday afternoon. That was the worst hour of my life. When they didn't call again, I thought they'd killed you."

"I can't believe that was yesterday," Peter said.

Harvey looked at his watch. "I know how you feel. Twelve hours ago, Eddie and I went to Cape Elizabeth to arrest the gangster Carter owed money to. He's looking good for putting a hit on your salesman."

"So that's what it was about." Peter sighed. "I knew it was something like that. So, what happened to the money?"

"It's back in the bank," Abby said. "Mr. Strickland was very good about the whole thing. We should send him a thank-you gift."

"Sounds like I owe a lot of people my thanks." Peter's eyelids drifted down.

"Maybe I should postpone the rest of the questions until tomorrow," Harvey said.

Peter's eyes snapped open. "Sorry. What did you say?"

Harvey smiled. "I'm going to let you sleep, Peter."

"No, no, if there's anything else that will help you. . .although, it sounds like you've got things under control."

"There's one loose end."

"Well? Fire away."

"Okay. What do you know about that house where they took you?"

"Nothing. Not even if it was within the city limits. I did wonder."

"It was," Harvey said. "In fact, it's for sale, and it's been listed with Redmond Realty."

Peter's frown returned. "Redmond? That's. . .No, no, no. Don't tell me Tom is mixed up in this."

"That's what I'm trying to figure out," Harvey replied. "We had him picked up in Boston, and my crew will go down and fetch him in the morning."

"Boston?" Peter looked blankly from him to Abby. "Was he on the run?"

"He had a real estate seminar this week," Abby said gently, "but he didn't leave town until Thursday morning."

Peter leaned his head back and gazed at the ceiling. "He could be the friend those two jokers called Wednesday night. They didn't know what to do with me, and neither one wanted to take me to his house. They called some buddy of theirs, and next thing I know, I'm chained up in that place."

"Any chance Tom was the buddy?" Harvey asked.

"I never saw him, never heard his voice distinctly," Peter said. "But he was upstairs in the house at one point that first night. I heard them moving around up there and talking while Mack was downstairs with me. Then the second man, Web, came down alone. I think the friend left. Web had the chain and—" He broke off suddenly and met Harvey's gaze. "Web had a gun then. He held it on me while Mack chained me up."

"Was it the same gun?"

"I don't know. Might have been."

247

"Well, don't stress about it. We recovered the gun that was used to kill Ulrich. That's the important one in this case. I wouldn't be surprised if those two both had guns when they went to your store to do him in." Harvey leaned over and patted Peter's right shoulder, the side with fewer injuries. "Look, I'm going home and get some sleep. You do the same, okay?"

"Yeah. Thanks, Harvey."

Harvey nodded and squeezed Abby's shoulder. "I'll be back in the morning. You going to stay, Abby?"

"Yes, I can't leave him now."

"I understand. If you need anything from the house, give me a call, anytime after six a.m."

"Thank you so much." Abby gave him a tremulous smile.

Twenty minutes later, Harvey was peeling off his gear and setting it out on top of his dresser.

"What time do you want to get up?" Jennifer asked.

"Sixish."

"Baby, it's after midnight."

"Okay, sevenish. And I want to have breakfast with Connor."

Jennifer wrapped her arms around him. "Me, too?"

"Of course you, too." Harvey pulled her close and kissed her.

Chapter 19

A timid tapping came on the patio door at quarter to seven. Jennifer grabbed her robe and hurried out through the sunroom. Andy stood on the step outside, shielding his eyes and looking in, with his face pressed up against the glass.

"Good morning." Jennifer grinned and opened the door.

Andy scrambled inside. "Auntie Jenn, me and Anna are up, and Aunt Beth said to tell you while she starts breakfast. If anybody wants to go over for pancakes, they can."

"Oh, okay. That's really nice of her. Is Uncle Jeff up yet?"

Andy shook his head. "He's sleeping. Aunt Beth said Anna and me have to be real quiet."

Hence the errand boy, instead of a quick call, Jennifer mused. "Hmm. I could have made you some breakfast over here." She leaned out and looked toward Beth and Jeff's house, but as usual, she couldn't see past the garage end and the entry that stuck out a little on the front of the stone house next door. "Come on in for a sec, Andy. I want to text Aunt Beth."

She took Andy to the kitchen. "Have a seat, buddy." She took a pint of blueberries from the refrigerator and set it on the table in front of him. "Help yourself."

Andy's eyes got huge, and he picked a couple of large berries off the top of the basket.

Jennifer made a quick trip into the bedroom for her cell phone. Harvey rolled over and blinked at her.

"What's up?" he asked.

"Not what, who. Andy's in the kitchen."

"Oh." Harvey squinted at the clock. "I might as well get up."

When she got back to the kitchen, Andy was still eating blueberries, and her brother Randy had joined him. He was dressed in jeans and a baseball jersey, and he looked ready for a full day.

"Hi," Jennifer said as she keyed in a quick message to Beth. *Sure u don't want me to feed Andy here?* "Was Connor awake?" she asked Randy.

"I don't think so. I tiptoed past his door, and I didn't hear anything."

"Okay, thanks." Her phone whirred, and Jennifer looked at Beth's reply. *Already got batter mixed. Send any hungry.* Jennifer smiled and texted back, *Want blueberries?* She glanced at the table, where Randy was scooping up a handful of berries. *Perfect,* came Beth's reply.

"You guys take the rest of those over to Beth, and she'll give you blueberry pancakes," she said.

"All right!" Randy picked up the container and hustled Andy out the back door. Jennifer heard the shower going in the master bath and started making coffee. By the time she pushed the start button, her mom stood in the doorway between the kitchen and the sunroom, with Connor in her arms. Wild-haired and blinking, he held out his arms to Jennifer.

"Mama!"

Jennifer laughed. "Hey, fluff-head. Come on, I'll get you some cereal." She kissed him and let him cling around her neck while she got out his baby spoon and bowl.

"Are we the first ones up?" her mother asked, looking around. "I thought I heard Randy."

"He went over to Beth's for pancakes. She says she'll serve anyone who's hungry."

"I guess I'll wait for your father," Marilyn replied. "He's getting up, too."

"I put coffee on. Want some while you wait? Or I can make you a cup of tea real quick."

"That sounds good, but I can get it." Marilyn went to the cupboard and got herself a floral-patterned mug. She filled it with water and stuck it in the microwave while Jennifer fixed Connor's cereal.

George Wainthrop was next. Marilyn had just retrieved her hot water and dropped a teabag in it.

"Hey," she said to her husband. "Pancakes at Beth's."

"Sounds good to me. Morning, Jenn."

"Morning, Dad."

"Are you going over?" he asked.

"I think it will be easier to feed Connor here. And Harvey's in the shower. I'm not sure yet what he'll do this morning. He may just grab a bite and head out."

"Okay. When can we take the boys to the hospital?"

"Abby hasn't called yet," Jennifer said. "I hope that means she's getting some sleep. But I'll let you know."

"Can I take my tea with me to Beth's?" her mother asked.

Jennifer laughed. "I think that's actually one of Beth's mugs."

Her parents were out the door, and Jennifer buckled Connor into the highchair. She was ready to sit down with him when Harvey came in, freshly shaved, showered, and dressed for the office.

"Hey, gorgeous." He kissed her. "Everybody cleared out?"

"Beth's serving pancakes. Do you want some?"

"No, thanks. Just coffee."

Jennifer put her hands on her hips and frowned at him. "You can't get away with that here, remember?"

He gave her a sheepish smile. "Okay. What's quick?"

"Scrambled eggs and toast? And a banana?"

"That's a lot," Harvey said.

"No, it's not. You'll give half of it to Connor, anyway." She poured his first cup of coffee and handed it to him. "Sit."

"Okay, boss woman."

Her smile drooped. She'd hardly seen him for days, and she really wasn't looking for trash talk.

Harvey eyed her closely and set the mug down. "Come here, Jenny."

She went into his arms and stayed there a minute and a half, until the wall phone rang and Connor let out a yip.

"You get the phone, and I'll get the boy?" Harvey asked.

251

"Good." Jennifer walked to the end of the counter and picked up the receiver.

"Jenn? It's Abby."

"Hi. How's Peter?"

"Good. He's eating frittata and strawberries, if you can believe it."

"Sounds pretty good for hospital food," Jennifer said.

"I think they have a new chef. Anyway, you can bring the boys anytime. The head nurse says she'll let them in for ten minutes."

"Okay. I know Mom and Dad want to come, too. Maybe I'll let them bring Gary and Andy, and I'll come over a little later?"

"Great," Abby said. "They're planning to do the cast around ten."

"We'll get the boys in and out before that."

"Is Harvey coming in?"

Jennifer held the receiver out toward Harvey, who was feeding Connor a spoonful of cereal. He took it and said, "Hey, Abby." After a pause, he said, "I was going to stop in at the office. Do you think I should go to the hospital first? Okay, I'll come by later. Glad Peter's doing well. . . .I'll tell her. Bye, kiddo."

He handed Jennifer the receiver. "She wants a clean blouse and unmentionables."

"Okay." Jennifer listened for a moment and realized Abby had signed off, so she hung up the phone.

"I hope she doesn't mind if I send some of my things instead of going over to her house to rummage."

"I'm sure she won't," Harvey said. Jennifer and Abby were interchangeable when it came to clothes.

"I'd better go tell Mom and Dad she's ready for the boys. Or maybe you can, while I cook your eggs."

"Yeah, okay." He stood and unbuckled Connor from his highchair seat. "I'll take the big guy with me."

"Don't be long."

"I won't." With a glance at the clock, he said, "I plan to be in the office in thirty minutes."

He went out the patio door carrying Connor, and Jennifer sighed. "Good luck with that." She opened the refrigerator and took out a carton of eggs.

Five minutes later, Harvey was back without the baby.

"Where's your sidekick?" Jennifer asked.

"I left him at Jeff's. Your mom's watching him. As soon as they're done eating, the boys will get cleaned up and she and George will take them to the hospital. Since it sounded like Randy didn't stand much of a chance of getting in to see Peter in the first round, he offered to bring Connor back here when he's done scarfing pancakes."

"Okay." Jennifer set his plate in front of him.

"You going to eat with me?" Harvey asked. "Or are you going to Beth's for flapjacks?"

"Wow. We have a full house, and yet we're all alone," she said. "That feels odd."

Harvey grinned. "Too bad I have to go to work. Come on, gorgeous. Grab a plate and a fork. You know I can't eat all this."

*****

Abby sat on the far side of Peter's bed so she could keep an eye on the door. Peter looked and sounded stronger today, and he was eager to see the boys.

Gary poked his head in first, blinking and searching the room. When his gaze landed on Peter, he yelped and hurried in, leading with his sling. Andy followed him, with Abby's parents close behind.

"Don't run, guys," Marilyn said.

Too late. Gary had reached the bed, and Andy slammed into the side, jarring Peter, but he didn't complain.

"Hey!" He reached clumsily to embrace the boys, bumping one of the monitor cords over Andy's head.

"Daddy, Daddy!" Andy's voice broke, and he climbed halfway onto the bed, burrowing his face into Peter's chest.

253

"Easy, honey," Abby said softly. "Daddy has some hurts."

Andy didn't reply, but lay clutching Peter's hospital gown and sobbing softly. Peter rubbed his head with his bandaged left hand, while he pulled Gary in for a fierce hug with his right arm.

"Hi, Dad," Gary murmured.

"Hello, son." Tears filled Peter's eyes. "I heard about your adventure." He nodded toward Gary's cast.

"Yeah." Two tears escaped Gary's eyes and trickled down his cheeks. "Sorry."

"It's okay. You can tell me all the details later."

Gary nodded and sniffed.

George stepped forward and smiled at Peter. "It's great to see you, Peter. How are you doing?"

"Not too bad, considering."

Abby got up and walked around the bed to hug her parents. Her mother's lips quivered as she smiled. She whispered, "He looks better than I expected. I tried to prepare the boys."

Abby smiled and gave her a squeeze. Chances were, all the preparations had scared the boys, and she wanted today to be a happy day.

"Jennifer sent this." Her mother handed her a bag.

"Oh, thanks!" Abby set it aside.

Marilyn walked around the bed with her and stood gazing at her son-in-law, as though looking for a place to pat him and finding none.

"Peter, we're so glad you're back," she said.

"Thanks," Peter replied. "So am I."

"How long are they going to keep you here?" George asked.

"A few days, I guess." Peter looked to Abby, and she nodded.

"He's got to get the leg taken care of. I hope he'll be able to come home Monday, but we'll see."

They chatted for a few more minutes, and then the nurse came in.

"Sorry, folks, but we need to do a little prep work on Mr. Hobart," she said with a smile.

Peter patted Andy's back. "Time to go, buddy."

"No!"

Andy held on, but Peter said gently, "Come on, Andy. You knew you couldn't stay long, right?"

"Ten minutes," Andy said with a stubborn edge to his voice.

"I think it's been that, but maybe you can come back this afternoon, after they're done poking me and wrapping up my leg." Peter arched his eyebrows at Abby.

"Yeah," she said. "You can come back later, I'm sure. Another short visit. Come on, guys. I'll walk out to the elevator with you."

*****

There was only so much Harvey could do on Saturday morning. He caught up on his reports and made sure all of their collars were in line to be scheduled for arraignment and hearings on Monday and Tuesday. He went over the reports John Hillman had sent him after the search in Cape Elizabeth and carefully read all of the Portland officers' reports that connected with the Ulrich murder and Peter's abduction.

About 10:30, Eddie called him from Boston.

"We got Merrick processed out. Tony and I will take him to the hotel to get his stuff and settle his bill. Then we'll hit I-95."

"Okay, good," Harvey said. "Did he say anything?"

"Not much. I figured you'd have everything together by the time we got there, and you'd want to question him."

"Sounds good. I'm going over to see Peter again when they're done putting his cast on. Call me when you're twenty minutes out, and I'll meet you at the office."

Harvey settled in for some time working his databases, hoping he could find out how Holden and McCafferty knew Tom.

He was back at the hospital with Peter, Abby, and Vickie Hobart when Eddie called him, around two o'clock.

"Where you been?" Harvey asked, stepping out of the room into the long hallway.

255

"We stopped for gas and lunch, but we'll be at the station in twenty minutes."

Harvey made his excuses to the family and wished Peter well. No one had mentioned Janelle or her absence from the group of relatives eager to see Peter.

Tony was in the office at his computer, and he jumped up when Harvey entered.

"Hey, Cap'n. Eddie's got Merrick in the interview room."

"Thanks." Harvey kept walking, into the small room where Eddie and Tom sat on opposite sides of the table.

"Harvey! I hope someone will tell me what this is all about." Tom's face was taut with strain.

"Hello, Tom. What did Eddie tell you?"

"Just that you needed to ask me some questions."

"Sit down, Tom. Janelle must have called you last night." Harvey settled in a chair beside Eddie.

"Well, yeah." Slowly, Tom resumed his seat, keeping his eyes on Harvey. "She called me. She told me you'd been to the house. Kind of shook her up."

"And?"

"She wanted to know why you were there looking for me. I'd like to know, too."

"I think you know," Harvey said.

Tom shook his head. "I have no idea."

"Really?"

"Yeah."

"I've had a couple of conversations with your boss."

"Mr. Redmond?" Tom's voice cracked.

"Yes, Mr. Redmond. On inspecting the company's records, he found that you'd signed out keys to one of the listed houses three times, but you only showed it twice."

Tom hesitated. "What house?"

"The brick ranch on Baldwin Place."

Tom swallowed hard but said nothing.

"Why did you check out the keys to that house Wednesday evening, Tom? You weren't scheduled to show it. In fact, you were leaving in the morning for Boston."

"I, uh, I figured I'd left something there, and needed to go look for it, see if I'd dropped it in the house. I put the keys back as soon as I was done."

"Oh, yeah, you left something there all right," Harvey said.

"I . . ." Tom shook his head as though at a loss.

"You left your friend Web Holden there, along with his pal Chad MacCafferty. Those two and your brother-in-law. We found Peter in that house last night, Tom."

"What?" Tom's face twisted. "What does Peter have to do with all this?"

"You tell me."

"I don't know." Tom shook his head vigorously. "I'll tell you what happened."

"Please do," Harvey said.

Tom fidgeted and looked around. "Can I smoke?"

"No."

"Okay." He took a deep breath. "This guy, Web Holden, called me Wednesday. I was on my way home from work. He asked me if I could give him a place to hold something. Storage, you know? Just overnight, he said. He promised not to make a mess." Tom eyed Harvey anxiously. "I thought he maybe had something hot."

"Stolen goods," Harvey said.

"Yeah. He didn't tell me what it was about, and I didn't ask."

"Why not?"

Tom let out a big sigh. "I owed him, okay?"

"You owed him a favor?"

"No. I owed him five hundred bucks. He said if I could give him a place in a quiet neighborhood, he'd cancel the debt."

"And you agreed and went back to the agency to get the keys," Harvey said.

"Yeah."

257

"Why? Five hundred dollars isn't that much. Why would you do something illegal for this guy for a measly five hundred?"

"I don't know." Tom shifted in his chair, took out a pack of cigarettes, looked at it, and put it away. "I was tired of him bothering me about it."

"Oh, so Holden had been after you to pay up?"

Tom shrugged.

Harvey sat forward, holding Tom's gaze. "Did you owe the money to Web Holden or to his boss?"

"His boss?"

"Davey Talbot."

Tom opened his mouth, but nothing came out. He shook his head.

"I've had conversations with Mr. Talbot, too," Harvey said. "I've also looked at some of his financial records. Your name is in one of his spreadsheets, Tom. It says you owe him two thousand dollars, not five hundred. Don't tell me Web offered to write off that debt to his boss if you'd get him into an empty house."

Tom sat still for a long moment. "I guess I need a lawyer."

Harvey sat back. "Okay, if you're sure. But you might help yourself more if you just tell me the truth, Tom."

They sat still for a moment. Eddie looked at Harvey and raised his eyebrows. Harvey gave him a minimal shrug.

Finally Tom met his gaze. "Okay, I owed Talbot. Holden said he was supposed to put the heat on me, but he would hold off for a couple of weeks if I helped him out that night. They were going to tell Janelle, and I couldn't let that happen. Holden said he wouldn't tell her, but if I didn't pay in two weeks, they would make me regret it."

"Meaning they would do you physical harm?"

"I didn't know, and I didn't want to find out."

"You know Janelle's brother was abducted," Harvey said.

"I know now. She told me late Thursday. But I didn't know anything about it when Web called me Wednesday night."

"Did you see Peter that night?"

258

"No. I had no idea he was involved."

"Did you know Holden and his friend had someone they wanted to hide?"

"No, no, no!" Tom hit the table with his hand. "They asked me for a quiet place that nobody would likely go into for a day or two. I checked the schedule, and nobody was down to show that house."

"So you gave him the keys."

"No, I signed out the front door key. I had to sign it out because one of the other agents was in the office, and she would have seen me open the lock box. I told her I had left something behind after I showed a place. I took the key to a store and made a copy in a machine, and I gave Holden the copy."

"What else did you give him?"

"What do you mean?"

"Padlocks? A chain, maybe?"

Tom shook his head.

"A sleeping bag?"

"No. I'm telling you, I gave him the key I'd made and took the original back to the office."

"Are you sure?" Harvey asked. "Because Peter heard you and Holden talking upstairs in the house while he was in the basement."

Tom's face blanched. "Okay, I want a lawyer."

Chapter 20

Abby stood back and let Randy and Jennifer take the chairs close to Peter. Her fatigue was catching up with her, but she enjoyed watching him engage with her siblings. Even though he was exhausted and in pain, Peter was gracious and agreeable. Realizing how close she had come to rejecting him and marrying another man gave her shivers.

Peter was the only man for her. She knew that now, and she sent up a fervent prayer of thanks. God in his mercy had kept her from making the wrong decision.

At first, she had feared he might not regain his usual laid-back, pleasant nature. But he hadn't changed. He still loved her fiercely, accepting all her foibles. Since the rescue, they hadn't had a lot of time together alone while he was conscious. When they did, she wanted to tell him how deeply she loved him. Unexpectedly, her love for him had grown during this ordeal, and she would make sure he knew that.

Randy was telling Peter about his summer job. He leaned forward, eager and at the same time a bit apprehensive.

"So, I'm going by there this afternoon, and he'll show me the setup at the store. I'll move down here next week and start right away."

"Sounds good," Peter said.

A light rap on the doorjamb drew everyone's attention, and Harvey walked in, smiling.

"Hi, Peter. How's it going?" He sidled up to Jennifer and slipped his arm around her.

"Okay," Peter said wearily.

"You look beat. Want me to toss out the rabble?"

"He does need rest," Abby said. Everybody in the family wanted to see Peter with their own eyes. She expected his mother

261

planned to bring Gary and Andy for their return visit in a couple of hours, and she hoped Peter would get a nap before that. Right now he looked almost as bad as when they'd brought him out of the cellar.

"I won't stay long." Harvey glanced at Jennifer. "Maybe you and Randy could take a little walk down the hall?"

"Sure," Jennifer said. "I'm sure we've overstayed our ten minutes, anyway."

Harvey gave her a quick kiss. "I should be home for dinner." Harvey waited until Abby had hugged Jennifer and Randy, and Peter had thanked them for coming in. Once they were out the door, he sat down next to the bed. Abby took the chair on the other side, wanting to hear whatever Harvey could tell them, but fearing it would not be happy news.

"Peter, there's no sense sugar-coating this," Harvey said. "We brought Tom home from Boston today, and he's in custody now."

"So he was in on it." Peter frowned. "I know he's been in some trouble in the past, but we all hoped he'd gotten past that."

"He admits he gave your abductors access to the house. His lawyer got him to clam up about anything else."

"I'm sorry, for Janelle's sake," Peter said.

Abby gently patted his arm as she gazed across at Harvey. "What happens now?"

"He'll be arraigned Monday or Tuesday. He'll probably be able to bail out until this mess comes to trial. The district attorney's office will handle it from here." Harvey pressed his lips together and shook his head. "If it's any consolation, we don't think he has any connection to the murder."

"Good," Peter said. "I'm sorry Tom's in it at all."

"I take it you two weren't very close," Harvey said.

Peter's sighed, his eyes drifting to Abby. "No, we never were. And Janelle is very defensive of him. I think she knows Mom and I never really felt he was the best match for her. But she won't talk about it, and she gets very upset if we imply that Tom's not perfect."

"Poor Janelle," Abby said softly. "Tom was kind of miffed last year, when Uncle Austin left you that land, and I'm not sure if he was just upset on principle, or if it was for Janelle's sake. But anyway, she's going to need a lot of support to get through this."

"Yeah." Peter looked down at his hands. "Let's push the doctor to let me out of here tomorrow. I've got a lot to do."

"But your P.T.," Abby protested.

"I can come in for the physical therapy, but I need to be home with you and the boys, and I need to be available for Janelle and Mom."

Abby inhaled slowly. "Okay. But if the doctor says you're not ready, please listen to him." Peter wasn't an irritable person, and he would usually listen to sound advice, but he was hurting inside, as well as out. He needed to be home in the familiar setting, where he could interact with his sons. She leaned forward and laid her hand against his cheek. "I'll take your side on that."

"Thank you."

"Tom claims he didn't know they had you when he gave them the house key. In fact, he says he didn't know you were missing until Janelle called him in Boston Thursday night."

"Why did they go to Tom, of all people?" Peter asked.

"Yeah, especially if they didn't know Tom and Peter were related." Abby frowned up at him.

Harvey sighed. "Tom had apparently taken some loans from Talbot and didn't want Janelle to find out. I also learned this morning that Tom helped sell Web Holden's mother's house last fall. That may be when they first met and why he thought of Tom. He knew he was in the real estate business."

"Well, that's crummy," Abby said.

Harvey stood. "Well, that's the most of it for now. I thought you'd want to know."

Peter nodded. "We appreciate it."

"Get some rest. Both of you."

When Harvey was gone, Peter's forehead furrowed as he gazed down at his right hand. "Can you unwrap this, please?"

"But your cuts," Abby said.

"This hand isn't as bad as the other. I don't need all the gauze, just the little bandages underneath." His anxious eyes met hers. "I want to hold on to you, Abigail."

That she could understand. She carefully undid the outer wrap of gauze and laid it aside. Tenderly, she touched the back of his hand. He turned it and lightly grasped her fingers. She could feel the warmth of his palm between the annoying bandages. No stitches in his right hand. Another thing to be thankful for.

"Peter, I love you so much."

He smiled and settled back on his pillow. "This may sound odd, but I'm very happy. Just let me gather my strength, and then I want to kiss you."

He closed his eyes, and Abby sat very still, watching him, savoring the moment.

*****

Harvey walked into his house expecting chaos. Instead, the scent of cinnamon hit him, and he found Jennifer in the kitchen baking. He walked over and hugged her. "Where is everyone?"

"Mom and Dad had lunch with Leeanne, and they're at Beth and Jeff's now. Vickie Hobart came and got Gary and Andy, and she's taking them in later to see Peter again." As she spoke, Jennifer plopped scoops of cookie dough on a baking sheet. "Randy's in the study, and Connor's having his nap. Did I miss anyone?"

Harvey smiled. "I don't think so. Sounds good to me. But shouldn't you be sacked out for a nap yourself?"

"No, I should be working on my Navy software, if you want the truth, but I had the feeling we'll need lots of extra food tonight and tomorrow."

"You don't have to cook everything. Randy and I can make a run to the store."

"No, just relax. Dad made the same offer, and I think he'll be here soon for my shopping list. Let me get these in the oven, and we can actually sit down for a few minutes."

264

Harvey went into the bedroom and peeled off his jacket and shoulder holster. He opted for jeans and a Fire Department T-shirt.

When he went back to the kitchen, Randy and Jennifer were seated at the table with milk and a plate of fresh oatmeal cookies.

"My favorite," Harvey said, reaching for a cookie as he sat down.

"I got to see Mr. Donnell this morning," Randy said.

"Oh, yeah? That's good."

"He showed me around the store. I'll start a week from Monday. Is that all right?"

"Perfect, so far as I'm concerned."

"Peter's looking pretty ragged out," Jennifer said.

"That's to be expected. Abby wants him to rest there a few days, but Peter wants to go home tomorrow."

"So soon?" She set down her glass and frowned.

"He feels the weight of responsibility."

"Why?" Randy asked. "It's not his fault someone kidnapped him."

"No, but right now he feels like he's caused his family a lot of stress, and wants to do whatever he can to ease that." Harvey took another cookie. Jennifer's oatmeal-raisin, when warm, basically melted in the eater's mouth. When cold, they were chewy. He liked them both ways.

"Are you talking about Gary being stressed?" Randy blinked behind his glasses. "I mean, yeah, Gary was looking for him, but he knew he shouldn't go out alone at night, right? I don't see how that's Peter's fault."

"It's not really," Jennifer said, "but if Peter was home, Gary wouldn't have done it. Therefore, Peter feels guilty. It's not logical, but it's very common."

"Oh." Randy took a big bite of his cookie.

"Actually, I was thinking more of Janelle," Harvey said. "She does blame Peter. Anyone but her husband."

"Oh, no." Jennifer shook her head. "She may blame Peter a little, but mostly she's blaming you."

"Me?" That really surprised Harvey.

"I got that straight from Abby's mouth."

Harvey scowled. "Like I forced Tom to make a copy of that key and give it to those moron kidnappers."

Jennifer shrugged. "Like you said, anyone but her husband."

The timer rang, and Jennifer rose to take out the next tray of cookies.

"Harvey? You got a minute?" Randy asked.

Harvey looked at him. "Sure. What's up?"

"I hope it's okay and I didn't mess anything up, but, uh, Jenn said you were looking for these people."

He held out a slip of paper, and Harvey took it. His stomach did a flip as he eyed the names he'd written. He must have left his notes on his desk.

"Yeah, I was, but it's nothing to worry about, Randy."

"I sort of. . .well, I asked Eddie about it. Probably I shouldn't have."

Harvey made himself inhale and exhale slowly. Randy was a kid. That didn't excuse Eddie.

"It's okay—but Eddie probably shouldn't have told you anything."

Randy winced. "Sorry. But he did. And, well, I thought maybe I'd do some detective work for you. Not that I could find out something you couldn't," he said quickly.

Harvey managed a tight smile. "Randy, I've been so stressed this week, I'm not sure I could find my own hand in front of my face."

From the counter, Jennifer said, "I didn't tell him anything, honey, but Randy knows not to blab about private stuff."

"Well, one would think Eddie did, too." Harvey took a swallow of milk, trying to tamp down his irritation. He had nothing to be embarrassed about, so why was he feeling so upset about this?

Randy tugged at the cuff of his sweatshirt, pulling the sleeve down. "Well, we don't have to talk about it. I'm sorry. I shouldn't have gotten into it."

"So, Eddie told you what these names are from?"

"He said it had to do with a birth certificate, and that Leah Viniard was the baby's name and you were trying to find something in common. I thought maybe I could make myself useful, only I couldn't find any connections."

"Sounds like you found about as much information as I did the other night," Harvey said.

Randy hesitated.

"What?" Harvey asked.

"Did you know there's another guy with the same name as you?"

Harvey stared at him. "No, I didn't. You giving it to me straight?"

"Yeah, I found his name in the *Boston Globe's* archives."

Harvey sat up straighter. "Another Harvey Alan Larson?"

Randy nodded.

Harvey looked over at Jennifer. She stood with the spatula in her hand, gazing at Randy.

"This is the first I've heard about it," she said.

Boston was a big city. Harvey had dealt with enough mistaken identity cases that he knew it could happen. "So, what did you find?"

"I bookmarked it," Randy said. "He was in the court news, like, twelve years ago. That was the only thing I found, but if I had more time—"

Harvey stood. "Show me the bookmark."

"Sure."

They went into the study, and Randy sat at his desk and clicked a few buttons on the keyboard. The *Boston Globe's* website came up. Harvey pulled Jennifer's desk chair over and sat down beside him. He leaned in over Randy's shoulder and read the brief notice, about halfway down a fifteen-inch column of police log entries. The man was two years younger than him. There was definitely another Harvey Alan Larson out there.

"Hmm. Arrested for drug possession. Anything else?"

"That's all I found," Randy replied. "I looked for more court news, or a trial or something, but I couldn't find anything. Maybe there's a different way to look for it."

"Don't worry about it. I have all kinds of software on my computer at work that will let me follow up on this and see if the guy went to jail or what, and if he had later arrests."

"Wouldn't they be in here?"

"Maybe not, if the charges were dropped. And not everything's online or accessible to the public." Harvey exhaled heavily. "Randy, my man, you just did me a big favor."

"Really?" Randy smiled, and behind his glasses his eyes brimmed with joy. "I hoped I wasn't messing up your research."

"No. In fact, this is a huge help." Harvey sat back in his chair. Now all he had to do was make the connection between the drug collar and Tara Ervin. "Print out a copy of that, would you?"

"Okay."

"Thanks." Harvey stood and clapped him on the shoulder. "I was so wound up with Peter's case that I never got back to that. It did occur to me that someone else could have the same name, but I tossed that out as too unlikely. I figured if someone in this area had the same name, I'd have run across him by now. Shows what I know."

"So you're not mad?"

Randy was peering up at him anxiously.

"No, I'm not mad. That guy may have been out of state all this time. But if he's the one on Leah's birth certificate, I'll find out."

Randy blinked. "Okay."

Harvey realized he hadn't had a decent conversation with Randy for a long time. He sat down again. "Catch me up. Were you accepted at the school you wanted?"

"Yeah, I was actually accepted at three."

Harvey smiled. "That doesn't surprise me. So, what did you pick?"

"Well, I thought about USM because they'd teach me how things are under Maine law."

"Are you sure you want to stay in Maine?"

"Not totally, but anyway, the counselors at the other schools said their programs would prepare me to work in any state. And I really would like to get some Bible classes. I feel pretty ignorant in that area."

"Yeah," Harvey said. "That's something I wish I had, too." He'd lived most of his life knowing next to nothing about God's Word. "I'm not saying you have to, but it's an opportunity you may never get again. And knowing the Bible is probably more important than your career path. It might not seem like it now, but trust an old duffer on this. If I'd gotten close to the Lord when I was your age. . ." He shook his head. It was too easy to get lost in regrets and what-ifs. "Let's just say, my life would have been a lot different."

Randy nodded soberly. "Yeah. I want to do what's right, but first I have to know what's right."

Chapter 20

Jennifer peeked around the end of the bestsellers display. The store manager was still talking to Leeanne.

"Ten more minutes until they start officially," her mother said.

Jennifer shifted Connor, putting most of his weight on her hip. "I know, but this guy's getting heavy."

"I can take him to the children's section until you're done, and then you can watch him while I get my books signed."

"No, I want us to be her first two customers."

At least Andy had gone to school that morning. Jennifer loved the little guy, but now that Peter was home, he needed to keep up in school.

She pulled in a deep breath. Bookstores were some of her favorite places, with all the glossy covers beckoning her to stories unread, and the smells of paper and coffee. Harvey had even proposed in a bookstore. She could lose herself in one for hours with no regrets.

The manager nodded, adjusted one of the tabletop easels holding a copy of Leeanne's book, gave Leeanne a big smile, and walked away.

"Now," Jennifer said.

She and Marilyn hurried toward the table, where Leeanne was seated behind two artfully stacked pyramids of *The House Next Door*. When she saw her mom and her sister, her eyes lit and she jumped up.

"Hey! Welcome!"

Marilyn set four copies of the hardbound book on the table in front of Leeanne. "We'd love to have you sign these for us."

"Wow, Mom. Four copies?"

"Two are mine and two are Jennifer's. We already paid."

Leeanne laughed and reached for Connor, who was flapping his hand and babbling at her. "Come here, big guy."

Jennifer pulled away, pivoting Connor away from her. "Oh, no. You're working. Let's see you get busy and start signing."

"Can't authors kiss babies?" Leeanne asked.

"No, that's politicians. I'll let you hold him if nobody else comes by before you're done, but. . ." Jennifer looked toward the store's front door and smiled. "But I have a feeling that's not happening."

Leeanne looked beyond her and spotted Eddie and Tony headed for the table with a striking red-haired young woman between them.

"Hi," Eddie said.

"Hi." Leeanne looked expectantly at the young woman.

"This is Laney," Tony said. "Laney, this is Eddie's wife, Leeanne."

Laney smiled. "It's great to meet you."

"Thanks."

"Hello, guys," Jennifer said. "Laney, I'm Leeanne's sister, Jennifer, this is our mom, Marilyn." When they'd greeted each other, Jennifer looked at Eddie. "Where's Harvey?"

"He and Jimmy are stuck in court," Eddie replied. "They said they'll try to get over here before two if they can."

Tony picked a book off the stack. "Impressive, Leeanne! Can you sign this for me?"

"Get in line," Jennifer said with make-believe offense.

Leeanne leaned toward Tony and Eddie and whispered, "You have to pay for it before I'm allowed to ink it."

"Oh, right. Be right back." Tony grabbed a second book and headed for the checkout.

"I don't need to buy one, right?" Eddie said.

"No, your wife's buying you one," Leeanne said, and they all laughed. Leeanne poised her pen over the title page of her mother's first volume. "Is this for you, Mom? I was going to give you one."

"Great. Sign that one for Grandpa and the other one for your Aunt Dorothy."

Jennifer touched Eddie's sleeve. "Aren't you proud of her?"

"You bet," Eddie said. "I want to bust my buttons today."

"Quit whispering," Leeanne said. As she started writing, two women approached with books in their hands. Eddie stepped aside with a sweep of his arm, and Laney fell back beside him.

"Step right up, ladies. I'm not in line," Eddie said. "I'm just the famous author's husband."

The women laughed and launched into conversation with Eddie. Leeanne seemed to take that in stride, but his mother-in-law arched her eyebrows. She leaned toward Jennifer.

"I suppose that's just Eddie being Eddie."

"Oh, yeah, he can't help flirting," Jennifer said. "I promise you it's innocent, but he may help sell a few books today." In fact, the handsome detective would probably draw more female shoppers than the colorful posters of Leeanne's book cover or the bowl of wrapped chocolates on the table.

Leeanne held up the two books she had signed and looked inquiringly at Jennifer.

"One for Mr. Bailey and one for John Macomber," Jennifer said. She knew that Everett Bailey, who had formerly owned her and Harvey's house, would welcome a copy, as would her partner in creating software.

Her mother had her cell phone out. "Can I snap a picture, real quick?"

"Of course," Leeanne said and frowned in concentration over the next book.

Marilyn snapped the shot. "Jennifer, get behind there with her."

"There's too many people waiting, Mom," Jennifer hissed.

Marilyn looked behind her. "Oh, all right. Aren't those your neighbors?"

Jennifer glanced over her shoulder. "Yeah, that's Bud and Janice Parker." She waved. Connor squealed and tossed his head.

"We'd better get him out of here. Looks like you're going to be busy, Leeanne."

"That's good." Leeanne finished her signature with a flourish and passed the books to her mother. "Thanks for coming."

"We wouldn't miss it," Marilyn said. As she put the books into her shopping bag, Jennifer shifted Connor's weight again. "Here, let me take him." Marilyn swapped the bag off to Jennifer and took Connor in her arms.

"Bye," Jennifer said. "Bye, Eddie. Laney, nice to meet you."

Eddie flashed his killer smile. "See you later."

As they walked toward the door, they met Mike Browning with half a dozen of Leeanne's books in his arms.

"Chief Browning," Marilyn said. "I think half the police department is here."

"I hope they're using their lunch hours for it," Mike said.

Jennifer eyed his stack. "You must know a lot of readers."

"Tons," he said. "This is the perfect gift. Goodbye, ladies."

Jennifer was still smiling as she pushed open the door. "Of course, he's in the book. He's probably giving one to each of his children and grandchildren." If she knew Mike, he would probably give one to the mayor as well.

"You're in it, too," her mother reminded her as they crossed the parking lot.

"Yeah—oh, look, there's John Russell."

"Who's he?"

"Leeanne's former boss at the newspaper. I wonder if he's going in to buy her book."

"I'll bet he is," Marilyn said.

Jennifer hit the unlock button on her key fob. "Well, Leeanne is going to have a lot to tell us about tonight."

*****

Abby opened the garage door, and Andy and Gary ducked past her, tearing for the master bedroom. By the time she reached it, Andy was climbing onto the bed, and Janelle was rising from her chair at Peter's side.

"Hi! How'd it go at school?" Peter asked, looking at Gary.

Gary edged up to the bed and held out a small, velvet-covered box. "I got a medal."

"Wow. That's great." Peter opened the box and looked down at the award. "This is for your dragon story?"

Gary nodded. "The school gave me that, and the bookstore gave me a fifty-dollar gift certificate."

"Fifty bucks?" Janelle cried. She looked to Abby for confirmation.

"He got the highest award in the school, plus first place in the fifth grade," Abby said.

"Pretty impressive, Gary," Peter said. "I'm really happy for you."

"Can I see it?" Janelle asked.

Gary walked over to her, displaying the open box. "Mom's got the gift certificate in her purse. She said we can go book shopping tomorrow."

"Not tomorrow," Abby said. "You're going to school tomorrow, remember?"

Gary's smile faded. "Oh, yeah."

"How's the arm?" Janelle asked.

"Okay. It hurts some." Gary looked up at Abby. "It hurts now."

"Yeah, you need to take your medicine. Daddy probably does, too."

"Does your leg hurt, Dad?" Gary asked anxiously.

"Yeah, it hurts some. Just one more thing we have in common, I guess."

Andy wiggled around to sit in the curve of Peter's arm and stared up at his aunt.

"Aunt Janelle, is Uncle Tom still in jail?"

Abby winced. She had specifically instructed the boys not to bring up the subject of Uncle Tom.

"Yeah." Janelle's upper lip quirked. "It looks like he may be there a while. At least until tomorrow, maybe longer."

"Will you stay for supper?" Abby asked.

275

"No, I'd better get going. I need to do some laundry." She glanced at Abby. "I'm going to the courthouse tomorrow, and then I'm going job hunting."

"Oh." Abby didn't know what else to say. Peter would fill her in after Janelle was gone, she supposed.

Janelle said her goodbyes all around, and Jennifer saw her to the door. She went to the kitchen and prepared the medications for Gary and Peter. When she got back to the bedroom, Andy was asking about his toy Mustang.

"I'm sorry," Peter said. "I lost the other wheel and the front axle. I think we're going to have to get you a new car."

Andy made a pouty face, but Gary took his pills without complaining. Abby handed Peter his and a glass of water.

"You boys go change into play clothes," she said.

"Can I wear my medal to supper?" Gary asked.

"You sure can."

Gary smiled. "Thanks, Mom."

Both boys ran out of the room, and she smiled down at Peter. "I got some wonderful kids when I married you."

"Yeah, I'll admit that. Top prize for the school. And he's calling you Mom now."

"Yeah. I noticed that, too. I think it started the night he broke his arm. We had a little talk about stepmothers."

"Aha."

Abby sat down gently on the edge of the bed. "Think Gary will be a writer?"

"I wouldn't be surprised," Peter said.

She took the glass from his hand and set it on the nightstand, then leaned over to kiss him. Peter held her there for a long moment.

She sat up and brushed her hair back. "I hope the boys end up doing something they love. If it's writing for Gary, that's great."

"He likes science, too," Peter said.

"Yeah." Abby pulled in a deep breath. "Do you ever think about selling the dealership?"

He held her gaze for several seconds. "I'd be lying if I said I didn't."

"Okay. Do you think you *could* sell it?"

"I know I could. At a profit."

Abby reached for his hand. They'd removed all the bandages on his right hand in the morning, and the cuts were healing nicely.

"I love you very much, Peter, and I'm good with whatever you want to do."

"I know. Thank you."

She smiled and stroked his hand gently. "I want you to do something you love, too. Even if it means going back to school."

He inhaled slowly, looking toward the door, then let out the breath. "I'll think about that."

"Good."

"Kiss me again," Peter said.

"Anytime."

Chapter 21

Tony glanced sideways at Laney. She caught him and smiled. He could feel his face heating. *Man!* He faced front, where Amy and her fiancé were lighting candles. He was sure this room was filled beyond capacity for fire safety. So many people were packed in for the wedding, it was hard to get a deep breath.

"You may kiss the bride," the minister said—finally. *Whew!*

It was bad enough being out with a woman for the first time. Tony hadn't considered the added pressure of being squeezed into the double parlor at the Blaine house with over a hundred other people and having all his relatives scrutinize Laney from head to toe. Not that she wouldn't pass muster. She looked terrific in the short blue-and-white dress she'd chosen. Stylish and chic. And the crush during the ceremony didn't seem to bother her, either. She looked perfectly comfortable. Of course, she had on a short-sleeved dress, not a jacket and tie. At least it wasn't raining. The reception was being held at a new resort hotel. Maybe they'd have more space there.

After Amy and Daniel had managed to squeeze down the narrow aisle between the folding chairs and into the state dining room, Tony seized Laney's hand.

"How about we step outside for a minute and let the crowd regroup?"

She laughed. "Sounds good."

Except his sister and at least half his numerous cousins had the same idea.

"Yo, Anthony," Theodore Johnson, sometimes known as Klutz or Thee-Odor, depending on whose company he was in, called from the lawn as soon as they stepped out onto the porch.

"Hey, Theo," Tony said, conscientiously choosing the least offensive of his cousin's nicknames when elderly relatives might be within earshot.

"Who you got with you?" Theo asked, sauntering toward them.

"This is Laney."

"Your girlfriend?" Theo frankly appraised her figure. The sun glinted off Laney's red hair.

"She's my friend," Tony said, unable to hold back a smile.

"Ha!"

Tony had the feeling Theo was about to try to muscle Laney away from him. He said quickly, "Laney, this is one of my cousins, Theodore Johnson. Laney is the police chief's secretary. I mean, office administrator."

"Hi," Laney said, but she kept hold of Tony's hand.

Theo's sister, Sarah, appeared in the doorway. She also homed in on them, but her smile was much more encouraging. "Hi, Laney. I'm Sarah." She held out her hand, and Laney grasped it, ignoring Theo.

"Pleased to meet you, Sarah. Are you Amy's sister?"

"Nope. Cousins. Our dads are brothers. And Tony's mom is their sister."

"Oh, okay." Laney shot him a glance, and Tony wondered if she was drawing a mental family tree.

"You heading over to the hotel?" Theo asked, looking at Tony.

"Yeah, but I want to touch base with my folks first." Tony tugged at his necktie. Could he get away with removing it and his jacket and leaving them in the car?

"Well, don't wait too long to get over there," Sarah said. "Uncle Bill wants us to circulate and make sure we greet everyone from Daniel's family."

A pencil-thin young woman with platinum blond hair and a skirt at least three inches shorter than Laney's came out of the house with a young man who looked happy to be at the hottest party in town. More than happy, he looked as though he thought he was really something.

"Oh, there's my sister and her boyfriend," Tony said. "You didn't get to meet them before." He steered Laney away from Sarah, toward Rachel and Clark. "Hey, Rach!"

Rachel smiled and nudged Clark, and they met Tony and Laney at the bottom of the porch steps.

"Hi," Rachel said. "I was afraid you weren't going to make it."

"We cut it a little close," Tony admitted. The worst part was being forced to park on the top floor of the nearby parking garage and walk over to the governor's mansion. But they'd made it in before Amy walked down the aisle. "Rachel, this is Laney Cross. Laney, my little sister and her escort, Clark Williamson."

Laney exchanged pleasantries with them, and Clark looked around.

"Where's the bar?" he asked.

"At the hotel," Tony said.

"Oh, yeah, we gotta drive over there. You ready, Rachel?"

"Not yet," she said.

"Where's Mom and Dad?" Tony asked.

"I think they're in the state dining room with Uncle Bill and Aunt Laura," Rachel said. "So, are you staying over tonight?"

"No, we're going right back after the reception," Tony said. He hoped the question didn't embarrass Laney. As if anyone would think they would stay overnight together. Or at the Blaine House. Or whatever Rachel meant—he wasn't sure he wanted to know. He hoped Laney didn't spill to anyone that this was their first date. The bookstore didn't count in his reckoning.

Laney was looking up at Rachel. Her four-inch heels made Rachel taller than Tony, which rankled him. She'd nearly caught him in height when he was in high school. Of course, Clark was over six feet, so she could wear high heels with him and not look out of proportion. Still. . .

"So, what do you do, Rachel?" Laney asked.

"I just finished my first year of law school."

281

"Oh. I'm impressed."

Rachel made a face. "I don't know if I'll stick with it."

"Really?"

"It's a lot of work. So, have you met our folks?"

"Not yet," Laney said. "I saw them during the ceremony." Tony had pointed out all his close family members.

"Why don't you go in and meet them now?" Rachel suggested. "Amy and Daniel are having some pictures done in the back yard. This might be a good time."

"Great idea. See you at the hotel." Tony walked Laney into the entry and leaned close to her ear. "My sister can be a little much."

"No, she's nice," Laney said.

He'd take that at face value and not get into a discussion about his siblings or his cousins. "Looks like she was right— Mom and Dad are in the dining room with Uncle Bill and Aunt Laura. You ready?"

Laney gritted her teeth for an instant. "You think? How's my hair?"

"You look terrific."

"Okay. Then, I guess let's get it over with."

He took her hand firmly and led her into the long state dining room. A cluster of people, mostly older relatives, surrounded the Johnsons, but Uncle Bill looked up and smiled broadly.

"Anthony! Glad you could come. And who is this beautiful young woman?"

Tony stepped forward. "Aunt Laura, Uncle Bill, this is Laney Cross." His mother nodded her approval. She'd made sure he learned the fourth-grade lessons on making introductions well, and the governor certainly took precedence in this situation.

"Pleased to meet you," Laney said.

"Thank you for coming," Aunt Laura replied.

Uncle Bill smiled at her confidentially. "I hear you're working in Mike Browning's office."

"Y-yes," Laney said.

"Great guy," Uncle Bill said. "You'll have to let me in on any secrets you've learned."

"Oh, I don't think—Chief Browning isn't a secretive kind of person."

The governor laughed. "You've got that right. Mike's an open book."

Tony's mom touched Laney's wrist gently. "Hello, Laney. We've looked forward to meeting you."

"Mom, Dad," Tony said quickly before Uncle Bill could launch into an anecdote about trout fishing with Chief Browning or facing down the Speaker of the House. "This is Laney. Laney, these are my parents, Roger and Linda Winfield."

"How do you do?" Laney asked.

"We're fine," his mother said. "I hope we get a chance to sit down later and have a chat. We see so little of Tony since he passed his detective exam." She eyed her son with mock sternness. "You really need to catch us up on all your adventures."

"Yes," his father said. "Were you in on that big kidnapping case a couple weeks ago?"

"Uh, yeah," Tony said. "It was my boss's brother-in-law who was abducted."

"Not Chief Browning," Laura said.

"No, Captain Larson. His wife's sister's husband. Well, anyway, he's home safe now."

"What are you working on now?" his father asked.

"Uh, something else."

His father scowled, but his mom said, "Now, Roger, don't make him talk about work on his day off."

"It's okay," Tony told her. "Eddie and I are still sorting out the indictments from the racket we busted in connection with the kidnapping, and we also caught a new homicide Thursday."

"And they let you leave Portland?" His dad sounded shocked.

"Well, yeah. We did the most of it yesterday. I'll be doing some interviews Monday. And reports."

"Take Laney over to the resort, and we'll see you there later," his mother said. "Amy and Daniel are having a few more photos done, but they left orders for the bar and the hors d'oeuvres table to be open. Get something to eat."

"Yeah, we'll talk later," his father added.

Laney smiled. "Nice to meet you both."

They made it outside without being accosted by any more relatives, and Tony nodded toward the street. "Ready to walk up to the garage? Or I can bring the car down here and pick you up."

"I'll go with you," Laney said.

He didn't blame her, not wanting to be left stranded for ten or fifteen minutes with this crazy family.

He slipped his jacket off. "Hope you don't mind."

"No, it's okay," Laney said. "It turned off warm this afternoon."

That was an understatement.

He cast about for something to talk about as they walked up the block. They'd about exhausted all the small talk topics he could think of on the drive from Portland.

"So, we're getting a new detective soon."

"Oh, right," Laney said. "Chief Browning mentioned it."

"Do you know who it is?" Tony asked. He and the other squad members had tried to pry the information out of Harvey for the last week, but the boss was tight-lipped about it.

"Well—" Laney broke off, and her cheeks reddened. "I don't think I'm supposed to talk about things I hear in the office. Sorry."

So she knew something.

"Sure," Tony said.

They reached the parking garage and stepped into the dim interior, out of the exuberant sun, and he was glad the structure had an elevator.

The drive to the hotel only took a few minutes. A resort employee directed them to the event room, and they found a couple dozen wedding guests already there, including several of

Tony's cousins. He ducked Theo and fifteen-year-old Jacey, who fancied herself a popular socialite because the governor was her uncle. A four-piece combo was playing, and people stood in small groups talking or sat at tables around the edge of the room.

Sarah approached them, towing a man Tony had never met. "Hey, guys," she said brightly. "This is Brett. He works for the retirement department."

"Hi." Tony shook hands. Sarah must have invited this guy for the reception. He looked as though he felt a little out of place.

To his relief, Tony saw that a bar had been set up on the far end of the room. "Would you girls like something to drink?" he asked.

"That sounds good," Sarah said, and she and Brett walked across the room with them. For a wonder, they eluded Thee-Odor and made it over to the bar without being stopped by anyone else.

"What can I get you?" the white-jacketed bartender asked.

"Champagne for me," Sarah said. "Laney?"

"Oh, I'll just have a soda," Laney said. "Anything diet."

"Here you go." The young man handed her Diet Sprite in a rocks glass.

"Uh, I'll have the same." Tony wondered if Laney eschewed alcohol as the devil's brew. Now wasn't he time to ask.

"What?" Sarah looked at him as if shocked. "You're tee-totaling now?"

"Gotta drive back to Portland later," Tony said with a grin. Sarah seemed to accept that, and Laney smiled with what he assessed as genuine approval. He'd gotten high marks in his training on reading body language, after all.

As they turned away with their glasses, Rachel and Clark approached the bar.

"Oh, hi, Sarah," Rachel stopped to talk to her cousin and said to her boyfriend, "Get me something, okay?"

Clark waved without looking back and went on toward the bar. Rachel turned to Laney. "That's probably the last you'll see of him for a while."

Laney's eyebrows shot up, but she didn't say anything. Tony had never especially liked Clark, and sometimes he wondered if Rachel did.

"They're serving hot hors d'oeuvres," Brett said.

"Are you hinting?" Sarah asked pointedly.

Brett shut his mouth so fast, Tony figured Sarah intimidated him big time. He gave the relationship about two hours, max.

"Well, I'm starved," he said. "Laney, want something to eat?"

"I'd love it." She smiled apologetically. "I had a sketchy lunch, and that was in Portland."

"Hey, Tony!"

"Great," he whispered.

Theo was bearing down on them. He grinned at Laney and then frowned at Rachel. "Did you bring that loser, Clark?"

"Shut up, Theo," Rachel said.

Laney caught her breath and moved a little closer to Tony.

"Let's go get that food," he said.

They fixed their plates at the buffet, and Tony found them a small table. Maybe they could have five minutes to themselves.

"Sorry about my cousin," he said, holding the back of her chair for her.

"That's okay. I like your parents."

"Yeah, they're good people. Theo's just spoiled. Well, I guess the truth is, we all are."

"You don't act it."

"Thanks."

Laney smiled. "And I'm sorry about before. I've been wondering how things were going in Priority, now that Detective Miller's gone."

"You were right not to say anything." Tony sighed. "We're stretched pretty thin. But Captain Larson says he's picked Nate's replacement. I was just hoping to get a little intel, but believe me, I understand. I shouldn't have asked about it."

"I think they're just waiting for a candidate to accept the position," she said.

"Yeah, they won't announce it until it's a done deal."

Laney nodded. "I hope it happens soon, and you guys get some help."

"Yeah." Tony sipped his Sprite and winced. Why had he asked for what Laney was drinking? He hated diet soda.

"Listen," she said, "if you want to drink something stronger, I don't mind. But I'll just have ginger ale or something when it comes to the champagne toast."

"That's okay," Tony said. "Gotta drive."

"Right."

So she was a total non-drinker. That was okay. He just wondered what other things they would disagree on. But that was what dates were for, getting to know each other.

"Hey, Tony. Can we sit here?"

He looked up to see his cousin Blake and his wife standing by the table with laden plates and wine glasses.

"Yeah, sure." Tony stood until Blake had seated Violet. "Laney, this is Amy's brother Blake and his wife, Violet."

How many introductions would he have to make today?

Violet and Blake gave Laney huge smiles.

"Is that shrimp any good?" Blake asked.

Laney had one speared on her fork. "Yeah, it's delicious. And the spinach puffs, too."

Violet sat down and adjusted her plate on the table before her. "So tell us, what's this guy really like when he's out from under the family watchdogs?" Violet actually looked eager to hear the answer.

Tony picked up his glass. Maybe Blake would think it was vodka. He leaned back in his chair, wondering what Laney would say. Getting to know Laney was harder than he'd thought. He should have taken her someplace quiet for dinner, not to this madhouse. Would they have a second date? He hoped so. They chatted easily while the room filled. His parents came in and started greeting people. Then Uncle Bill and Aunt Laura arrived.

"Can I get you a refill?" he asked Laney.

"Sure. Thank you." She handed him her empty glass. He went to the bar and ordered her a diet Sprite and Moxie for himself.

"Here comes the bride and groom," Violet said as he rejoined them at the table.

Good. Maybe after a while they'd get to dance.

Amy and Daniel made their way slowly around the room, accepting kisses and best wishes. They were almost to Tony and Laney's corner when a loud voice said, "Buzz off, Thee-Odor!"

"Oh, boy," Blake said, shrinking down in his chair. "Here we go."

"What? I just asked when you're going to pay me." Theo sounded like he'd already had too many drinks.

Tony glanced apprehensively at Laney. Before he could say anything, a sharp crack, the sound of bone on bone, reached them. He whipped around. Theo had flown backward, apparently bowling down Aunt Heather and a waiter with a tray full of glasses. Clark Williamson was standing next to a stricken Rachel, rubbing his knuckles.

"Do something, Tony," Violet said.

"Me?" Tony croaked out. "Both those guys are bigger than me."

"Well, you're a cop," Violet said.

Tony pulled in a breath and made a quick decision. "Not my jurisdiction."

Uncle Bill stepped up. He stood between the two young men, holding up his hands.

"You boys settle down, you hear me? Theo, I'm ashamed of you."

"Me?" Theo roared. He got to his feet. "I'm the one who got sucker-punched."

"Yeah, I guess that makes you the sucker," Clark said.

"Hey!" Uncle Bill turned his glare on Clark. "You two can leave."

"Aw, Uncle Bill," Theo whined.

288

"That's it, Theo. I've had enough. This is Amy's day." The governor's bodyguards moved in closer to him.

Clark nodded. "I'm sorry, sir. I'll leave now." He headed for the door with Rachel trailing him.

"Will your sister leave, too?" Laney whispered.

"I hope not, but maybe," Tony said. He was glad he hadn't gotten in the middle of it.

Theo was limping toward the door between two of the Executive Protection Unit agents, while Aunt Laura helped Aunt Heather up off the floor and four waiters hastened to clean up the spilled liquids and broken glassware.

Blake gave Laney a crooked smile. "Never a dull moment in this family."

Tony leaned toward Laney. "Do you want to leave?"

"Now? We can't. They haven't cut the cake. And besides, somebody said there would be dancing later."

"Tony's a great dancer," Violet said, and he realized she was eagerly listening to every word.

Amy and Daniel sidled up to their table. "Well, hi, Tony," Amy said with a wide smile. "This must be Laney."

"Yeah." Tony stood up. "Laney, this is my cousin Amy John—I mean, Amy Forkner."

Amy grinned. "Yeah, I like the sound of that. This is Daniel."

"I'm so happy to meet you," Laney said. "The wedding was gorgeous."

"Thanks." Amy leaned toward Tony. "Dad's still got it, huh? Who needs a bouncer?"

"Yeah," Tony said with a forced chuckle.

Amy spoke to her brother and his wife and moved on.

The combo started to play, and someone said, "Mr. and Mrs. Daniel Fortner in their first dance as husband and wife." Amy and Daniel moved out to the center of the floor to waltz.

Tony let out his breath. He looked over at Laney. "Still glad you came?"

"Are you kidding? It's a little stressful, but it's a fun kind of stressful."

Tony picked up his glass. "I'll remind you that you said that when the next fist fight breaks out."

Chapter 22

Tears gushed from Leah's eyes and down her face.

"Oh, honey." Jennifer reached toward her, and Leah sank back into Jennifer's arms with a deep sob.

"I was hoping."

"Of course you were." Jennifer met Harvey's gaze. What kid wouldn't want to be his child?

"There's no mistake, Leah," he said gently.

"I hoped you were wrong. That maybe you'd forgotten something."

Harvey cleared his throat. "I wouldn't forget something like that."

No, Jennifer thought, he wouldn't. He'd wanted a child badly while he was married to Carrie, but she made sure that didn't happen.

"So, who *is* my dad?" Leah crumpled the letter she'd received from the lab. It matched Harvey's letter exactly, except for their addresses. If only their data had matched more closely, too, she would be overjoyed, not heartbroken. Jennifer patted her shoulder.

"It took some digging," Harvey said, "but I was able to locate him through some law enforcement data bases."

"Law enforcement?" Leah's chin jerked up. "He's a cop, too?"

"No. I'm sorry."

She crumpled in the chair. "He has a police record, then."

"Yes."

"Is he in jail now?"

Harvey nodded reluctantly.

Leah blinked a couple of times. "Can I meet him?"

Harvey glanced toward the doorway to the living room, where Mr. and Mrs. Viniard waited while giving them the few minutes Harvey had requested alone with Leah. Jennifer had expected to stay and chat with them, but Harvey had asked her to come with him and Leah, so she'd left them apologetically with coffee and ginger snaps.

"That would be up to your parents until you turn eighteen. But I'm not sure it would be a good idea."

"Why not?" Leah's eyes challenged him. "Don't I have a right?"

"No. Not now. Not until you're of age, and only if he wants to then."

Leah looked away, her face drooping. She didn't ask why her biological father wouldn't want to meet her. He'd had almost sixteen years to do that, and he hadn't wanted to.

"What did he do, anyway?"

"A lot of things, it turns out, all of them bad."

"I want to know."

Harvey looked bleakly at Jennifer.

"Leah, it's pretty grim stuff," she said softly. "He's in prison for life."

Leah sucked in a breath. "And my mother knew this? She got close to him anyway."

"A lot of it happened after you were born," Harvey said. "She may have thought he was a decent guy. Or maybe she didn't know him at all."

Leah was silent for several seconds. "I still want to meet him."

Harvey sighed. "I'll explain the situation to your parents, but I doubt they'll want you anywhere near this man. Besides, he's in another state."

"Where?"

He hesitated. "West of the Mississippi."

Her eyes narrowed. "Why won't you tell me?"

"Because I don't want you to try to find him. Not yet."

"Did he kill someone?"

"Probably."

"What does that mean?" She sat up, her posture rigid. "People don't go to jail for probably doing something. They have to be proven guilty."

"Yes," Harvey said. "And he was. Of other things. But he's suspected of committing more crimes than he was convicted for."

After a long moment, she rose stiffly. "Okay. Thanks. Sorry I bothered you with this mess."

"Leah. . ." Harvey stood.

She waved a hand in dismissal and walked out into the living room.

Jennifer reached for his arm. "Pray, Harvey."

"I feel like I made things worse."

"Maybe for a while. But Leah's smart. She'll see the wisdom of what you said after she calms down."

He exhaled heavily. "Yeah, maybe. Okay, send her father in."

"Don't you want her mom, too?"

"Only if you think you can keep Leah in this house while I talk to them. I don't want her taking off or doing some other stupid thing."

"Right." Jennifer squeezed his arm and went to the living room doorway.

Leah sat on the couch wrapped in her mother's arms, weeping while her father stood nearby with his hands hanging at his sides as though he was ready to help but didn't know how. To Jennifer's surprise, Randy was sitting in one of the armchairs, eyeing the family with concern.

Jennifer walked over to him and touched his shoulder.

Randy looked up at her. "Hi."

"I didn't hear you come in," Jennifer said.

"I parked at Jeff's when I saw the extra car in the driveway. Didn't want to block them."

"So, you met Mr. and Mrs. Viniard?"

Randy nodded.

Leah's sobs subsided, and her mother handed her a tissue.

"It's going to be okay, sweetie."

Leah sniffed and wiped her nose. In the quiet moment, Jennifer heard Connor babbling and squealing, not unhappily, upstairs.

"Harvey would like to talk to you folks," Jennifer said. "Leah, I'm going to go get the baby. It sounds like he's done with his nap. Then maybe you'd like to join my brother and me for some milk and cookies."

Leah pulled another tissue from the box on the coffee table and dabbed at her eyes. She blinked at Randy. "That's your brother?"

"Yes." Jennifer smiled. "Families are funny, aren't they? This is my brother, Randy Wainthrop. Randy, I don't think you've met Leah."

"Hi," Randy said, standing awkwardly.

"How old are you?" Leah asked, her eyebrows lowered.

"Leah," her mother said gently.

"It's okay," Randy said. "I'm sixteen."

She glanced at Jennifer. "You're a lot younger than her."

Jennifer said, "There are three more kids between us, and one older than me."

"Oh. Big family."

Connor's happy shriek reached them.

"I'll get Connor," Randy said and hurried toward the stairs.

"Well, Leah," Mr. Viniard said, "are you going to be okay if we go talk to Captain Larson for a few minutes?"

"Whatever."

"Leah," her mother said reproachfully, but her husband touched her sleeve.

"We'll be fine," Jennifer said, though she had no idea what she would do if Leah bolted for the door. She hoped Randy and Connor would help distract her for as long as it took Harvey to explain the situation and impress on the couple how important it was that their daughter not try to establish a relationship with a serial rapist now incarcerated in Arizona.

294

The Viniards went into the study with Harvey, and Jennifer said, "Come on in the kitchen, Leah. I think it's the busiest room in our house."

Leah followed her and looked around. "Does that boy live here?"

"Randy? Just for the summer. He's got a job here. He'll go back to Skowhegan before school starts."

"Oh. Can I use your bathroom?"

"Of course." Jennifer led her to the bath off the entry, a little uneasy because it was so close to the breezeway door. "You should find everything you need." She went back to the kitchen and set out a plate of cookies, glasses, and napkins, but listened closely for the bathroom door to open.

Randy came in with Connor squirming and laughing in his arms.

Jennifer smiled. "Did you change him?"

"Yeah."

"Thanks. Just put him in the highchair."

"Can I hold him?" Randy asked.

"Yeah, if you want to."

Randy looked toward the entry. "Hey, Leah, have you seen Connor yet? He's a really neat kid."

Leah came hesitantly back to the kitchen. "Is he, like, your little brother?"

"No, he's my nephew. He's Jennifer and Harvey's kid."

"Oh, yeah. I forgot." Leah slid into the chair Jennifer indicated and studied Connor critically. "He's cute. I never had a baby around."

"Me either, much," Randy said. "I was the youngest. But I spend as much time as I can with him and my brother Jeff's baby."

Jennifer was going to ask if Leah wanted milk, but she didn't want to interrupt the conversation. She set a full glass in front of Randy. When Leah didn't say anything, she poured another and put it down near Leah, who promptly picked it up and took a sip.

"Thanks," Leah said.

"You're welcome. Help yourself to cookies." Jennifer puttered around, putting a few dishes into the dishwasher and wiping down the counter, half listening to the two teens talk.

"Are you on Facebook?" Randy asked. "Or Instagram, or—"

Leah whipped a phone out of her pocket. "What's your number? I'll text you."

After a few minutes, Leah was holding Connor, feeding him tiny bites of cookie. Randy had told a funny story about a woman who came into the store that morning, and they were now discussing school and their college plans.

"You know, judging from what I learned about my birth parents, I probably wouldn't be able to go to college if I hadn't been adopted," Leah said quietly.

"That's rough," Randy said. "I guess you were blessed to be adopted."

Leah was silent for a moment. "Maybe. I don't know. I need to think about it some more."

"Well, your parents seem like good people," Randy said.

"Yeah. Lucky me."

The study door opened.

"Da-da-da!" Connor held out his arms as soon as he spotted Harvey, lunging forward.

Leah caught him and pulled him back. "Oh, easy. You almost jumped right off my lap!"

Harvey came over and scooped him up. "Hey, buddy."

Connor hugged him ferociously and planted a sloppy kiss on his cheek.

"Well, I see you made a couple of new friends," Denise Viniard said.

"Isn't he adorable?" Leah said, smiling widely. "He's fourteen months old."

"He's precious," her mother said.

Harvey winked at Jennifer. "So, more coffee, folks?"

"No, I think we'd better head home," Steve said. "But thank you both so much. I know this hasn't been the most pleasant thing for you."

"Hey, we're fine," Harvey said. "I'm glad we could help Leah get some answers."

"I'll just get my purse." Denise headed for the living room.

"Dad, I want a little brother for my birthday," Leah said.

Steve laughed. "I thought you wanted a horse."

"Well, it's getting kind of late for that. I've got to start thinking about college, you know."

"Oh, college." He gave Harvey a sage nod. "We're at that stage now."

"Yeah, Randy here's going through it—filing applications, looking for financial aid. It's an exciting time."

Jennifer held out a plastic bag of cookies to Leah. "Why don't you take these home, Leah? I think I made too many."

"Thanks," Leah said. "I wish I lived close enough to babysit Connor for you."

"That's a nice thought." Jennifer gave her hand a squeeze. "Thank you. You call us anytime, okay?"

"Thanks."

Harvey put his arm around Jennifer. "She means it, and so do I. I gave you our home number here. If you need to talk about something, give one of us a call."

"Just don't call him if you get arrested," Randy said drily.

Leah made her face into an exaggerated frown. "I don't do stupid things that will get me arrested."

"Glad to hear it," her father said.

"Yeah, somebody taught me how to behave," she said.

Steve laughed as Denise returned. "Come on, girls. Let's go home."

When they'd waved them off, Randy went up to his room.

"It's three o'clock on a Saturday afternoon, and nobody's demanding you go to work," Jennifer said. They walked slowly into the living room with Harvey carrying Connor.

"Imagine that," he said.

297

"What do you want to do?"

"I want to sit down here with you and Connor and not move until suppertime."

"Your wish is granted." Jennifer kissed him and pushed him down into his favorite armchair. "I hope you meant it when you said you're okay with Leah keeping in touch."

"I did."

"Good. Because she and Randy are now online buddies."

"Oh, boy."

"Yeah. We're at *that* stage with him, too."

Harvey looked up at the ceiling. "Randy and girls. Are we ready?"

"I know I'm not," Jennifer said.

Harvey absently patted Connor's back. "She's kind of funny looking, with all that bushy hair, but she's kind of cute, don't you think?"

"I think Randy found her interesting."

He chuckled. "Yeah. Well, I think she's interesting, too. She took it hard about her father, though."

"Wouldn't you?"

He nodded. "Tough thing to lay on a kid that age."

"Do you think she'll try to contact him?"

"I hope not. I laid it on the line with Steve and Denise. If they can help it, she won't. At least not until she older."

"Even then, he could be a horrible influence on her."

"Yeah," Harvey said. "I hope she'll have sense enough to stay away from him."

"She says she doesn't do stupid things."

"Oh, I have no doubt she thinks that. But I also know every kid has that yearning." He held Connor closer.

Someone knocked on the patio door.

"I'll get it," Jennifer said. She walked into the sunroom. Eddie and Jeff stood on the back steps, and Jeff was holding a basketball. She slid the door open.

"Can Harv come out and play?" Jeff asked in a little-boy voice.

She sighed. "I'll ask him."

She walked over to the connecting doorway. "Eddie and Jeff want to shoot hoops."

"Tell them I'm staying in with you. I've hardly seen you all week."

She turned around and looked at them. "You heard?"

Eddie frowned. "Yeah. What about Randy? Is he home?"

"I'll let him know you asked." She went to the stairs and called up to Randy. "Hey, Randy, you want to play ball with Jeff and Eddie?"

Randy came pounding down the stairs in cutoff shorts and a T-shirt.

"They're out there." Jennifer pointed toward the sunroom.

After she made sure he shut the patio door tightly, she went back to Harvey chair. He shifted Connor to make room for her, and she sat down on his lap.

They sat for a minute in silence, except for Connor's happy little burbles as he patted Harvey's scratchy cheek. The repeated thud of the basketball on the pavement in front of the garage made her smile.

"This is nice," she said.

"Mmm."

"Are you asleep?"

"No," Harvey said. "Just filing the paperwork."

"On what?"

He tightened his arm around her. "This moment."

The End

Dear Reader,

Thank you for choosing *Ransom of the Heart*. This is Book 7 in the Maine Justice Series, which features the men of the Priority Unit and their families. This story focuses on Abby Wainthrop Hobart and her husband, Peter, who are part of the extended family for Harvey Larson and Eddie Thibodeau. Harvey and Eddie are married to Abby's sisters, Jennifer and Leeanne. I hope you enjoyed their adventure. Group discussion questions are just a few pages away. If you haven't read the earlier books in the series, you would enjoy starting with *The Priority Unit,* Book 1, and follow their story to this point.

This story deals with the abduction of an adult and a demand for ransom. It also finds Harvey confronted by a teenager who thinks he is her father. Because of the urgency of the kidnapping case, Harvey doesn't have much time for other concerns for a few days, but he gets some help on other matters from the family.

If you enjoy the Maine Justice Series, I hope you will tell other readers and perhaps post a review on Amazon, Barnes & Noble, Goodreads, BookBub, or other venues of your choice.

I hope to continue the series, God willing. In the meanwhile, I am working on other books and will continue to re-issue some more of my backlist books.

Breaking News has been available only as an e-book for several years, but I recently released it as a paperback. Kurt Borden sends his star reporter out to do a feature on a senator who disappeared decades earlier. Then the reporter vanishes. If you haven't read this mystery solved by newspaper editor Kurt and his wife, Janet, take a look at the excerpt at the end of this book. I hope you love it.

Sincerely,
Susan Page Davis

About the author:

Susan Page Davis is the author of more than eighty published novels. She's a two-time winner of the Faith, Hope & Love Readers' Choice Award and the Will Rogers Medallion, and also a winner of the Carol Award and a finalist in the WILLA Literary Awards. A Maine native, she now lives in Kentucky with her husband Jim, one of their six grown children, and two cats, sweet Sora and naughty Arthur. Visit her website at: www.susanpagedavis.com , where you can see all her books, sign up for her occasional newsletter, and read a short story on her romance page.

Find Susan at:
Website: www.susanpagedavis.com
Twitter:@SusanPageDavis
Facebook:
https://www.facebook.com/susanpagedavisauthor
Sign up for Susan's occasional newsletter at
https://madmimi.com/signups/118177/join

Discussion questions for *Ransom of the Heart*
for Book Clubs and other groups

1. Do you think adopted children should have access to information about their birth parents? Could Harvey have handled his first meeting with Leah better? What safeguards would you recommend in a situation like this, for him and for Leah?

2. Why do you think it was easier for Andy to call Abby "Mom" than it was for Gary?

3. Abby's family members wanted to visit her to show their support. Are there situations when well-meaning friends and family could be more hindrance than help?

4. Gary felt an overwhelming need to look for his father. How could Abby and Grandma Vickie have better helped the two boys when they learned their father was missing?

5. Harvey is once more procrastinating choosing a new detective for his squad. Whom do you think he should choose? Sarah? Someone else in the Portland department? Someone from outside?

6. Harvey discovered there was another Harvey Alan Larson. Have you ever known of anyone with the same name as you?

7. Tom Merrick used his job as a realtor to make extra money on the sly. Have you known of situations where an employee takes advantage of an employer?

8. How might Abby and Peter help Janelle at the end of this story?

9. Abby wants Peter and the boys to have careers they love, but not everyone can do that. Should Peter sell his business? Have you ever had a moment in your life where you wanted a complete change of occupation?

10. Harvey offered his handkerchief to Abby to wipe her tears. She seemed surprised that anyone still carried one. Can you think of similar items that could seem old-fashioned to young people?

11. Do you think Holden and Mack would have released Peter if they had received the ransom money?

12. Can you recall a time where you felt helpless and had to completely trust in God for help?

Excerpt from Susan Page Davis's novel
Breaking News

Kurt couldn't stand to put it off any longer. After the morning news meeting with his staff, he lost no time getting to the police station.

He stopped at the window and gave the dispatcher a brief version of his mission, and she immediately called the patrol sergeant. The uniformed sergeant opened a door farther down the hall and guided Kurt into a tiny office that was more a niche than a room.

"I know Mick Tyler. How long has he been missing?" Sergeant Bedard opened a small notebook and sat with his pen ready. He was young, in his early thirties, clean cut, and exhibited the right amount of concern and efficiency.

"Since Monday morning." As Bedard wrote, Kurt felt as if something was finally being done, and things would turn out all right. He had come prepared with all the contact information he had for Mick—Callie's phone number and address, Mick's cell phone, Lionel's phone and address, a description of Mick's car.

"Do you have the license plate number?" Bedard scrutinized the memo sheet Kurt had given him.

Competent and thorough, Kurt thought with relief. "No, sorry. Callie might have some records at the house."

"I can check it." Bedard wrote something else in his notebook, then looked up at Kurt. "Pardon my asking, but is there a chance Tyler is hiding from you?"

"Oh, I don't think so. He never has before."

"But isn't he a hard drinker on the weekends?"

"I guess he can be, but I saw him for a minute Monday morning, and he was sober." Kurt watched the sergeant, waiting for an expert opinion on Mick's erratic behavior. "He was upbeat that day," he added. "I had put him on a new assignment last Thursday."

304

"What was it?"

"A nostalgic piece about an old family that used to live in Belgrade. He went out there Friday and scoped the house involved. One of our photographers, Wally Reed—"

"I know him."

Kurt nodded. Sgt. Bedard apparently knew everyone at the paper. "Wally was going to meet him there at ten Monday morning and take some photos for the story. But when he got to Belgrade, Mick wasn't there. Wally waited a while and then came back. But Mick hasn't checked in since, and as I told you, his wife and the friend he was staying with haven't heard from him either."

Bedard frowned and studied his notes. "You say he and Mrs. Tyler were having some problems."

"Well, I don't know any details." Kurt shifted in his chair, uncomfortable to be revealing another's private affairs. "All he told me was that he wasn't currently living at home. And when I stopped by the house yesterday, Callie seemed..."

The sergeant zeroed in on his hesitation. "How did she seem?"

Kurt groped for the right word.

"Mr. Borden, if Tyler's in trouble, any little thing could be important."

"Well, to be honest, she was pretty bitter. Sort of a *good riddance* attitude. She said ... she said he'd been a no-show for lots of family events."

"So she considered this part of a pattern."

"I don't know. I only know that at work he either shows up or he calls in. But not this time."

Bedard nodded. "I'll have one of our officers do some checking. Could be he decided to get away for a few days and forgot to let you know."

Kurt doubted that. "If he was involved in an accident, wouldn't his car show up in your reports?"

"Depends on where it happened. Sometimes it takes a while for our system to get updates from other agencies. But I'll put

305

someone on it right away. Meanwhile, if there's any word from him, you let us know."

"Of course." Kurt stood, wishing he'd come in sooner to file the report. Now to tell Grant. He wished he didn't have to, but they needed to inform the newspaper staff right away. Terry Fallon, the reporter covering Mick's former police beat, would find out soon anyhow, when he went to collect the daily reports from the police log. Kurt didn't want the employees to find out that way.

~~~~

On Thursday morning Janet went next door to help Sharon prepare for her daughter's arrival.

"Tory ought to be here by suppertime," Sharon said with a smile.

"I'm glad she's coming." Janet stood on the opposite side of an old, oak-framed double bed from Sharon, tucking in the sheets.

"So am I. I'd rattle around in this big old house all by my lonesome, now that Andrew is gone."

"Oh, he left this morning?" Janet asked.

"Yes. He was the last. I was surprised he stayed this long, but I'm glad he did."

"What does he do? He lives in Knoxville, right?

"Yes, Tennessee." Sharon reached for a pillowcase. "He's a city planner. They've had a lot of growth in that area. I think he's good at it. At least, he's always busy. He doesn't call me very often, and I have to admit I don't know that much about his work."

Janet nodded, thankful again for her close, loving family. Although her only brother lived in Idaho, they kept in touch, and she and Kurt received phone calls from their three married children often.

"He was a bit put out that he couldn't get hold of his school friend again before he left." Sharon smiled ruefully. "At least he got to see Dad conscious."

"I'm so glad your father's improving," Janet said.

Sharon's smile widened. "Me, too. He's not saying much yet, just a few words here and there, and I can tell by the look in his eyes sometimes that he's terribly frustrated."

Janet nodded and picked up a pillow. "Can't communicate the way he wants to."

"Right. But the doctors are optimistic. They say that with time and therapy, he may regain a lot of his speech and mobility."

"That's wonderful." Sharon didn't say anything about Elwood's previous attempts to convey messages to his children, and Janet didn't bring it up. It would only add to Sharon's stress. They were both aware of it, and if Elwood was able to shed any light on the mysterious events he had mentioned earlier, Sharon would tell her.

"Today I started looking into options for long-term care," Sharon said. "The doctors aren't sure if he'll be able to come home, and he certainly can't live alone anymore."

"I'm sorry."

Sharon shrugged. "Part of life. But I can't stay forever. Vic says he needs me. He's getting way behind on the financials for the company. So I figured I'd better start making arrangements. You know, tie up loose ends as soon as I can. I told him it may take me another week, and he wasn't happy, but he said to do what I have to for Dad."

"That's nice of him," Janet said.

"Yes, he's pretty good about things like that. But I could tell he wished I was home. I suggested he might have our accountant help out a little extra, but that would be expensive." She laughed. "I work cheap."

"Is Tory flying up?" Janet asked.

"No, she's driving. She lives in Providence now, and she got the rest of the week off, and all of next week."

"Why don't the two of you have supper with us?"

"Oh, thank you, but Tory asked me especially if we could eat at the seafood restaurant in Waterville after she sees her grandfather tonight. Dad took her there the last time she was in

Maine, and she hasn't forgotten the scallops. Maybe another time?"

"Sure. Have you got another blanket for this bed? The nights are getting colder."

~~~~

Kurt and Janet sat in the family room watching the tail end of Jeopardy. The final category was "U.S. Presidents." Janet thought she might have a chance of guessing the answer if the relevant president lived before 1920. She enjoyed reading historical novels and dabbled in genealogy, which had taken her on some lively forays into colonial and early American history. But if the question involved a more recent President, Kurt surely had the advantage with his exhaustive news background.

"He was the youngest man ever to be President of the United States," Alex Trebek said.

Kurt smiled at her. "You know this."

"Hmm. Kennedy?" She squinted at the screen. "Does it say *elected*?"

"I don't think so, but I don't have my glasses on."

"Then it must be Theodore Roosevelt," Janet said with certainty. "He was younger, but he wasn't elected to his first term. He inherited the job from McKinley."

"In a manner of speaking," Kurt agreed.

The music ended, and they listened carefully to the responses. Kennedy … wrong … Kennedy … wrong …Roosevelt … correct!

"There you go," said Kurt, pushing the off button on the remote. "You win tonight. If you'd been on the show, you'd have almost forty thousand dollars."

Janet laughed. "If I'd been on there, I wouldn't have made it to Final Jeopardy. All those questions about business moguls and rock music! Besides, you knew it before I did."

"Speaking of the Kennedys," Kurt said, rising and picking up his empty coffee mug, "Do you remember the summer of '68? Bobby Kennedy's assassination?"

"Well, sure. I was in school when we heard the news. Why?"

He frowned. "Nothing. Just something Mick Tyler said to me a few days before he went missing."

"About Robert Kennedy?"

"Well, about Senator Jacobs."

Janet eyed him in confusion. "The man who used to own the house down the road."

"Right. He said Jacobs disappeared the same year Robert Kennedy was shot, so no one thinks of it anymore. All they remember is Kennedy's assassination."

She nodded slowly. "I sure don't remember much about the Senator's disappearance. Just Kennedy and Martin Luther King, Jr. But I was pretty young. Kurt, don't you think it's strange that Jacobs disappeared, and when Mick started digging into the story, he disappeared, too?"

The doorbell rang, and they looked at each other in surprise.

"Must be Sharon." Janet hurried to the entry and flipped the switch for the outside light. She could see Sharon through the glass in the door. A young woman was with her.

"Well, hi!" Janet swung the door wide. "Been to the hospital? You must be Tory. Come on in."

The two women spilled into the hallway, and Sharon clutched Janet's arm.

"Thank heaven you're home! Call the police!" Sharon's eyes were wide with fear.

"What's wrong?" Janet asked.

Tory smiled at her in wan apology. "We just got back from dinner, and someone has broken into Grandpa's house."

End of Excerpt

More of SUSAN PAGE DAVIS'S Mystery and Suspense books that you might enjoy:

Other Books in this Series:
The Priority Unit
Fort Point
Found Art
Heartbreaker Hero
The House Next Door
The Labor Day Challenge

The Frasier Island Series:
  Frasier Island
  Finding Marie
  Inside Story

Hearts in the Crosshairs
The Saboteur
The Mainely Mysteries Series (coauthored by Susan's daughter, Megan Elaine Davis)
    Homicide at Blue Heron Lake
    Treasure at Blue Heron Lake
    Impostors at Blue Heron Lake
  Trail to Justice
  Tearoom Mysteries (from Guideposts, books written by several authors)
    Tearoom for Two
    Trouble Brewing
    Steeped in Secrets

A selection of Susan's Historical Novels:

Echo Canyon (set in 1860)
River Rest (set in 1918)
My Heart Belongs in the Superstition Mountains (set in 1866)

The Crimson Cipher (set in 1915)
The Outlaw Takes a Bride (western)
Mrs. Mayberry Meets Her Match
The Seafaring Women of the Vera B. (Co-authored with Susan's son James S. Davis)
The Ladies' Shooting Club Series (westerns)
   The Sheriff's Surrender
   The Gunsmith's Gallantry
   The Blacksmith's Bravery
Captive Trail (western)
Cowgirl Trail (western)
Heart of a Cowboy (western collection)
The Prairie Dreams series (set in the 1850s)
   The Lady's Maid
   Lady Anne's Quest
   A Lady in the Making
   The Prisoner's Wife
   The Castaway's Bride
   The Lumberjack's Lady
Mountain Christmas Brides
Seven Brides for Seven Texans
See all of her books at www.susanpagedavis.com.

CPSIA information can be obtained
at www.ICGtesting.com
Printed in the USA
LVHW05s0319270718
585116LV00007B/240/P

9 781947 079076